# ADVENTURE STORIES FROM THE 'STRAND'

# ADVENTURE STORIES FROM THE 'STRAND'

*Selected by* **Geraldine Beare**

*Introduction by* **Tim Heald**

*Illustrations by* **David Eccles**

LONDON
THE FOLIO SOCIETY
1995

## ACKNOWLEDGEMENTS

Every effort has been made to contact copyright holders; in the event of an
inadvertent omission or error, the editorial department should be notified at
The Folio Society, 44 Eagle Street, London WC1R 4AP.

The editor wishes to thank the following writers, publishers and literary
representatives for their permission to use copyright material:

'Lost Tommy Jepps' by Arthur Morrison, reproduced by permission of
A. P. Watt Ltd on behalf of the National Society for the Prevention of
Cruelty to Children and Special Trustees of Westminster and Roehampton
Hospitals.

'The Land Ironclads' by H. G. Wells, reproduced by permission of A. P.
Watt Ltd on behalf of The Literary Executors of the Estate of H. G. Wells.

'An Eventful Day in the Life of Miss Faversham' by Richmal Crompton,
reproduced by permission of A. P. Watt Ltd on behalf of Richmal Ashbee.

'Mirage' by W. Somerset Maugham, reproduced by permission of A. P.
Watt Ltd on behalf of The Royal Literary Fund and William Heinemann.

'Magic' by A. E. W. Mason, reproduced by permission of A. P. Watt Ltd on
behalf of Trinity College, Oxford.

'The News in English' by Graham Greene. Copyright © 1940 Verdant
S. A.

SET IN EHRHARDT BY FAKENHAM PHOTOSETTING LTD
PRINTED AND BOUND AT THE BATH PRESS, AVON
DESIGN OF TEXT AND BINDING BY DAVID ECCLES

# Contents

# Introduction

I CAN SEE him now, that slightly fleshy, patrician face, the aquiline nose, the headmasterly manner which was at once authoritative and yet fond. The grand piano, the oar which he had won rowing for a Cambridge eight in the days of his youth. Outside, the distant sound of summer harvesting or lawn-mowing. Twenty or thirty of us little boys crouched on the carpet in grey flannel shorts and ties of navy and gold stripes; the evening sun shafting through the windows, the echoes of evensong and his wife's inimitable rendering on the school organ of 'The Day Thou Gavest' fresh in our ears and in our minds.

My brother was at the same school, in the blissful lee of the Quantocks, at about much the same time, and he shares the memories. On a hot summer day we would decamp to the weeping beech and squat in its shade while Randall Hoyle or his wife, Grizel, read to us. As they did so they transported us out of our rural captivity into a wonderful escapist world. There were heroes and heroines and heroics; there were exotic foreign locations and exotic foreign villains; there was a world of adventure where explorers and duellists and men of the world triumphed over the forces of evil whether in the form of killer ants or the infamous Professor Moriarty.

I asked my brother what he best remembered, and he came up with Kipling and Conan Doyle. Those to me, too, seemed the keynote authors. Everyone associates Doyle with Sherlock Holmes, but I remember a romance called *The White Company* and another called *Micah Clarke*. In 1955, unexpectedly, I won the school essay prize and was rewarded with *The Lonsdale Book of Cricket* and Volume Two of Doyle's Historical Romances. Half of the latter was devoted to the 'Exploits' and the 'Adventures' of Brigadier Gerard. I see that the first 'Exploit' was 'How the Brigadier Came to the Castle of Gloom', which turns out to be the one piece by Doyle represented in this selection of adventure stories from the *Strand*.

I used to love the Brigadier in my early teens, though I suspect that

I might now find him a bit of an old bore. 'In me you see one of the last of those wonderful men, the men who were veterans when they were yet boys, who learned to use a sword earlier than a razor, and who during a hundred battles had never once let the enemy see the colour of their knapsacks.' Oh, come on, old boy! You can't have been that wonderful.

As for Kipling, one of whose Raj adventures is here – I like to think, though I cannot be sure, that it was Randall who first read me 'The Maltese Cat', which I still think is the best of all Kipling's short yarns. I really came to appreciate him properly a little later, in 1958, when *Kim* was the set book for a prize exam in my first year at public school.

Of the other writers in this collection there are several other friends: the prescient though mildly tiresome H. G. Wells, doing some military crystal ball gazing; Graham Greene, whose taut tale of wartime propaganda I thought the best piece in the book; Somerset Maugham, teetering on the edge of self-parody with his expatriate former medical student, smoking opium and living in a dingy room with a native woman in Haiphong; 'Sapper', with Bulldog Drummond in characteristically hearty, not to say blokeish, mode – 'Great heavens, Jackson! What is this ghastly thing I see before my eyes? Have you got a charabanc party coming?'; A. E. W. Mason, who I think was another prep. school discovery (Randall may have read us *The Four Feathers*).

I had, however, never heard of several of the authors here, a failure which prompted sober thoughts about the transitory nature of fame and popularity. Was Fred M. White, who has written a straightforward if upsetting story involving man-eating purple orchids, a great name in his day? Or his namesake, William C. White, who has two secret agents in Berlin competing for the hand of a French diplomat?

I had vaguely heard of F. Anstey, author of *Vice Versa*, though I think the manner in which his Lincoln's Inn lawyer slays a dragon is distinctly unsporting. I knew nothing of Conan Doyle's friend Grant Allen until reading Geraldine Beare's words on him, and I thought his story of the attempted jewel heist in a French railway station a little coy. Hilton Brown (man-eating ants), Arthur Morrison (lost boy at seaside) and F. Britten Austin (adventure at sea with novel twist of new-fangled radio, and one of the first aeroplane hijacks) were all strangers. Edgar Wallace, of course, was not. I had forgotten how good he could be. His code-cracking Secret Service is not only adroit, but has one or two cruelly perceptive asides. I particularly like the judgement on a Chief Secretary hanging on for retirement and pension. He had, writes Wallace, 'reached that delicate stage of a man's career which is represented by the interregnum between the end of a period of usefulness and the consciousness of the fact.'

Rider Haggard is not represented, though Geraldine Beare mentions him in her preface. I asked a friend of mine who is descended from him and who has been adapting one of his novels for the screen about this, and she said that her ancestor was not one for short stories. Not least because 'he went on a bit'. Two of the other yarn-spinners I remember with pleasure were the incomparable G. A. Henty, whose rather beautifully bound historical romances I still seem to see on the bookshelves of many middle-aged friends, and Percy F. Westerman. Not many people now remember Percy F. Westerman, but I used to devour him when I was about eleven.

Leafing through these yarns, mostly while overlooking the harbour in the Cypriot port of Paphos, my principal thought was a gentle nostalgia. 'They don't write stories like these any more' was my original reaction, closely followed by the thought that they don't make little boys like we were. We always had our faces stuck in books, and our teachers enjoyed reading to us and communicating the pleasure of words and plots. Much of our early reading was from the fields of what would now be called 'crime' and 'thrillers' – Dorothy L. Sayers, perhaps, on the one hand, and John Buchan on the other.

There are plenty of lineal descendants of Dorothy Sayers in Britain in the nineties but many fewer of John Buchan. I suppose Le Carré and Deighton are of that tradition, but they are very much novelists of espionage rather than writers of adventure in the style of, say, Hammond Innes, who is one of the last practitioners, it seems to me, of this particular school.

Who, though, would claim today to be the modern Conan Doyle or Kipling, Somerset Maugham or even 'Sapper'? I can think of one or two novelists who might push themselves forward, though I wouldn't take their claims tremendously seriously. The writing was of the clean-limbed, middle-brow sort now so little in fashion that there are hardly any short-story writers in this vein.

This is partly because there is no *Strand Magazine* or modern equivalent. Anyone in Britain aspiring to write short stories nowadays has only a limited and very competitive market. Some glossy magazines publish fiction, but seldom more than one story per issue. Women's magazines use slightly more, but they tend to deal in romance rather than what Le Carré once laconically described to me as 'shooty-bangs'. The *London Magazine* publishes interesting 'literary' fiction as, in a different vein, does *Granta*. British crime-writers find a regular home in the American *Ellery Queen's Mystery Magazine*, but there is no equivalent for mini-thrillers or yarns.

Perhaps television is the reason for this. Or radio. Or the video. Anything rather than the labour of reading words off the printed page – particularly for those with relatively undemanding tastes. The best of these stories, while highly polished and crafted, didn't require an enormous amount of hard work on the part of the reader. I should have thought there would still be a market. Nevertheless, there obviously isn't – or is not perceived to be one. Are yesterday's Bulldog Drummond fans working out their fantasies with computer games? I guess some of them must be.

I have a strong feeling that the writers, however, are out there lurking at their keyboards and waiting for the call. Indeed, a few years ago I edited a book of yarns nearly all of which would, I think, have fitted comfortably into the pages of a latter-day *Strand*. The conceit was that I had been put in touch with a retired British spy called Dorothy Rigby. Dorothy had been at the centre of practically every web of intrigue from her adolescence in pre-war Simla and Munich at the time of Chamberlain's piece of paper (she became friendly with Hitler) to the 1979 election campaign (she impersonated Mrs Thatcher).

The writers in my selection included such names as H. R. F. Keating, Peter Lovesey, Paul Gosling, Michael Gilbert, Richard Martin Stern, William Haggard (now alas deceased), Duncan Kyle, James Leasor, Anthony Price, John Ehrlichman and the *Sunday Telegraph* columnist, Minette Marrin, who does have one excellent, though little-known, novel to her credit.

This is very much the sort of cast list one would expect if there were a modern *Strand Magazine*. It would have been good to have included more women writers but, as this selection from the *Strand* suggests, yarn-spinning, unlike detection, has always tended to be a male preserve. Perhaps some of the jokes were a little arch – the idea of getting Ehrlichman to write about Nixon and Watergate was perhaps conceptually a bit much. But then, such diverse writers as 'Sapper', Somerset Maugham and Conan Doyle were more than prone to jokes, some of which were only appreciated by themselves. Indeed, sometimes, for this sort of writer, the more private the joke the better it becomes.

The writers were all perfectly at home with such prerequisites as exotic foreign settings, fiendish foreigners and twists in the tale. My experience of editing that modern-day selection of adventure short stories confirmed my feeling that if an opportunity arises the talent is there. But the opportunity seldom does. Publishing wisdom is that 'short stories do not sell', and, generally speaking, if and when a publisher is persuaded to put out a collection of stories by a 'genre' writer, then they don't sell nearly as well as a full-length novel by the same author. The same perceived wisdom applies in the world of magazines.

I mentioned the word 'genre' in the preceding paragraph and am, in a sense, sorry to have done so, though it raises an important point. At the time they were writing I do not believe that H. G. Wells, say, or A. E. W. Mason would have considered themselves 'genre' writers. They wouldn't have known what the word meant, and Wells in particular had such a wonderfully inflated sense of his own worth and importance that there is no way he would have ceded best to another writer, in or outside any 'genre'.

In the 1990s, however, the Lit. Crit. establishment has invented a whole series of more or less arbitrary and pejorative classifications. I have a first-hand sense of this because for some years I reviewed 'thrillers' for *The Times* while Marcel Berlins reviewed 'crime'. The Literary Editor distinguished between the two forms largely on the grounds of bulk: big fat books were 'thrillers', especially if they had swastikas on the cover, while short slim ones, especially if the word 'inspector' appeared on the outside, were 'crime'.

In the old days, by and large, such distinctions were unknown. Books were books, authors were authors and short stories, short stories. Some were better than others and some sold more but they weren't divided up into genres and sub-genres. Today the H. G. Wells story would be classified as 'Sci-Fi', the Richard Marsh about meeting a girl at the seaside would be 'Romance', the Conan Doyle would be 'Historical', the Kipling 'Thriller' and the Richmal Crompton (yes, the same who created William) would be 'Crime'. By the same token, 'the author, Arthur Conan Doyle' would often now be described as 'the crime-writer Arthur Conan Doyle' and Wells would be 'the science-fiction writer H. G. Wells'. Both men are clearly beyond such classification, but we have become manic about pigeonholes. Worse still, we have created a literary pyramid where the 'genre' material, including short stories for the *Strand*, clusters at the bottom, while 'Literary Fiction', no matter how poor, sits at the top. So, in a modern climate, authors such as, say, Aldous Huxley or D. H. Lawrence would, because of their intellectual and literary pretension, be at the top, even though their work was so very uneven, whereas men like Doyle or Wells would be scorned despite their obvious talents, craft and ingenuity.

I should not perhaps labour this point, but it does seem to me that the fact that there is now a *Granta* and a *London Magazine* but no *Strand* or *Argosy* does say something about literary snobbery. I am not criticising the serious literary survivors, but there should be a place too for the sort of story-telling practised by the best of those who contributed to the *Strand*.

It goes without saying that many of these stories have a dated feel to them. Edgar Wallace, for instance, says: 'The Secret Service never call themselves anything so melodramatic. If they speak at all, it is vaguely of "The Department" – not even "The Intelligence Department."' A little later he says that 'the Big Game was played by men who "chew ciphers in the cradle"'. Those of us familiar with George Smiley and his cronies and antagonists know that the world has changed, but Wallace was writing in 1916, and at the time he was probably spot on.

Similarly, F. Britten Austin's story has a marvellous description of 'the busy departure hour of the morning at the London terminus used by all the half-dozen competing aerial transportation companies'. Of course habitués of today's Heathrow and Gatwick will find this quaint. But he was writing in May 1920. Oddly, it is not just the facts which date. There is also a manner of writing belonging to an author not quite in the top notch which has the same sort of dated charm. F. Britten Austin was never in the same league as, say, Somerset Maugham or Kipling, and like other similar writers he compensates by using an engaging overblown lyricism. Too many words and often too long, but sometimes they have great charm, particularly seventy-odd years on.

Listen to him describing that early morning take-off:

One by one the machines ran forward from the long line of hangars where the stocking-cap wind-indicators ballooned stiffly horizontal from their staffs. One by one they scudded across the rank turf of the great aerodrome, and one by one, repeating each other's movement like rooks rising from a field, they swung round into the wind, hurled themselves against it, and were borne upward in long, slow spirals until, their height attained, they sped onward, in rapid diminution of size, upon their diverse courses.

I find Britten Austin's sheer effort in producing this piece of 'fine writing' very endearing. I like to picture him at his desk, brow furrowed, pen scratching across the paper and then the hand once more scrunching it into a ball and throwing it into the waste-paper basket. I like too the awe of the grace and power of those early flying machines which to us now seem rickety beyond belief.

Most of all I submit the view – and this may be special pleading – that this sort of writing and this sort of writer impart a whiff of everyday life and reality which the great writers often miss. Where else in the twentieth century can you find a first-hand word picture of the early Croydon aerodrome?

'Lost Tommy Jepps' by Arthur Morrison is my least favourite of all these stories. It appears coy and winsome, and when someone gets dialect wrong, it jars horribly. Morrison, it seems to me, has a tin ear: 'What 'a' you bin an' done with the ticket now?' surely can't have been an accurate piece of speech even then.

Notwithstanding these strictures, I find that Morrison manages to describe, with some precision and a great eye for detail, just what it must have been like to go to Southend-on-Sea on a Bank Holiday in 1902. The volume of people, the size of the extended family complete with cousins and aunts and hangers-on; and on the beach, the swings, the roundabouts, the shooting gallery and, suddenly, without warning, 'a band of niggers'. This pulled me up short and gave me pause for reflection. And so did much else besides.

By the same token, even in his short story 'The Lost Legion', Kipling marvellously evokes the smell and sound of a dawn raid on the Indian frontier:

... the men reined up, but the horses, blown as they were, refused to halt. There was unchristian language, the worse for being delivered in a whisper, and you heard the saddles squeaking in the darkness as the horses plunged.

You can sniff the sweat, the leather, the fear and the confusion even a hundred years away.

Providing ammunition for future social historians is perhaps a peripheral reason for bringing back 'the yarn' from the *Strand*, yet I think it's a plausible one. At their best these stories have a punctilious sense of time and place often absent from the work of better and more 'literary' writers.

I do believe that we are the poorer for being without this sort of tight, exotic, twisty, robust and gripping story. For me I suppose it is because this sort of ripping yarn helped to make me aware of the English language and what it could do, how it could lull you and entertain you, and transport you to a far-off world. Sitting cross-legged in my grey flannel shorts in Somerset forty years ago I had my first English lessons. I learned how you could tell stories and weave spells and make magic out of simple words. Those Sunday evenings with Conan Doyle and Kipling and the Hoyles, they live to haunt me still.

I should hate to think the art is lost.

TIM HEALD

# Editor's Preface

'A SOMEWHAT DULL YEAR' wrote the historian R. H. Gretton as he surveyed 1891, and who, in all honesty, can deny that he was correct. True, the Prince of Wales was involved in a baccarat scandal and Charles Stuart Parnell, the fiery Irishman whose liaison with Kitty O'Shea had shocked his parliamentary colleagues, died in October of that year, but on the whole 1891 passed away uneventfully. That is to say, politically and socially it was no more or less exciting than the years on either side. Yet in January 1891 an event took place that was to have a profound effect on the world of periodical and newspaper publishing. The *Strand Magazine*, brainchild of Sir George Newnes and Herbert Greenhough Smith, appeared on the bookstalls, priced at sixpence. The distinctive blue cover designed by G. H. Haite, a founder member of the London Sketch Club, showed a bustling street scene on the corner of Southampton Street and the Strand with an arrow pointing to the offices of *Tit-Bits* (Newnes' first successful publication) from where the *Strand Magazine* was first produced.

This new magazine, prepared in just four months, proved to be the most successful periodical of its kind, outliving all its rivals. The combination of fiction, articles and, above all, illustration, proved to be a winning formula. Greenhough Smith, its editor for forty years, was a tall, lean man known to his fellow clubmen as 'Calamity' Smith. He loved his job, but would have resigned rather than admit it. He had a 'nose' for stories and always made prompt decisions, on the grounds that it was not fair to writers to keep them waiting. This surprised not a few contributors including Gerard Fairlie who, in 1926, was an unknown author. He was paid fifteen guineas which 'so enchanted [him] that [he] spent twenty guineas of that straight away'. Fairlie was a life-long friend of 'Sapper' (H. C. McNeile) and the inspiration for that most famous of adventurous Englishmen, Bulldog Drummond.

Bulldog Drummond was born in the clubhouse on Nairn golf-course, 'the parentage by Beer out of Tankard', in the early summer of 1919. 'Sapper' had just finished a round of golf with a man he had never seen before, and devoutly prayed he would never see again. This man had grumbled and groused his way round the course delivering himself of hoarse noises on the green just as 'Sapper' was putting. It occurred to 'Sapper' how wonderful it would be if a society could be formed for the extermination of unpleasant individuals. A 'delightful girl' ('Sapper''s words) with whom he discussed the creation of an arch-villain said, 'Of course, you must make him ugly. I adore ugly men!' A suitable rogue was found in the person of Carl Petersen, and Bulldog Drummond, his adversary, made his appearance the following year. After the 'death' of Petersen 'Sapper' continued the story, concentrating on Irma Petersen and entitling it *The Female of the Species*. This was serialised in the *Strand Magazine* in 1928.

Before the Great War, adventure came in many guises. Women were more self-sufficient – able to do their own 'thing'. Grant Allen, a familiar name to *Strand* readers of the 1890s, created two female heroines: Hilda Wade, a nurse whose intuition serves her well, and Miss Cayley, whose adventurous spirit persuades her to travel round the world on the day she finds she has just 'twopence in her pocket'. Grant Allen and Sir Arthur Conan Doyle were old friends, and when the former died in October 1899 after a painful illness, it was the latter who undertook to finish the final episode of Hilda Wade: 'a beautiful and pathetic act of friendship', wrote Greenhough Smith, 'which it is a pleasure to record'.

Conan Doyle himself, when not engaged in writing about the most famous detective of them all, enjoyed penning historical novels. For the *Strand*, he wrote two series concerning Etienne Gerard, soldier of the Napoleonic Wars. When asked about his method of work, Conan Doyle replied that it varied according to the subject. 'In short stories it has always seemed to me that so long as you produce your dramatic effect, accuracy of detail matters little. It is otherwise where history is brought in. Even in a short story one should be accurate. In the Brigadier Gerard stories, even the uniforms are correct.'

In the early years of the century, F. Anstey was enjoying success as a children's writer. *Vice Versa* had been published in 1882, and he was a well-known contributor to *Punch*. For the *Strand* he wrote *The Brass Bottle*, *Only Toys* and half a dozen short stories all with fantastic or magical themes, of which 'The Snowing Globe' is an example. In contrast, Richard Marsh, perhaps influenced by both Grant Allen and

Conan Doyle, introduced the adventures of Judith Lee, a teacher of the deaf and dumb who uses her talents in the art of detection, and a delightful character by the name of Sam Briggs. Created in 1904, Briggs was used to considerable effect during the first two years of the Great War demonstrating how the common man became embroiled in the conflict and came out of it a hero. Sadly, Marsh himself died in 1915 at the age of fifty-eight. In attitude he was typical of many writers of his generation, claiming to be 'a clumsy but enthusiastic student of whatever made for proficiency in the fine art of doing nothing'.

Rudyard Kipling and H. G. Wells were also familiar names in the *Strand* index of contributors. Kipling's first story for the *Strand* appeared in 1892 ('The Lost Legion') and his final one 'Teem – a Treasure Hunter' in January 1936, the month of his death. By all accounts, Kipling was not without his critics, and in 1906 a Yale Professor was reported as saying: 'Mr Kipling's great mistake was that he did not die of pneumonia when he was ill in New York seven or eight years ago.'

H. G. Wells, in his 'Auto-Obituary' written for the *Strand* in 1943, declared that 'he had a flair for "what is coming"', and evidence of this can be found in his story 'The Land Ironclads', in which Wells forecast the use of tanks in warfare. This story was reprinted in the *Strand* in November 1916 and, apart from Conan Doyle's 'A Scandal in Bohemia' and Kipling's 'Proofs of Holy Writ' (both of which can be found in previous Folio volumes), was the only other story to have been printed twice in the magazine.

Arthur Morrison had a writing career that spanned no more than twenty years. As an employee of the Charity Commission he witnessed at first hand life in the East End of London. These experiences resulted in his *Tales of Mean Streets*, which was published in the same year (1894) as *Martin Hewitt, Investigator*. The stories that made up this latter volume had been written for the *Strand*, and introduced the first of many detectives based on Sherlock Holmes. Morrison's tale 'Lost Tommy Jepps' is typical of those featuring resilient, adventurous children capable of fending for themselves in an often violent, if ultimately benign, adult world.

Adventure is often juxtaposed with travel, and stories of Empire, sea voyages and treasure-seeking abound. Series such as *Gleams from the Dark Continent* by Charles J. Mansford, the Stingaree tales by E. W. Hornung, who had yet to write about Raffles, the gentleman burglar, and stories of the Wild West by Bret Harte can all be found within the pages of the *Strand*.

A. E. W. Mason represents another kind of adventure writer. Reginald Pound, the penultimate editor of the *Strand*, described him as 'one of our greatest tribal story-tellers'. When asked how the idea of *The Four Feathers* had come to him, Mason replied that it was 'the fear of fear carried to the point of disgrace, with the subsequent realisation that the highly-strung once put to it will go farther than the rest'. His stories were immensely popular in their day and he was a regular contributor to the *Strand* from before the First World War until his death in 1948.

Somerset Maugham needs little introduction. His tales, set in the Far East, were written after the Great War, during which he had worked as a Secret Service agent. His first story for the *Strand* appeared in 1904, and the money paid enabled him to take a much needed holiday. During the early 1920s he spent several years away from England. On his return he delighted in telling the story of the greeting he received from an elderly fellow-clubman who exclaimed: 'Hello Maugham, I haven't seen your face lately. Been to Brighton I suppose . . .'

Two authors now largely forgotten, but who deserve to be re-read, are F. Britten Austin and Stacy Aumonier. Austin echoed 'Sapper''s dictum on how to write a rattling good yarn ('you must start with a bang; the interest must continue in an ever-increasing trajectory; and then finish as quickly as possible in one paragraph which should contain an unexpected twist'), saying that he liked 'a story to march logically and swiftly from an opening note to a climax, and resolve rapidly from that climax to a last word that is all the better if it can, in some way, echo the note of the first'.

Aumonier's entry on to the literary scene was due in no small measure to the fortuitous intervention of Curtis Brown, the literary agent. Aumonier had submitted some stories which the manager of the magazine department had turned down as having no market value. One of them, 'The Friends', was rescued by Brown, and on publication turned out to be one of the most famous stories of its decade, being reprinted many times on both sides of the Atlantic. There followed a succession of indifferent tales until 'A Source of Irritation', which Brown considered one of the greatest stories written. This was first published in the *Strand*, and was succeeded by many more gems such as 'Where Was Wych Street?', 'The Kidnapped "General"' and 'One Sunday Morning'.

In choosing these stories I was once again faced with the task of deciding which should go in and which should not. What indeed was adventure? As a child I had read Enid Blyton's Famous Five and

Adventure series with relish. These were quickly followed by Baroness Orczy's *Scarlet Pimpernel*, Rider Haggard's *Allan Quatermain* and, best of all, 'Sapper''s *Bulldog Drummond*. Along the way I had also picked up Dennis Wheatley's matchless Duke de Richleau/Rex Van Ryn stories and F. Van Wyck Mason's sea tales. I thought I knew what adventure was all about and I thought the selection would be easy. Of course it wasn't. Unrelieved 'excitement' becomes tedious, and, as a friend pointed out, 'Adventure is something that can happen to ordinary people that is outside their normal experience.' It can be as varied as a lost child finding his parents, a repressed spinster finding herself stealing a vase or a secret agent killing an adversary. In the end the stories had to represent adventure as it was perceived through sixty eventful years, from the late Victorian period of Rider Haggard and Rudyard Kipling to 1950 and the imminent arrival of Ian Fleming's James Bond and the hard-hitting adventure-thrillers of Alistair Maclean and John Le Carré. Excitement is present in all of them – but the context may surprise. Read and enjoy!

*Adventure Stories
from the 'Strand'*

# THE LOST LEGION

## *By Rudyard Kipling*

WHEN THE Indian Mutiny broke out, and a little time before the siege of Delhi, a regiment of Native Irregular Horse was stationed at Peshawur on the frontier of India. That regiment caught what John Lawrence called at the time 'the prevalent mania', and would have thrown in its lot with the mutineers, had it been allowed to do so. The chance never came, for, as the regiment swept off down south, it was headed off by a remnant of an English corps into the hills of Afghanistan, and there the tribesmen, newly conquered by the English, turned against it as wolves turn against buck. It was hunted for the sake of its arms and accoutrements from hill to hill, from ravine to ravine, up and down the dried beds of rivers and round the shoulders of bluffs, till it disappeared as water sinks in the sand – this officer-less, rebel regiment. The only trace left of its existence today is a nominal roll drawn up in neat round-hand and counter-signed by an officer who called himself 'Adjutant, late —— Irregular Cavalry'. The paper is yellow with years and dirt, but on the back of it you can still read a pencil note by John Lawrence, to this effect: 'See that the two native officers who remained loyal are not deprived of their estates.—J. L.' Of six hundred and fifty sabres only two stood the strain, and John Lawrence in the midst of all the agony of the first months of the Mutiny found time to think about their merits.

That was more than thirty years ago, and the tribesmen across the Afghan border who helped to annihilate the regiment are now old men. Sometimes a greybeard speaks of his share in the massacre. 'They came', he will say, 'across the border, very proud, calling upon us to rise and kill the English, and go down to the sack of Delhi. But we who had just been conquered by the same English knew that they were over-bold, and that the Government could account easily for those down-country dogs. This Hindustani regiment, therefore, we treated with fair words, and kept standing in one place till the red-coats came after them very hot and angry. Then this regiment ran forward a little more into our hills to avoid the wrath of the English, and we lay upon their flanks watching from the sides of the hills till we were well assured that their path was lost behind them. Then we came down, for we desired their clothes, and their bridles, and their rifles, and their boots – more especially their boots. That was a great killing – done slowly.' Here the old man will rub his nose, and shake his snaky locks, and lick his bearded lips, grinning till the yellow tooth-stumps show. 'Yea, we killed them because we needed their gear, and we knew that their lives had been forfeited to God on account of their sin – the sin of treachery to the salt which they had eaten. They rode up and down the valleys, stumbling and rocking in their saddles, and howling for mercy. We drove them slowly like cattle till they were all assembled in one place, the flat, wide valley of Sheor-Kôt. Many had died from want of water, but there still were many left, and they could not make any stand. We went among them pulling them down with our hands two at a time, and our boys killed them who were new to the sword. My share of the plunder was such and such – so many guns, and so many saddles. The guns were good in those days. Now we steal the Government rifles, and despise smooth barrels. Yes, beyond doubt we wiped that regiment from off the face of the earth, and even the memory of the deed is now dying. But men say—'

At this point the tale would stop abruptly, and it was impossible to find out what men said across the border. The Afghans were always a secretive race, and vastly preferred doing something wicked to saying anything at all. They would for months be quiet and well-behaved, till one night, without word or warning, they would rush a police post, cut the throats of a constable or two, dash through a village, carry away three or four women, and withdraw, in the red glare of burning thatch, driving the cattle and goats before them to their desolate hills. The Indian Government would become almost tearful on these occasions. First it would say, 'Please be good and we'll forgive you.' The tribe concerned in the latest depredation would collectively put its thumb to its nose and answer rudely. Then the Government would say: 'Hadn't you better pay up a little money for those few corpses you left behind you the other night?' Here the tribe would temporise, and lie and bully, and some of the younger men, merely to show contempt of authority, would raid another police post and fire into some frontier mud fort, and, if lucky, kill a real English officer. Then the Government would say: 'Observe; if you persist in this line of conduct, you will be hurt.' If the tribe knew exactly what was going on in India, it would apologise or be rude, according as it learned whether the

Government was busy with other things or able to devote its full attention to their performances. Some of the tribes knew to one corpse how far to go. Others became excited, lost their heads, and told the Government to 'come on'. With sorrow and tears, and one eye on the British taxpayer at home, who insisted on regarding these exercises as brutal wars of annexation, the Government would prepare an expensive little field-brigade and some guns, and send all up into the hills to chase the wicked tribe out of the valleys, where the corn grew, into the hilltops, where there was nothing to eat. The tribe would turn out in full strength and enjoy the campaign, for they knew that their women would never be touched, that their wounded would be nursed, not mutilated, and that as soon as each man's bag of corn was spent they could surrender and palaver with the English General as though they had been a real enemy. Afterwards, years afterwards, they would pay the blood-money, driblet by driblet, to the Government, and tell their children how they had slain the redcoats by thousands. The only drawback to this kind of picnic-war was the weakness of the redcoats for solemnly blowing up with powder the Afghan fortified towers and keeps. This the tribes always considered mean.

Chief among the leaders of the smaller tribes – the mean little clans who knew to one penny the expense of moving white troops against them – was a priestly bandit-chief whom we will call the Gulla Kutta Mullah. His enthusiasm for border murder as an art was almost dignified. He would cut down a mail-runner in pure wantonness, or bombard a mud fort with rifle fire when he knew that our men needed sleep. In his leisure moments he would go on circuit among his neighbours, and try to incite other tribes to devilry. Also, he kept a kind of hotel for fellow-outlaws in his village, which lay in a valley called Bersund. Any respectable murderer of that section of the frontier was sure to lie up at Bersund, for it was reckoned an exceedingly safe place. The sole entry to it ran through a narrow gorge which could be converted into a death-trap in five minutes. It was surrounded by high hills, reckoned inaccessible to all save born mountaineers, and here the Gulla Kutta Mullah lived in great state, the head of a colony of mud and stone huts, and in each mud hut hung some portion of a red uniform and the plunder of dead men. The Government particularly wished for his capture, and once invited him formally to come out and be hanged on account of seventeen murders in which he had taken a direct part. He replied:

'I am only twenty miles, as the crow flies, from your border. Come and fetch me.'

'Some day we will come,' said the Government, 'and hanged will you be.'

The Gulla Kutta Mullah let the matter from his mind. He knew that the patience of the Government was as long as a summer day; but he did not realise that its arm was as long as a winter night.

Months afterwards, when there was peace on the border, and all India was quiet, the Indian Government turned in its sleep and remembered the Gulla Kutta Mullah at Bersund, with his thirteen outlaws. The movement against him of one single regiment – which the telegrams would have translated as brutal war – would have been highly impolitic. This was a time for silence and speed, and, above all, absence of bloodshed.

You must know that all along the north-west frontier of India is spread a force of some thirty thousand foot and horse, whose duty it is to quietly and unostentatiously shepherd the tribes in front of them. They move up and down, and down and up, from one desolate little post to another; they are ready to take the field at ten minutes' notice; they are always half in and half out of a difficulty somewhere along the monotonous line; their lives are as hard as their own muscles, and the papers never say anything about them. It was from this force that the Government picked its men.

One night at a station where the mounted night-patrol fire as they challenge, and the wheat rolls in great blue-green waves under our cold northern moon, the officers were playing billiards in the mud-walled club-house, when orders came to them that they were to go on parade at once for a night drill. They grumbled, and went to turn out their men – a hundred English troops, let us say, two hundred Goorkhas, and about a hundred of the finest native cavalry in the world.

When they were on the parade-ground, it was explained to them in whispers that they must set off at once across the hills to Bersund. The English troops were to post themselves round the hills at the side of the valley; the Goorkhas would command the gorge and the death-trap, and the cavalry would fetch a long march round and get to the back of the circle of hills, whence, if there were any difficulty, they could charge down on the Mullah's men. But the orders were very strict that there should be no fighting and no noise. They were to return in the morning with every round of ammunition intact, and the Mullah and the thirteen outlaws bound in their midst. If they were successful, no one would know or care anything about their work; but failure meant probably a small border war, in which the Gulla Kutta Mullah would be posed in the English newspapers as a popular leader against a big, bullying power, instead of a common border murderer.

Then there was silence, broken only by the clicking of the compass needles and snapping of watch-cases, as the heads of columns compared bearings and made appointments for the rendezvous. Five minutes later the parade-ground was empty; the green coats of the Goorkhas and the overcoats of the English troops had faded into the darkness, and the cavalry were cantering away in the face of a blinding drizzle.

What the Goorkhas and the English did will be seen later on. The heavy work lay with the horse, for it had to go far and pick its way clear of habitations. Many of the troopers were natives of that part of the world, ready and anxious to fight against their kin, and some of the officers had made private and unofficial excursions into those hills before. They crossed the border, found a dried river-bed, cantered up that, walked through a stony gorge, risked crossing a low hill under cover of the darkness, skirted another hill, leaving their hoof-marks deep in some ploughed ground, felt their way along another water-course, ran over the neck of a spur praying that no one would hear their horses grunting, and so worked on in the rain and the darkness, till they had left Bersund and its crater of hills a little behind them, and to the left, and it was time to swing round. The ascent commanding the back of Bersund was steep, and they halted to draw breath in a broad level valley below the height. That is to say, the men reined up, but the horses, blown as they were, refused to halt. There was unchristian language, the worse for being delivered in a whisper, and you heard the saddles squeaking in the darkness as the horses plunged.

The subaltern at the rear of one troop turned in his saddle and said very softly:

'Carter, what the blessed heavens are you doing at the rear? Bring your men up, man.'

There was no answer, till a trooper replied:

'Carter Sahib is forward – not there. There is nothing behind us.'

'There is,' said the subaltern. 'The squadron's walking on its own tail.'

Then the Major in command moved down to the rear, swearing softly and asking for the blood of Lieutenant Halley – the subaltern who had just spoken.

'Look after your rearguard,' said the Major. 'Some of your infernal thieves have got lost. They're at the head of the squadron, and you're a several kinds of idiot.'

'Shall I tell off my men, sir?' said the subaltern sulkily, for he was feeling wet and cold.

'Tell 'em off!' said the Major. '*Whip* 'em off, by Gad! You're squandering them all over the place. There's a troop behind you *now*!'

'So I was thinking,' said the subaltern calmly. 'I have all my men here, sir. Better speak to Carter.'

'Carter Sahib sends salaam and wants to know why the squadron is stopping,' said a trooper to Lieutenant Halley.

'Where under heaven *is* Carter?' said the Major.

'Forward, with his troop,' was the answer.

'Are we walking in a ring, then, or are we the centre of a blessed brigade?' said the Major.

By this time there was silence all along the column. The horses were still; but, through the drive of the fine rain, men could hear the feet of many horses moving over stony ground.

'We're being stalked,' said Lieutenant Halley.

'They've no horses here. Besides they'd have fired before this,' said the Major. 'It's—it's villagers' ponies.'

'Then our horses would have neighed and spoilt the attack long ago. They must have been near us for half an hour,' said the subaltern.

'Queer that we can't smell the horses,' said the Major, damping his finger and rubbing it on his nose as he sniffed up-wind.

'Well, it's a bad start,' said the subaltern, shaking the wet from his overcoat. 'What shall we do, sir?'

'Get on,' said the Major; 'we shall catch it tonight.'

The column moved forward very gingerly for a few paces. Then there was an oath, a shower of blue sparks as shod hoofs crashed on small stones, and a man rolled over with a jangle of accoutrements that would have waked the dead.

'Now we've gone and done it,' said Lieutenant Halley. 'All the hillside awake, and all the hillside to climb in the face of musketry fire. This comes of trying to do night-hawk work.'

The trembling trooper picked himself up and tried to explain that his horse had fallen over one of the little cairns that are built of loose stones on the spot where a man has been murdered. There was no need to go on. The Major's big Australian charger blundered next, and the men came to a halt in what seemed to be a very graveyard of little cairns all about two feet high. The manoeuvres of the squadron are not reported. Men said that it felt like mounted quadrilles without the training and without the music; but at last the horses, breaking rank and choosing their own way, walked clear of the cairns, till every man of the squadron re-formed and drew rein a few yards up the slope of the hill. Then, according to Lieutenant Halley, there began another scene very like the one which has been described. The Major and Carter insisted that all the men had not joined ranks, and that there were more of them in the rear clicking and blundering among the dead men's cairns. Lieutenant Halley told off his own troopers for the second or third time, and resigned himself to wait. Later on he said to me:

'I didn't much know, and I didn't much care, what was going on. The row of that trooper falling ought to have scared half the country, and I would take my oath that we were being stalked by a full regiment in the rear, and *they* were making row enough to rouse all Afghanistan. I sat tight, but nothing happened.'

The mysterious part of the night's work was the silence on the hillside. Everybody knew that the Gulla Kutta Mullah had his outpost huts on the reverse side of the hill, and everybody expected, by the time that the Major had sworn himself into a state of quiet, that the watchmen there would open fire. When nothing occurred, they thought that the gusts of the rain had deadened the sound of the horses, and thanked Providence. At last the Major satisfied himself (*a*) that he had left no one behind among the cairns, and (*b*) that he was not being taken in rear by a large and powerful body of cavalry. The men's tempers were thoroughly spoiled, the horses were lathered and unquiet, and one and all prayed for the daylight.

They set themselves to climb up the hill, each man leading his mount carefully. Before they had covered the lower slopes or the breastplates had begun to tighten, a thunderstorm came up behind, rolling across the low hills and drowning any noise less than that of cannon. The first flash of the lightning showed the bare ribs of the ascent, the hill-crest standing steely blue against the black sky, the little falling lines of the rain, and, a few yards to their left flank, an Afghan watchtower, two-storeyed, built of stone, and entered by a ladder from the upper storey. The ladder was up, and a man with a rifle was leaning from the window. The darkness and the thunder rolled down in an instant, and, when the lull followed, a voice from the watchtower cried, 'Who goes there?'

The cavalry were very quiet, but each man gripped his carbine and stood to his horse. Again the voice called, 'Who goes there?' and in a louder key, 'O brothers, give the alarm!' Now, every man in the cavalry would have died in his long boots sooner than have asked for quarter; but it is a fact that the answer to the second call was a long wail of 'Marf karo! Marf karo!' which means, 'Have mercy! Have mercy!' It came from the climbing regiment.

The cavalry stood dumbfounded, till the big troopers had time to whisper one to another: 'Mir Khan, was that thy voice? Abdullah, didst *thou* call?' Lieutenant Halley stood beside his charger and waited. So long as no firing was going on he was content. Another flash of lightning showed the horses with heaving flanks and nodding heads, the men, white eyeballed, glaring beside them, and the stone watchtower to the left. This time there was no head at the window, and the rude iron-clamped shutter that could turn a rifle-bullet was closed.

'Go on, men,' said the Major. 'Get up to the top at any rate.'

The squadron toiled forward, the horses wagging their tails and the men pulling at the bridles, the stones rolling down the hillside and the sparks flying. Lieutenant Halley declares that he never heard a squadron make so much noise in his life. They scrambled up, he said, as though each horse had eight legs and a spare horse to follow him. Even then there was no sound from the watchtower, and the men stopped exhausted on the ridge that overlooked the pit of darkness in which the village of Bersund lay. Girths were loosed, curb-chains shifted, and saddles adjusted, and the men dropped down among the stones. Whatever might happen now, they held the upper ground of any attack.

The thunder ceased, and with it the rain, and the soft, thick darkness of a winter night before the dawn covered them all. Except for the sound of running water among the ravines, everything was still. They heard the shutter of the watchtower below them thrown back with a clang, and the voice of the watcher calling: 'Oh, Hafiz Ullah!'

The echoes took up the call – 'La-la-la!' – and an answer came from a watchtower hidden round the curve of the hill, 'What is it, Shahbaz Khan?'

Shahbaz Khan replied, in the high-pitched voice of the mountaineer: 'Hast thou seen?'

The answer came back: 'Yes. God deliver us from all evil spirits!'

There was a pause, and then: 'Hafiz Ullah, I am alone! Come to me!'

'Shahbaz Khan, I am alone also; but I dare not leave my post!'

'That is a lie; thou art afraid.'

A longer pause followed, and then: 'I am afraid. Be silent! They are below us still. Pray to God and sleep.'

The troopers listened and wondered, for they could not understand what save earth and stone could lie below the watchtowers.

Shahbaz Khan began to call again: 'They are below us. I can see them. For the pity of God, come over to me, Hafiz Ullah! My father slew ten of them. Come over!'

Hafiz Ullah answered to the darkness in a very loud voice, 'Mine was guiltless. Hear, ye Men of the Night, neither my father nor my blood had any part in that sin. Bear thou thine own punishment, Shahbaz Khan.'

'Oh, someone ought to stop those two chaps crowing away like cocks there,' said Lieutenant Halley, shivering under his rock.

He had hardly turned round to expose a new side of him to the rain before a long-locked, evil-smelling Afghan rushed up the hill, and tumbled into his arms. Halley sat upon him, and thrust as much of a sword-hilt as could be spared down the man's gullet. 'If you cry out, I kill you,' he said, cheerfully.

The man was beyond any expression of terror: he lay and quaked, gasping. When Halley took the sword-hilt from between his teeth, he was still inarticulate, but clung to Halley's arm, feeling it from elbow to wrist.

'The Rissala! the dead Rissala!' he gulped at last. 'It is down there!'

'No; the Rissala, the very much alive Rissala. It is up here,' said Halley, unshipping his watering-bridle, and fastening the man's hands. 'Why were you in the towers so foolish as to let us pass?'

'The valley is full of the dead,' said the Afghan. 'It is better to fall into the hands of the English than the hands of the dead. They march to and fro below there. I saw them in the lightning.'

He recovered his composure after a little, and whispering, because Halley's pistol was at his stomach, said: 'What is this? There is no war between us now, but the Mullah will kill me for not seeing you pass!'

'Rest easy,' said Halley; 'we are coming to kill the Mullah, if God please. His teeth have grown too long. No harm will come to thee unless the daylight shows thine as a face which is desired by the gallows for crime done. But what of the dead regiment?'

'I only kill within my own border,' said the man, immensely relieved. 'The dead regiment is below. The men must have passed through it on their journey – four hundred dead on horses, stumbling among their own graves, among the little heaps – dead men all, whom we slew.'

'Whew!' said Halley. 'That accounts for my cursing Carter and the Major cursing me. Four hundred sabres, eh? No wonder we thought there were a few extra men in the troop. Kurruk Shah,' he whispered to a grizzled native officer that lay within a few feet of him, 'hast thou heard anything of a dead Rissala in these hills?'

'Assuredly,' said Kurruk Shah with a chuckle. 'When I was a young man I saw the killing in the valley of Sheor-Kôt there at our feet, and I know the tale that grew up therefrom. But how can the ghosts of unbelievers prevail against us who are of the Faith? Strap that dog's hands a little tighter, Sahib. An Afghan is like an eel.'

'But a dead Rissala,' said Halley, jerking his captive's wrist. 'That is foolish talk, Kurruk Shah. The dead are dead. Hold still, *sag*.' The Afghan wriggled.

'The dead are dead, and for that reason they walk at night. What need to talk? We be men, we have our eyes and ears. Thou canst both see and hear them, down the hillside,' said Kurruk Shah.

Halley stared and listened long and intently. The valley was full of stifled noises, as every valley must be at night; but whether he saw or heard more than was natural Halley alone knows, and he does not choose to speak on the subject.

At last, and just before the dawn, a green rocket shot up from the far side of the valley of Bersund, at the head of the gorge, to show that the Goorkhas were in position. A red light from the infantry at left and right answered it, and the cavalry burnt a white flare. Afghans in winter are late sleepers, and it was not till full day that the Gulla Kutta Mullah's men began to straggle from their huts, rubbing their eyes. They saw men in green, and red, and brown uniforms, leaning on their arms, neatly arranged all round the crater of the village of Bersund, in a cordon that not a wolf could have broken. They rubbed their eyes the more when a pink-faced young man, who was not even in the Army, but represented the Political Department, tripped down the hillside with two orderlies, rapped at the door of the Gulla Kutta Mullah's hut, and told him quietly to step out and be tied up for safe transport. That same young man passed on through the huts, tapping here one cateran, and there another lightly with his cane; and as each was pointed out, so he was tied up, staring hopelessly at the crowned heights around where the English soldiers looked down with incurious eyes. Only the Mullah tried to carry it off by curses and high words, till a soldier who was tying his hands, said:

'None o' your lip! Why didn't you come out when you was ordered, instead o' keepin' us awake all night? You're no better than my own barrick-sweeper, you white-'eaded old polyanthus! Kim up!'

Half an hour later the troops had gone away with the Mullah and his thirteen friends; the dazed villagers were looking ruefully at a pile of broken muskets and snapped swords, and wondering how in the world they had come so to miscalculate the forbearance of the Indian Government.

It was a very neat little affair, neatly carried out, and the men concerned were unofficially thanked for their services.

Yet it seems to me that much credit is also due to another regiment whose name did not appear in the Brigade Orders, and whose very existence is in danger of being forgotten.

# HOW THE BRIGADIER CAME TO THE CASTLE OF GLOOM

*By A. Conan Doyle*

YOU DO VERY WELL, my friends, to treat me with some little reverence, for in honouring me you are honouring both France and yourselves. It is not merely an old, grey-moustached officer whom you see eating his omelette or draining his glass, but it is a piece of history, and of the most glorious history which our own or any country has ever had. In me you see one of the last of those wonderful men, the men who were veterans when they were yet boys, who learned to use a sword earlier than a razor, and who during a hundred battles had never once let the enemy see the colour of their knapsacks. For twenty years we were teaching Europe how to fight, and even when they had learned their lesson it was only the thermometer, and never the bayonet, which could break the Grand Army down. Berlin, Naples, Vienna, Madrid, Lisbon, Moscow – we stabled our horses in them all. Yes, my friends, I say again that you do well to send your children to me with flowers, for these ears have heard the trumpet calls of France, and these eyes have seen her standards in lands where they may never be seen again.

Even now, when I doze in my armchair, I can see those great warriors stream before me – the green-jacketed chasseurs, the giant cuirassiers, Poniatowsky's lancers, the white-mantled dragoons, the nodding bearskins of the horse grenadiers. And then there comes the thick, low rattle of the drums, and through wreaths of dust and smoke I see the line of high bonnets, the row of brown faces, the swing and toss of the long, red plumes amid the sloping lines of steel. And there rides Ney with his red head, and Lefebvre with his bulldog jaw, and Lannes with his Gascon swagger; and then amidst the gleam of brass and the flaunting feathers I catch a glimpse of *him*, the man with the pale smile, the rounded shoulders, and the far-off eyes. There is an

15

end of my sleep, my friends, for up I spring from my chair, with a cracked voice calling and a silly hand outstretched, so that Madame Titaux has one more laugh at the old fellow who lives among the shadows.

Although I was a full Chief of Brigade when the wars came to an end, and had every hope of soon being made a General of Division, it is still rather to my earlier days that I turn when I wish to talk of the glories and the trials of a soldier's life. For you will understand that when an officer has so many men and horses under him, he has his mind full of recruits and remounts, fodder and farriers, and quarters, so that even when he is not in the face of the enemy, life is a very serious matter for him. But when he is only a lieutenant or a captain, he has nothing heavier than his epaulettes upon his shoulders, so that he can clink his spurs and swing his dolman, drain his glass and kiss his girl, thinking of nothing save of enjoying a gallant life. That is the time when he is likely to have adventures, and it is most often to that time that I shall turn in the stories which I may have for you. So it will be tonight when I tell you of my visit to the Castle of Gloom; of the strange mission of Sub-Lieutenant Duroc, and of the horrible affair of the man who was once known as Jean Carabin, and afterwards as the Baron Straubenthal.

You must know, then, that in the February of 1807, immediately after the taking of Danzig, Major Legendre and I were commissioned to bring four hundred remounts from Prussia into eastern Poland.

The hard weather, and especially the great battle at Eylau, had killed so many of the horses that there was some danger of our beautiful Tenth of Hussars becoming a battalion of light infantry. We knew, therefore, both the Major and I, that we should be very welcome at the front. We did not advance very rapidly, however, for the snow was deep, the roads detestable, and we had but twenty returning invalids to assist us. Besides, it is impossible, when you have a daily change of forage, and sometimes none at all, to move horses faster than a walk. I am aware that in the story-books the cavalry whirls past at the maddest of gallops; but for my own part, after twelve campaigns, I should be very satisfied to know that my brigade could always walk upon the march and trot in the presence of the enemy. This I say of the hussars and chasseurs, mark you, so that it is far more the case with cuirassiers or dragoons.

For myself I am fond of horses, and to have four hundred of them, of every age and shade and character, all under my own hands, was a very great pleasure to me. They were from Pomerania for the most part, though some were from Normandy and some from Alsace, and it amused us to notice that they differed in character as much as the people of those provinces. We observed also, what I have often proved since, that the nature of a horse can be told by his colour, from the coquettish light bay full of fancies and nerves, to the hardy chestnut, and from the docile roan to the pig-headed rusty-black. All this has nothing in the world to do with my story, but how is an officer of cavalry to get on with his tale when he finds four hundred horses waiting for him at the outset? It is my habit, you see, to talk of that which interests myself, and so I hope that I may interest you.

We crossed the Vistula opposite Marienwerder, and had got as far as Riesenberg, when Major Legendre came into my room in the post house with an open paper in his hand.

'You are to leave me,' said he, with despair upon his face.

It was no very great grief to me to do that, for he was, if I may say so, hardly worthy to have such a subaltern. I saluted, however, in silence.

'It is an order from General Lasalle,' he continued; 'you are to proceed to Rossel instantly, and to report yourself at the headquarters of the regiment.'

No message could have pleased me better. I was already very well thought of by my superior officers, although I may say that none of them had quite done me justice. It was evident to me, therefore, that this sudden order meant that the regiment was about to see service once more, and that Lasalle understood how incomplete my squadron would be without me. It is true that it came at an inconvenient moment, for the keeper of the post house had a daughter – one of those ivory-skinned, black-haired Polish girls – whom I had hoped to have some further talk with. Still, it is not for the pawn to argue when the fingers of the player move him from the square; so down I went, saddled my big black charger, Rataplan, and set off instantly upon my lonely journey.

My word, it was a treat for those poor Poles and Jews, who have so little to brighten their dull lives, to see such a picture as that before their doors. The frosty morning air made Rataplan's great black limbs and the beautiful curves of his back and sides gleam and shimmer with every gambade. As for me, the rattle of hoofs upon a road, and the jingle of bridle chains which comes with every toss of a saucy head, would even now set my blood dancing through my veins. You may think, then, how I carried myself in my five-and-twentieth year – I, Etienne Gerard, the picked horseman and surest blade in the ten regiments of hussars. Blue was our colour in the Tenth – a sky-blue dolman and pelisse with a scarlet front – and it was said of us in the army that we could set a whole population running, the women towards us, and the men away. There were bright eyes in the Riesenberg windows that morning, which seemed to beg me to tarry; but what can a soldier do, save to kiss his hand and shake his bridle as he rides upon his way?

It was a bleak season to ride through the poorest and ugliest country in Europe, but there was a cloudless sky above, and a bright, cold sun, which shimmered on the huge snowfields. My breath reeked into the frosty air, and Rataplan sent up two feathers of steam from his nostrils, while the icicles drooped from the side-irons of his bit. I let him trot to warm his limbs, while for my own part I had too much to think of to give much heed to the cold. To north and south stretched the great plains, mottled over with dark clumps of fir and lighter patches of larch. A few cottages peeped out here and there, but it was only three months since the Grand Army had passed that way, and you know what that meant to a country. The Poles were our friends, it was true, but out of a hundred thousand men, only the Guard had wagons, and the rest had to live as best they might. It did not surprise me, therefore, to see no signs of cattle and no smoke from the silent houses. A weal had been left across the country where the great host had passed and it was said that even the rats were starved wherever the Emperor had led his men.

By midday I had got as far as the village of Saalfeldt, but as I was on the direct road for Osterode, where the Emperor was wintering, and also for the main camp of the seven divisions of infantry, the highway was choked with carriages and carts. What with artillery caissons and wagons and couriers, and the ever-thickening stream of recruits and stragglers, it seemed to me that it would be a very long time before I should join my comrades. The plains, however, were five feet deep in snow, so there was nothing for it but to plod upon our way. It was with joy, therefore, that I found a second road which branched away from the other, trending through a fir-wood towards the north. There was a small auberge at the crossroads, and a patrol of the Third Hussars of Conflans – the very regiment of which I was afterwards Colonel – were mounting their horses at the door. On the steps stood their officer, a slight, pale young man, who looked more like a young priest from a seminary than a leader of the devil-may-care rascals before him.

'Good day, sir,' said he, seeing that I pulled up my horse.

'Good day,' I answered. 'I am Lieutenant Etienne Gerard, of the Tenth.'

I could see by his face that he had heard of me. Everybody had heard of me since my duel with the six fencing-masters. My manner, however, served to put him at his ease with me.

'I am Sub-Lieutenant Duroc, of the Third,' said he.

'Newly joined?' I asked.

'Last week.'

I had thought as much, from his white face and from the way in which he let his men lounge upon their horses. It was not so long, however, since I had learned myself what it was like when a schoolboy has to give orders to veteran troopers. It made me blush, I remember, to shout abrupt commands to men who had seen more battles than I had years, and it would have come more natural for me to say, 'With your permission, we shall now wheel into line,' or, 'If you think it best, we shall trot.' I did not think the less of the lad, therefore, when I observed that his men were somewhat out of hand, but I gave them a glance which stiffened them in their saddles.

'May I ask, monsieur, whether you are going by this northern road?' I asked.

'My orders are to patrol it as far as Arensdorf,' said he.

'Then I will, with your permission, ride so far with you,' said I. 'It is very clear that the longer way will be the faster.'

So it proved, for this road led away from the army into a country which was given over to Cossacks and marauders, and it was as bare as the other was crowded. Duroc and I rode in front, with our six troopers clattering in the rear. He was a good boy, this Duroc, with his head full of the nonsense that they teach at St Cyr, knowing more about Alexander and Pompey than how to mix a horse's fodder or care for a horse's feet. Still, he was, as I have said, a good boy, unspoiled as yet by the camp. It pleased me to hear him prattle away about his sister Marie and about his mother in Amiens. Presently we found ourselves at the village of Hayenau. Duroc rode up to the post house and asked to see the master.

'Can you tell me,' said he, 'whether the man who calls himself the Baron Straubenthal lives in these parts?'

The postmaster shook his head, and we rode upon our way.

I took no notice of this, but when, at the next village, my comrade repeated the same question, with the same result, I could not help asking him who this Baron Straubenthal might be.

'He is a man,' said Duroc, with a sudden flush upon his boyish face, 'to whom I have a very important message to convey.'

Well, this was not satisfactory, but there was something in my companion's manner which told me that any further questioning would be distasteful to him. I said nothing more, therefore, but Duroc would still ask every peasant whom we met whether he could give him any news of the Baron Straubenthal.

For my own part I was endeavouring, as an officer of light cavalry should, to form an idea of the lay of the country, to note the course of the streams, and to mark the places where there should be fords. Every step was taking us farther from the camp round the flanks of which we were travelling. Far to the south a few plumes of grey smoke in the frosty air marked the position of some of our outposts. To the north, however, there was nothing between ourselves and the Russian winter quarters. Twice on the extreme horizon I caught a glimpse of the glitter of steel, and pointed it out to my companion. It was too distant for us to tell whence it came, but we had little doubt that it was from the lance-heads of marauding Cossacks.

The sun was just setting when we rode over a low hill and saw a small village upon our right, and on our left a high black castle, which jutted out from amongst the pine-woods. A farmer with his cart was approaching us – a matted-haired, downcast fellow, in a sheepskin jacket.

'What village is this?' asked Duroc.

'It is Arensdorf,' he answered, in his barbarous German dialect.

'Then here I am to stay the night,' said my young companion. Then, turning to the farmer, he asked his eternal question, 'Can you tell me where the Baron Straubenthal lives?'

'Why, it is he who owns the Castle of Gloom,' said the farmer, pointing to the dark turrets over the distant fir-forest.

Duroc gave a shout like the sportsman who sees his game rising in front of him. The lad seemed to have gone off his head – his eyes shining, his face deathly white, and such a grim set about his mouth as made the farmer shrink away from him. I can see him now, leaning forward on his brown horse, with his eager gaze fixed upon the great black tower.

'Why do you call it the Castle of Gloom?' I asked.

'Well, it's the name it bears upon the countryside,' said the farmer. 'By all accounts there have been some black doings up yonder. It's not for nothing that the wickedest man in Poland has been living there these fourteen years past.'

'A Polish nobleman?' I asked.

'Nay, we breed no such men in Poland,' he answered.

'A Frenchman, then?' cried Duroc.

'They say that he came from France.'

'And with red hair?'

'As red as a fox.'

'Yes, yes, it is my man,' cried my companion, quivering all over in his excitement. 'It is the hand of Providence which has led me here. Who can say that there is not justice in this world? Come, Monsieur Gerard, for I must see the men safely quartered before I can attend to this private matter.'

He spurred on his horse, and ten minutes later we were at the door of the inn of Arensdorf, where his men were to find their quarters for the night.

Well, all this was no affair of mine, and I could not imagine what the meaning of it might be. Rossel was still far off, but I determined to ride on for a few hours and take my chance of some wayside barn in which I could find shelter for Rataplan and myself. I had mounted my horse, therefore, after tossing off a cup of wine, when young Duroc came running out of the door and laid his hand upon my knee.

'Monsieur Gerard,' he panted, 'I beg of you not to abandon me like this!'

'My good sir,' said I, 'if you would tell me what is the matter and what you would wish me to do, I should be better able to tell you if I could be of any assistance to you.'

'You can be of the very greatest,' he cried. 'Indeed, from all that I have heard of you, Monsieur Gerard, you are the one man whom I should wish to have by my side tonight.'

'You forget that I am riding to join my regiment.'

'You cannot, in any case, reach it tonight. Tomorrow will bring you to Rossel. By staying with me you will confer the very greatest kindness upon me, and you will aid me in a matter which concerns my own honour and the honour of my family. I am compelled, however, to confess to you that some personal danger may possibly be involved.'

It was a crafty thing for him to say. Of course, I sprang from Rataplan's back and ordered the groom to lead him back into the stables.

'Come into the inn,' said I, 'and let me know exactly what it is that you wish me to do.'

He led the way into a sitting-room, and fastened the door lest we should be interrupted. He was a well-grown lad, and as he stood in the glare of the lamp, with the light beating upon his earnest face and upon his uniform of silver grey, which suited him to a marvel, I felt my heart warm towards him. Without going so far as to say that he carried himself as I had done at his age, there was at least similarity enough to make me feel in sympathy with him.

'I can explain it all in a few words,' said he. 'If I have not already satisfied your very natural curiosity, it is because the subject is so painful a one to me that I can hardly bring myself to allude to it. I cannot, however, ask for your assistance without explaining to you exactly how the matter lies.

'You must know, then, that my father was the well-known banker, Christophe Duroc, who was murdered by the people during the September massacres. As you are aware, the mob took possession of the prisons, chose three so-called judges to pass sentence upon the unhappy aristocrats, and then tore them to pieces when they were passed out into the street. My father had been a benefactor of the poor all his life. There were many to plead for him. He had the fever, too, and was carried in, half-dead, upon a blanket. Two of the judges were in favour of acquitting him; the third, a young Jacobin, whose huge body and brutal mind had made him a leader among these wretches, dragged him, with his own hands, from the litter, kicked him again and again with his heavy boots, and hurled him out of the door, where in an instant he was torn limb from limb under circumstances which are too horrible for me to describe. This, as you perceive, was murder, even under their own unlawful laws, for two of their own judges had pronounced in my father's favour.

'Well, when the days of order came back again, my elder brother began to make enquiries about this man. I was only a child then, but it was a family matter, and it was discussed in my presence. The fellow's name was Carabin. He was one of Sansterre's Guard, and a noted duellist. A foreign lady named the Baroness Straubenthal having been dragged before the Jacobins, he had gained her liberty for her on the promise that she with her money and estates should be his. He had married her, taken her name and title, and escaped out of France at the time of the fall of Robespierre. What had become of him we had no means of learning.

'You will think, doubtless, that it would be easy for us to find him, since we had both his name and his title. You must remember, however, that the Revolution left us without money, and that without money such a search is very difficult. Then came the Empire, and it became more difficult still, for, as you are aware, the Emperor considered that the 18th Brumaire brought all accounts to a settlement, and that on that day a veil had been drawn across the past. None the less, we kept our own family story and our own family plans.

'My brother joined the army, and passed with it through all Southern Europe, asking everywhere for the Baron Straubenthal. Last October he was killed at Jena, with his mission still unfulfilled. Then it became my turn, and I have the good fortune to hear of the very man of whom I am in search at one of the first Polish villages which I have to visit, and within a fortnight of joining my regiment. And then, to make the matter even better, I find myself in the company of one whose name is never mentioned throughout the army save in connection with some daring and generous deed.'

This was all very well, and I listened to it with the greatest interest, but I was none the clearer as to what young Duroc wished me to do.

'How can I be of service to you?' I asked.

'By coming up with me.'

'To the Castle?'

'Precisely.'

'When?'

'At once.'

'But what do you intend to do?'

'I shall know what to do. But I wish you to be with me, all the same.'

Well, it was never in my nature to refuse an adventure, and, besides, I had every sympathy with the lad's feelings. It is very well to forgive one's enemies, but one wishes to give them something to forgive also. I held out my hand to him, therefore.

'I must be on my way for Rossel tomorrow morning, but tonight I am yours,' said I.

We left our troopers in snug quarters, and, as it was but a mile to the Castle, we did not disturb our horses. To tell the truth, I hate to see a cavalry man walk, and I hold that just as he is the most gallant thing upon earth when he has his saddle-flaps between his knees, so he is the most clumsy when he has to loop up his sabre and his sabretache in one hand and turn in his toes for fear of catching the rowels of his spurs. Still, Duroc and I were of the age when one can carry things off, and I dare swear that no woman at least would have quarrelled with the appearance of the two young hussars, one in blue and one in grey, who set out that night from the Arensdorf post house. We both carried our swords, and for my own part I slipped a pistol from my holster into the inside of my pelisse, for it seemed to me that there might be some wild work before us.

The track which led to the Castle wound through a pitch-black fir-wood, where we could see nothing save the ragged patch of stars above our head. Presently, however, it opened up, and there was the Castle right in front of us, about as far as a carbine would carry. It was a huge, uncouth place, and bore every mark of being exceedingly old, with turrets at every corner, and a square keep on the side which was nearest to us. In all its great shadow there was no sign of light save for a single window, and no sound came from it. To me there was something awful in its size and its silence, which corresponded so well with its sinister name. My companion pressed on eagerly, and I followed him along the ill-kept path which led to the gate.

There was no bell or knocker upon the great, iron-studded door, and it was only by pounding with the hilts of our sabres that we could attract attention. A thin, hawk-faced man, with a beard up to his temples, opened it at last. He carried a lantern in one hand, and in the other a chain which held an enormous black hound. His manner at the first moment was threatening, but the sight of our uniforms and of our faces turned it into one of sulky reserve.

'The Baron Straubenthal does not receive visitors at so late an hour,' said he, speaking in very excellent French.

'You can inform Baron Straubenthal that I have come eight hundred leagues to see him, and that I will not leave until I have done so,' said my companion. I could not myself have said it with a better voice and manner.

The fellow took a sidelong look at us, and tugged at his black beard in his perplexity.

'To tell the truth, gentlemen,' said he, 'the Baron has a cup or two of wine in him at this hour, and you would certainly find him a more entertaining companion if you were to come again in the morning.'

He had opened the door a little wider as he spoke, and I saw by the light of the lamp in the hall behind him that three other rough fellows were standing there, one of whom held another of these monstrous hounds. Duroc must have seen it also, but it made no difference to his resolution.

'Enough talk,' said he, pushing the man to one side. 'It is with your master that I have to deal.'

The fellows in the hall made way for him as he strode in among them, so great is the power of one man who knows what he wants over several who are not sure of themselves. My companion tapped one of them upon the shoulder with as much assurance as though he owned him.

'Show me to the Baron,' said he.

The man shrugged his shoulders, and answered something in Polish. The fellow with the beard, who had shut and barred the front door, appeared to be the only one among them who could speak French.

'Well, you shall have your way,' said he, with a sinister smile. 'You shall see the Baron. And perhaps, before you have finished, you will wish that you had taken my advice.'

We followed him down the hall, which was stone-flagged and very spacious, with skins scattered upon the floor, and the heads of wild beasts upon the walls. At the farther end he threw open a door, and we entered.

It was a small room, scantily furnished, with the same marks of neglect and decay which met us at every turn. The walls were hung with discoloured tapestry, which had come loose at one corner, so as to expose the rough stonework behind. A second door, hung with a curtain, faced us upon the other side. Between lay a square table, strewn with dirty dishes and the sordid remains of a meal. Several bottles were scattered over it. At the head of it, and facing us, there sat a huge man, with a lion-like head and a great shock of orange-coloured hair. His beard was of the same glaring hue; matted and tangled and coarse as a horse's mane. I have seen some strange faces in my time, but never one more brutal than that, with its small, vicious, blue eyes, its white, crumpled cheeks, and the thick, hanging lip which protruded over his monstrous beard. His head swayed about on his shoulders, and he looked at us with the vague, dim gaze of a drunken man. Yet he was not so drunk but that our uniforms carried their message to him.

'Well, my brave boys,' he hiccuped. 'What is the latest news from Paris, eh? You're going to free Poland, I hear, and have meantime all become slaves yourselves – slaves to a little aristocrat with his grey coat and his three-cornered hat. No more citizens either, I am told, and nothing but monsieur and madame. My faith, some more heads will have to roll into the sawdust basket some of these mornings.'

Duroc advanced in silence, and stood by the ruffian's side.

'Jean Carabin,' said he.

The Baron started, and the film of drunkenness seemed to be clearing from his eyes.

'Jean Carabin,' said Duroc, once more.

He sat up and grasped the arms of his chair.

'What do you mean by repeating that name, young man?' he asked.

'Jean Carabin, you are a man whom I have long wished to meet.'

'Supposing that I once had such a name, how can it concern you, since you must have been a child when I bore it?'

'My name is Duroc.'

'Not the son of—?'

'The son of the man you murdered.'

The Baron tried to laugh, but there was terror in his eyes.

'We must let bygones be bygones, young man,' he cried. 'It was our life or theirs in those days: the aristocrats or the people. Your father was of the Gironde. He fell. I was of the mountain. Most of my comrades fell. It was all the fortune of war. We must forget all this and learn to know each other better, you and I.' He held out a red, twitching hand as he spoke.

'Enough,' said young Duroc. 'If I were to pass my sabre through you as you sit in that chair, I should do what is just and right. I dishonour my blade by crossing it with yours. And yet you are a Frenchman, and have even held a commission under the same flag as myself. Rise, then, and defend yourself!'

'Tut, tut!' cried the Baron. 'It is all very well for you young bloods—'

Duroc's patience could stand no more. He swung his open hand into the centre of the great orange beard. I saw a lip fringed with blood, and two glaring blue eyes above it.

'You shall die for that blow.'

'That is better,' said Duroc.

'My sabre!' cried the other; 'I will not keep you waiting, I promise you!' and he hurried from the room.

I have said that there was a second door covered with a curtain. Hardly had the Baron vanished when there ran from behind it a woman, young and beautiful. So swiftly and noiselessly did she move that she was between us in an instant, and it was only the shaking curtains which told us whence she had come.

'I have seen it all,' she cried. 'Oh, sir, you have carried yourself splendidly.' She stooped to my companion's hand, and kissed it again and again ere he could disengage it from her grasp.

'Nay, madame, why should you kiss my hand?' he cried.

'Because it is the hand which struck him on his vile, lying mouth. Because it may be the hand which will avenge my mother. I am his stepdaughter. The woman whose heart he broke was my mother. I loathe him, I fear him. Ah, there is his step!' In an instant she had vanished as suddenly as she had come. A moment later, the Baron entered with a drawn sword in his hand, and the fellow who had admitted us at his heels.

'This is my secretary,' said he. 'He will be my friend in this affair. But we shall need more elbow-room than we can find here. Perhaps you will kindly come with me to a more spacious apartment.'

It was evidently impossible to fight in a chamber which was blocked by a great table. We followed him out, therefore, into the dimly-lit hall. At the farther end a light was shining through an open door.

'We shall find what we want in here,' said the man with the dark beard. It was a large, empty room, with rows of barrels and cases round the walls. A strong lamp stood upon a shelf in the corner. The floor was level and true, so that no swordsman could ask for more. Duroc drew his sabre and sprang into it. The Baron stood back with a bow and motioned me to follow my companion. Hardly were my heels over the threshold when the heavy door crashed behind us and the key screamed in the lock. We were taken in a trap.

For a moment we could not realise it. Such incredible baseness was outside all our experiences. Then, as we understood how foolish we had been to trust for an instant a man with such a history, a flush of rage came over us, rage against his villainy and against our own stupidity. We rushed at the door together, beating it with our fists and kicking with our heavy boots. The sound of our blows and of our execrations must have resounded through the Castle. We called to this villain, hurling at him every name which might pierce even into his hardened soul. But the door was enormous – such a door as one finds in medieval castles – made of huge beams clamped together with iron. It was as easy to break as a square of the Old Guard. And our cries appeared to be of as little avail as our blows, for they only brought for answer the clattering echoes from the high roof above us. When you have done some soldiering, you soon learn to put up with what cannot be altered. It was I, then, who first recovered my calmness, and prevailed upon Duroc to join with me in examining the apartment which had become our dungeon.

There was only one window, which had no glass in it and was so narrow that one could not so much as get one's head through. It was high up, and Duroc had to stand upon a barrel in order to see from it.

'What can you see?' I asked.

'Fir-woods, and an avenue of snow between them,' said he. 'Ah!' he gave a cry of surprise.

I sprang upon the barrel beside him. There was, as he said, a long, clear strip of snow in front. A man was riding down it, flogging his horse and galloping like a madman. As we watched, he grew smaller and smaller, until he was swallowed up by the black shadows of the forest.

'What does that mean?' asked Duroc.

'No good for us,' said I. 'He may have gone for some brigands to cut our throats. Let us see if we cannot find a way out of this mousetrap before the cat can arrive.'

The one piece of good fortune in our favour was that beautiful lamp. It was nearly full of oil, and would last us until morning. In the dark our situation would have been far more difficult. By its light we proceeded to examine the packages and cases which lined the walls.

In some places there was only a single line of them, while in one corner they were piled nearly to the ceiling. It seemed that we were in the storehouse of the Castle, for there were a great number of cheeses, vegetables of various kinds, bins full of dried fruits, and a line of wine barrels. One of these had a spigot in it, and as I had eaten little during the day, I was glad of a cup of claret and some food. As to Duroc, he would take nothing, but paced up and down the room in a fever of anger and impatience. 'I'll have him yet!' he cried, every now and then. 'The rascal shall not escape me!'

This was all very well, but it seemed to me, as I sat on a great round cheese eating my supper, that this youngster was thinking rather too much of his own family affairs and too little of the fine scrape into which he had got me. After all, his father had been dead fourteen years, and nothing could set that right; but here was Etienne Gerard, the most dashing lieutenant in the whole Grand Army, in imminent danger of being cut off at the very outset of his brilliant career. Who was ever to know the heights to which I might have risen if I were knocked on the head in this hole-and-corner business, which had nothing whatever to do with France or the Emperor? I could not help thinking what a fool I had been, when I had a fine war before me and everything which a man could desire, to go off upon a hare-brained expedition of this sort, as if it were not enough to have a quarter of a million Russians to fight against, without plunging into all sorts of private quarrels as well.

'That is all very well,' I said at last, as I heard Duroc muttering his threats. 'You may do what you like to him when you get the upper hand. At present the question rather is, what is *he* going to do to us?'

'Let him do his worst!' cried the boy. 'I owe a duty to my father.'

'That is mere foolishness,' said I. 'If you owe a duty to your father, I owe one to my mother, which is to get out of this business safe and sound.'

My remark brought him to his senses.

'I have thought too much of myself!' he cried. 'Forgive me, Monsieur Gerard. Give me your advice as to what I should do.'

'Well,' said I, 'it is not for our health that they have shut us up here among the cheeses. They mean to make an end of us if they can. That is certain. They hope that no one knows that we have come here, and that none will trace us if we remain. Do your hussars know where you have gone to?'

'I said nothing.'

'Hum! It is clear that we cannot be starved here. They must come to us if they are to kill us. Behind a barricade of barrels we could hold our own against the five rascals whom we have seen. That is, probably, why they have sent that messenger for assistance.'

'We must get out before he returns.'

'Precisely, if we are to get out at all.'

'Could we not burn down this door?' he cried.

'Nothing could be easier,' said I. 'There are several casks of oil in the corner. My only objection is that we should ourselves be nicely toasted, like two little oyster pâtés.'

'Can you not suggest something?' he cried, in despair. 'Ah, what is that?'

There had been a low sound at our little window, and a shadow came between the stars and ourselves. A small, white hand was stretched into the lamplight. Something glittered between the fingers.

'Quick! quick!' cried a woman's voice.

We were on the barrel in an instant.

'They have sent for the Cossacks. Your lives are at stake. Ah, I am lost! I am lost!'

There was the sound of rushing steps, a hoarse oath, a blow, and the stars were once more twinkling through the window. We stood helpless upon our barrel with our blood cold with horror. Half a minute afterwards we heard a smothered scream, ending in a choke. A great door slammed somewhere in the silent night.

'Those ruffians have seized her. They will kill her,' I cried.

Duroc sprang down with the inarticulate shouts of one whose reason had left him. He struck the door so frantically with his naked hands that he left a blotch of blood with every blow.

'Here is the key!' I shouted, picking one from the floor. 'She must have thrown it in at the instant that she was torn away.'

My companion snatched it from me with a shriek of joy. A moment later he dashed it down upon the boards. It was so small that it was lost in the enormous lock. Duroc sank upon one of the boxes with his head between his hands. He sobbed in his despair. I could have sobbed, too, when I thought of the woman and how helpless we were to save her.

But I am not easily baffled. After all, this key must have been sent to us for a purpose. The lady could not bring us that of the door, because this murderous stepfather of hers would most certainly have it in his pocket. Yet this other must have a meaning, or why should she risk her life to place it in our hands? It would say little for our wits if we could not find out what that meaning might be.

I set to work moving all the cases out from the wall, and Duroc, gaining new hope from my courage, helped me with all his strength. It was no light task, for many of them were large and heavy. On we went, working like maniacs, slinging barrels, cheeses, and boxes pell-mell into the middle of the room. At last there only remained one huge barrel of vodki, which stood in the corner. With our united strength we rolled it out, and there was a little low wooden door in the wainscot behind it. The key fitted, and with a cry of delight we saw it swing open before us. With the lamp in my hand, I squeezed my way in, followed by my companion.

We were in the powder-magazine of the Castle – a rough, walled cellar, with barrels all round it, and one with the top staved in in the centre. The powder from it lay in a black heap upon the floor. Beyond there was another door, but it was locked.

'We are no better off than before,' cried Duroc. 'We have no key.'

'We have a dozen,' I cried.

'Where?'

I pointed to the line of powder barrels.

'You would blow this door open?'

'Precisely.'

'But you would explode the magazine.'

It was true, but I was not at the end of my resources.

'We will blow open the store-room door,' I cried.

I ran back and seized a tin box which had been filled with candles. It was about the size of my shako – large enough to hold several pounds of powder. Duroc filled it while I cut off the end of a candle. When we had finished, it would have puzzled a colonel of engineers to make a better petard. I put three cheeses on the top of each other and placed it above them, so as to lean against the lock. Then we lit our candle-end and ran for shelter, shutting the door of the magazine behind us.

It is no joke, my friends, to lie among all those tons of powder, with the knowledge that if the flame of the explosion should penetrate through one thin door our blackened limbs would be shot higher than the Castle keep. Who could have believed that a half-inch of candle could take so long to burn? My ears were straining all the time for the thudding of the hoofs of the Cossacks who were coming to destroy us. I had almost made up my mind that the candle must have gone out when there was a smack like a bursting bomb, our door flew to bits, and pieces of cheese, with a shower of turnips, apples, and splinters of cases, were shot in among us. As we rushed out we had to stagger through an impenetrable smoke, with all sorts of debris beneath our feet, but there was a glimmering square where the dark door had been. The petard had done its work.

In fact, it had done more for us than we had even ventured to hope. It had shattered gaolers as well as gaol. The first thing that I saw as I came out into the hall was a man with a butcher's axe in his hand, lying flat upon his back, with a gaping wound across his forehead. The second was a huge dog, with two of its legs broken, twisting in agony upon the floor. As it raised itself up I saw the two broken ends flapping like flails. At the same instant I heard a cry, and there was Duroc, thrown against the wall, with the other hound's teeth in his throat. He pushed it off with his left hand, while again and again he passed his sabre through its body, but it was not until I blew out its brains with my pistol that the iron jaws relaxed, and the fierce, blood-shot eyes were glazed in death.

There was no time for us to pause. A woman's scream from in front – a scream of mortal terror – told us that even now we might be too late. There were two other men in the hall, but they cowered away from our drawn swords and furious faces. The blood was streaming from Duroc's neck and dyeing the grey fur of his pelisse. Such was the lad's fire, however, that he shot in front of me, and it was only over his shoulder that I caught a glimpse of the scene as we rushed into the chamber in which we had first seen the master of the Castle of Gloom.

The Baron was standing in the middle of the room, with his tangled mane bristling like an angry lion. He was, as I have said, a huge man, with enormous shoulders; and as he stood there, with his face flushed with rage and his sword advanced, I could not but think that, in spite of all his villainies, he had a proper figure for a grena-dier. The lady lay cowering in a chair behind him. A weal across one of her white arms and a dog-whip upon the floor were enough to show that our escape had hardly been in time to save her from his brutality. He gave a howl like a wolf as we broke in, and was upon us in an instant, hacking and driving, with a curse at every blow.

I have already said that the room gave no space for swordsmanship. My young companion was in front of me in the narrow passage between the table and the wall, so that I could only look on without being able to aid him. The lad knew something of his weapon, and was as fierce and active as a wild cat, but in so narrow a space the weight and strength of the giant gave him the advantage. Besides, he was an admirable swordsman. His parade and riposte were as quick as lightning. Twice he touched Duroc upon the shoulder, and then, as the lad slipped up on a lunge, he whirled up his sword to finish him before he could recover his feet. I was quicker than he, however, and took the cut upon the pommel of my sabre.

'Excuse me,' said I, 'but you have still to deal with Etienne Gerard.'

He drew back and leaned against the tapestry-covered wall, breathing in little, hoarse gasps, for his foul living was against him.

'Take your breath,' said I. 'I will await your convenience.'

'You have no cause of quarrel against me,' he panted.

'I owe you some little attention,' said I, 'for having shut me up in your store-room. Besides, if all other were wanting, I see cause enough upon that lady's arm.'

'Have your way, then!' he snarled, and leaped at me like a madman. For a minute I saw only the blazing blue eyes, and the red glazed point which stabbed and stabbed, rasping off to right or to left, and yet ever back at my throat and my breast. I had never thought that such good sword-play was to be found at Paris in the days of the Revolution. I do not suppose that in all my little affairs I have met six men who had a better knowledge of their weapon. But he knew that I was his master. He read death in my eyes, and I could see that he read it. The flush died from his face. His breath came in shorter and in thicker gasps. Yet he fought on, even after the final thrust had come, and died still hacking and cursing, with foul cries upon his lips, and his blood clotting upon his orange beard. I who speak to you have seen so many battles, that my old memory can scarce contain their names, and yet of all the terrible sights which these eyes have rested upon, there is none which I care to think of less than of that orange beard with the crimson stain in the centre, from which I had drawn my sword point.

It was only afterwards that I had time to think of all this. His monstrous body had hardly crashed down upon the floor before the woman in the corner sprang to her feet, clapping her hands together and screaming out in her delight. For my part I was disgusted to see a woman take such delight in a deed of blood, and I gave no thought as to the terrible wrongs which must have befallen her before she could so far forget the gentleness of her sex. It was on my tongue to tell her sharply to be silent, when a strange, choking smell took the breath from my nostrils, and a sudden, yellow glare brought out the figures upon the faded hangings.

'Duroc, Duroc!' I shouted, tugging at his shoulder. 'The Castle is on fire!'

The boy lay senseless upon the ground, exhausted by his wounds. I rushed out into the hall to see whence the danger came. It was our explosion which had set alight to the dry framework of the door. Inside the store-room some of the boxes were already blazing. I glanced in, and as I did so my blood was turned to water by the sight of the powder barrels beyond, and of the loose heap upon the floor. It might be seconds, it could not be more than minutes, before the flames would be at the edge of it. These eyes will be closed in death, my friends, before they cease to see those crawling lines of fire and the black heap beyond.

How little I can remember what followed. Vaguely I can recall how I rushed into the chamber of death, how I seized Duroc by one limp hand and dragged him down the hall, the woman keeping pace with me and pulling at the other arm. Out of the gateway we rushed, and on down the snow-covered path until we were on the fringe of the fir-forest. It was at that moment that I heard a crash behind me, and, glancing round, saw a great spout of fire shoot up into the wintry sky. An instant later there seemed to come a second crash far louder than the first. I saw the fir trees and the stars whirling round me, and I fell unconscious across the body of my comrade.

It was some weeks before I came to myself in the post house of Arensdorf, and longer still before I could be told all that had befallen me. It was Duroc, already able to go soldiering, who came to my bedside and gave me an account of it. He it was who told me how a piece of timber had struck me on the head and had laid me almost dead upon the ground. From him, too, I learned how the Polish girl had run to Arensdorf, how she had roused our hussars, and how she had only just brought them back in time to save us from the spears of the Cossacks who had been summoned from their bivouac by that same black-bearded secretary whom we had seen galloping so swiftly over the snow. As to the brave lady who had twice saved our lives, I could not learn very much about her at that moment from Duroc, but when I chanced to meet him in Paris two years later, after the campaign of Wagram, I was not very much surprised to find that I needed no introduction to his bride, and that by the queer turns of fortune he had himself, had he chosen to use it, that very name and title of the Baron Straubenthal, which showed him to be the owner of the blackened ruins of the Castle of Gloom.

# THE ADVENTURE OF THE CANTANKEROUS OLD LADY

## By *Grant Allen*

ON THE DAY when I found myself with twopence in my pocket, I naturally made up my mind to go round the world.

It was my stepfather's death that drove me to it. I had never seen my stepfather. Indeed, I never thought of him as anything more than even Colonel Watts-Morgan. I owed him nothing except my poverty. He married my dear mother when I was a girl at school in Switzerland; and he proceeded to spend her little fortune, left at her sole disposal by my father's will, in paying his gambling debts. After that, he carried my dear mother off to Burma; and when he and the climate between them had succeeded in killing her, he made up for his appropriations cheaply by allowing me just enough to send me to Girton. So, when the Colonel died, in the year I was leaving college, I did not think it necessary to go into mourning for him. Especially as he chose the precise moment when my allowance was due, and bequeathed me nothing but his consolidated liabilities.

'Of course you will teach,' said Elsie Petheridge, when I explained my affairs to her. 'There is a good demand just now for high-school teachers.'

I looked at her, aghast. '*Teach!* Elsie,' I cried. (I had come up to town to settle her in at her unfurnished lodgings.) 'Did you say *teach?* That's just like you dear good schoolmistresses! You go to Cambridge, and get examined till the heart and life have been examined out of you; then you say to yourselves at the end of it all, "Let me see; what am I good for now? I'm just

35

about fit to go away and examine other people!" That's what our Principal would call "a vicious circle" – if one could ever admit there was anything vicious at all about you, dear. No, Elsie, my child, I do *not* propose to teach. Nature did not cut me out for a high-school teacher. I couldn't swallow a poker if I tried for weeks. Pokers don't agree with me. My dear, between ourselves, I am a bit of a rebel.'

'You are, Brownie,' she answered, pausing in her papering, with her sleeves rolled up – they called me 'Brownie', partly because of my complexion, but partly because they could never understand me. 'We all knew that long ago.'

I laid down the paste-brush and mused.

'Do you remember, Elsie,' I said, staring hard at the paper-board, 'when I first went to Girton, how all you girls wore your hair quite straight, in neat smooth coils, plaited up at the back about the size of a pancake; and how of a sudden I burst in upon you, like a tropical hurricane, and demoralised you; and how, after three days of me, some of the dear innocents began with awe to cut themselves artless fringes, while others went out in fear and trembling and surreptitiously purchased a pair of curling-tongs? I was a bombshell in your midst in those days; why, you yourself were almost afraid at first to speak to me.'

'You see, you had a bicycle,' Elsie put in, smoothing the half-papered wall; 'and in those days, of course, ladies didn't yet bicycle. You must admit, Brownie, dear, it *was* a startling innovation. You terrified us so. And yet, after all, there isn't much harm in you.'

'I hope not,' I said, devoutly. 'I was before my time, that was all; at present, even a curate's wife may blamelessly bicycle.'

'But if you don't teach,' Elsie went on, gazing at me with those wondering big blue eyes of hers, 'whatever will you do, Brownie?' Her horizon was bounded by the scholastic circle.

'I haven't the faintest idea,' I answered, continuing to paste. 'Only, as I can't trespass upon your elegant hospitality for life, whatever I mean to do, I must begin doing this morning, when we've finished the papering. I couldn't teach' (teaching, like mauve, is the refuge of the incompetent); 'and I don't, if possible, want to sell bonnets.'

'As a milliner's girl?' Elsie asked, with a face of red horror.

'As a milliner's girl; why not? 'Tis an honest calling. Earl's daughters do it now. But you needn't look so shocked. I tell you, just at present, I am not contemplating it.'

'Then what *do* you contemplate?'

I paused and reflected. 'I am here in London,' I answered, gazing rapt at the ceiling; 'London, whose streets are paved with gold –

though it *looks* at first sight like muddy flagstones; London, the greatest and richest city in the world, where an adventurous soul ought surely to find some loophole for an adventure. (That piece is hung crooked, dear; we must take it down again.) I have a Plan, therefore. I submit myself to fate; or, if you prefer it, I leave my future in the hands of Providence. I shall go out this morning, as soon as I've "cleaned myself", and embrace the first stray enterprise that offers. Our Baghdad teems with enchanted carpets. Let one but float my way, and, hi, presto, I seize it. I go where glory or a modest competence waits me. I snatch at the first offer, the first hint of an opening.'

Elsie stared at me, more aghast and more puzzled than ever. 'But, how?' she asked. 'Where? When? You *are* so strange! What will you do to find one?'

'Put on my hat and walk out,' I answered. 'Nothing could be simpler. This city bursts with enterprises and surprises. Strangers from east and west hurry through it in all directions. Omnibuses traverse it from end to end, even, I am told, to Islington and Putney; within, folk sit face to face who never saw one another before in their lives, and who may never see one another again, or, on the contrary, may pass the rest of their days together.'

I had a lovely harangue all pat in my head, in much the same strain, on the infinite possibilities of entertaining angels unawares, in cabs, on the Underground, in the Aërated Bread shops; but Elsie's widening eyes of horror pulled me up short like a hansom in Piccadilly when the inexorable upturned hand of the policeman checks it. 'Oh, Brownie,' she cried, drawing back, 'you *don't* mean to tell me you're going to ask the first young man you meet in an omnibus to marry you?'

I shrieked with laughter. 'Elsie,' I cried, kissing her dear yellow little head, 'you are *impayable.* You never will learn what I mean. You don't understand the language. No, no; I am going out, simply in search of adventure. What adventure may come, I have not at this moment the faintest conception. The fun lies in the search, the uncertainty, the toss-up of it. What is the good of being penniless – with the trifling exception of twopence – unless you are prepared to accept your position in the spirit of a masked ball at Covent Garden?'

'I have never been to one,' Elsie put in.

'Gracious heavens, neither have I! What on earth do you take me for? But I mean to see where fate will lead me.'

'I may go with you?' Elsie pleaded.

'Certainly *not*, my child,' I answered – she was three years older than I, so I had the right to patronise her. 'That would spoil all. Your dear little face would be quite enough to scare away a timid adventure.' She knew what I meant. It was gentle and pensive, but it lacked initiative.

So, when we had finished that wall, I put on my best hat, and strolled out by myself into Kensington Gardens.

I am told I ought to have been terribly alarmed at the straits in which I found myself – a girl of twenty-one, alone in the world, and only twopence short of penniless, without a friend to protect, a relation to counsel, her. (I don't count Aunt Susan, who lurked in ladylike indigence at Blackheath, and whose counsel was given away too profusely to everybody to allow one's placing any very high value upon it.) But, as a matter of fact, I must admit I was not in the least alarmed. Nature had endowed me with a profusion of crisp black hair, and plenty of high spirits. If my eyes had been like Elsie's – that liquid blue which looks out upon life with mingled pity and amazement – I might have felt as a girl ought to feel under such conditions; but having large dark eyes, with a bit of a twinkle in them, and being as well able to pilot a bicycle as any girl of my acquaintance, I have inherited or acquired an outlook on the world which distinctly leans rather towards cheeriness than despondency. I croak with difficulty. So I accepted my plight as an amusing experience, affording full scope for the congenial exercise of courage and ingenuity.

How boundless are the opportunities of Kensington Gardens – the Round Pond, the winding Serpentine, the mysterious seclusion of the Dutch brick Palace. Genii swarm there. It is a land of romance, bounded on the north by the Abyss of Bayswater, and on the south by the Amphitheatre of the Albert Hall. But for a centre of adventure I chose the Long Walk; it beckoned me somewhat as the North-West Passage beckoned my seafaring ancestors – the buccaneering mariners of Elizabethan Devon. I sat down on a chair at the foot of an old elm with a poetic hollow, prosaically filled by a utilitarian plate of galvanised iron. Two ancient ladies were seated on the other side already – very grand-looking dames, with the haughty and exclusive ugliness of the English aristocracy in its later stages. For frank hideousness, commend me to the noble dowager. They were talking confidentially as I sat down; the trifling episode of my approach did not suffice to stem the full stream of their conversation. The great ignore the intrusion of their inferiors.

'Yes, it's a terrible nuisance,' the eldest and ugliest of the two observed – she was a high-born lady, with a distinctly cantankerous cast of countenance. She had a Roman nose, and her skin was wrinkled like a wilted apple; she wore coffee-coloured point-lace in her bonnet, with a complexion to match. 'But what could I do, my dear? I simply *couldn't* put up with such insolence. So I looked her straight back in the face – oh, she quailed, I can tell you; and I said to her, in my iciest voice – you know how icy I can be when occasion demands it' – the second old lady nodded an ungrudging assent, as if perfectly prepared to admit her friend's gift of iciness – 'I said to her, "Célestine, you can take your month's wages, and half an hour to get out of this house." And she dropped me a deep reverence, and she answered: "*Oui, madame; merci beaucoup, madame; je ne désire pas mieux, madame.*" And out she flounced. So there was the end of it.'

'Still, you go to Schlangenbad on Monday?'

'That's the point. On Monday. If it weren't for the journey, I should have been glad enough to be rid of the minx. I'm glad as it is, indeed; for a more insolent, independent, answer-you-back-again young woman, with a sneer of her own, *I* never saw, Amelia – but I *must* get to Schlangenbad. Now, there the difficulty comes in. On the one hand, if I engage a maid in London, I have the choice of two evils. I must either take a trapesing English girl – and I know by experience that an English girl on the Continent is a vast deal worse than no maid at all: *you* have to wait upon *her*, instead of her waiting upon you; she gets seasick on the crossing, and when she reaches France or Germany, she hates the meals, and she can't speak the language, so that she's always calling you in to interpret for her in her private differences with the *fille-de-chambre* and the landlord: or else I must pick up a French maid in London, and I know equally by experience that the French maids one engages in London are invariably dishonest – more dishonest than the rest even; they've come here because they have no character elsewhere, and they think you aren't likely to write and enquire of their last mistress in Toulouse or St Petersburg. Then, again, on the other hand, I can't wait to get a Gretchen, an unsophisticated little Gretchen of the Taunus at Schlangenbad – I suppose there *are* unsophisticated girls in Germany still – made in Germany – they don't make 'em any longer in England, I'm sure – like everything else, the trade in rustic innocence has been driven from the country. I can't wait to get a Gretchen, as I should like to do, of course, because I simply *daren't* undertake to cross the Channel alone and go all that long journey by Ostend or Calais, Brussels and Cologne, to Schlangenbad.'

'You could get a temporary maid,' her friend suggested, in a lull of the tornado.

The Cantankerous Old Lady flared up. 'Yes, and have my jewel-case stolen! Or find she was an English girl without one word of

German. Or nurse her on the boat when I want to give my undivided attention to my own misfortunes. No, Amelia, I call it positively unkind of you to suggest such a thing. You're *so* unsympathetic! I put my foot down there. I will *not* take any temporary person.'

I saw my chance. This was a delightful idea. Why not start for Schlangenbad with the Cantankerous Old Lady?

Of course, I had not the slightest intention of taking a lady's-maid place for a permanency. Nor even, if it comes to that, as a passing expedient. But *if* I wanted to go round the world, how could I do better than set out by the Rhine country? The Rhine leads you on to the Danube, the Danube to the Black Sea, the Black Sea to Asia; and so by way of India, China and Japan, you reach the Pacific and San Francisco; whence one returns quite easily by New York and the White Star Liners. I began to feel like a globe-trotter already; the Cantankerous Old Lady was the thin end of the wedge – the first rung of the ladder!

I leaned around the corner of the tree and spoke. 'Excuse me,' I said, in my suavest voice, 'but I think I see a way out of your difficulty.'

My first impression was that the Cantankerous Old Lady would go off in a fit of apoplexy. She grew purple in the face with indignation and astonishment, that a casual outsider should venture to address her; so much so, indeed, that for a second I almost regretted my well-meant interposition. Then she scanned me up and down, as if I were a girl in a mantle shop, and she contemplated buying either me or the mantle. At last, catching my eye, she thought better of it, and burst out laughing.

'What do you mean by this eavesdropping?' she asked.

I flushed up in turn. 'This is a public place,' I replied, with dignity; 'and you spoke in a tone which was hardly designed for the strictest privacy. Besides, I desired to do you a service.'

The Cantankerous Old Lady regarded me once more from head to foot. I did not quail. Then she turned to her companion. 'The girl has spirit,' she remarked, in an encouraging tone, as if she were discussing some absent person. 'Upon my word, Amelia, I rather like the look of her. Well, my good woman, what do you want to suggest to me?'

'Merely this,' I replied, bridling up and crushing her. 'I am a Girton girl, an officer's daughter, and I have nothing in particular to do for the moment. I don't object to going to Schlangenbad. I would convoy you over, as companion, or lady-help, or anything else you choose to call it; I would remain with you there for a week, till you could arrange with your Gretchen, presumably unsophisticated; and then I would leave you. Salary is unimportant; my fare suffices. I accept the chance as a cheap opportunity of attaining Schlangenbad.'

The yellow-faced old lady put up her long-handled tortoise-shell eyeglasses and inspected me all over again. 'Well, I declare,' she murmured. 'What are girls coming to, I wonder? Girton, you say; Girton! That place at Cambridge! You speak Greek, of course; but how about German?'

'Like a native,' I answered, with cheerful promptitude. 'I was at school in Canton Berne; it is a mother tongue to me.'

'No, no,' the old lady went on, fixing her keen small eyes on my mouth. 'Those little lips could never frame themselves to "schlecht" or "wunderschön"; they were not cut out for it.'

'Pardon me,' I answered, in German. 'What I say, that I mean. The never-to-be-forgotten music of the Fatherland's-speech has on my infant ear from the first-beginning impressed itself.'

The old lady laughed aloud.

'Don't jabber it to me, child,' she cried. 'I hate the lingo. It's the one tongue on earth that even a pretty girl's lips fail to render attractive. You yourself make faces over it. What's your name, young woman?'

'Lois Cayley.'

'Lois! *What* a name! I never heard of any Lois in my life before, except Timothy's grandmother. *You're* not anybody's grandmother, are you?'

'Not to my knowledge,' I answered, gravely.

She burst out laughing again.

'Well, you'll do, I think,' she said, catching my arm. 'That big mill down yonder hasn't ground the originality altogether out of you. I adore originality. It was clever of you to catch at the suggestion of this arrangement. Lois Cayley, you say; any relation of a madcap Captain Cayley whom I used once to know, in the Forty-second Highlanders?'

'His daughter,' I answered, flushing. For I was proud of my father.

'Ha! I remember; he died, poor fellow; he was a good soldier – and his' – I felt she was going to say 'his fool of a widow', but a glance from me quelled her; 'his widow went and married that good-looking scapegrace, Jack Watts-Morgan. Never marry a man, my dear, with a double-barrelled name and no visible means of subsistence: above all, if he's generally known by a nickname. So you're poor Tom Cayley's daughter, are you? Well, well, we can settle this little matter between us. Mind, I'm a person who always expects to have my own way. If you come with *me* to Schlangenbad, you must do as I tell you.'

'I *think* I could manage it – for a week,' I answered, demurely.

She smiled at my audacity. We passed on to terms. They were quite satisfactory. She wanted no references. 'Do I look like a woman who cares about a reference? You take my fancy; that's the point! And poor Tom Cayley! But, mind, I will *not* be contradicted.'

'And your name and address?' I asked, after we had settled preliminaries.

A faint red spot rose quaintly in the centre of the Cantankerous Old Lady's sallow cheek. 'My dear', she murmured, 'my name is the one thing on earth I'm really ashamed of. My parents chose to inflict upon me the most odious label that human ingenuity ever devised for a Christian soul; and I've not had courage enough to burst out and change it.'

A gleam of intuition flashed across me. 'You don't mean to say,' I exclaimed, 'that you're called Georgina?'

The Cantankerous Old Lady gripped my arm hard. 'What an unusually intelligent girl!' she broke in. 'How on earth did you guess? It *is* Georgina.'

'Fellow-feeling,' I answered. 'So is mine, Georgina Lois. But as I quite agree with you as to the atrocity of such conduct, I have suppressed the Georgina. It ought to be made penal to send innocent girls into the world so burdened.'

'My opinion to a T! You are really an exceptionally sensible young woman. There's my name and address; I start on Monday.'

I glanced at her card. The very copperplate was noisy. 'Lady Georgina Fawley, 49 Fortescue Crescent, W.'

It had taken us twenty minutes to arrange our protocols. As I walked off, well pleased, Lady Georgina's friend ran after me quickly.

'You must take care,' she said, in a warning voice. 'You've caught a Tartar.'

'So I suspect,' I answered. 'But a week in Tartary will be at least an experience.'

'She has an awful temper.'

'That's nothing. So have I. Appalling, I assure you. And if it comes to blows, I'm bigger and younger and stronger than she is.'

'Well, I wish you well out of it.'

'Thank you. It is kind of you to give me this warning. But I think I can take care of myself. I come, you see, of a military family.'

I nodded my thanks, and strolled back to Elsie's. Dear little Elsie was in transports of surprise when I related my adventure.

'Will you really go? And what will you do, my dear, when you get there?'

'I haven't a notion,' I answered; 'but, anyhow, I shall have got there.'

'Oh, Brownie, you might starve!'

'And I might starve in London. In either place, I have only two hands and one head to help me.'

'But, then, here you are among friends. You might stop with me for ever.'

I kissed her fluffy forehead. 'You good, generous little Elsie,' I cried; 'I won't stop here one moment after I have finished the painting and papering. I came here to help you. I couldn't go on eating your hard-earned bread and doing nothing. I know how sweet you are; but the last thing I want is to add to your burdens. Now let us roll up our sleeves again and get on with the dado.'

'But, Brownie, you'll want to be getting your own things ready. Remember, you're off to Germany on Monday.'

I shrugged my shoulders. 'Tis a foreign trick I picked up in Switzerland. 'What have I got to get ready?' I asked. 'I can't go out and buy a complete summer outfit in Bond Street for twopence. Now, don't look at me like that: be practical, Elsie, and let me help you paint the dado.' For unless I helped her, poor Elsie could never have finished it herself. I cut out half her clothes for her; her own ideas were almost entirely limited to differential calculus. And cutting out a blouse by differential calculus is weary, uphill work for a high-school teacher.

By Monday I had papered and furnished the rooms, and was ready to start on my voyage of exploration. I met the Cantankerous Old Lady at Charing Cross, by appointment, and proceeded to take charge of her luggage and tickets.

Oh my, how fussy she was! 'You will drop that basket! I hope you have got through tickets, *via* Malines, *not* by Brussels – I won't go by Brussels. You have to change there. Now, mind you notice how much the luggage weighs in English pounds, and make the man at the office give you a note of it to check those horrid Belgian porters. They'll charge you for double the weight, unless you reduce it at once to kilogrammes. *I* know their ways. Foreigners have no consciences. They just go to the priest and confess, you know, and wipe it all out, and start fresh again on a career of crime next morning. I'm sure I don't know why I *ever* go abroad. The only country in the world fit to live in is England. No mosquitoes, no passports, no – goodness gracious, child, don't let that odious man bang about my hat-box! Have you no immortal soul, porter, that you crush other people's property as if it was black-beetles? No, I will *not* let you take this, Lois; this is my jewel-box – it contains all that remains of the Fawley family jewels. I positively decline to appear at Schlangenbad without a diamond to my back. This never leaves my hands. It's hard enough nowadays to keep body and skirt together. *Have* you secured that *coupé* at Ostend?'

We got into our first-class carriage. It was clean and comfortable; but the Cantankerous Old Lady made the porter mop the floor, and fidgeted and worried till we slid out of the station. Fortunately, the only other occupant of the compartment was a most urbane and obliging Continental gentleman – I say Continental, because I never quite made out whether he was French, German, or Austrian – who was anxious in every way to meet Lady Georgina's wishes. Did madame desire to have the window open? Oh, certainly, with pleasure; the day was so sultry. Closed a little more? *Parfaitement*, there *was* a current of air, *il faut l'admettre*. Madame would prefer the corner? No? Then perhaps she would like this valise for a footstool? *Permettez* – just thus. A cold draught runs so often along the floor in railway carriages. This is Kent that we traverse; ah, the garden of England! As a diplomat, he knew every nook of Europe, and he echoed the *mot* he had accidentally heard drop from madame's lips on the platform: no country in the world so delightful as England!

'Monsieur is attached to the Embassy in London?' Lady Georgina enquired, growing affable.

He twirled his grey moustache: a waxed moustache of great distinction. 'No, madame; I have quitted the diplomatic service; I inhabit London now *pour mon agrément*. Some of my compatriots call it *triste*; for me, I find it the most fascinating capital in Europe. What gaiety! What movement! What poetry! What mystery!'

'If mystery means fog, it challenges the world,' I interposed.

He gazed at me with fixed eyes. 'Yes, mademoiselle,' he answered, in quite a different and markedly chill voice. 'Whatever your great country attempts – were it only a fog – it achieves consummately.'

I have quick intuitions. I felt the foreign gentleman took an instinctive dislike to me.

To make up for it, he talked much, and with animation, to Lady Georgina. They ferreted out friends in common, and were as much surprised at it as people always are at that inevitable experience.

'Ah, yes, madame, I recollect him well in Vienna. I was there at the time, attached to our Legation. He was a charming man; you read his masterly paper on the Central Problem of the Dual Empire?'

'You were in Vienna then!' the Cantankerous Old Lady mused back. 'Lois, my child, don't stare' – she had covenanted from the first to call me Lois, as my father's daughter, and I confess I preferred it to being Miss Cayley'd. 'We must surely have met. Dare I ask your name, monsieur?'

I could see the foreign gentleman was delighted at this turn. He had played for it, and carried his point. He meant her to ask him. He had a card in his pocket, conveniently close; and he handed it across to her. She read it, and passed it on: 'M. le Comte de Laroche-sur-Loiret.'

'Oh, I remember your name well,' the Cantankerous Old Lady broke in. 'I think you knew my husband, Sir Evelyn Fawley, and my father, Lord Kynaston.'

The Count looked profoundly surprised and delighted. 'What! you are then Lady Georgina Fawley!' he cried, striking an attitude. 'Indeed, miladi, your admirable husband was one of the very first to exert his influence in my favour at Vienna. Do I recall him, *ce cher* Sir Evelyn? If I recall him! What a fortunate rencounter! I must have seen you some years ago at Vienna, miladi, though I had not then the great pleasure of making your acquaintance. But your face had impressed itself on my sub-conscious self!' (I did not learn till later that the esoteric doctrine of the sub-conscious self was Lady Georgina's favourite hobby.) 'The moment chance led me to this carriage this morning, I said to myself, "That face, those features: so vivid, so striking: I have seen them somewhere. With what do I connect them in the recesses of my memory? A high-born family; genius; rank; the diplomatic service; some unnameable charm; some faint touch of eccentricity. Ha! I have it. Vienna, a carriage with footmen in red livery, a noble presence, a crowd of wits – poets, artists, politicians – pressing eagerly round the landau." That was my mental picture as I sat and confronted you: I understand it all now; this is Lady Georgina Fawley!'

I thought the Cantankerous Old Lady, who was a shrewd person in her way, must surely see through this obvious patter; but I had underestimated the average human capacity for swallowing flattery. Instead of dismissing his fulsome nonsense with a contemptuous smile, Lady Georgina perked herself up with a conscious air of coquetry, and asked for more. 'Yes, they were delightful days in Vienna,' she said, simpering; 'I was young then, Count; I enjoyed life with a zest.'

'Persons of miladi's temperament are always young,' the Count retorted, glibly, leaning forward and gazing at her. 'Growing old is a foolish habit of the stupid and the vacant. Men and women of *esprit* are never older. One learns as one goes on in life to admire, not the obvious beauty of mere youth and health' – he glanced across at me disdainfully – 'but the profounder beauty of deep character in a face – that calm and serene beauty which is imprinted on the brow by experience of the emotions.'

'I have had my moments,' Lady Georgina murmured, with her head on one side.

'I believe it, miladi,' the Count answered, and ogled her.

Thenceforward to Dover, they talked together with ceaseless animation. The Cantankerous Old Lady was capital company. She had a tang in her tongue, and in the course of ninety minutes she had flayed alive the greater part of London society, with keen wit and sprightliness. I laughed against my will at her ill-tempered sallies; they were too funny not to amuse, in spite of their vitriol. As for the Count, he was charmed. He talked well himself, too, and between them, I almost forgot the time till we arrived at Dover.

It was a very rough passage. The Count helped us to carry our nineteen hand-packages and four rugs on board; but I noticed that, fascinated as she was with him, Lady Georgina resisted his ingenious efforts to gain possession of her precious jewel-case as she descended the gangway. She clung to it like grim death, even in the chops of the Channel. Fortunately I am a good sailor, and when Lady Georgina's sallow cheek began to grow pale, I was steady enough to supply her with her shawl and her smelling-bottle. She fidgeted and worried the whole way over. She *would* be treated like a vertebrate animal. Those horrid Belgians had no right to stick their deck-chairs just in front of her. The impertinence of the hussies with the bright red hair – a grocer's daughters, she felt sure – in venturing to come and sit on the same bench with *her* – the bench 'for ladies only', under the lee of the funnel! 'Ladies only,' indeed! Did the baggages pretend they considered themselves ladies? Oh, that placid old gentleman in the episcopal gaiters was their father, was he? Well, a bishop should bring up his daughters better, having his children in subjection with all gravity. Instead of which – 'Lois, my smelling-salts!' This was a beastly boat; such an odour of machinery; they had no decent boats nowadays; with all our boasted improvements, she could remember well when the cross-Channel service was much better conducted than it was at present. But *that* was before we had compulsory education. The working classes were driving trade out of the country, and the consequence was, we couldn't build a boat which didn't reek like an oil-shop. Even the sailors on board were French – jabbering idiots; not an honest British Jack-tar among the lot of them; though the stewards were English, and very inferior Cockney English at that, with their off-hand ways, and their School Board airs and graces. *She'd* School

Board them if they were her servants; *she'd* show them the sort of respect that was due to birth and education. But the children of the lower classes never learnt their catechism nowadays; they were too much occupied with literatoor, jography, and free-'and drawrin'. Happily for my nerves, a good lurch to leeward put a stop for a while to the course of her thoughts on the present distresses.

At Ostend, the Count made a second gallant attempt to capture the jewel-case, which Lady Georgina automatically repulsed. She had a fixed habit, I believe, of sticking fast to that jewel-case; for she was too overpowered by the Count's urbanity, I feel sure, to suspect for a moment his honesty of purpose. But whenever she travelled, I fancy, she clung to her case as if her life depended upon it: it contained the whole of her valuable diamonds.

We had twenty minutes for refreshments at Ostend, during which interval my old lady declared with warmth that I *must* look after her registered luggage; though, as it was booked through to Cologne, I could not even see it till we crossed the German frontier; for the Belgian *douaniers* seal up the van as soon as the through baggage for Germany is unloaded. To satisfy her, however, I went through the formality of pretending to inspect it, and rendered myself hateful to the head of the *douane* by asking various foolish and inept questions, on which Lady Georgina insisted. When I had finished this silly and uncongenial task – for I am not by nature fussy, and it is hard to assume fussiness as another person's proxy – I returned to our *coupé* which I had arranged for in London. To my great amazement, I found the Cantankerous Old Lady and the egregious Count comfortably seated there. 'Monsieur has been good enough to accept a place in our carriage,' she observed, as I entered.

He bowed and smiled. 'Or, rather, madame has been so kind as to offer me one,' he corrected.

'Would you like some lunch, Lady Georgina?' I asked, in my chilliest voice. 'There are ten minutes to spare, and the *buffet* is excellent.'

'An admirable inspiration,' the Count murmured. 'Permit me to escort you, miladi.'

'You will come, Lois?' Lady Georgina asked.

'No, thank you,' I answered, for I had an idea. 'I am a capital sailor, but the sea takes away my appetite.'

'Then you'll keep our places,' she said, turning to me. 'I hope you won't allow them to stick in any horrid foreigners! They will try to force them on you unless you insist. *I* know their tricky ways. You have the tickets, I trust? And the *bulletin* for the *coupé*? Well, mind you don't lose the paper for the registered luggage. Don't let those dreadful porters touch my cloaks. And if anybody attempts to get in, be sure you stand in front of the door as they mount to prevent them.'

The Count handed her out; he was all high courtly politeness. As Lady Georgina descended, he made yet another dexterous effort to relieve her of the jewel-case. I don't think she noticed it, but automatically once more she waved him aside. Then she turned to me. 'Here, my dear,' she said, handing it to me, 'you'd better take care of it. If I lay it down in the *buffet* while I am eating my soup, some rogue may run away with it. But mind, don't let it out of your hands on any account. Hold it so, on your knee; and, for Heaven's sake, don't part with it.'

By this time my suspicions of the Count were profound. From the first I had doubted him; he was so blandly plausible. But as we landed at Ostend, I had accidently overheard a low whispered conversation when he passed a shabby-looking man, who had travelled in a second-class carriage from London. 'That succeeds?' the shabby-looking man had muttered under his breath in French, as the haughty nobleman with the waxed moustache brushed by him.

'That succeeds admirably,' the Count had answered, in the same soft undertone. *'Ça réussit à merveille.'*

I understood him to mean that he had prospered in his attempt to impose on Lady Georgina.

They had been gone five minutes at the *buffet*, when the Count came back hurriedly to the door of the *coupé* with a *nonchalant* air. 'Oh, mademoiselle,' he said, in an off-hand tone, 'Lady Georgina has sent me to fetch her jewel-case.'

I gripped it hard with both hands. *'Pardon*, M. le Comte,' I answered; 'Lady Georgina entrusted it to *my* safe keeping, and, without her leave, I cannot give it up to anyone.'

'You mistrust me?' he cried, looking black. 'You doubt my honour? You doubt my word when I say that miladi has sent me?'

*'Du tout,'* I answered, calmly. 'But I have Lady Georgina's order to stick to this case; and till Lady Georgina returns, I stick to it.'

He murmured some indignant remark below his breath, and walked off. The shabby-looking passenger was pacing up and down the platform outside in a badly-made dust-coat. As they passed, their lips moved. The Count's seemed to mutter, *'C'est un coup manqué.'*

However, he did not desist even so. I saw he meant to go on with his dangerous little game. He returned to the *buffet* and rejoined Lady Georgina. I felt sure it would be useless to warn her, so completely had the Count succeeded in gulling her; but I took my own steps. I examined the jewel-case closely. It had a leather outer covering; within was a strong steel box, with stout bands of metal to bind it. I took my cue at once, and acted for the best on my own responsibility.

When Lady Georgina and the Count returned, they were like old friends together. The quails in aspic and the sparkling hock had evidently opened their hearts to one another. As far as Malines, they laughed and talked without ceasing. Lady Georgina was now in her finest vein of spleen: her acid wit grew sharper and more caustic each moment. Not a reputation in Europe had a rag left to cover it as we steamed in beneath the huge iron roof of the main central junction.

I had observed all the way from Ostend that the Count had been anxious lest we might have to give up our *coupé* at Malines. I assured him more than once that his fears were groundless, for I had arranged at Charing Cross that it should run right through to the German frontier. But he waved me aside, with one lordly hand. I had not told Lady Georgina of his vain attempt to take possession of her jewel-case; and the bare fact of my silence made him increasingly suspicious of me.

'Pardon me, mademoiselle,' he said, coldly; 'you do not understand these lines as well as I do. Nothing is more common than for those rascals of railway clerks to sell one a place in a *coupé* or a *wagon-lit*, and then never reserve it, or turn one out half way. It is very possible miladi may have to descend at Malines.'

Lady Georgina bore him out by a large variety of selected stories concerning the various atrocities of the rival companies which had stolen her luggage on her way to Italy. As for *trains de luxe*, they were dens of robbers.

So when we reached Malines, just to satisfy Lady Georgina, I put out my head and enquired of a porter. As I anticipated, he replied that there was no change; we went through to Verviers.

The Count, however, was still unsatisfied. He descended, and made some remarks a little further down the platform to an official in the gold-banded cap of a *chef-de-gare*, or some such functionary. Then he returned to us, all fuming. 'It is as I said,' he exclaimed, flinging open the door. 'These rogues have deceived us. The *coupé* goes no further. You must dismount at once, miladi, and take the train just opposite.'

I felt sure he was wrong, and I ventured to say so. But Lady Georgina cried, 'Nonsense, child! The *chef-de-gare* must know. Get out at once! Bring my bag and the rugs! Mind that cloak! Don't forget the sandwich-tin! Thanks, Count; will you kindly take charge of my umbrellas? Hurry up, Lois; hurry up; the train is just starting!'

I scrambled after her, with my fourteen bundles, keeping a quiet eye meanwhile on the jewel-case.

We took our seats in the opposite train, which I noticed was marked 'Amsterdam, Bruxelles, Paris.' But I said nothing. The Count jumped in, jumped about, arranged our parcels, jumped out again. He spoke to a porter: then he rushed back excitedly. '*Mille pardons*, miladi,' he cried. 'I find the *chef-de-gare* has cruelly deceived me. You were right, after all, mademoiselle! We must return to the *coupé*!'

With singular magnanimity, I refrained from saying, 'I told you so.'

Lady Georgina, very flustered and hot by this time, tumbled out once more, and bolted back to the *coupé*. Both trains were just starting. In her hurry, at last, she let the Count take possession of her jewel-case. I rather fancy that as he passed one window he handed it in to the shabby-looking passenger; but I am not certain. At any rate, when we were comfortably seated in our own compartment once more, and he stood on the footboard just about to enter, of a sudden, he made an unexpected dash back, and flung himself wildly into a Paris carriage. At the self-same moment, with a piercing shriek, both trains started.

Lady Georgina flung up her hands in a frenzy of horror. 'My diamonds!' she cried aloud. 'Oh, Lois, my diamonds!'

'Don't distress yourself,' I answered, holding her back, or I verily believe she would have leapt from the train. 'He has only taken the outer shell, with the sandwich-case inside it. *Here* is the steel box!' And I produced it, triumphantly.

She seized it, overjoyed. 'How did this happen?' she cried, hugging it, for she loved those diamonds.

'Very simply,' I answered. 'I saw the man was a rogue, and that he had a confederate with him in another carriage. So, while you were gone to the *buffet* at Ostend, I slipped the box out of the case, and put in the sandwich-tin, that he might carry it off, and we might have proofs against him. All you have to do now is to inform the conductor, who will telegraph to stop the train to Paris. I spoke to him about that at Ostend, so that everything is ready.'

She positively hugged me. 'My dear,' she cried, 'you are the cleverest little woman I ever met in my life! Who on earth could have suspected such a polished gentleman? Why, you're worth your weight in gold. Whatever shall I do without you at Schlangenbad?'

# THE PURPLE TERROR

## By Fred M. White

I

LIEUTENANT WILL SCARLETT'S instructions were devoid of problems, physical or otherwise. To convey a letter from Captain Driver of the *Yankee Doodle*, in Porto Rico Bay, to Admiral Lake on the other side of the isthmus, was an apparently simple matter.

'All you have to do,' the Captain remarked, 'is to take three or four men with you in case of accidents, cross the isthmus on foot, and simply give this letter into the hands of Admiral Lake. By so doing we shall save at least four days, and the aborigines are presumably friendly.'

The aborigines aforesaid were Cuban insurgents. Little or no strife had taken place along the neck lying between Porto Rico and the north bay where Lake's flagship lay, though the belt was known to be given over to the disaffected Cubans.

'It is a matter of fifty miles through practically unexplored country,' Scarlett replied; 'and there's a good deal of the family quarrel in this business, sir. If the Spaniards hate us, the Cubans are not exactly enamoured of our flag.'

Captain Driver roundly denounced the whole pack of them.

'Treacherous thieves to a man', he said. 'I don't suppose your progress will have any brass bands and floral arches to it. And they tell me the forest is pretty thick. But you'll get there all the same. There is the letter, and you can start as soon as you like.'

'I may pick my own men, sir?'

'My dear fellow, take whom you please. Take the mastiff, if you like.'

'I'd like the mastiff,' Scarlett replied; 'as he is practically my own, I thought you would not object.'

Will Scarlett began to glow as the prospect of adventure stimulated his imagination. He was rather a good specimen of West Point naval dandyism. He had brains at the back of his smartness, and his geological and botanical knowledge were going to prove of considerable service to a grateful country when said grateful country should have passed beyond the rudimentary stages of colonisation. And there was some disposition to envy Scarlett on the part of others floating for the past month on the liquid prison of the sapphire sea.

A warrant officer, Tarrer by name, plus two ABs of thews and sinews, to say nothing of the dog, completed the exploring party. By the time that the sun kissed the tip of the feathery hills they had covered some six miles of their journey. From the first Scarlett had been struck by the absolute absence of the desolation and horror of civil strife. Evidently the fiery cross had not been carried here; huts and houses were intact; the villagers stood under sloping eaves, and regarded the Americans with a certain sullen curiosity.

'We'd better stop for the night here,' said Scarlett.

They had come at length to a village that boasted some pretensions. An adobe chapel at one end of the straggling street was faced by a wine-house at the other. A padre, with hands folded over a bulbous, greasy gabardine, bowed gravely to Scarlett's salutation. The latter had what Tarrer called 'considerable Spanish'.

'We seek quarters for the night,' said Scarlett. 'Of course, we are prepared to pay for them.'

The sleepy padre nodded towards the wine-house.

'You will find fair accommodation there,' he said. 'We are friends of the Americanos.'

Scarlett doubted the fact, and passed on with florid thanks. So far, little sign of friendliness had been encountered on the march. Coldness, suspicion, a suggestion of fear, but no friendliness to be embarrassing.

The keeper of the wine-shop had his doubts. He feared his poor accommodation for guests so distinguished. A score or more of picturesque, cut-throat-looking rascals with cigarettes in their mouths lounged sullenly in the bar. The display of a brace of gold dollars enlarged mine host's opinion of his household capacity.

'I will do my best, *señors*,' he said. 'Come this way.'

So it came to pass that an hour after twilight Tarrer and Scarlett were seated in the open amongst the oleanders and the trailing gleam of the fireflies, discussing cigars of average merit and a native wine that was not without virtues. The long bar of the wine-house was brilliantly illuminated; from within came shouts of laughter mingled with the ting, tang of the guitar and the rollicking clack of the castanets.

'They seem to be happy in there,' Tarrer remarked. 'It isn't all daggers and ball in this distressful country.'

A certain curiosity came over Scarlett.

'It is the duty of a good officer', he said, 'to lose no opportunity of acquiring useful information. Let us join the giddy throng, Tarrer.'

Tarrer expressed himself with enthusiasm in favour of any amusement that might be going. A month's idleness on shipboard increases the appetite for that kind of thing wonderfully. The long bar was comfortable, and filled with Cubans who took absolutely no notice of the intruders. Their eyes were turned towards a rude stage at the far end of the bar, whereon a girl was gyrating in a dance with a celerity and grace that caused the wreath of flowers around her shoulders to resemble a trembling zone of purple flame.

'A wonderfully pretty girl and a wonderfully pretty dance,' Scarlett murmured, when the motions ceased and the girl leapt gracefully to the ground. 'Largesse, I expect. I thought so. Well, I'm good for a quarter.'

The girl came forward, extending a shell prettily. She curtsied before Scarlett and fixed her dark, liquid eyes on his. As he smiled and dropped his quarter-dollar into the shell, a coquettish gleam came into the velvety eyes. An ominous growl came from the lips of a bearded ruffian close by.

'Othello's jealous,' said Tarrer. 'Look at his face.'

'I am better employed,' Scarlett laughed. 'That was a graceful dance, pretty one. I hope you are going to give us another one presently—'

Scarlett paused suddenly. His eyes had fallen on the purple band of flowers the girl had twined round her shoulder. Scarlett was an enthusiastic botanist; he knew most of the gems in Flora's crown, but he had never looked upon such a vivid wealth of blossom before.

The flowers were orchids, and orchids of a kind unknown to collectors anywhere. On this point Scarlett felt certain. And yet this part of the world was by no means a difficult one to explore in comparison with New Guinea and Sumatra, where the rarer varieties had their homes.

The blooms were immensely large, far larger than any flower of the kind known to Europe or America, of a deep pure purple, with a blood-red centre. As Scarlett gazed upon them he noticed a certain cruel expression on the flower. Most orchids have a kind of face of their own; the purple blooms had a positive expression of ferocity and cunning. They exhumed, too, a queer, sickly fragrance. Scarlett had smelt something like it before, after the Battle of Manila. The perfume was the perfume of a corpse.

'And yet they are magnificent flowers,' said Scarlett. 'Won't you tell me where you got them from, pretty one?'

The girl was evidently flattered by the attention bestowed upon her by the smart young American. The bearded Othello alluded to edged up to her side.

'The *señor* had best leave the girl alone,' he said, insolently.

Scarlett's fist clenched as he measured the Cuban with his eyes. The Admiral's letter crackled in his breast-pocket, and discretion got the best of valour.

'You are paying yourself a poor compliment, my good fellow,' he said, 'though I certainly admire your good taste. Those flowers interested me.'

The man appeared to be mollified. His features corrugated in a smile.

'The *señor* would like some of those blooms?' he asked. 'It was I who procured them for little Zara here. I can show you where they grow.'

Every eye in the room was turned in Scarlett's direction. It seemed to him that a kind of diabolical malice glistened on every dark face there, save that of the girl, whose features paled under her healthy tan.

'If the *señor* is wise,' she began, 'he will not—'

'Listen to the tales of a silly girl,' Othello put in, menacingly. He grasped the girl by the arm, and she winced in positive pain. 'Pshaw, there is no harm where the flowers grow, if one is only careful. I will take you there, and I will be your guide to Port Anna, where you are going, for a gold dollar.'

All Scarlett's scientific enthusiasm was aroused. It is not given to every man to present a new orchid to the horticultural world. And this one would dwarf the finest plant hitherto discovered.

'Done with you,' he said; 'we start at daybreak. I shall look to you to be ready. Your name is Tito? Well, good-night, Tito.'

As Scarlett and Tarrer withdrew, the girl suddenly darted forward. A wild word or two fluttered from her lips. Then there was a sound as of a blow, followed by a little stifled cry of pain.

'No, no,' Tarrer urged, as Scarlett half turned. 'Better not. They are ten to one, and they are no friends of ours. It never pays to interfere in these family quarrels. I dare say, if you interfered, the girl would be just as ready to knife you as her jealous lover.'

'But a blow like that, Tarrer!'

'It's a pity, but I don't see how we can help it. Your business is the quick dispatch of the Admiral's letter, not the squiring of dames.'

Scarlett owned with a sigh that Tarrer was right.

II

It was quite a different Tito who presented himself at daybreak the following morning. His insolent manner had disappeared. He was cheerful, alert, and he had a manner full of the most winning politeness.

'You quite understand what we want,' Scarlett said. 'My desire is to reach Port Anna as soon as possible. You know the way?'

'Every inch of it, *señor*. I have made the journey scores of times. And I shall have the felicity of getting you there early on the third day from now.'

'Is it so far as that?'

'The distance is not great, *señor*. It is the passage through the woods. There are parts where no white man has been before.'

'And you will not forget the purple orchids?'

A queer gleam trembled like summer lightning in Tito's eyes. The next instant it had gone. A time was to come when Scarlett was to recall that look, but for the moment it was allowed to pass.

'The *señor* shall see the purple orchid,' he said; 'thousands of them. They have a bad name amongst our people, but that is all nonsense. They grow in the high trees, and their blossoms cling to long, green tendrils. These tendrils are poisonous to the flesh, and great care should be taken in handling them. And the flowers are quite harmless, though we call them the devil's poppies.'

To all of this Scarlett listened eagerly. He was all-impatient to see and handle the mysterious flower for himself. The whole excursion was going to prove a wonderful piece of luck. At the same time he had to curb his impatience. There would be no chance of seeing the purple orchid today.

For hours they fought their way along through the dense tangle. A heat seemed to lie over all the land like a curse – a blistering, swelter-ing, moist heat with no puff of wind to temper its breathlessness. By the time that the sun was sliding down, most of the party had had enough of it.

They passed out of the underwood at length, and, striking upwards, approached a clump of huge forest trees on the brow of a ridge. All kinds of parasites hung from the branches; there were ropes and bands of green, and high up a fringe of purple glory that caused Scarlett's pulses to leap a little faster.

'Surely that is the purple orchid?' he cried.

Tito shrugged his shoulders contemptuously.

'A mere straggler or two,' he said, 'and out of our reach in any case. The *señor* will have all he wants and more tomorrow.'

'But it seems to me,' said Scarlett, 'that I could—'

Then he paused. The sun like a great glowing shield was shining full behind the tree with its crown of purple, and showing up every green rope and thread clinging to the branches with the clearness of liquid crystal. Scarlett saw a network of green cords like a huge spider's web, and in the centre of it was not a fly, but a human skeleton!

The arms and legs were stretched apart as if the victim had been crucified. The wrists and ankles were bound in the cruel web. Fragments of tattered clothing fluttered in the faint breath of the evening breeze.

'Horrible,' Scarlett cried, 'absolutely horrible!'

'You may well say that,' Tarrer exclaimed, with a shudder. 'Like the fly in the amber or the apple in the dumpling, the mystery is how he got there.'

'Perhaps Tito can explain the mystery,' Scarlett suggested.

Tito appeared to be uneasy and disturbed. He looked furtively from one to the other of his employers as a culprit might who feels he has been found out. But his courage returned as he noted the absence of suspicion in the faces turned upon him.

'I can explain,' he exclaimed, with teeth that chattered from some unknown terror or guilt. 'It is not the first time that I have seen the skeleton. Some plant-hunter doubtless who came here alone. He climbed into the tree without a knife, and those green ropes got twisted round his limbs, as a swimmer gets entangled in the weeds. The more he struggled, the more the cords bound him. He would call in vain for anyone to assist him here. And so he must have died.'

The explanation was a plausible one, but by no means detracted from the horror of the discovery. For some time the party pushed their way on in the twilight, till the darkness descended suddenly like a curtain.

'We will camp here,' Tito said; 'it is high, dry ground, and we have this belt of trees above us. There is no better place than this for miles around. In the valley the miasma is dangerous.'

As Tito spoke he struck a match, and soon a torch flamed up. The little party were on a small plateau, fringed by trees. The ground was dry and hard, and, as Scarlett and his party saw to their astonishment, littered with bones. There were skulls of animals and skulls of human beings, the skeletons of birds, the frames of beasts, both great and small. It was a weird, shuddering sight.

'We can't possibly stay here,' Scarlett exclaimed.

Tito shrugged his shoulders.

'There is nowhere else,' he replied. 'Down in the valley there are many dangers. Further in the woods are the snakes and jaguars. Bones are nothing. Peuf, they can be easily cleared away.'

They had to be cleared away, and there was an end of the matter. For the most part the skeletons were white and dry as air and sun could make them. Over the dry, calcined mass the huge fringe of trees nodded mournfully. With the rest, Scarlett was busy scattering the mocking frames aside. A perfect human skeleton lay at his feet. On one finger something glittered – a signet ring. As Scarlett took it in his hand he started.

'I know this ring!' he exclaimed; 'it belonged to Pierre Anton, perhaps the most skilled and intrepid plant-hunter the Jardin des Plantes ever employed. The poor fellow was by way of being a friend of mine. He met the fate that he always anticipated.'

'There must have been a rare holocaust here,' said Tarrer.

'It beats me,' Scarlett responded. By this time a large circle had been shifted clear of human and other remains. By the light of the fire loathsome insects could be seen scudding and straddling away. 'It beats me entirely. Tito, can you offer any explanation? If the bones were all human, I could get some grip of the problem. But when one comes to birds and animals as well! Do you see that the skeletons lie in a perfect circle, starting from the centre of the clump of trees above us? What does it mean?'

Tito professed utter ignorance of the subject. Some years before a small tribe of natives invaded the peninsula for religious rites. They came from a long way off in canoes, and wild stories were told concerning them. They burnt sacrifices, no doubt.

Scarlett turned his back contemptuously on this transparent tale. His curiosity was aroused. There must be some explanation, for Pierre Anton had been seen of men within the last ten years.

'There's something uncanny about this,' he said, to Tarrer. 'I mean to get to the bottom of it, or know why.'

'As for me,' said Tarrer, with a cavernous yawn, 'I have but one ambition, and that is my supper, followed by my bed.'

### III

Scarlett lay in the light of the fire looking about him. He felt restless and uneasy, though he would have found it difficult to explain the reason. For one thing, the air trembled to strange noises. There seemed to be something moving, writhing in the forest trees above his head. More than once it seemed to his distorted fancy that he could see a squirming knot of green snakes in motion.

Outside the circle, in a grotto of bones, Tito lay sleeping. A few moments before his dark, sleek head had been furtively raised, and his eyes seemed to gleam in the flickering firelight with malignant cunning. As he met Scarlett's glance he gave a deprecatory gesture and subsided.

'What the deuce does it all mean?' Scarlett muttered. 'I feel certain yonder rascal is up to some mischief. Jealous still because I paid his girl a little attention. But he can't do us any real harm. Quiet, there!'

The big mastiff growled and then whined uneasily. Even the dog seemed to be conscious of some unseen danger. He lay down again, cowed by the stern command, but he still whimpered in his dreams.

'I fancy I'll keep awake for a spell,' Scarlett told himself.

For a time he did so. Presently he began to slide away into the land of poppies. He was walking amongst a garden of bones which bore masses of purple blossoms. Then Pierre Anton came on the scene, pale and resolute as Scarlett had always known him; then the big mastiff seemed in some way to be mixed up with the phantasm of the dream, barking as if in pain, and Scarlett came to his senses.

He was breathing short, a beady perspiration stood on his forehead, his heart hammered in quick thuds – all the horrors of nightmare were still upon him. In a vague way as yet he heard the mastiff howl, a real howl of real terror, and Scarlett knew that he was awake.

Then a strange thing happened. In the none too certain light of the fire, Scarlett saw the mastiff snatched up by some invisible hand, carried far on high towards the trees, and finally flung to the earth with a crash. The big dog lay still as a log.

A sense of fear born of the knowledge of impotence came over Scarlett; what in the name of evil did it all mean? The smart scientist had no faith in the occult, and yet what *did* it all mean?

Nobody stirred. Scarlett's companions were soaked and soddened with fatigue; the rolling thunder of artillery would have scarce disturbed them. With teeth set and limbs that trembled, Scarlett crawled over to the dog.

The great, black-muzzled creature was quite dead. The full chest was stained and soaked in blood; the throat had been cut apparently with some jagged, saw-like instrument away to the bone. And, strangest thing of all, scattered all about the body was a score or more of the great purple orchid flowers broken off close to the head. A hot, pricking sensation travelled slowly up Scarlett's spine and seemed to pass out at the tip of his skull. He felt his hair rising.

He was frightened. As a matter of honest fact, he had never been so horribly scared in his life before. The whole thing was so mysterious, so cruel, so bloodthirsty.

Still, there must be some rational explanation. In some way the matter had to do with the purple orchid. The flower had an evil reputation. Was it not known to these Cubans as the devil's poppy?

Scarlett recollected vividly now Zara's white, scared face when Tito had volunteered to show the way to the resplendent bloom; he remembered the cry of the girl and the blow that followed. He could see it all now. The girl had meant to warn him against some nameless horror to which Tito was leading the small party. This was the jealous Cuban's revenge.

A wild desire to pay this debt to the uttermost fraction filled Scarlett, and shook him with a trembling passion. He crept along in the drenching dew to where Tito lay, and touched his forehead with the chill blue rim of a revolver barrel. Tito stirred slightly.

'You dog!' Scarlett cried. 'I am going to shoot you.'

Tito did not move again. His breathing was soft and regular. Beyond a doubt the man was sleeping peacefully. After all he might be innocent; and yet, on the other hand, he might be so sure of his quarry that he could afford to slumber without anxiety as to his vengeance.

In favour of the latter theory was the fact that the Cuban lay beyond the limit of what had previously been the circle of dry bones. It was just possible that there was no danger outside that pale. In that case it would be easy to arouse the rest, and so save them from the horrible death which had befallen the mastiff. No doubt these were a form of upas tree, but that would not account for the ghastly spectacle in mid-air.

'I'll let this chap sleep for the present,' Scarlett muttered.

He crawled back, not without misgivings, into the ring of death. He meant to wake the others and then wait for further developments. By now his senses were more alert and vigorous than they had ever been before. A preternatural clearness of brain and vision possessed him. As he advanced he saw suddenly falling a green bunch of cord that straightened into a long, emerald line. It was triangular in shape, fine at the apex, and furnished with hooked spines. The rope appeared to dangle from the tree overhead; the broad, sucker-like termination was evidently soaking up moisture.

A natural phenomenon evidently, Scarlett thought. This was some plant new to him, a parasite living amongst the tree-tops and drawing life and vigour by means of these green, rope-like antennae designed by Nature to soak and absorb the heavy dews of night.

For a moment the logic of this theory was soothing to Scarlett's distracted nerves, but only for a moment, for then he saw at regular intervals along the green rope the big pure blossoms of the devil's poppy.

He stood gasping there, utterly taken aback for the moment. There must be some infernal juggling behind all this business. He saw the rope slacken and quiver, he saw it swing forward like a pendulum, and the next minute it had passed across the shoulders of a sleeping seaman.

Then the green root became as the arm of an octopus. The line shook from end to end like the web of an angry spider when invaded by a wasp. It seemed to grip the sailor and tighten, and then, before Scarlett's affrighted eyes, the sleeping man was raised gently from the ground.

Scarlett jumped forward with a desire to scream hysterically. Now that a comrade was in danger he was no longer afraid. He whipped a jack-knife from his pocket and slashed at the cruel cord. He half expected to meet with the stoutness of a steel strand, but to his surprise the feeler snapped like a carrot, bumping the sailor heavily on the ground.

He sat up, rubbing his eyes vigorously.

'That you, sir?' he asked. 'What is the matter?'

'For the love of God, get up at once and help me to arouse the others,' Scarlett said, hoarsely. 'We have come across the devil's workshop. All the horrors of the inferno are invented here.'

The bluejacket struggled to his feet. As he did so, the clothing from his waist downwards slipped about his feet, clean cut through by the teeth of the green parasite. All around the body of the sailor blood oozed from a zone of teeth-marks.

Two-o'clock-in-the-morning courage is a virtue vouchsafed to few. The tar, who would have faced an ironclad cheerfully, fairly shivered with fright and dismay.

'What does it mean, sir?' he cried. 'I've been—'

'Wake the others,' Scarlett screamed; 'wake the others.'

Two or three more green tangles of rope came tumbling to the ground, straightening and quivering instantly. The purple blossoms stood out like a frill upon them. Like a madman Scarlett shouted, kicking his companions without mercy.

They were all awake at last, grumbling and moaning for their lost slumbers. All this time Tito had never stirred.

'I don't understand it at all,' said Tarrer.

' Come from under those trees,' said Scarlett, 'and I will endeavour to explain. Not that you will believe me for a moment. No man can be expected to believe the awful nightmare I am going to tell you.'

Scarlett proceeded to explain. As he expected, his story was followed with marked incredulity, save by the wounded sailor, who had strong evidence to stimulate his otherwise defective imagination.

'I can't believe it,' Tarrer said, at length. They were whispering together beyond earshot of Tito, whom they had no desire to arouse for obvious reasons. 'This is some diabolical juggling of yonder rascally Cuban. It seems impossible that those slender green cords could—'

Scarlett pointed to the centre of the circle. 'Call the dog,' he said, grimly, 'and see if he will come.'

'I admit the point as far as the poor old mastiff is concerned. But at the same time I don't – however, I'll see for myself.'

By this time a dozen or more of the slender cords were hanging pendent from the trees. They moved from spot to spot as if jerked up by some unseen hand and deposited a foot or two farther. With the great purple blooms fringing the stem, the effect was not unlovely save to Scarlett, who could see only the dark side of it. As Tarrer spoke, he advanced in the direction of the trees.

'What are you going to do?' Scarlett asked.

'Exactly what I told you. I am going to investigate this business for myself.'

Without wasting further words Scarlett sprang forward. It was no time for the niceties of an effete civilisation. Force was the only logical argument to be used in a case like this, and Scarlett was the more powerful man of the two.

Tarrer saw and appreciated the situation.

'No, no,' he cried; 'none of that. Anyway, you're too late.'

He darted forward and threaded his way between the slender emerald columns. As they moved slowly and with a certain stately deliberation there was no great danger to an alert and vigorous individual. As Scarlett entered the avenue he could hear the soak and suck as the dew was absorbed.

'For Heaven's sake, come out of it,' he cried.

The warning came too late. A whip-like trail of green touched Tarrer from behind, and in a lightning flash he was in the toils. The tendency to draw up anything and everything gave the cords a terrible power. Tarrer evidently felt it, for his breath came in great gasps.

'Cut me free,' he said, hoarsely; 'cut me free. I am being carried off my feet.'

He seemed to be doomed for a moment, for all the cords there were apparently converging in his direction. This, as a matter of fact, was a solution of the whole sickening, horrible sensation. Pulled here and there, thrust in one direction and another, Tarrer contrived to keep his feet.

Heedless of possible danger to himself, Scarlett darted forward, calling to his companions to come to the rescue. In less time than it takes to tell, four knives were at work ripping and slashing in all directions.

'Not all of you,' Scarlett whispered. So tense was the situation that no voice was raised above a murmur. 'You two keep your eyes open for fresh cords, and cut them as they fall, instantly. Now then.'

The horrible green spines were round Tarrer's body like snakes. His face was white, his breath came painfully, for the pressure was terrible. It seemed to Scarlett to be one horrible dissolving view of green, slimy cords and great weltering, purple blossoms. The whole of the circle was strewn with them. They were wet and slimy underfoot.

Tarrer had fallen forward half unconscious. He was supported now by but two cords above his head. The cruel pressure had been relieved. With one savage sweep of his knife Scarlett cut the last of the lines, and Tarrer fell like a log unconscious to the ground. A feeling of nausea, a yellow dizziness, came over Scarlett as he staggered beyond the dread circle. He saw Tarrer carried to a place of safety, and then the world seemed to wither and leave him in the dark.

'I feel a bit groggy and weak,' said Tarrer an hour or so later: 'but beyond that this idiot of a Richard is himself again. So far as I am concerned, I should like to get even with our friend Tito for this.'

'Something with boiling oil in it,' Scarlett suggested, grimly. 'The callous scoundrel has slept soundly through the whole of this business. I suppose he felt absolutely certain that he had finished with us.'

'Upon my word, we ought to shoot the beggar!' Tarrer exclaimed.

'I have a little plan of my own,' said Scarlett, 'which I am going to put in force later on. Meanwhile we had better get on with breakfast. When Tito wakes a pleasant little surprise will await him.'

Tito roused from his slumbers in due course and looked around him. His glance was curious, disappointed, then full of a white and yellow fear. A thousand conflicting emotions streamed across his dark face. Scarlett read them at a glance as he called the Cuban over to him.

'I am not going into any unnecessary details with you,' he said. 'It has come to my knowledge that you are playing traitor to us. Therefore we prefer to complete our journey alone. We can easily find the way now.'

'The *señor* may do as he pleases,' he replied. 'Give me my dollar and let me go.'

Scarlett replied grimly that he had no intention of doing anything of the kind. He did not propose to place the lives of himself and his comrades in the power of a rascally Cuban who had played false.

'We are going to leave you here till we return,' he said. 'You will have plenty of food, you will be perfectly safe under the shelter of these trees, and there is no chance of anybody disturbing you. We are going to tie you up to one of these trees for the next four-and-twenty hours.'

All the insolence died out of Tito's face. His knees bowed, a cold dew came out over the ghastly green of his features. From the shaking of his limbs he might have fared disastrously with ague.

'The trees,' he stammered, 'the trees, *señor*! There is danger from snakes, and – and from many things. There are other places—'

'If this place was safe last night, it is safe today,' Scarlett said, grimly. 'I have quite made up my mind.'

Tito fought no longer. He fell forward on his knees, he howled for mercy, till Scarlett fairly kicked him up again.

'Make a clean breast of it,' he said, 'or take the consequences. You know perfectly well that we have found you out, scoundrel.'

Tito's story came in gasps. He wanted to get rid of the Americans. He was jealous. Besides, under the Americanos would Cuba be any better off? By no means and assuredly not. Therefore it was the duty of every good Cuban to destroy the Americanos where possible.

'A nice lot to fight for,' Scarlett muttered. 'Get to the point.'

Hastened to the point by a liberal application of stout shoe-leather, Tito made plenary confession. The *señor* himself had suggested death by medium of the devil's poppies. More than one predatory plant-hunter had been lured to his destruction in the same way. The skeleton hung on the tree was a Dutchman who had walked into the clutch of the purple terror innocently. And Pierre Anton had done the same. The suckers of the devil's poppy only came down at night to gather moisture; in the day they were coiled up like a spring. And anything that they touched they killed. Tito had watched more than one bird or small beast crushed and mauled by these cruel spines with their fringe of purple blossoms.

'How do you get the blooms?' Scarlett asked.

'That is easy,' Tito replied. 'In the daytime I moisten the ground under the trees. Then the suckers unfold, drawn by the water. Once the suckers unfold, one cuts several of them off with long knives. There is danger, of course, but not if one is careful.'

'I'll not trouble the devil's poppy any further at present,' said Scarlett, 'but I shall trouble you to accompany me to my destination as a prisoner.'

Tito's eyes dilated.

'They will not shoot me?' he asked, hoarsely.

'I don't know,' Scarlett replied. 'They may hang you instead. At any rate, I shall be bitterly disappointed if they don't end you one way or the other. Whichever operation it is, I can look forward to it with perfect equanimity.'

# LOST TOMMY
# JEPPS

## By Arthur Morrison

I

AT STRATFORD Main railway station there are about half-a-dozen platforms, with stairs and an underground passage to join them; and on bank-holiday all these platforms, as well as the stairs and the passage and the booking-offices, are packed so closely with excited people that there seems to be no room for one single walking-stick more, even a thin one. The fortunate persons in front stick to the edge of the platform somehow by their heels, in defiance of all natural laws. When a train arrives, the people in the booking-office rush at the passage, the people in the passage rush at the stairs, the people on the stairs rush at the platform, and nothing seems left for the people on the platform but slaughter and destruction, beginning with the equilibrists at the edge. And yet nobody gets killed. Half the people seem to be on the wrong platforms, but are wholly unable to struggle through to the right ones; and I believe the other half are on the wrong platforms too, but don't know it. And yet everybody seems to get somewhere, eventually.

Jepps's family party was one of a hundred others in Stratford station, and in most respects very like ninety-five of them at least. There was Thomas Jepps himself, head of the family by courtesy, but now struggling patiently at its tail, carrying the baby always, and sometimes also carrying Bobby, aged four. There was Mrs Jepps, warm and short of temper; there were Aunt Susan, rather stout, and Cousin Jane, rather thin; and there was Cousin Jane's sister's young man's aunt, warmer than 'Tilda Jepps and stouter than Aunt Susan, and perpetually losing something, or losing herself, or getting into original difficulties in the crowd. And then, beside the baby and Bobby, there were Tommy and Polly, whose ages were eight and five respectively, though it was Polly who tyrannised. It was the way of this small woman to rate her bigger brother in imitation of her mother's manner; and Tommy, who had the makings of a philosopher, was, as a rule, moodily indifferent to the scolding of both, so long as he judged himself beyond the radius of his mother's arm and hand.

'What 'a' you bin an' done with the tickets now?' demanded Mrs Jepps of her husband in the midst of the wrestle in the booking-office.

'Me?' asked Jepps, innocently, from behind the baby's frills. 'Me? I – I dunno. Ain't you got 'em?'

'Yes,' piped Tommy, partly visible beneath the capacious lunch-bag of Cousin Jane's sister's young man's aunt. 'Yes, Mother's got 'em!'

'You look after your little brother an' don't go contradictin' me!' snapped Mrs Jepps. 'Of course I ain't got 'em,' she went on to Jepps. 'You've bin an' lost 'em, that's what you've done!'

'Don't contradict Mother,' Polly echoed, pragmatically, to her wicked brother. 'You be a good boy an' look after Bobby. That's what you've got to do. Ain't it, Mother?'

'Oh, don't worrit me!' answered the distracted parent. 'Where's them tickets? Did he give 'em to you, Aunt Susan?'

Aunt Susan hadn't seen them, and passed the question on to Cousin Jane. Cousin Jane, with a reproachful look at the unhappy Jepps, declared that he had never given them to *her*, whatever he might say or fancy; and her sister's young man's aunt gasped and stared and swayed in the crowd, and disclaimed all knowledge of the tickets; also she announced that whatever had become of them she expected to be taken to Southend, and that whatever happened she wasn't going to pay again. Poor Jepps defended himself weakly, but he was generally held to have spoiled the day's pleasure at the beginning. 'I think you've got 'em, really, 'Tilda,' he protested; 'look in your purse!'

'Yes,' piped Tommy once more, this time from behind Aunt Susan; 'I see Mother put 'em in her purse!'

Mrs Jepps's plunge at Tommy was interrupted by Jepps. 'You might look, at least,' he pleaded.

'Look!' she retorted, tearing open her bag and snatching the purse from within. 'Look yourself, if you won't believe your own wife!' She spread the purse wide, and displayed – the tickets; all in a bunch, whole tickets and halves mixed together.

'He'd better not let me get hold of him,' said Mrs Jepps, a moment later, nodding fiercely at Tommy. 'Aggravatin' little wretch! He'll drive me mad one o' these days, that's what he'll do!'

With that the family was borne full drive against the barrier, and struggled and tumbled through the gate, mingled with stray members of other parties; all to an accompaniment of sad official confusion in the matter of what ticket belonged to which. But there was no easy rallying in the subway. The crowd pressed on, and presently Cousin Jane's sister's young man's aunt got into a novel complication by reason of her umbrella (which she grasped desperately in the middle) somehow drifting away horizontally into the crowd at her full arm's length, so that in a moment she was carried irresistibly up the first steps of the wrong staircase, clinging to her property with might and main, trailing her lunch-bag behind her, and expostulating with much clamour. Jepps, with the baby, watched her helplessly; but Tommy, ducking and dodging among the legs of the crowd, got ahead of her, twisted the umbrella into a vertical position, and, so releasing it, ducked and dodged back again. Cousin Jane's sister's young man's aunt was very angry, and the crowd disregarded her scolding altogether – laughed at it, in fact; so that Tommy, scrambling back triumphantly through the crush, came very handy for it.

'If I was yer mother I'd give you a good sound hidin', that's what *I'd* do,' said Cousin Jane's sister's young man's aunt.

Tommy began to feel resentful, philosopher as he was. And when his mother, having with difficulty been convinced that the staircase she insisted on was another wrong one, and that the one advised by Tommy was right, forthwith promised him one for himself when she got him home, he grew wholly embittered, while his sister Polly openly triumphed over him. And so, with a few more struggles and family separations (Cousin Jane's sister's young man's aunt was lost and recovered twice), the party at length found itself opposite an open third-class carriage door, and climbed in with all the speed it might.

'Ah, well,' said Aunt Susan, 'here we are at last, an' no more bother till we get to Southend, any'ow.'

'There'll be a lot afore you get there in this train, Mum,' observed a cynical coster, who had been greatly impressed – on the toes – by Aunt Susan's weight.

'What!' exclaimed Cousin Jane; 'this is the Southend train, ain't it?'

'No, Mum,' replied the coster, calmly; 'it ain't.'

Mrs Jepps caught at the door, but it was too late. The train was gathering speed, and in a few seconds it was out of the station. 'There,' said Mrs Jepps, desperately, 'I knew it was the wrong platform!'

'Then you was wrong again, Mum,' pursued the sardonic coster; ''cos it was the right 'un. But this 'ere's the wrong train.'

'Mother!' squeaked Polly, viciously, 'Tommy says – go away, I *will* tell – Tommy says he knew it was the wrong train when we got in.'

'What! You young—you didn't! How did you know?'

'Read it on the board,' said Tommy, sulkily. 'Board in front of the engine. C.O.L. Col, C.H.E.S.T. chest, E—'

'Take him away, somebody,' yelped Mrs Jepps. 'Take the little imp out o' my sight or I'll kill him – I know I shall! Knew it was the wrong train an' let us get in! I—oh!'

'Why,' pleaded Tommy, in doleful bewilderment, 'when I told you about tickets you said I was drivin' you mad, an' when I told you about the platform you said you'd whop me when you got me home, an' now 'cos I didn't tell you about the train—'

'He's a saucy young varmint, that's what *he* is,' interrupted Cousin Jane's sister's young man's aunt, whose misfortunes were telling on her temper as well as reddening her face. 'Lucky for him he ain't a child o' mine, that's all. I'd show him!'

'So would I!' added Cousin Jane.

'He's a perfect noosance to bring out,' said Aunt Susan; 'that's what he is!'

'You're a naughty, wicked boy, Tommy!' said his superior little sister.

Tommy's spirits sank to the lowest stage of dejection. There was no understanding these grown-up people and no pleasing them. They were all on to him except his father, and even he seemed sadly grieved, in his mild fashion.

The cynical coster had been chuckling in a quiet, asthmatic sort of way, rather as though some small but active animal was struggling in his chest. Now he spoke again.

'It's all right, Mum,' he said. 'Don't be rough on the kid. You can change at Shenfield, jest as good as if you come in the right train all the way.'

This was better, and the spirits of the party rose accordingly; though their relief was balanced by a feeling of undignified stultification.

'Givin' us all a fright for nothing,' said Aunt Susan, with an acid glare at the unhappy Tommy. 'It's a pity some children ain't taught to keep their mouths shut!'

'Why, so I did, an' Mother said she'd—'

'Be quiet, now!' interrupted Mrs Jepps. 'Be quiet! You've done quite enough mischief with your clatter. Catch me bringing you out again on a holiday, that's all!'

And so for the rest of the journey Tommy remained in the lowest depths of despondency, never exhibiting the smallest sign of rising to the surface without being instantly shoved down again by a reproof from somebody.

The cynical coster got out at Romford, with another asthmatic chuckle and an undisguised wink at Tommy. The train jogged along through Harold Wood and Brentwood to Shenfield Junction, and there the party found the Southend train at last. With the people already there they more than filled the compartment, and Tommy had to stand, a distinction which cost him some discomfort; for when he stood by the door he was blamed for interfering with Polly's and Bobby's enjoyment of the landscape, and when he moved up the carriage his efforts to maintain his equilibrium seriously disturbed the repose of Aunt Susan's corns.

The day was bright, and Southend was crowded thick everywhere with holiday-makers. Mrs Jepps rallied her party and adjured Tommy. 'Now you, Tommy, see if you can't begin to behave yourself, an' take care of your little brother an' sister. S'pose a man was to come and take *them* away! Then I s'pose you'd wish you'd been a better boy, when it was too late!'

'I'd make him wish it a quicker way than that!' said Cousin Jane's sister's young man's aunt, spitefully; for she had not yet got over her earlier misfortunes.

As the words left her mouth a horrible squeak rent her ears, and a long pink 'trunk' – one of those paper tubes which, when blown, extend suddenly to a yard long and as suddenly retreat into a little curl – shot over her shoulder into her eye, and was gone again. With a gasp and a bounce she let go umbrella and lunch-bag together; and, while a grinning boy went dancing and trumpeting away in the crowd, a trickle of fragrant liquor, which would have smelt much the same if it had been gin, issued from the lunch-bag and wandered across the pavement. And Tommy Jepps, startled in the depth of his gloom, hastily stuffed his fist against his mouth, and spluttered irrepressibly over his knuckles. For indeed, in his present state of exasperation, Tommy had little sympathy for the misfortunes of so very distant a relation as Cousin Jane's sister's young man's aunt.

Tommy's father was mildly horrified, and murmured deprecatingly from among the baby's frills. 'Tommy!' he said, in an awe-struck whisper. 'Tommy! Nothing to laugh at!'

'Get out o' my sight,' cried Mrs Jepps, making a miss at Tommy's head with her own bag. 'Get out of my sight before I—'

Tommy got out of it with all possible celerity, and took his place in the extreme rear of the procession which formed as soon as the lunch-bag had been recovered and cleared of broken glass. The procession, with a score of others like it, went straggling along the High Street towards the beach, where the crowd was thicker than ever.

There were large open spaces, with shows, and swings, and round-

abouts, and stalls, and coconut shies, and among these the Jepps
column wound its way, closing up and stopping here, and tailing out
lengthily there. It stopped for a moment before a shooting-gallery,
and then lengthened out in the direction of a band of niggers; arrived
opposite the niggers, it closed up once more, and Mrs Jepps looked
about to survey her forces. There was Jepps, perspiring freely under
the burden of the baby, for the day was growing hot; there were Aunt
Susan, Cousin Jane, and Cousin Jane's sister's young man's aunt,
whose shorter name was Mrs Lunn, red and ruffled; there were Polly
and Bobby; but – Mrs Jepps gave a second glance round before she
would believe it – there was *not* Tommy.

Mrs Jepps's chin dropped suddenly, and she began darting and
dodging, looking this way and that, among the crowd. 'Tommy!' she
cried, 'You Tommy!' with a voice still a little angry, but mainly
anxious. 'Mercy on us, where's the child gone?'

Jepps came back, with blank alarm on so much of his face as was
visible above the baby and its clothes, and the rest of the party started
dodging also. But all to no purpose. Their calls were drowned in the
general hubbub, and their questings to and fro were fruitless; Tommy
was lost!

'Oh! my child!' cried Mrs Jepps; 'my lovely, darling boy! What
shall I do? He's lost! He's been stole! The best child as ever was!'

'Such a little dear!' said Cousin Jane.

'Such a jool of a duck!' said Aunt Susan, affected almost to tears.

'Oh, oh!' gasped Mrs Jepps, with signs of flopping and fainting;
'an' – an' – you called him a noosance!'

'An' you called him an imp!' retorted Aunt Susan. 'You should ha'
treated him better when you had him.'

'If he was a child of mine,' said Cousin Jane's sister's young man's
aunt, sententiously, 'I'd ha' been a little more patient with him.'

Jepps was off to the nearest stall to ask the stall-keeper if he had
seen a boy. It seemed that the stall-keeper had seen a good many boys
that morning. But had he seen Jepps's own boy? This conundrum the
stall-keeper gave up without hesitation.

But Jepps's example did something, and presently the whole party
scattered for the hunt. Jepps was left with the baby in his arms and the
other two children about his knees, and he had strict orders not to
lose any of them nor to wander far from a certain indicated point,
near which the rest of the party might find him on occasion. He was
not allowed to join in the search because somebody must take care of
the children and Mrs Jepps felt that she would die of suspense if
condemned to wait inactive.

Mrs Jepps was anything but inactive, and the other ladies were as busy as Mrs Jepps. Before they separated they seized on a wandering apple-woman, who was confused and badgered into a cloudy admission that she *had* seen a boy with a man somewhere a little while ago, or perhaps rather before that, and, her replies being considered evasive, she was unanimously suspected of complicity.

It speedily grew apparent that small boys with men, together with small boys plain, were rather numerous in the many crowds; and one mistaken pursuit followed another for a sad long time, while Aunt Susan narrowly escaped a visit to the police station on a charge preferred by the indignant parent of a child whom she chased and seized violently from behind because of a supposed resemblance to Tommy when viewed from that aspect.

So it came to pass that, Aunt Susan having rejoined Mrs Jepps, the two, fatigued and a trifle hysterical, returned to where they had left Jepps. As they turned the last corner, a red-headed man, with his hat in his hand, came running past them and vanished in the crowd, while they almost immediately perceived Jepps in the distance striving his utmost to raise a gallop, while Polly and Bobby hung to his coat-tails, and the baby tumbled and struggled in his arms.

'Stop him!' cried Jepps, choking with the breathlessness of his trot and the flapping of the baby's cape over his mouth. 'Stop him! It's him! He's stole my—'

'The villain!' cried Mrs Jepps, turning and charging the crowd. 'Stop him! He's stole my child!'

'Stop him!' gasped Jepps again. 'He snatched my—'

But Mrs Jepps and Aunt Susan were deep in the crowd, chasing and grabbing this time at red-headed men. Red-headed men, however, were scarce in that particular corner just at the moment, and the scarcest of all was the particular red-headed man who had rushed past them.

Jepps, gasping still, came up with his wife and Aunt Susan in the midst of a knot of people, answering the enquiries of curious sympathisers as he came along.

'Was it a good 'un?' asked another family man, with another baby in his arms, just as Jepps reached his wife.

'Yes,' answered Jepps, 'a real good 'un!'

'The best in the world!' sobbed Mrs Jepps.

'I won it in a raffle,' Jepps added.

'What?' cried Aunt Susan, 'won it in a raffle? What do you mean? Is this a time for sich jokes, Thomas?'

'Jokes?' bleated poor Jepps. 'It ain't no joke! He stole my watch, I tell you! Snatched it while I was a-trying to keep baby quiet!'

'Your watch!' Mrs Jeps exclaimed. 'Your watch! Thomas Jepps, you ain't fit to be trusted neither with a watch nor a family, you ain't!'

## II

Tommy had lagged behind a little at the rifle-gallery, a place where you shot into a sort of tunnel with a target at the other end. The tunnels – there were four of them – interested him deeply, and he walked round to the side of the establishment to see how they were built. They were long, tapering metal tubes, it seemed, painted red. Tommy walked along to the very end, hoping to see something of the target mechanism, but that was boxed in. Here, at some little distance from where his wandering started, his attention was arrested by a man in a little crowd, who offered to eat a lighted newspaper for the small subscription of two shillings. It seemed to Tommy that so handsome an offer must be closed with at once, so he pushed into the crowd.

And that was how Tommy Jepps was lost. For each individual member of that crowd agreed with Tommy, feeling convinced that some of the others would be sure to subscribe so reasonable a sum without delay, so that the subscription was a long time beginning. And when at last it did begin it grew so slowly that at last the champion fire-swallower of the world and elsewhere was fain to be content with eighteenpence, at which very reasonable sum his contract was completed. Having witnessed this, Tommy's eyeballs retired to their normal place in his head, and his mouth, which had been wider open than the fire-swallower's, closed slowly. The crowd opened out, and Tommy, who had been effectually buried in it for half an hour, awoke to the realisation that the rest of his party were nowhere to be seen.

For the moment it seemed a rather serious thing. Then, with a pause of reflection, he saw his misfortune in quite another light. He looked cautiously about him, and, after a little more consideration, he resolved that he would not be found – just yet, at any rate. He had enjoyed the society of his family for some time, and he resolved on a temporary change.

Tommy was not only a philosopher, but a sagacious boy of business. He had come out for a day's pleasure, but he must attend to business first; and one piece of business must needs be transacted to make things quite secure. So he started off back to the railway station, keeping a wary eye for his relations as he went.

The station was just a little less crowded now, though it was busy enough still. Tommy had not quite settled how, exactly, he should set about his business, but he kept his eyes open and looked out for a friend. Grown-up people, as a rule, were difficult to negotiate with; you never could tell for certain what they would do or say next, and it was apt to be something unpleasant when it came. But there was a sort of grown-up persons – Tommy could never have described them – who were quite excellent, and always behaved like bricks to boys. And they were not such a rare sort of people, either. So he kept watch for some person of this kind, resolved to ask help and advice. Presently he saw one – a stout, red-faced man in a staring tweed suit, with a big gold watch-chain. Several other stout men were with him, and they were all laughing and chuckling together at a joke one of them had made about half an hour before.

'Please, sir!' said Tommy, craning his neck up at the red-faced man.

'Eh! Hallo!' said the man, almost falling over him. 'Well, young 'un, what's up?'

'Please sir, will they give me another ticket home, and who ought I to go and ask for it?'

'Another ticket home? What for? Lost your own?'

'No, sir – Mother's got it. But I've lost Mother.'

'O–o–o–oh! Lost your mother, eh? Well, would you know your way home if you had the ticket?'

'Yes, sir. But' – this with a sudden apprehension – 'but I don't want to go home yet.'

'No? Why not?'

'I come out to have a holiday, sir.'

The red face broadened into a wide grin, and some of the stout men laughed outright. 'So you're goin' off on the spree all by yourself, are you?' said the red-faced man. 'That's pluck. But if you go asking for another ticket they'll keep you in the office till your mother comes for you, or take you to the police station. *That* wouldn't be much of a holiday, would it?'

Tommy was plainly dismayed at the idea, and at his doleful face several stout men laughed aloud. 'Come, Perkins,' said one, 'it's only one and a penny, half single. I'll toss you who pays!'

'Done!' replied the red-faced man. 'Sudden death – you call,' and he spun a shilling.

'Heads!' called the challenger.

'Tails it is,' was the answer. 'You pay. What station, young 'un?'

'Stratford, sir.'

'That's all right,' said the loser, moving off with his hand in his pocket. 'I was a bit rash. It might ha' been Manchester!'

'That's saved me one d.,' observed the red-faced man, spinning his shilling again, and dexterously transferring it to Tommy's startled palm. 'You go an' buy the town, you desp'rit young rip! An' take care you don't go losing the last train!'

Tommy was almost more amazed than delighted. This was magnificent – noble. As soon as he could, he began to think. It was plain that being lost had its advantages – decided advantages. Those stout men wouldn't have looked at him a second time in ordinary circumstances, but because he was lost – behold the shilling and the railway ticket! Here was a discovery: nothing less than a new principle in holiday-making. Get lost, and make your holiday self-supporting.

He did not buy the town, but began modestly with a penn'orth of bulls'-eyes, to stimulate thought. He sucked them pensively, and thought his hardest: thought so hard, indeed, that in his absence of mind he swallowed a bull's-eye prematurely, and stood staring, with a feeling as of a red-hot brick passing gradually through his chest, and an agonised effort to remember if he had heard of people dying through swallowing bulls'-eyes whole. The pain in the chest presently passed off, however, and he found himself staring at a woman with a basket of apples and oranges.

'Apples, three a penny,' said the woman, enticingly. 'Oranges, a ha'penny each. There's nice ripe 'uns, my dear!'

'I've lost my mother,' replied Tommy irrelevantly.

'Lost yer mother!' responded the woman, with much sympathy. 'Why, I wonder if you're the little boy as I was asked about? Has yer father got pale whiskers an' a round 'at, an' a baby which knocks it off, an' yer mother an' three other ladies an' yer little brother an' sister?'

Tommy nodded – perhaps rather guiltily.

The woman swung her basket on her arm and gave him an energetic push on the shoulder. 'You go straight along down there, my dear,' she said, pointing, 'an' then round to the left, an' yer father's waiting by the second turning. Don't forget! Here – have an apple!' And she thrust one into his hand. 'And an orange,' she added, impulsively, stuffing one into his jacket-pocket.

This was really very satisfactory. He had half expected the apple, but the orange was quite an extra – in fact, the whole contribution had been wrung from the honest apple-woman by the pathetic look occasioned by the swallowing of the bull's-eye. Tommy went off in the direction she indicated, but somehow made the mistake of turning to the right instead of to the left at the critical point, being much occupied with thought. For he was resolving to look, all day, as pathetic as could be expected of a boy with a holiday all to himself, and an entirely new invention to make it pay.

And, indeed, the invention paid very well. Tommy perambulated the crowded beach on a system of scouting devised for the occasion. He made a halt at each convenient booth or stand, and from behind it carefully reconnoitred the crowd in front. No doubt he was searching anxiously for his sorrowing relatives; but somehow, though he altogether failed to meet them, he never seemed disappointed.

And meantime, as I have said, the invention worked excellently. He did not always set it in motion by the mere crude statement that he had lost his mother – he led up to it. He asked people if they had seen her. In this way he procured a short sea voyage, by interesting the mother of an embarking family which did not quite fill the boat. He had his railway ticket, he explained, and could get home, but meantime he must make his holiday as best he might. That excellent family yielded a penny and a bun, as well as the experience in navigation. A similar family was good for a turn on a roundabout.

'Got no change,' said the roundabout man, as roundabout men do. For it is their custom, if possible, to postpone giving change, in the hope of their patrons emerging from the machine too sick and giddy to remember it. 'Got no change. I'll give it you when you come off.'

'Not you,' retorted paterfamilias, made cunning by experience. 'You'll be too busy, or forget, or something. Here's a boy what's looking for his mother; we'll make up the tanner with him.'

So the morning went; and Tommy acquired a high opinion of the generosity of his fellow-creatures, and a still higher one of his own diplomacy. Not that it always succeeded. It failed sometimes altogether. There was a coconut-shy proprietor, for instance, whose conduct led Tommy to consider him a very worthless person indeed. He began by most cordially inviting Tommy to try his luck – called him a young sportsman, in fact. Tommy was much gratified, and selected a stick.

'Money first,' said the man, extending a dirty palm.

'Lost my mother,' replied Tommy, confidently, having come to regard this form of words as the equivalent of coin of the realm.

'What?' The man's face expressed furious amazement.

'Lost my mother,' Tommy repeated, a little louder, surprised to find anybody so dull of comprehension.

''Ere, get out!' roared the outraged tradesman, who was not educated to the point of regarding a coconut-shy a necessity of life for a lost boy. 'Get out!' And he snatched the stick with such energy that Tommy got out with no delay.

He was so far cast down by this ruffian's deplorable ignorance of the rules of the game that his next transaction was for cash.

He saw a man selling paper 'trunks' of the sort that had so seriously startled Mrs Lunn on the family's first arrival, and he greatly desired one for himself. But the trunk-merchant was an unpromising-looking person – looked, in fact, rather as though he might be the coconut man's brother. So Tommy paid his penny, and set out to amuse himself.

The toy was quite delightful for a while, and utterly confounded and dismayed many respectable persons. But after a little time it began to pall; chiefly, perhaps, because it interfered with business. If you wish to appeal to the pity of any lady or gentleman in the character of a lost child, it is not diplomatic to begin by blowing a squeaking paper 'trunk' into that lady's or gentleman's face. It strikes the wrong note, so to speak: doesn't seem to lead up to the subject. So presently Tommy tired of the 'trunk', and devised a new use for it. For he was a thrifty boy, and wasted nothing.

He looked about to find some suitable person to whom to offer the article for sale, and at length he fixed on a comfortable old lady and gentleman who were sitting on a newspaper spread on the sand, eating sandwiches. Now to the superficial it might seem that a stout and decorous old couple of about sixty-five years of age, and thirty-two stone total weight, were not precisely the most likely customers on Southend beach for such an implement as Tommy had to offer. But Tommy was not superficial, and he knew his business.

'Please would you like to buy that?' he asked, looking as interesting and as timid as he could manage. 'Only a ha'penny. It cost a penny.'

'Why, bless the child!' cried the old lady; 'we don't want a thing like that!' And the old gentleman sat speechless – partly because his mouth was full of sandwich.

'I've lost my mother,' said Tommy.

For a moment more the old couple continued to stare, and then the old lady realised the pathos of the situation in a flash. Tommy suddenly found himself snatched into a sitting position beside her and kissed. And the next moment he was being fed with sandwiches.

'Poor little chap!' said the nice old lady. 'Poor little chap! Lost his mother and tried to sell his toy to buy something to eat! Have another sandwich, my dear.'

Tommy did not really need the sandwiches, having been eating a good deal all day, and being even now conscious of sundry pockets distended by an apple, a paper of bulls'-eyes, several biscuits, and a large piece of toffee. But he wished to be polite, so he ate as much as he could and answered the old lady's questions to the best of his ability. He told her his name, his age, where he lived, and what sums he could do. He assured her that he knew his way home and had his ticket safe; and he eased her mind wonderfully by his confidence that he could find his mother very soon, and particularly because of his absolute certainty of meeting her, at latest, at the railway station. And finally, not without difficulty, he tore himself away, bearing with him not only the rejected 'trunk', but also added wealth to the amount of fourpence.

He did very well with the 'trunk' – very well indeed. He never got quite so much as fourpence again; but he got some pennies, one twopence, and several halfpennies. He continued to select his customers with care, and rarely made a mistake. Some selections were unfortunate and unproductive, however, but that he quite expected; and it surprised him to find what a number of benevolent persons, made liberal by a fine bank-holiday, were ready to give a copper for a thing and then let him keep it. But he never fell into the inartistic error of offering his stock-in-trade to any person in the least likely to use it. Persons of sufficient age and dignity were easily to be found by a boy of discrimination, even on Southend beach.

But everything must come to an end at last, and so did the trunk. Having carefully observed a large, good-tempered-looking woman sitting under an umbrella, and having convinced himself that she was not likely to need a paper trunk for personal entertainment, he proceeded to business in the usual manner.

'Lost yer mother?' said the woman, affably. 'All right, you'll soon find her. Here's yer ha'penny.'

And with that this unscrupulous female actually *took* the trunk, and handed it over to some children who were playing hard by.

Tommy felt deeply injured. He had no idea those children were hers. It was shameful, he thought, to take advantage of a lost boy in such an unexpected fashion as that. And he had really begun quite to like that trunk, too.

But it had paid excellently, on the whole; and, at any rate, with his accumulated capital, he could make an excellent holiday for the rest of the day: to say nothing of what he might still come in for on the strength of his distressful situation.

So he went on combining business with pleasure, till he was driven to absolute flight by an excellent but over-zealous old gentleman who insisted on taking him to the police station. It was a narrow squeak, and it was a most fortunate circumstance that the zealous old gentleman was wholly unable to run. As it was, the adventure so disconcerted Tommy that he concluded to relinquish business altogether for a time, and seek some secluded spot where he might at leisure transfer some of his accumulated commissariat from his bursting pockets to a more interior situation.

The cliffs at Southend, as you may know, are laid out as public gardens, traversed by precipitous paths, embushed with shrubs, and dotted with convenient seats. But Tommy did not want a seat. He was, in fact, a little tired of keeping a constant look-out, and since there were his own party, the apple-woman, whom he had espied in the distance twice since their first encounter, and the zealous old gentleman, all at large somewhere in Southend, he judged it safest to lie under a convenient bush, in some place commanding an interesting view, and there begin a leisurely picnic.

He found a capital bush, just behind one of the seats; a thick bush that no eye could penetrate from without, yet from between the twigs of which he had an excellent view of the sea and some part of the gardens. It was almost as good as a pirate's cave, which was very proper, for, on the whole, he felt something of a pirate himself today. He began his picnic with toffee.

Presently his attention was drawn to a man who came up the path with a very laboured air of casual indifference, although he was puffing visibly as he came, as if he had been running. He was a red-headed man, and, as he walked, he glanced anxiously over his shoulder. The seat before Tommy's retreat was empty, and the man threw himself upon it, so that his legs obstructed Tommy's view. And then, to Tommy's utter amazement, the man's hand came stealing out behind him into the bush, and there deposited on the ground, absolutely under Tommy's nose – two watches!

The hand was withdrawn as stealthily as it came, and the man began with some difficulty to whistle a tune. And now up the same path there came another man, plainly following the first: a tall, well-set-up man who walked like a policeman, which, indeed, was exactly what he was – a policeman in plain clothes.

'Well, Higgs,' said the newcomer, suspiciously, 'what's your game today?'

'Game?' whined the red-headed man, in an injured tone. 'Why, no game at all, guv'nor, not today. Can't a bloke come out for a 'oliday?'

'Oh, of course,' replied the other, 'anybody can come out for a holiday. But there's some as does rum things on their holidays. I've got my eye on you, my fine feller!'

'S'elp me, guv'nor, it's all right,' protested the red-headed man, rising and moving off a little way. 'I'm on'y 'avin' a 'oliday, guv'nor! You can turn me over if you like!'

Now Tommy did not know that to turn a man over meant to search him, but he did not stop to wonder. For what occupied the whole of his attention now, even to the exclusion of the very toffee in his mouth, was the astounding fact that one of the watches was his own father's!

There was no mistake about it. There were initials on the silver case – not his father's initials, for, indeed, he had won the watch in a raffle; but Tommy knew the letters well enough. Plainly the man had stolen it; and, in fact, three links of a broken chain were still hanging to the bow; and Tommy knew the chain as well as he knew the watch.

Tommy was a boy of business, a philosopher, and a practical person. He knew nothing of the second watch, whether it was the red-headed man's or another's. But he did know that this with the broken chain was his father's – he had had it in his hands a hundred times. So with no more ado he put it in his trousers-pocket, on top of the bag of bulls'-eyes, and then quietly withdrew from the bush, leaving the red-headed man and his enemy talking some yards away on the opposite side.

'I can't go home without him!' cried Mrs Jepps that evening in the booking-office of Southend station. 'My darling child! I can't! I can't!'

'But come an' ask the station-master,' reasoned her husband. 'He might ha' come here to see about gettin' home. We never thought o' that!'

A small boy, who had been mistakenly trying to weigh himself by clinging desperately to the arm of the machine used for luggage, let go as he recognised the voices, and came out of the dim corner, looking uncommonly bulky about the pockets.

'Hallo, Mother!' said Tommy, 'I've been waiting for you since – well, I've been waiting a long time!'

This time, Mrs Jepps really did faint. But it was not for long. When she came to herself, with water from the waiting-room bottle in her hair and down her back, she recovered her customary energy with surprising rapidity. 'Tommy, you wicked, ungrateful little wretch!' she said; 'a nice holiday you've made o' this for me! Wait till I get you home, that's all!'

'Why, Tommy,' said his father, 'wasn't there no party as stole you, after all?'

'I don't believe parties steal boys at all,' said Tommy; 'but parties steal watches.' And with that he hauled out what Jepps had never expected to see again.

This phenomenon completed the demoralisation of the party; it also dissipated the storm that was gathering about Tommy's head.

'Lawks, child!' cried all the ladies at once. And Cousin Jane's sister's young man's aunt clung for support to the nearest object, which was a porter.

'Come!' squeaked Tommy, with a new importance in his voice, rattling the money in his trousers-pockets. 'Got your tickets? Keep close to me, an' I'll show you the right train.'

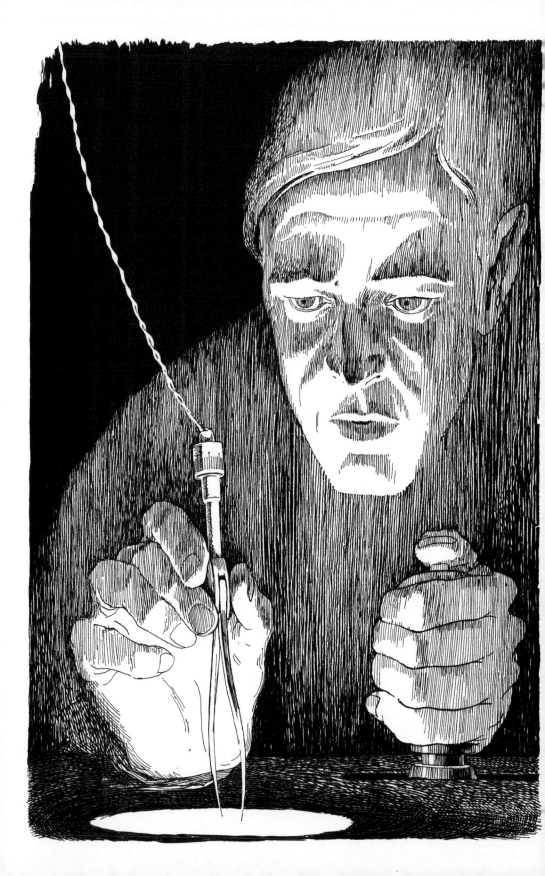

# THE LAND IRONCLADS

## By H. G. Wells

### I

THE YOUNG LIEUTENANT lay beside the war correspondent and admired the idyllic calm of the enemy's lines through his field-glass.

'So far as I can see,' he said, at last, 'one man.'

'What's he doing?' asked the war correspondent.

'Field-glass at us,' said the young lieutenant.

'And this is war!'

'No,' said the young lieutenant; 'it's Bloch.'

'The game's a draw.'

'No! They've got to win or else they lose. A draw's a win for our side.'

They had discussed the political situation fifty times or so, and the war correspondent was weary of it. He stretched out his limbs. 'Aaai s'pose it *is!*' he yawned.

'*Flut!*'

'What was that?'

'Shot at us.'

The war correspondent shifted to a slightly lower position 'No one shot at him,' he complained.

'I wonder if they think we shall get so bored we shall go home?'

The war correspondent made no reply.

'There's the harvest, of course . . .'

They had been there a month. Since the first brisk movements after the declaration of war things had gone slower and slower, until it seemed as though the whole machine of events must have run down. To begin with, they had had almost a scampering time; the invader had come across the frontier on the very dawn of the war in half a dozen parallel columns behind a cloud of cyclists and cavalry, with a

87

general air of coming straight on the capital, and the defender-horsemen had held him up, and peppered him and forced him to open out to outflank, and had then bolted to the next position in the most approved style, for a couple of days, until in the afternoon, bump! they had the invader against their prepared lines of defence. He did not suffer so much as had been hoped and expected: he was coming on it seemed with his eyes open, his scouts winded the guns, and down he sat at once without the shadow of an attack and began grubbing trenches for himself, as though he meant to sit down there to the very end of time. He was slow, but much more wary than the world had been led to expect, and he kept convoys tucked in and shielded his slow marching infantry sufficiently well, to prevent any heavy adverse scoring.

'But he ought to attack,' the young lieutenant had insisted.

'He'll attack us at dawn, somewhere along the lines. You'll get the bayonets coming into the trenches just about when you can see,' the war correspondent had held until a week ago.

The young lieutenant winked when he said that.

When one early morning the men the defenders sent to lie out five hundred yards before the trenches, with a view to the unexpected emptying of magazines into any night attack, gave way to causeless panic and blazed away at nothing for ten minutes, the war correspondent understood the meaning of the wink.

'What would you do if you were the enemy?' said the war correspondent, suddenly.

'If I had men like I've got now?'

'Yes.'

'Take these trenches.'

'How?'

'Oh – dodges! Crawl out half-way at night before moonrise and get into touch with the chaps we send out. Blaze at 'em if they tried to shift, and so bag some of 'em in the daylight. Learn that patch of ground by heart, lie all day in squatty holes, and come on nearer next night. There's a bit over there, lumpy ground, where they could get across to rushing distance – easy. In a night or so. It would be a mere game for our fellows; it's what they're made for . . . Guns? Shrapnel and stuff wouldn't stop good men who meant business.'

'Why don't *they* do that?'

'Their men aren't brutes enough; that's the trouble. They're a crowd of devitalised townsmen, and that's the truth of the matter. They're clerks, they're factory hands, they're students, they're civilised men. They can write, they can talk, they can make and do all sorts of things, but they're poor amateurs at war. They've got no physical staying power, and that's the whole thing. They've never slept in the open one night in their lives; they've never drunk anything but the purest water-company water; they've never gone short of three meals a day since they left their devitalising feeding-bottles. Half their cavalry never cocked leg over horse till it enlisted six months ago. They ride their horses as though they were bicycles – you watch 'em! They're fools at the game, and they know it. Our boys of fourteen can give their grown men points . . . Very well—'

The war correspondent mused on his face with his nose between his knuckles.

'If a decent civilisation,' he said 'cannot produce better men for war than—'

He stopped with belated politeness. 'I mean—'

'Than our open-air life,' said the young lieutenant, politely.

'Exactly,' said the war correspondent. 'Then civilisation has to stop.'

'It looks like it,' the young lieutenant admitted.

'Civilisation has science, you know,' said the war correspondent. 'It invented and it makes the rifles and guns and things you use.'

'Which our nice healthy hunters and stockmen and so on, rowdy-dowdy cow-punchers and nigger-whackers, can use ten times better than— *What's that?*'

'What?' said the war correspondent, and then seeing his companion busy with his field-glass he produced his own. 'Where?' said the war correspondent, sweeping the enemy's lines.

'It's nothing,' said the young lieutenant, still looking.

'What's nothing?'

The young lieutenant put down his glass and pointed. 'I thought I saw something there, behind the stems of those trees. Something black. What it was I don't know.'

The war correspondent tried to get even by intense scrutiny.

'It wasn't anything,' said the young lieutenant, rolling over to regard the darkling evening sky, and generalised: 'There never will be anything any more for ever. Unless—'

The war correspondent looked enquiry.

'They may get their stomachs wrong, or something – living without proper drains.'

A sound of bugles came from the tents behind. The war correspondent slid backward down the sand and stood up. 'Boom!' came from somewhere far away to the left. 'Hallo!' he said, hesitated, and crawled back to peer again. 'Firing at this time is jolly bad manners.'

The young lieutenant was uncommunicative again for a space.

Then he pointed to the distant clump of trees again. 'One of our big guns. They were firing at that,' he said.

'The thing that wasn't anything?'

'Something over there, anyhow.'

Both men were silent, peering through their glasses for a space. 'Just when it's twilight,' the lieutenant complained. He stood up.

'I might stay here a bit,' said the war correspondent.

The lieutenant shook his head. 'There's nothing to see,' he apologised, and then went down to where his little squad of sun-brown, loose-limbed men had been yarning in the trench. The war correspondent stood up also, glanced for a moment at the businesslike bustle below him, gave perhaps twenty seconds to those enigmatical trees again, then turned his face toward the camp.

He found himself wondering whether his editor would consider the story of how somebody thought he saw something black behind a clump of trees, and how a gun was fired at this illusion by somebody else, too trivial for public consumption.

'It's the only gleam of a shadow of interest,' said the war correspondent, 'for ten whole days.'

'No,' he said, presently; 'I'll write that other article, "Is War Played Out?".'

He surveyed the darkling lines in perspective, the tangle of trenches one behind another, one commanding another, which the defender had made ready. The shadows and mists swallowed up their receding contours, and here and there a lantern gleamed, and here and there knots of men were busy about small fires. 'No troops on earth could do it,' he said . . .

He was depressed. He believed that there were other things in life better worth having than proficiency in war; he believed that in the heart of civilisation, for all its stresses, its crushing concentrations of forces, its injustice and suffering, there lay something that might be the hope of the world, and the idea that any people by living in the open air, hunting perpetually, losing touch with books and art and all the things that intensify life, might hope to resist and break that great development to the end of time, jarred on his civilised soul.

Apt to his thought came a file of the defender soldiers and passed him in the gleam of a swinging lamp that marked the way.

He glanced at their red-lit faces, and one shone out for a moment, a common type of face in the defender's ranks: ill-shaped nose, sensuous lips, bright clear eyes full of alert cunning, slouch hat cocked on one side and adorned with the peacock's plume of the rustic Don Juan turned soldier, a hard brown skin, a sinewy frame, an open, tireless stride, and a master's grip on the rifle.

The war correspondent returned their salutations and went on his way.

'Louts,' he whispered. 'Cunning, elementary louts. And they are going to beat the townsmen at the game of war!'

From the red glow among the nearer tents came first one and then half-a-dozen hearty voices, bawling in a drawling unison the words of a particularly slab and sentimental patriotic song.

'Oh, *go* it!' muttered the war correspondent, bitterly.

## II

It was opposite the trenches called after Hackbone's Hut that the battle began. There the ground stretched broad and level between the lines, with scarcely shelter for a lizard, and it seemed to the startled, just-awakened men who came crowding into the trenches that this was one more proof of that green inexperience of the enemy of which they had heard so much. The war correspondent would not believe his ears at first, and swore that he and the war artist, who, still imperfectly roused, was trying to put on his boots by the light of a match held in his hand, were the victims of a common illusion. Then, after putting his head in a bucket of cold water, his intelligence came back as he towelled. He listened. 'Gollys!' he said; 'that's something more than scare firing this time. It's like ten thousand carts on a bridge of tin.'

There came a sort of enrichment to that steady uproar. 'Machine guns!'

Then, 'Guns!'

The artist, with one boot on, thought to look at his watch, and went to it hopping.

'Half an hour from dawn,' he said. 'You were right about their attacking, after all . . .'

The war correspondent came out of the tent, verifying the presence of chocolate in his pocket as he did so. He had to halt for a moment or so until his eyes were toned down to the night a little. 'Pitch!' he said. He stood for a space to season his eyes before he felt justified in striking out for a black gap among the adjacent tents. The artist coming out behind him fell over a tent-rope. It was half-past two o'clock in the morning of the darkest night in time, and against a sky of dull black silk the enemy was talking searchlights, a wild jabber of searchlights. 'He's trying to blind our riflemen,' said the war correspondent with a flash, and waited for the artist and then set off with a sort of discreet haste again. 'Whoa!' he said, presently. 'Ditches!'

They stopped.

'It's the confounded searchlights,' said the war correspondent.

They saw lanterns going to and fro, nearby, and men falling in to march down to the trenches. They were for following them, and then the artist began to feel his night eyes. 'If we scramble this,' he said, 'and it's only a drain, there's a clear run up to the ridge.' And that way they took. Lights came and went in the tents behind, as the men turned out, and ever and again they came to broken ground and staggered and stumbled. But in a little while they drew near the crest. Something that sounded like the impact of a very important railway accident happened in the air above them, and the shrapnel bullets seethed about them like a sudden handful of hail. 'Right-ho!' said the war correspondent, and soon they judged they had come to the crest and stood in the midst of a world of great darkness and frantic glares, whose principal fact was sound.

Right and left of them and all about them was the uproar, an army-full of magazine fire, at first chaotic and monstrous and then, eked out by little flashes and gleams and suggestions, taking the beginnings of a shape. It looked to the war correspondent as though the enemy must have attacked in line and with his whole force – in which case he was either being or was already annihilated.

'Dawn and the Dead,' he said, with his instinct for headlines. He said this to himself, but afterwards, by means of shouting, he conveyed an idea to the artist. 'They must have meant it for a surprise,' he said.

It was remarkable how the firing kept on. After a time he began to perceive a sort of rhythm in this inferno of noise. It would decline – decline perceptibly, droop towards something that was comparatively a pause – a pause of enquiry. 'Aren't you all dead yet?' this pause seemed to say. The flickering fringe of rifle-flashes would become attenuated and broken, and the whack-bang of the enemy's big guns two miles away there would come up out of the deeps. Then suddenly, east or west of them, something would startle the rifles to a frantic outbreak again.

The war correspondent taxed his brain for some theory of conflict that would account for this, and was suddenly aware that the artist and he were vividly illuminated. He could see the ridge on which they stood, and before them in black outline a file of riflemen hurrying down towards the nearer trenches. It became visible that a light rain was falling, and farther away towards the enemy was a clear space with men – 'our men?' – running across it in disorder. He saw one of those men throw up his hands and drop. And something else black and shining loomed up on the edge of the beam-coruscating flashes; and behind it and far away a calm, white eye regarded the world. 'Whit, whit, whit,' sang something in the air, and then the artist was running for cover, with the war correspondent behind him. Bang came shrapnel, bursting close at hand as it seemed, and our two men were lying flat in a dip in the ground, and the light and everything had gone again, leaving a vast note of interrogation upon the night.

The war correspondent came within bawling range. 'What the deuce was it? Shooting our men down!'

'Black,' said the artist, 'and like a fort. Not two hundred yards from the first trench.'

He sought for comparisons in his mind. 'Something between a big blockhouse and a giant's dish-cover,' he said.

'And they were running!' said the war correspondent.

'*You'd* run if a thing like that, with a searchlight to help it, turned up like a prowling nightmare in the middle of the night.'

They crawled to what they judged the edge of the dip and lay regarding the unfathomable dark. For a space they could distinguish nothing, and then a sudden convergence of the searchlights of both sides brought the strange thing out again.

In that flickering pallor it had the effect of a large and clumsy black insect, an insect the size of an ironclad cruiser, crawling obliquely to the first line of trenches and firing shots out of portholes in its back. And on its carcass the bullets must have been battering with more than the passionate violence of hail on a roof of tin.

Then in the twinkling of an eye the curtain of the dark had fallen again and the monster had vanished, but the crescendo of musketry marked its approach to the trenches.

They were beginning to talk about the thing to each other, when a flying bullet kicked dirt into the artist's face, and they decided abruptly to crawl down into the cover of the trenches. They had got down with an unobtrusive persistence into the second line, before the dawn had grown clear enough for anything to be seen. They found themselves in a crowd of expectant riflemen, all noisily arguing about the thing that would happen next. The enemy's contrivance had done execution upon the outlying men, it seemed, but they did not believe it would do any more. 'Come the day and we'll capture the lot of them,' said a burly soldier.

'Them?' said the war correspondent.

'They say there's a regular string of 'em, crawling along the front of our lines . . . Who cares?'

The darkness filtered away so imperceptibly that at no moment could one declare decisively that one could see. The searchlights ceased to sweep hither and thither. The enemy's monsters were dubious patches of darkness upon the dark, and then no longer dubious, and so they crept out into distinctness. The war correspondent, munching chocolate absent-mindedly, beheld at last a spacious picture of battle under the cheerless sky, whose central focus was an array of fourteen or fifteen huge clumsy shapes lying in perspective on the very edge of the first line of trenches, at intervals of perhaps three hundred yards, and evidently firing down upon the crowded riflemen. They were so close in that the defender's guns had ceased, and only the first line of trenches was in action.

The second line commanded the first, and as the light grew the war correspondent could make out the riflemen who were fighting these monsters, crouched in knots and crowds behind the transverse banks that crossed the trenches against the eventuality of an enfilade. The trenches close to the big machines were empty save for the crumpled suggestions of dead and wounded men; the defenders had been driven right and left as soon as the prow of this land ironclad had loomed up over the front of the trench. He produced his field-glass, and was immediately a centre of enquiry from the soldiers about him.

They wanted to look, they asked questions, and after he had announced that the men across the traverses seemed unable to advance or retreat, and were crouching under cover rather than fighting, he found it advisable to loan his glasses to a burly and incredulous corporal. He heard a strident voice, and found a lean and sallow soldier at his back talking to the artist.

'There's chaps down there caught,' the man was saying. 'If they retreat they got to expose themselves, and the fire's too straight . . .'

'They aren't firing much, but every shot's a hit.'

'Who?'

'The chaps in that thing. The men who're coming up—'

'Coming up where?'

'We're evacuating them trenches where we can. Our chaps are coming back up the zigzags . . . No end of 'em hit . . . But when we get clear our turn'll come. Rather! Those things won't be able to cross a trench or get into it: and before they can get back our guns'll smash 'em up. Smash 'em right up. See?' A brightness came into his eyes. 'Then we'll have a go at the beggar inside,' he said.

The war correspondent thought for a moment, trying to realise the idea. Then he set himself to recover his field-glasses from the burly corporal . . .

The daylight was getting clearer now. The clouds were lifting, and a gleam of lemon yellow amidst the level masses to the east portended sunrise. He looked again at the land ironclad. As he saw it in the bleak, grey dawn, lying obliquely upon the slope and on the very lip of the foremost trench, the suggesion of a stranded vessel was very great indeed. It might have been from eighty to a hundred feet long – it was about two hundred and fifty yards away – its vertical side was ten feet high or so, smooth for that height, and then with a complex patterning under the eaves of its flattish turtle cover. This patterning was a close interlacing of portholes, rifle barrels, and telescope tubes – sham and real – indistinguishable one from the other. The thing had come into such a position as to enfilade the trench, which was empty now, so far as he could see, except for two or three crouching knots of men and the tumbled-looking dead. Behind it, across the plain, it had scored the grass with a train of linked impressions, like the dotted tracings sea-things leave in sand. Left and right of that track dead men and wounded men were scattered – men it had picked off as they fled back from their advanced positions in the searchlight glare from the invader's lines. And now it lay with its head projecting a little over the trench it had won, as if it were a single sentient thing planning the next phase of its attack . . .

He lowered his glasses and took a more comprehensive view of the situation. These creatures of the night had evidently won the first line of trenches and the fight had come to a pause. In the increasing light he could make out by a stray shot or a chance exposure that the defender's marksmen were lying thick in the second and third line of trenches up towards the low crest of the position, and in such of the zigzags as gave them a chance of a converging fire. The men about him were talking of guns. 'We're in the line of the big guns at the crest, but they'll soon shift one to pepper them,' the lean man said, reassuringly.

'Whup,' said the corporal.

'Bang! bang! bang! Whir-r-r-r!' it was a sort of nervous jump, and all the rifles were going off by themselves. The war correspondent found himself and the artist, two idle men crouching behind a line of preoccupied backs, of industrious men discharging magazines. The monster had moved. It continued to move regardless of the hail that splashed its skin with bright new specks of lead. It was singing a mechanical little ditty to itself, 'Tuf-tuf, tuf-tuf, tuf-tuf,' and

squirting out little jets of steam behind. It had humped itself up, as a
limpet does before it crawls; it had lifted its skirt and displayed along
the length of it – *feet!* They were thick, stumpy feet, between knobs
and buttons in shape – flat, broad things, reminding one of the feet of
elephants or the legs of caterpillars; and then, as the skirt rose higher,
the war correspondent, scrutinising the thing through his glasses
again, saw that these feet hung, as it were, on the rims of wheels. His
thoughts whirled back to Victoria Street, Westminster, and he saw
himself in the piping times of peace, seeking matter for an interview.

'Mr – Mr Diplock,' he said; 'and he called them Pedrails . . . Fancy
meeting them here!'

The marksman beside him raised his head and shoulders in a
speculative mood to fire more certainly – it seemed so natural to
assume the attention of the monster must be distracted by this trench
before it – and was suddenly knocked backwards by a bullet through
his neck. His feet flew up, and he vanished out of the margin of the
watcher's field of vision. The war correspondent grovelled tighter,
but after a glance behind him at a painful little confusion, he resumed
his field-glass, for the thing was putting down its feet one after the
other, and hoisting itself farther and farther over the trench. Only a
bullet in the head could have stopped him looking just then.

The lean man with the strident voice ceased firing to turn and
reiterate his point. 'They can't possibly cross,' he bawled. 'They—'

'Bang! Bang! Bang, bang!' – drowned everything.

The lean man continued speaking for a word or so, then gave it up,
shook his head to enforce the impossibility of anything crossing a
trench like the one below, and resumed business once more.

And all the while that great bulk was crossing. When the war
correspondent turned his glass on it again it had bridged the trench,
and its queer feet were rasping away at the farther bank, in the
attempt to get a hold there. It got its hold. It continued to crawl until
the greater bulk of it was over the trench – until it was all over. Then
it paused for a moment, adjusted its skirt a little nearer the ground,
gave an unnerving 'toot, toot', and came on abruptly at a pace of,
perhaps, six miles an hour straight up the gentle slope towards our
observer.

The war correspondent raised himself on his elbow and looked a
natural enquiry at the artist.

For a moment the men about him stuck to their position and fired
furiously. Then the lean man in a mood of precipitancy slid backwards, and the war correspondent said 'Come along' to the artist, and
led the movement along the trench.

As they dropped down, the vision of a hillside of trench being rushed by a dozen vast cockroaches disappeared for a space, and instead was one of a narrow passage, crowded with men, for the most part receding, though one or two turned or halted. He never turned back to see the nose of the monster creep over the brow of the trench; he never even troubled to keep in touch with the artist. He heard the 'whit' of bullets about him soon enough, and saw a man before him stumble and drop, and then he was one of a furious crowd fighting to get into a transverse zigzag ditch that enabled the defenders to get under cover up and down the hill. It was like a theatre panic. He gathered from signs and fragmentary words that on ahead another of these monsters had also won to the second trench.

He lost his interest in the general course of the battle for a space altogether; he became simply a modest egotist, in a mood of hasty circumspection, seeking the farthest rear, amidst a dispersed multitude of disconcerted riflemen similarly employed. He scrambled down through trenches, he took his courage in both hands and sprinted across the open, he had moments of panic when it seemed madness not to be quadrupedal, and moments of shame when he stood up and faced about to see how the fight was going. And he was one of many thousand very similar men that morning. On the ridge he halted in a knot of scrub, and was for a few minutes almost minded to stop and see things out.

The day was now fully come. The grey sky had changed to blue, and of all the cloudy masses of the dawn there remained only a few patches of dissolving fleeciness. The world below was bright and singularly clear. The ridge was not, perhaps, more than a hundred feet or so above the general plain, but in this flat region it sufficed to give the effect of extensive view. Away on the north side of the ridge, little and far, were the camps, the ordered wagons, all the gear of a big army; with officers galloping about and men doing aimless things. Here and there men were falling-in, however, and the cavalry was forming up on the plain beyond the tents. The bulk of men who had been in the trenches were still on the move to the rear, scattered like sheep without a shepherd over the farther slopes. Here and there were little rallies and attempts to wait and do – something vague; but the general drift was away from any concentration. Then on the southern side was the elaborate lacework of trenches and defences, across which these iron turtles, fourteen of them spread out over a line of perhaps three miles, were now advancing as fast as a man could trot, and methodically shooting down and breaking up any persistent knots of resistance. Here and there stood little clumps of men, outflanked and unable to get away, showing the white flag, and the invader's cyclist infantry was advancing now across the open, in open order but unmolested, to complete the work of the machines. So far as the day went, the defenders already looked a beaten army. A mechanism that was effectually ironclad against bullets, that could at a pinch cross a thirty-foot trench, and that seemed able to shoot out rifle-bullets with unerring precision, was clearly an inevitable victor against anything but rivers, precipices, and guns.

He looked at his watch. 'Half-past four! Lord! What things can happen in two hours. Here's the whole blessed army being walked over, and at half-past two—

'And even now our blessed louts haven't done a thing with their guns!'

He scanned the ridge right and left of him with his glasses. He turned again to the nearest land ironclad, advancing now obliquely to him and not three hundred yards away, and then scanned the ground over which he must retreat if he was not to be captured.

'They'll do nothing,' he said, and glanced again at the enemy.

And then from far away to the left came the thud of a gun, followed very rapidly by a rolling gun-fire.

He hesitated and decided to stay.

### III

The defender had relied chiefly upon his rifles in the event of an assault. His guns he kept concealed at various points upon and behind the ridge ready to bring them into action against any artillery preparations for an attack on the part of his antagonist. The situation had rushed upon him with the dawn, and by the time the gunners had their guns ready for motion, the land ironclads were already in among the foremost trenches. There is a natural reluctance to fire into one's own broken men, and many of the guns, being intended simply to fight an advance of the enemy's artillery, were not in positions to hit anything in the second line of trenches. After that the advance of the land ironclads was swift. The defender-general found himself suddenly called upon to invent a new sort of warfare, in which guns were to fight alone amidst broken and retreating infantry. He had scarcely thirty minutes in which to think it out. He did not respond to the call, and what happened that morning was that the advance of the land ironclads forced the fight, and each gun and battery made what play its circumstances dictated. For the most part it was poor play.

Some of the guns got in two or three shots, some one or two, and the percentage of misses was unusually high. The howitzers, of course, did nothing. The land ironclads in each case followed much the same tactics. As soon as a gun came into play the monster turned itself almost end on, so as to get the biggest chance of a glancing hit, and made not for the gun, but for the nearest point on its flank from which the gunners could be shot down. Few of the hits scored were very effectual; only one of the things was disabled, and that was the one that fought the three batteries attached to the brigade on the left wing. Three that were hit when close upon the guns were clean shot through without being put out of action. Our war correspondent did not see that one momentary arrest of the tide of victory on the left; he saw only the very ineffectual fight of half-battery 96B close at hand upon his right. This he watched some time beyond the margin of safety.

Just after he heard the three batteries opening up upon his left he became aware of the thud of horses' hoofs from the sheltered side of the slope, and presently saw first one and then two other guns galloping into position along the north side of the ridge, well out of sight of the great bulk that was now creeping obliquely towards the crest and cutting up the lingering infantry, beside it and below, as it came.

The half-battery swung round into line – each gun describing its curve – halted, unlimbered, and prepared for action . . .

'Bang!'

The land ironclad had become visible over the brow of the hill, and just visible as a long black back to the gunners. It halted, as though it hesitated.

The two remaining guns fired, and then their big antagonist had swung round and was in full view, end on, against the sky, coming at a rush.

The gunners became frantic in their haste to fire again. They were so near the war correspondent could see the expression of their excited faces through his field-glass. As he looked he saw a man drop, and realised for the first time that the ironclad was shooting.

For a moment the big black monster crawled with an accelerated pace towards the furiously active gunners. Then, as if moved by a generous impulse, it turned its full broadside to their attack, and scarcely forty yards away from them. The war correspondent turned his field-glass back to the gunners and perceived it was now shooting down the men about the guns with the most deadly rapidity.

Just for a moment it seemed splendid and then it seemed horrible. The gunners were dropping in heaps about their guns. To lay a hand on a gun was death. 'Bang!' went the gun on the left, a hopeless miss, and that was the only second shot the half-battery fired. In another moment half-a-dozen surviving artillerymen were holding up their hands amidst a scattered muddle of dead and wounded men, and the fight was done.

The war correspondent hesitated between stopping in his scrub and waiting for an opportunity to surrender decently, or taking to an adjacent gully he had discovered. If he surrendered, it was certain he would get no copy off; while, if he escaped, there were all sorts of chances. He decided to follow the gully, and take the first offer in the confusion beyond the camp of picking up a horse.


I V


Subsequent authorities have found fault with the first land ironclads in many particulars, but assuredly they served their purpose on the day of their appearance. They were essentially long, narrow, and very strong steel frameworks carrying the engines, and borne upon eight pairs of big pedrail wheels, each about ten feet in diameter, each a driving wheel and set upon long axles free to swivel round a common axis. This arrangement gave them the maximum of adaptability to the contours of the ground. They crawled level along the ground with one foot high upon a hillock and another deep in a depression, and they could hold themselves erect and steady sideways upon even a steep hillside. The engineers directed the engines under the command of the captain, who had look-out points at small ports all round the upper edge of the adjustable skirt of twelve-inch iron-plating which protected the whole affair, and who could also raise or depress a conning-tower set about the portholes through the centre of the iron top cover. The riflemen each occupied a small cabin of peculiar construction, and these cabins were slung along the sides of and before and behind the great main framework, in a manner suggestive of the slinging of the seats of an Irish jaunting-car. Their rifles, however, were very different pieces of apparatus from the simple mechanisms in the hands of their adversaries.

These were in the first place automatic, ejected their cartridges and loaded again from a magazine each time they fired, until the ammunition store was at an end, and they had the most remarkable sights imaginable, sights which threw a bright little camera-obscura picture into the light-tight box in which the rifleman sat below. This camera-obscura picture was marked with two crossed lines, and whatever was covered by the intersection of these two lines, that the rifle hit. The sighting was ingeniously contrived. The rifleman stood at the table with a thing like an elaboration of a draughtsman's dividers in his hand, and he opened and closed these dividers, so that they were always at the apparent height – if it was an ordinary-sized man – of the man he wanted to kill. A little twisted strand of wire like an electric-light wire ran from this implement up to the gun, and as the dividers opened and shut the sights went up or down. Changes in the clearness of the atmosphere, due to changes of moisture, were met by an ingenious use of that meteorologically sensitive substance, catgut, and when the land ironclad moved forward the sights got a compensatory deflection in the direction of its motion. The rifleman stood up in his pitch-dark chamber and watched the little picture before him. One hand held the dividers for judging distance, and the other grasped a big knob like a door-handle. As he pushed this knob about, the rifle above swung to correspond, and the picture passed to and fro like an agitated panorama. When he saw a man he wanted to shoot, he brought him up to the cross-lines, and then pressed a finger upon a litle push like an electric bell-push, conveniently placed in the centre of the knob. Then the man was shot. If by any chance the rifleman missed his target, he moved the knob a trifle, or readjusted his dividers, pressed the push, and got him the second time.

This rifle and its sights protruded from a porthole, exactly like a great number of other portholes that ran in a triple row under the eaves of the cover of the land ironclad. Each porthole displayed a rifle and sight in dummy, so that the real ones could only be hit by a chance shot, and if one was, then the young man below said 'Pshaw!' turned on an electric light, lowered the injured instrument into his camera, replaced the injured part, or put up a new rifle if the injury was considerable.

You must conceive these cabins as hung clear above the swing of the axles, and inside the big wheels upon which the great elephant-like feet were hung, and behind these cabins along the centre of the monster ran a central gallery into which they opened, and along which worked the big compact engines. It was like a long passage into which this throbbing machinery had been packed, and the captain stood about the middle, close to the ladder that led to his conning-tower, and directed the silent, alert engineers – for the most part by signs. The throb and noise of the engines mingled with the reportsof the rifles and the intermittent clangour of the bullet hail upon the armour. Ever and again he would touch the wheel that raised his conning-tower, step up his ladder until his engineers could see nothing of him above the waist, and then come down again with orders. Two small electric lights were all the illumination of this space – they were placed to make him most clearly visible to his subordinates; the air was thick with the smell of oil and petrol, and had the war correspondent been suddenly transferred from the spacious dawn outside to the bowels of this apparatus he would have thought himself fallen into another world.

The captain, of course, saw both sides of the battle. When he raised his head into his conning-tower there were the dewy sunrise, the amazed and disordered trenches, the flying and falling soldiers, the depressed-looking groups of prisoners, the beaten guns; when he bent down again to signal 'Half speed', 'Quarter speed', 'Half circle round towards the right', or what not, he was in the oil-smelling twilight of the ill-lit engine-room. Close beside him on either side was the mouthpiece of a speaking-tube, and ever and again he would direct one side or other of his strange craft to 'Concentrate fire forward on gunners', or to 'Clear out trench about a hundred yards on our right front'.

He was a young man, healthy enough but by no means sun-tanned, and of a type of feature and expression that prevails in His Majesty's Navy: alert, intelligent, quiet. He and his engineers and his riflemen all went about their work, calm and reasonable men. They had none of that flapping strenuousness of the half-wit in a hurry, that excessive strain upon the blood-vessels, that hysteria of effort which is so frequently regarded as the proper state of mind for heroic deeds. If their machine had demanded anything of the sort, they would, of course, have improved their machine. They were all perfectly sober and in good training, and if any of them had begun to ejaculate nonsense or bawl patriotic airs, the others would probably have gagged him and tied him up as a dangerous, unnerving sort of fool. And if they were free from hysteria they were equally free from that stupid affectation of nonchalance which is the refuge of the thoroughly incapable in danger. Death was abroad, and there were marginal possibilities of the unforeseen, but it is no good calculating upon the incalculable, and so beyond a certain unavoidable tightening up of nerve and muscle, a certain firmness of the lips, this affected them not at all.

For the enemy these young engineers were defeating they felt a certain qualified pity and a quite unqualified contempt. They regarded these big, healthy men they were shooting down precisely as these same big, healthy men might regard some inferior kind of nigger. They despised them for making war; despised their bawling patriotisms and their emotionality profoundly; despised them, above all, for the petty cunning and the almost brutish want of imagination their method of fighting displayed. 'If they *must* make war,' these young men thought, 'why in thunder don't they do it like sensible men?' They resented the assumption that their own side was too stupid to do anything more than play their enemy's game, that they were going to play this costly folly according to the rules of un-imaginative men. They resented being forced to the trouble of making man-killing machinery; resented the alternative of having to massacre these people or endure their truculent yappings; resented the whole unfathomable imbecility of war.

Meanwhile, with something of the mechanical precision of a good clerk posting a ledger, the riflemen moved their knobs and pressed their buttons . . .

The captain of Land Ironclad Number Three had halted on the crest close to his captured half-battery. His lined-up prisoners stood hard by and waited for the cyclists behind to come for them. He surveyed the victorious morning through his conning-tower.

He read the general's signals. 'Five and Four are to keep among the guns to the left and prevent any attempt to recover them. Seven and Eleven and Twelve, stick to the guns you have got; Seven, get into position to command the guns taken by Three. Then we're to do something else, are we? Six and One, quicken up to about ten miles an hour and walk round behind that camp to the levels near the river – we shall bag the whole crowd of them,' interjected the young man. 'Ah, here we are! Two and Three, Eight and Nine, Thirteen and Fourteen, space out to a thousand yards, wait for the word, and then go slowly to cover the advance of the cyclist infantry against any charge of mounted troops. That's all right. But where's Ten? Hallo! Ten to repair and get movable as soon as possible. They've broken up Ten!'

The discipline of the new war machines was businesslike rather than pedantic, and the head of the captain came down out of the conning-tower to tell his men. 'I say, you chaps there. They've broken up Ten. Not badly, I think; but anyhow, he's stuck!'

But that still left thirteen of the monsters in action to finish up the broken army.

The war correspondent stealing down his gully looked back and saw them all lying along the crest and talking fluttering congratulatory flags to one another. Their iron sides were shining golden in the light of the rising sun.

V

The private adventures of the war correspondent terminated in sur-render about one o'clock in the afternoon, and by that time he had stolen a horse, pitched off it, and narrowly escaped being rolled upon; found the brute had broken its leg, and shot it with his revolver. He had spent some hours in the company of a squad of dispirited riflemen, who had commandeered his field-glass and whose pedes-trianism was exemplary, and he had quarrelled with them about topography at last, and gone off by himself in a direction that should have brought him to the banks of the river and didn't. Moreover, he had eaten all his chocolate and found nothing in the whole world to drink. Also, it had become extremely hot. From behind a broken, but attractive, stone wall he had seen far away in the distance the defender horsemen trying to charge cyclists in open order, with land ironclads outflanking them on either side. He had discovered that cyclists could retreat over open turf before horsemen with a sufficient margin of speed to allow of frequent dismounts and much terribly effective sharpshooting; and he had a sufficient persuasion that those horsemen, having charged their hearts out, had halted just beyond his range of vision and surrendered. He had been urged to sudden activity by a forward movement of one of those machines that had threatened to enfilade his wall. He had discovered a fearful blister on his heel.

He was now in a scrubby gravelly place, sitting down and meditat-ing on his pocket-handkerchief, which had in some extraordinary way become in the last twenty-four hours extremely ambiguous in hue. 'It's the whitest thing I've got,' he said.

He had known all along that the enemy was east, west, and south of him, but when he heard war ironclads Numbers One and Six stalking in their measured, deadly way not half a mile to the north he decided to make his own little unconditional peace without any further risks. He was for hoisting his white flag to a bush and taking up a position of modest obscurity near it, until someone came along. He became aware of voices, clatter, and the distinctive noises of a body of horse, quite near, and he put his handkerchief in his pocket again and went to see what was going forward.

The sound of firing ceased, and then as he drew near he heard the deep sounds of many simple, coarse, but hearty and noble-hearted soldiers of the old school swearing with vigour.

He emerged from his scrub upon a big level plain, and far away a fringe of trees marked the banks of the river.

In the centre of the picture was a still intact road bridge, and a big railway bridge a little to the right. Two land ironclads rested, with a general air of being long, harmless sheds, in a pose of anticipatory peacefulness right and left of the picture, completely commanding two miles and more of the river levels. Emerged and halted a little from the scrub was the remainder of the defender's cavalry, dusty, a little disordered and obviously annoyed, but still a very fine show of men. In the middle distance three or four men and horses were receiving medical attendance, and a little nearer a knot of officers regarded the distant novelties in mechanism with profound distaste. Everyone was very distinctly aware of the twelve other ironclads, and of the multitude of townsmen soldiers, on bicycles or afoot, encumbered now by prisoners and captured war-gear but otherwise thoroughly effective, who were sweeping like a great net in their rear.

'Checkmate,' said the war correspondent, walking out into the open. 'But I surrender in the best of company. Twenty-four hours ago I thought war was impossible – and these beggars have captured the whole blessed army! Well! Well!' He thought of his talk with the young lieutenant. 'If there's no end to the surprises of science, the civilised people have it, of course. As long as their science keeps going they will necessarily be ahead of open-country men. Still . . .'

He wondered for a space what might have happened to the young lieutenant.

The war correspondent was one of those inconsistent people who always want the beaten side to win. When he saw all these burly, sun-tanned horsemen, disarmed and dismounted and lined up; when he saw their horses unskilfully led away by the singularly not equestrian cyclists to whom they had surrendered; when he saw these truncated Paladins watching this scandalous sight, he forgot altogether that he had called these men 'cunning louts' and wished them beaten not four-and-twenty hours ago. A month ago he had seen that regiment in its pride going forth to war, and had been told of its terrible prowess, how it could charge in open order with each man firing from his saddle, and sweep before it anything else that ever came out to battle in any sort of order, foot or horse. And it had had to fight a few score of young men in atrociously unfair machines!

'Manhood *versus* Machinery' occurred to him as a suitable head-line. Journalism curdles all one's mind to phrases.

He strolled as near the lined-up prisoners as the sentinels seemed disposed to permit and surveyed them and compared their sturdy proportions with those of their lightly-built captors.

'Smart degenerates,' he muttered. 'Anaemic cockneydom.'

The surrendered officers came quite close to him presently, and he could hear the colonel's high-pitched tenor. The poor gentleman had spent three years of arduous toil upon the best material in the world perfecting that shooting-from-the-saddle charge, and he was enquiring with phrases of blasphemy, natural under the circumstances, what one could be expected to do against this suitably consigned iron-mongery.

'Guns,' said someone.

'Big guns they can walk round. You can't shift big guns to keep pace with them, and little guns in the open they rush. I saw 'em rushed. You might do a surprise now and then – assassinate the brutes, perhaps—'

'You might make things like 'em.'

'What? *More* ironmongery? Us? . . .'

'I'll call my article,' meditated the war correspondent, ' "Mankind *versus* Ironmongery", and quote the old boy at the beginning.'

And he was much too good a journalist to spoil his contrast by remarking that the half-dozen comparatively slender young men in blue pyjamas who were standing about their victorious land ironclad, drinking coffee and eating biscuits, had also in their eyes and carriage something not altogether degraded below the level of a man.

# THE GIRL ON
# THE SANDS

## By *Richard Marsh*

TALK ABOUT ADVENTURES! I had an adventure which beat anything I ever heard of, either in a novel or a play. It was last year at Sandbythesea. I was there for my holiday – ten days altogether. It happened on the Saturday before the Monday on which it was to be a case of first train up to town. I had been doing myself a fair treat – riding on charabancs, sailing-boats, rowing-boats, steamers; in fact, everything that was going. I give you my word that I'd missed nothing. That sort of thing makes the pieces fly. So that Saturday afternoon I was on the look-out for something that would provide the most amusement at the smallest cost. I was looking for it on the sands.

A lot of cheap excursions had come down that day – twenty-four in a compartment for half a crown – that kind of thing. And the crowds! You couldn't see the sands because of the people. As for getting near the pierrots, or any one of the entertainments, it was not to be done, unless you were an acrobat, and could stand on any head that was handy. No doubt there were plenty who were enjoying themselves, but having been there all the week it was nothing new to me, and I was just beginning to feel that it would have to be a case of another twopence for the pier – the money a pier does run away with, what with the twopence every time you go on, and the feeling that you must spend something when you are on! – when – the adventure began.

She was a girl. Not much to look at. Certainly nothing in the way of dress. Plain brown holland – that was what she had on. One of those cloth caps with peaks. A bit of blue ribbon worn as a necktie. No gloves. Black shoes. Not one single article that could be called stylish. So it was not her get-up that drew me. She had two pockets in her skirt – queer-cut skirt I thought it. With a hand in each she was looking about her with a sort of a kind of a smile. I stood by her for about a minute, just to see how the land was lying; then I looked at her with a twinkle in my eye. She looked me straight in the face, and she smiled. So then, of course, I broke the ice.

'Fine weather, isn't it?' I remarked, just by way of a beginning.

She kept on looking me straight in the face; I never was looked at straighter. Then she said:

'It rained last month.'

There was something about the way she said it which took me a little aback. It was a second or two before I gave the conversation another turn.

'I dare say it did; but as that was some time ago I can't say I remember much about it. Good many people on the sands today.'

She kept on looking me straight in the face, and a fine pair of eyes she had to do it with.

'I've counted ten during the last five minutes – you make eleven.'

Then I caught her drift.

'You're fond of your joke, I see.'

'I always have been fond of a joke.'

She smiled till she showed as nice a set of teeth as anyone could want.

'Same here. Ever since I was a nipper.'

'A what?'

'A nipper; don't you know what that is?'

She shook her head.

'I haven't had your opportunities.'

'That's very likely. Though I say it myself, I've seen as much as most and a good deal more than some.'

'You look as if you were a person who knew his world.'

'You may take it from me that anybody will have to know a bit who wants to teach Sam Briggs.'

'Sam Briggs?'

'Yours obediently. Allow me to introduce you to Samuel Briggs, Esquire.' I took my Panama off and did the graceful. 'Staying here?' She nodded. 'Cheerful place, I call it.'

'At this time of the year it is – cheerful.'

She kept looking about her, still with that sort of a kind of a smile.

'I mean at this time of the year. In the winter it must be awful.'

'You think so?'

'I'm told that after September there's hardly a soul about the place – no, thank you! None of your Nature for me; I like life. The study of humanity – that's my hobby. Not, mind you, that after a time you don't begin to have enough of it. I've been here ten days.'

'So long as that?'

'Ten days Monday. Then it's back to the nuts and oranges.'

'Nuts and oranges?'

'I'm in the dry fruit trade – wholesale; at least, my governor is. Been there four years. Started with five shillings a week. Now I'm getting thirty. Mean to have three pounds before very long.'

'Three pounds a week?'

'I don't mean to marry till I have got it. If a girl cares for a man she'll wait for him. I say the same to you that I say to every young lady – I don't hold with love in a cottage.'

'How old are you, Mr Briggs?'

'Twenty-one the year after next. And up to now I've never been so much as engaged. How old are you?'

'There's not much difference between us.'

'That's what I thought. Might I ask if you're engaged?'

'I can't say that I am – as yet.'

'Ah! You will be. He'll find you. You'll know him when he comes. There's time.'

'I think myself that there still is time.'

'You may take it from me that there is. That's a subject on which I'm allowed, by those who know me best, to be something of a judge. What might be your line?'

'My line?'

'What do you do for a living?'

She gave what you might describe as a sigh.

'I'm afraid that I'm not doing anything at present.'

'Out of a berth, are you? That's hard lines. My sister, she was out most of last year. Fretted something cruel, she did. It's not nice for a girl to have nothing coming in of her own, even when she has a good home.'

She sighed again. A sudden idea struck me. There was something about her I liked. So I did what I had never meant to do when I came out; as you might put it, I dropped a hint.

'It's a bit thick on the sands. Would you like to come on the pier? I'll pay.'

'You'll pay?' She looked at me with those twinkling eyes of hers for I dare say a good half minute; they were twinkling more than ever. 'That is very good of you. Do you know I have never been on the pier. Is it very exciting?'

That did tickle me. I suppose there are people who never do a turn on the pier because of what it costs; but it did seem rough on a girl like her.

'You'll enjoy yourself if you never have been, I give you my word. For one thing, it's much more classy on the pier than it is down here; but, of course, it would be. In fact, in my opinion, in the whole place there's not a more agreeable way of spending an afternoon or evening.'

Off we went. I shelled out for the two. Before I started I hadn't meant to spend so much as a copper; but when I saw the way she was enjoying herself I didn't begrudge the money – not a mite. Soon as we had passed the turnstile she sort of laughed. I didn't know what she was laughing at, but I liked to hear her; it made you feel that she was having a real good time. Presently we came to some automatic machines. The way she went on you would think that she had never seen anything like them in her life before. Nothing would suit her but that she should have a go at them. She had several goes. Bang went fivepence – of mine – in what you might call the twinkling of an eye. From what I could see she was game for a go at every blessed machine there was on the pier. A nice treat for me that would have been; especially considering that after I had paid my bill, and such like, I did not know how there was going to be more than four shillings, at the outside, to see me through my next week's dinners, and everything else as well. So when she wanted to have another try at the cricket machine, which was supposed to return your penny if you hit a boundary, but which, so far as I could make out, would not act as it ought, I said, casual like: 'You don't happen to have twelve coppers for a shilling on you, do you?'

She shook her head.

'I'm afraid I haven't.'

'Ah, that's a pity, because these machines only take coppers.'

A party who was standing close to me said, as I felt, most officiously:

'I can give you twelve coppers for a shilling.'

'Thank you,' I replied. 'I'll get them from the proper person who's appointed to give change, if you don't mind.'

And off we went. Before we had gone very far I began to wonder if I wasn't in for more than I had bargained for. I never saw anything like her for those automatic machines. There was not one she did not want to have a go at – or several goes, for all I could tell. And there was that party who kept on offering to give me change till I could have hit him, he made me so mad. There are a lot of people in this world who'll hang about an automatic machine all day long waiting for someone else to put a penny in; and when he does, they'll crowd round it and spoil his show. I know: I'm not so simple. It would not have taken much to tell that party that if he kept on wanting to give me change I'd give him change. But I kept myself in.

At last we got to the end, where they were having tea out in the open air. Then I had it full in the face. When she saw the people eating and drinking, she sang out:

'Oh, I should like to have some tea! Couldn't we have some tea?'

That was what you might term a straight tip; so far as I am personally concerned I have never had one straighter. I felt in my pocket to make sure that there was still something there. Coming across a shilling and sixpence, I made the best of things.

'Of course we could. And I'll pay. Let's find a table.'

We found a nice little marble table, and we had it to ourselves. After waiting maybe ten minutes she began to fidget.

'Where are all the attendants? Why doesn't somebody come?'

I tried to take advantage of what I thought might be an opening.

'If they're too busy to care for our custom we won't force it on them. What do you say to going? Being kept waiting don't suit me.'

But evidently she wasn't one of those birds which are to be caught with salt. I'd got hold of a Tartar. My luck all over.

'Oh,' she went on, 'but I want some tea. It's ever so much past tea-time.'

I looked at my watch. Sure enough she was right. They would just be about finishing tea up at my boarding-house. Not only was I not having any, though I should have to pay for it, but here was I having to pay for two more teas as well. Next time I took a young lady on the pier I'd give her to understand that I was not going to keep on forking out. But there was something about her which made it difficult for me to even drop a distant hint. When the waitress did come up I asked her what she would have, hoping, I don't mind owning, that she wouldn't have much.

'Oh,' she said, 'tea, and cakes, and anything nice they have. Let them bring us all sorts of things.'

Good hearing for me. I fingered my eighteenpence, and wondered if I had not better mention, before things had gone too far, what was the exact amount I ran to. While I was bringing myself to the point, back came the waitress with a whole tray full; pastry enough for a dozen, and not cheap-looking stuff either.

'Shall I give you a cup of tea?' says my young lady, as free as if she was doing it all on her own. 'Milk? Do you like it sweet?'

She handed me my cup of tea; it seemed that a nice cup of tea I was going to find it. I had not meant to have any, feeling that it would take me all my time to pay for what she had; but she had such an off-handed way about her that I was sipping away almost before I knew it. She took hold of a plateful of pastry.

'What funny-looking cakes!'

'I shouldn't be surprised if they were twopence each.'

I just managed to slip it in; so as to give her an idea of how things were going.

'Are they? Twopence each? Really?' There were three children looking on, as some children will when there's food about. 'Do you like cakes?' she said to them. 'Would you like one of these?'

If you will believe me she gave them a whole cake each. I thought I should have choked. There was another sixpence gone to three strange kids! Saucy little monkeys as ever I saw. I was making up my mind as to whether I had not better plank down my eighteenpence, and say, 'There you are. You can do what you like with that little bit; but you won't get any more out of me, because that happens to be all I've got,' and then walk right off, and leave her to do as she pleased; when back came those three youngsters – stuffing themselves with twopenny cakes – and with them were two more – boys!

'These are my brothers,' said one of them. My young lady was quick enough at taking a hint, when it was of the wrong sort.

'Are they? And do they like cakes?' She gave them one apiece; I suppose just to find out. Fourpence more; that left eightpence. She went on. 'What a number of children there do seem to be about! And they all look as if they liked cake. Shall I try?'

She tried. She gave a cake to every kid that came crowding round till she had cleared two platefuls. I was speechless. By the time I had thought of something to say the plates were empty. Then I said it.

'Excuse me. I don't want to seem unpleasant; but I don't know who's going to pay for this little treat of yours, eighteenpence being every farthing I've got on me.'

The waitress, who was standing by, must have heard me. She slapped a bill down on the table.

'Four-and-eightpence, if you please, sir.'

My young lady had given away two dozen cakes at twopence each; the eightpence was for the tea.

'You'll have to take eighteenpence on account. I'll bring you round the rest when I get to my boarding-house. There's been a mistake.'

My young lady laughed, though I didn't know what at. Her ideas of a joke were different to mine. I never felt so small in my life – or so done.

'I think I have some money,' she said.

She put her hand into one of her pockets and she pulled out a sovereign. I tell you I stared. She gave the waitress a shilling out of the change too; I saw her do it.

'You don't seem stony,' I said, 'although you are out of a situation.

Considering that there's nothing coming in aren't you a bit fond of throwing it about?'

'Oh,' she answered, 'I get my money out of other people's pockets.'

'I don't understand.'

I did not. She leaned her elbows on the table, and she laughed again. Dead nuts she seemed on laughing; particularly as half the time it puzzled me what there was to laugh at.

'You see, it's easier than working for it – getting it out of other people's pockets.'

'I don't see how you're going to do that.'

'Why, by putting your hand in, of course.'

'Putting your hand in? That sounds like pickpocketing.'

'Well, some people might call it that. So much depends on a name.'

Whether she was in earnest or not I could not tell. I did not half like the look of it. I wished more than ever that I had kept myself to my own society. The feeling was growing on me strong that she was the sort who was capable of anything. On she went:

'Mr Briggs, I have to thank you for a very delightful afternoon. And now I propose that, as a pleasant finish, we should go for a little ride together.'

'I'm sorry; but eighteenpence don't go far when it comes to riding, and I never let a young lady pay for me under any circs. To my mind, it ought to be the other way about; and where I'm concerned it's always going to be. And, anyhow, the charabancs have left off before this.'

'I didn't mean in a charabanc. I was thinking of a motor.'

'A motor? Why, that costs more than a charabanc.'

'As it happens, a motor has been waiting for me all this time.'

'What motor?'

'Well,' she pressed the tips of her fingers together, smiling more than ever, 'if it comes to that, I suppose it's my governor's.'

'Your governor's? I thought you hadn't got one.'

'I mean my father.'

'Is your father in the motor trade?'

'I can't say that he is, exactly. Please Mr Briggs, do come for a ride with me.'

She had such a I-lay-you'll-do-as-I-want-you sort of way about her it fairly knocked me. Before I had made up my mind to do anything like it I found myself walking beside her down the pier. I didn't half fancy what she had said about taking money out of other people's pockets. There cannot be the slightest doubt that in such places there are any amount of bad characters. It would not suit me to get myself mixed up with a female swell-mobsman, not though she was as pretty as paint. I tell you I kept a sharp eye on her – without her knowing it – while we were going down the pier. Nice figure I should cut if she was to get up to any of her pranks, or get herself locked up, while she was in my society. She kept her hand clear of other people's pockets while she was with me. But you never can be sure. That class of person is so artful.

I had been a bit doubtful about that motor of which she had been speaking; being more than a bit doubtful about her altogether. But when we got to the road there was a little car – one of those small ones with a single seat, and room for two. In it was sitting a young man about my age – a gentlemanly young fellow, so far as looks went. When he saw her he hopped out on to the road as if he was pressed for time.

'Get in, Mr Briggs,' she said.

I got in. She got in also, paying no more heed to that young man than if he was not there.

'There's plenty of room for your friend,' I said, squeezing to one side so that he could get between us.

'My friend? Oh!' She glanced at the young man. 'It doesn't matter about him. He understands.'

It was more than I did. I had not had a chance of saying another word when she had caught hold of a handle and we were off, leaving the young man standing in the road as if he was carved out of stone.

'I hope I haven't turned your friend out of his seat,' I remarked. I never had seen anybody treated more off-handish.

'You have,' she said.

'Then if you don't mind going back he can either have my place or there's plenty of room for him between us.'

'Aren't you comfortable as you are?'

'I'm not very eager to go for a ride anyhow, seeing how the time's getting on. I want to get back to my boarding-house for dinner before six; we dine late at my place. By then I shall feel like handling a knife and fork. And, if you'll excuse my saying so, if you was to treat me as you've treated that friend of yours I shouldn't like it; and I shouldn't forget to let you know it too.'

'Dear Mr Briggs!'

If I was to try for a month I could not explain how she said it. It was just like they do it on the stage. She looked at me out of the corners of her eyes, with her face turned just a little up, and a smile that killing – and, I may say, crushing – it left me speechless. It was as if she was on the very tiptop of St Paul's Cathedral and I was down in the crypt. I dare say we had gone a mile before I found my tongue, feeling bound to make some sort of conversation.

'Fancy your being able to drive a motor,' I said. 'I should never have thought it.'

'Would you like to drive?' she asked.

'Me? I catch myself at it. Why, we should be over the hedge and goodness alone knows where else before I'd properly started.'

'I sometimes have accidents – particulary when I go like this.'

I am not prepared to take my affidavit as to what she quite did, but she gave a twist to the handle; the car gave a sort of jump, and, my word – were we not moving!

'Aren't we going a bit fast?' I asked.

'We are going over the legal limit. We shall get into trouble if a policeman sees us; let's hope we shan't, or that nothing will turn up unexpectedly for us to run into.'

'Excuse me, but I don't care myself for going quite so fast as this. If it's all the same to you perhaps you'll go a little slower.'

'Don't you really like going fast? I do; as fast as one possibly can. I like to feel that one carries one's life in one's hand; that it all depends on the way in which one crooks one's little finger whether or not one's in for a glorious smash.'

'Then all I can say is that I don't agree with you.'

I very much did not. To tell the truth, the way we were whizzing and bumping along was beginning to give me a nasty feeling in the small of the back. I was not made more comfortable by the way she talked.

'I think I've got as far as I care to go; so if you'll turn round now, and start off back, I shall feel obliged.'

'Turn round?' she said. 'Why should I do that? I'm not obliged to take you back.'

'Not going to take me back?'

'Of course I'm not, Mr Briggs – the idea! I'm going to take you on, and on, and on.'

I stared. There was something about her I fancied less and less.

'I know you're fond of your joke,' I said; 'but there's such a thing as carrying a joke too far. When I tell you that at my boarding-house they dine at six, and that if you're not there to time the chances are that there won't be much food left, and what is left isn't worth having, you'll understand how it is.'

'I assure you, Mr Briggs, that you won't dine at your boarding-house this evening. I am not going to turn, either now or ever. I tell you again that I am going to take you on, and on, and on; unless, that is, you choose to drive yourself – and I shouldn't advise you to try – because I'm perfectly certain you'll come to everlasting grief if you do.'

In a general way I am not one to use what I call strong language; but I could have used some then. Out loud, too. To think that a man like me should have let myself get into a mess like that; trust myself alone with a strange young female in a motor-car – a thing I never had had a fancy for. I was beginning to suspect every moment more and more that she was not altogether right in her head, to speak of nothing else. I was so helpless. What she said was right enough. I might as well break my neck right off as try to drive the thing. All I could do was to sit still; while, as she put it, we went on, and on, and on; farther and farther from my boarding-house and my dinner. I give you my word that I was not feeling cheerful.

'How long are you going to keep this up?' I asked, when we had gone goodness alone knew how far.

'Your tone is not very flattering, Mr Briggs,' she said. 'No one to look at you, or to listen to you, would think that you were enjoying yourself very much.'

'I am not. Don't you make any mistake about it. This may be your idea of fun, but it's not mine. I never did care for practical jokes; and when it comes to this sort of thing it seems to me that it's a case for the police. You've got me here by means of a trick, that's what you've done; and if that's not against the law I don't know what is. If I'd thought you were going to carry on like this before I set foot in it I'd have—'

'Yes; you'd have—?'

'Never mind what I'd have done. I'd have kept out of it; you can take that from me. No wonder that friend of yours didn't mind being left behind. He knew a good thing when he saw it. How far have we come?'

'Fifteen or sixteen miles.'

'Fifteen or sixteen miles! Great smoke! Where's the nearest railway station?'

'There are practically no railway stations round about here. You see, we are getting to a part of the world which may be said to be remote from civilisation.'

I had not noticed, as we went flying along, that houses seemed to be getting fewer, and the country – from what you could catch of it – wilder and wilder. With eighteenpence in my pocket, when she did put me down what was I going to do in a place like that? I never was much of a hand at walking. It was growing dusk. It would soon be dark. The idea of me walking fifteen or sixteen miles, and maybe twenty, and maybe more, through the pitch darkness, when I had no more idea than anything where I was, was most ridiculous. And in my boarding-house that greedy crowd was putting away my dinner. In my mind's eye I could see them at it. So that I was being got at both ends.

A kind of desperation came over me. I believe in another half-minute I should have made a grab at the handle, no matter what happened, because nothing much worse could happen than was happening already. Only just as I was bringing myself to do it the car gave a sudden twist, we went whizzing through a pair of great gates – which, as luck had it, were open – and she was flying along what looked like an avenue of trees.

'This is private property,' she said. 'If trespassers are seen on it the gamekeepers pepper them with shot, or if the police catch them they lock them up.'

'So far as I'm concerned,' I gasped, hanging on to my seat by my eyelids, that sudden twist having all but jerked me on to the road, 'the gamekeepers can do all the peppering they want to; and if it comes to locking up it won't be me who'll get the worst of that.'

On we whizzed – anything like the pace I never saw or heard of. All at once we came to a huge house; it was that big at first sight I took it for a public institution. She gave the car another twirl – almost jerking me off it again. Then, before I quite knew if I was off or on, she brought it to a sudden dead standstill right in front of the very hall door. Out of it she hopped. There was a party standing close by.

'Mr Briggs,' she said, 'allow me to introduce you to my governor.'

The party raised his hat.

'Very glad to see you, Mr Briggs.'

I got a sort of general idea that he was a tall, handsome, straight-standing old party, with a stick under his arm. But I was in such a state of fluster that, so far as keeping my head went, I was not worth a row of pins.

'Pater,' she said, 'Mr Briggs is staying at Sandbythesea. He's given me a most delightful afternoon, including tea on the pier. As I told Mr Briggs, before today I was never on the pier; so he was so sorry for me he took me on it there and then. Wasn't it good of him? So I took him for a run in my car. We had a charming run, didn't we, Mr Briggs?'

I could not answer her; just then I could not have said 'Boo!' to a goose. I would never have believed that a man could have felt as I felt then, as if all the bone had gone out of my back and all the sense out of my head.

'Are you fond of motoring, Mr Briggs?' asked the old party. I had to stammer out something.

'I can't say that I've seen much of it, so to speak.'

He looked me up and down. Then he turned to her.

'Is Mr Briggs an old friend of yours?'

'No; he introduced himself to me on the sands this afternoon.'

'Introduced himself to you on the sands, did he?'

'And he has been so kind to me; I must leave you to thank him properly. But in the first place you must persuade him to stop for dinner; his own dinner-hour is at six.'

'At six, is it? Mr Briggs, you must dine with us.'

I could no more have refused than I could have flown. There was a commanding way about him which settled it. I mumbled something about being very glad and tried to look it, though I cannot honestly say it was much of a success.

'We dine at eight,' she said. 'Pater, I'll leave you to entertain Mr Briggs till then.'

Off she skipped up the steps towards the house.

'Come back!' he shouted. 'What do you mean by leaving me to – to bore your young friend?'

'Oh, Pater, you won't bore Mr Briggs. Mr Briggs isn't so easily bored. Why, even I haven't bored him. I've lots of things which I must do, and I'm quite sure Mr Briggs will be quite safe in your hands till dinner.'

'You – you—!'

He shook his stick at her. She kissed her hand, laughed, and went into the house. And there was him and me left alone together. I would have given the eighteenpence I had in my pocket a good many times over to have been somewhere else. He had a way of looking at you which made you feel as if you were all over pimples, and as if he was wondering how on earth you got them.

'Well, Mr Briggs,' he said, when he had had about enough of looking, and I had had a great deal too much, 'what shall we do to amuse each other?'

'I'm sure I don't know,' I said.

'Would you like me to show you round the place?'

'I don't mind,' I said. 'It doesn't take much to amuse me.'

'Doesn't it? That is fortunate. Because, in that case, even I may succeed. Perhaps it's rather late for a tour of inspection. What do you say to a game of billiards?'

I can play billiards. Many is the game I have played at the Crown and Anchor. I can give my friend, Tom Pope, fifteen out of a hundred, and beat him every time; if I am on my game, and he keeps off his fluking. So I thought I could manage my end up in a game of billiards.

We went into the house. Talk about Buckingham Palace! Not that I have ever actually been there; but from what I have heard and read I should say it was not a bit better than that was. And the servants there were about! All men – powdered heads – and such liveries! Why, the hall alone was big enough to hold a couple of houses like ours – that is a solemn fact. And the furniture – and the pictures – and the wonderful things there were all over the place. But there, it is no use my trying to describe what I only saw in a kind of a dream. And the passages we went through – pictures on every wall – not to speak of statues, and men in armour. Holding on one side a velvet curtain, and opening a door which was beyond, the old party led the way into the finest room I was ever in in all my days. It was a billiard-room. He touched the button of an electric bell. Someone came in at another door. Turning, I saw my young cousin, Bob Williams, dressed like some sort of a page, getting out the billiard balls. At sight of him I felt more than ever that I must be dreaming.

'Bob!' I cried.

He never said a word or moved a muscle, but stared straight past me as if I was not there. I could have almost bet it was a nightmare I was having.

'If you will choose a cue which suits you, Mr Briggs,' said the old party, 'and will amuse yourself by knocking the balls about, I will return to you in a very few minutes.'

Directly his back was turned Bob burst out:

'Sam Briggs, what in goodness' name are you doing here?'

'That's what I want to know,' I answered. 'I never had such a day! Before you ask another question or say another word, you just tell me this – where am I?'

Bob did stare.

'Where are you? Why, you're at Woodgarde.'

'Woodgarde? Is that the name of the house? And who's the old party who just went out?'

'You'd better not let anyone hear you call him an old party. That's the Duke of ——.'

I do not want to mention names – so far as that goes, this is private and confidential – but he mentioned the name of one of the best-known dukes of all England, who, I have been told, is descended from Royalty itself. As the saying is, you might have knocked me down with a feather – and no wonder.

'And who's the girl?'

'What girl?'

'In a sort of holland dress, with big, brown eyes and a saucy smile; I believe she's his daughter.'

'If she's his daughter you must be talking about the Lady Adeline Beaumanoir.'

'Then I took the Lady Adeline Beaumanoir on the pier, so as to give her a bit of a treat.'

'Sam Briggs!'

'I thought she was one of them cheap excursionists, till she herself put the idea into my head that her lay was picking pockets.'

'Well, Mr Briggs, have you found a cue to your liking?'

There was the old – I beg pardon, the Duke back again. Bob Williams, all at once, was as if he was a wooden image. I was all over confusion; but then that was nothing fresh. I got hold of some sort of a cue, then we started playing. I soon found out that the Duke did not play the kind of game I was used to at the Crown and Anchor. He made hay of me – simply. There was only one person in that game, and it was not me.

What with being all of a tremor, the way he had of looking at me every time I opened my mouth or made a stroke, and the feeling I had that Bob Williams's eyes were piercing me like corkscrews, it was all I could do to hit the balls. I do not know how many I scored; I only know that he kept on scoring like a house on fire, while most of my time was taken up by making misses. After, I suppose, he had had about enough of making rings round me he told Bob to ring the bell. A party appeared with powder on his head.

'Show Mr Briggs into a room where he can dress for dinner.'

Off I toddled with this party till we came to what I have reason to believe was meant for a dressing-room, though it was more like a drawing-room than some I have seen. There was silver lying every-where – every brush had got a silver back to it. There were lots of silver-topped bottles with goodness only knows what inside them; not to speak of half a dozen different kinds of soaps, and, for all I know, a dozen different kinds of water. Why, the very water came out of silver taps.

'Is there anything I can do for you, sir?' asked the powdered party.

'No,' I said, 'I don't think there is.'

'When you are quite ready, sir, if you will ring I will come and show you downstairs.'

And off he went. When I came to have a glimpse at myself in a looking-glass – there were a few of them! – I felt worse than ever. My collar was not extra clean, nor my shirt either – the next day being Sunday. My suit of flannels, which I gave twenty-two and six for just before I left home, I had worn ever since I had been away, and, somehow, it did not look so fresh as it might have done. Altogether, I not only felt cheap, but, what was much worse, I had a sort of suspicion that I looked it; and, mind you, in a general way I rather prided myself on my appearance. When I had tidied myself up I never rang the bell; I had not got the nerve to do it. At last that powdered person came back of his own accord.

'If you are quite ready, sir.' I was not quite ready, far from it; but as I should never have been more ready in that place I went with him. 'I think, sir, that Lady Adeline is in the small drawing-room.'

If he called that a small drawing-room I wondered what he would have called the drawing-room in our house at Walham Green. She was there, but – changed! My word! She looked that beautiful – a queen she looked – a queen of beauty, if nothing else. And in a dress – I never saw one like it, not even in the shop windows. Now, if she had come on to the sands in that dress, or anything like it, I should not have made of myself the idiot I had done; I should have known her for what she was. It fairly dazzled you to turn your eyes her way. In front of her I felt as if I were nothing at all; I do not mind owning it. Especially with the Duke looming high overhead, in about a square yard of shirt front. We went in to dinner, me with the Lady Adeline on my arm. A pretty pair I lay we made. It did not make me feel any better when, on entering the dining-room, I all but ran into my Uncle Williams – with powder on his head. I stared at him, but, like Bob, he stared at me as if I was not there. Somehow it did not seem homelike to have your own uncle handing you the soup from over your shoulder, and you not daring to ask him how he was. I knew that Uncle Williams was in good service in high families, but I never had realised that he was in a place like that. And, between ourselves, I am rather partial to my cousin Susan Ann.

That was something like a dinner, fit for Windsor Castle, and that is where it was; it was above me, clean. I cannot say truly that I enjoyed myself on the whole. Lady Adeline was affability itself, and the Duke was all politeness; yet all the while I could not get rid of the idea that they were cutting me up between them. Afterwards we went back to the drawing-room. Lady Adeline played and sang. Hers was singing! Talk of the pierrots, or that young lady who drew such crowds to hear her on the beach – it was not the same thing! Presently another powdered person appeared in the doorway.

'The carriage is waiting,' he said. And almost before I knew it I was saying goodbye to the Duke and Lady Adeline, and walking along a wide passage to the front door, where there was a carriage waiting – an electric brougham, if you please! And in it I was whizzed back to my boarding-house. I do not mind admitting that I enjoyed that drive more than anything that had happened since I first spoke to her on the sands.

Some of the boarders were still hanging about the front door of my boarding-house; kept pretty late hours some of them did.

'Where have you been?' asked one of them, as I got out of the electric brougham.

Like his sauce it was to ask it, too; it being no business of his where I went.

'I've been dining with the Duke of —— and Lady Adeline Beaumanoir,' I said.

'Go on! What ho! Cheese it!' That is what he answered. 'Tell your tales to your uncle, and ask him what he'll lend you on them.'

He was a vulgar monkey. Not that he was the last who doubted me when I told the simple truth. My own family, when I told them exactly what had happened, they would hardly believe me; at least, until there came a letter from Uncle Williams. And it was not a very civil letter either. I have felt a coolness towards him ever since it came. But I had the laugh of them, when a few days afterwards there arrived a parcel addressed to 'Mr Sam Briggs, Junior.' In it was her photograph, in a silver frame, and on it she had written, in her own handwriting:

> *To Mr Sam Briggs,*
> *In memory of an Afternoon's Entertainment,*
> *from Lady Adeline Beaumanoir.*

It is hanging in my bedroom at the present moment. It will hang in my drawing-room, some day, when I have a house of my own. And to think I took her for a tripper!

# THE ADVENTURE OF THE SNOWING GLOBE

## By F. Anstey

BEFORE BEGINNING TO relate an experience which, I am fully
aware, will seem to many so singular as to be almost, if not quite,
incredible, it is perhaps as well to state that I am a solicitor of several
years' standing, and that I do not regard myself – nor, to the best of
my knowledge and belief, have I ever been regarded – as a person in
whom the imaginative faculty is at all unduly prominent.

It was in Christmas week of last year. I was walking home from my
office in New Square, Lincoln's Inn, as my habit is – except on
occasions when the state of the weather renders such open-air exercise too imprudent – and on my way I went into a toy-shop; with a
view to purchasing some seasonable present for a small godchild of
mine.

As was only to be expected at that time of year, the shop was
crowded with customers, and I had to wait until one of the assistants
should be at liberty. While waiting, my attention was attracted to a toy
on the counter before me.

It was a glass globe, about the size of a moderately large orange.
Inside it was a representation of what appeared to be the façade of a
castle, before which stood a figure holding by a thread a small, pear-
shaped air-ball striped red and blue. The globe was full of water
containing a white sediment in solution, which when agitated produced the effect of a miniature snowstorm.

I cannot account for such a childish proceeding, except by the
circumstance that I had nothing better to occupy me at the moment,
but I employed myself in shaking the globe and watching the tiny
snowflakes circulating in the fluid, till I became so engrossed as to be
altogether oblivious of my surroundings. So that I was not particularly
surprised when I found, as I presently did, that the flakes were falling

and melting on my coat-sleeve. Before me was a heavy gateway belonging to a grim, castellated edifice, which I thought at first must be Holloway Gaol, though how I could have wandered so far out of my way was more than I could understand.

But on looking round I saw no signs of any surburban residences, and recognised that I had somehow strayed into a locality with which I was totally unacquainted, but which was evidently considerably beyond the Metropolitan radius. It seemed to me that my best plan would be to knock at the gate and ask the lodge-keeper where I was and my way to the nearest railway station; but before I could carry out my intention a wicket in one of the gates was cautiously opened by a person of ancient and venerable appearance. He did not look like an ordinary porter, but was in a peculiar livery, which I took to be a seneschal's – not that I have ever seen a seneschal, but that was my impression of him. Whoever he was, he appeared distinctly pleased to see me. 'You are right welcome, fair sir!' he said, in a high, cracked voice. 'Well knew I that my hapless lady would not lack a protector in her sad plight, though she had well-nigh abandoned all hope of your coming!'

I explained that I had not called by appointment, but was simply a stranger who found himself in the neighbourhood by the merest chance.

''Tis no matter,' he replied, in his old-fashioned diction, 'seeing that you have come, for truly, sir, she is in sore need of anyone who is ready to undertake her cause!'

I said that I happened to be a member of the legal profession, and that if, as I gathered, his mistress was in any difficulty in which she desired my assistance, I was quite prepared to advise her to the best of my ability, and to act for her, should her case be one which, in my opinion, required it.

'That does it, indeed!' he said; 'but I pray you stand no longer parleying without, which, since I perceive you are but ill-protected at present,' he added, fussily, 'may be fraught with unnecessary danger. Come within without further delay!'

I did not think there was any real risk of catching cold, but I did wonder why it had not occurred to me to put up my umbrella, until I discovered that my right hand was already engaged in holding a cord to which was attached a gaudily-coloured balloon that floated above my head.

This was so unsuitable an appendage to any solicitor, especially to one about to offer his services in an affair which was apparently serious, that I was somewhat disconcerted for the moment. But I soon recollected having gone into a toy-shop sometime previously, and concluded that I must have purchased this air-ball as a present for my godchild.

I was about to explain this to the old man, when he pulled me suddenly through the wicket-gate, shutting the door so sharply that it snapped the string of the balloon. I saw it soaring up on the other side of the wall till a whirl of snow hid it from my sight.

'Trouble not for its loss,' said the seneschal; 'it has fulfilled its purpose in bringing you to our gates.'

If he really supposed that anybody was at all likely to adopt so eccentric a means of conveyance, he must, I thought, be in his dotage, and I began to have a misgiving that, by accepting his invitation to step in, I might have placed myself in a false position.

However, I had gone too far to retract now, so I allowed him to conduct me to his mistress. He took me across a vast courtyard to a side-entrance, and then up a winding stair, along deserted corridors, and through empty antechambers, until we came into a great hall, poorly lighted from above, and hung with dim tapestries. There he left me, saying that he would inform his mistress of my arrival.

I had not long to wait before she entered by an opposite archway.

I regret my inability – owing partly to the indifferent manner in which the apartment was lit – to describe her with anything like precision. She was quite young – not much, I should be inclined to say, over eighteen; she was richly but fantastically dressed in some shimmering kind of robe, and her long hair was let down and flowing loose about her shoulders, which (although I am bound to say that the effect, in her case, was not unbecoming) always has, to my mind at least, a certain air of untidiness in a grown-up person, and almost made me doubt for a moment whether she was quite in her right senses.

But, while she was evidently in a highly emotional state, I could detect nothing in her manner or speech that indicated any actual mental aberration. Her personal appearance, too, was distinctly pleasing, and altogether I cannot remember ever to have felt so interested at first sight in any female client.

'Tell me,' she cried, 'is it really true? Have you indeed come to my deliverance?'

'My dear young lady,' I said, perceiving that any apology for what I had feared must seem a highly irregular intrusion was unnecessary, 'I have been given to understand that you have some occasion for my services, and if that is correct I can only say that they are entirely at your disposal. Just try to compose yourself and tell me, as clearly and concisely as you can, the material facts of your case.'

'Alas! sir,' she said, wringing her hands, which I remember no-ticing were of quite remarkable beauty, 'I am the unhappiest princess in the whole world.'

I trust I am as free from snobbishness as most people, but I admit to feeling some gratification in the fact that I was honoured by the confidence of a lady of so exalted a rank.

'I am extremely sorry to hear it, ma'am,' I said, recollecting that that was the proper way to address a princess. 'But I am afraid', I added, as I prepared to take her instructions, 'that I can be but of little assistance to you unless you can bring yourself to furnish me with somewhat fuller particulars.'

'Surely', she said, 'you cannot be ignorant that I am in the power of a wicked and tyrannous uncle?'

I might have explained that I was far too busy a man to have leisure to keep up with the latest Court scandals, but I refrained.

'I may take it, then,' I said, 'that you are an orphan, and that the relative you refer to is your sole guardian?'

She implied by a gesture that both these inferences were correct. 'He has shut me up a close prisoner in this gloomy place,' she declared, 'and deprived me of all my attendants one by one, save the aged but faithful retainer whom you have beheld.'

I replied, of course, that this was an unwarrantable abuse of his authority, and enquired whether she could assign any motive for such a proceeding on his part.

'He is determined that I shall marry his son,' she explained, 'whom I detest with an unutterable loathing!'

'Possibly', I ventured to hint, 'there is someone else who—'

'There is none,' she said, 'since I have never been permitted to look upon any other suitor, and here I am held in durance until I consent to this hated union – and I will die sooner! But you will save me from so terrible a fate! For what else are you here?'

'I should be incompetent indeed, ma'am,' I assured her, 'if I could not see a way out of what is really a very ordinary predicament. By attempting to force you into a marriage against your will, your guard-ian has obviously shown himself a totally unfit person to have you in his custody. You have the law entirely on your side.'

'Unfit is he, truly!' she agreed. 'But I care not who else is on my side, so long as you will be my champion. Only, how will you achieve my rescue?'

'Under all the circumstances,' I told her, 'I think our best course would be to apply for a *habeas corpus*. You will then be brought up to the Courts of Justice, and the judge could make any order he thought advisable. In all probability he would remove your uncle from his position and have you made a ward of Court.'

There is always a difficulty in getting ladies to understand even the simplest details of legal procedure, and my princess was no exception to the rule. She did not seem in the least to realise the power which every Court possesses of enforcing its own decrees.

'Sir, you forget', she said, 'that my uncle, who has great renown in these parts as a sorcerer and magician, will assuredly laugh any such order to scorn.'

'In that case, ma'am,' said I, 'he will render himself liable for contempt of Court. Besides, should his local reputation answer your description, we have *another* hold on him. If we can only prove that he has been using any subtle craft, means, or device to impose on any of His Majesty's subjects, he could be prosecuted under the Vagrancy Act of 1824 as a rogue and a vagabond. He might get as much as six months for it!'

'Ah, sir,' she cried – rather peevishly, I thought – 'we do but waste precious time in idle talk such as this, of which I comprehend scarce a word! And the hour is nigh when I must meet my uncle face to face, and should I still refuse to obey his will his wrath will be dire indeed!'

'All you have to do is to refer him to *me*,' I said. 'I think I shall be able, in the course of a personal interview, to bring him to take a more reasonable view of his position. If you are expecting him shortly, perhaps I had better remain here till he arrives?'

'Happily for us both,' she replied, 'he is still many leagues distant from here! Can you not see that, if my rescue is to be accomplished at all, it must be ere his return, or else am I all undone? Is it possible that, after coming thus far, you can tarry here doing naught?'

I took a little time for reflection before answering. 'After careful reconsideration,' I said, at last, 'I have come to the conclusion that, as you are evidently under grave apprehension of some personal violence from your uncle, in the event of his finding you on the premises, I should be fully justified in dispensing with the usual formalities and removing you from his custody at once. At all events, I will take that responsibility on myself – whatever risk I may incur.'

'I crave your pardon for my seeming petulance,' she said, with a pretty humility. 'I should have known right well that I might safely rely on the protection of so gallant and fearless a knight!'

'You will understand, I am sure, ma'am,' I said, 'that I cannot, as a bachelor, offer you shelter under my own roof. What I propose (subject, of course, to your approval) is that I should place you under the care of an old aunt of mine at Croydon until some other arrangement

can be made. I presume it will not take you long to make your preparations for the journey?'

'What need of preparation?' she cried. 'Let us delay no longer, but
fly this instant!'

'I should recommend you to take at least a dressing-bag,' I said;
'you will have time to pack all you may require while your retainer is
fetching us a fly. Then I know of nothing to hinder us from leaving at
once.'

'Nothing?' she exclaimed. 'Do you dread a dragon so little, then,
that you can speak thus lightly?'

I could not help smiling; it was so surprising to find a princess of
her age who still retained a belief in fairy-tales. 'I think, ma'am,' I
said, 'that at this time of day a dragon is not an obstacle which we
need take into serious consideration. You have evidently not been
informed that such a monster has long since ceased to exist. In other
words, it is undoubtedly extinct.'

'And you have slain it!' she cried, and her eyes blazed with admiration. 'I might have guessed as much! It is slain – and now even my
uncle has no longer power to detain me here! For many a long month
I have not dared to look from out my casements, but now I may
behold the light of day once more without shrinking!' She drew back
some hangings as she spoke, disclosing a large oriel window, and the
next moment she cowered away with a cry of abject terror.

'Why have you deceived me?' she demanded, with indignant re-
proach. 'It is *not* extinct. It is still there. Look for yourself!'

I did look; the window commanded the rear of the castle, which I
had not hitherto seen, and now I saw something else so utterly
unexpected that I could hardly trust the evidence of my own eyesight.

Towering above the battlemented outer wall I saw a huge horny
head, poised upon a long and flexible neck, and oscillating slowly
from side to side with a sinister vigilance. Although the rest of the
brute was hidden by the wall, I saw quite enough to convince me that
it could not well be anythihg else than a dragon – and a formidable
one at that. I thought I understood now why the seneschal had been
so anxious to get me inside, though I wished he had been rather more
explicit.

I stood there staring at it – but I made no remark. To tell the truth,
I did not feel equal to one just then.

The Princess spoke first. 'You seem astonished, sir,' she said, 'yet
you can hardly have been in ignorance that my uncle has set this
ferocious monster to guard these walls and devour me should I strive
to make my escape.'

'I can only say, ma'am,' I replied, 'that this is the first intimation I have had of the fact.'

'Still, you are wise and strong,' she said. 'You will surely devise some means whereby to rid me of this baleful thing!'

'If you will permit me to draw the curtain again,' I said, 'I will endeavour to think of something . . . Am I right in assuming that the brute is the property of your uncle?'

She replied that that was so.

'Then I think I see a way,' I said. 'Your uncle could be summoned for allowing such a dangerous animal to be at large, since it is clearly not under proper control. And if an application were made to a magistrate, under the Act of 1871, he might be ordered to destroy it at once.'

'You little know my uncle', she said, with a touch of scorn, 'if you deem that he would destroy his sole remaining dragon at the bidding of any person whatever!'

'He will incur a penalty of twenty shillings a day till he *does*,' I replied. 'In any case, I can promise you that, if I can only manage to get out of this place, you shall not be exposed to this annoyance very much longer.'

'You will?' she cried. 'Are you quite sure that you will succeed?'

'Practically I am,' I said. 'I shall apply – always supposing I can get home safely – the first thing tomorrow morning, and, if I can only convince the Bench that the terms of the Act are wide enough to include not only dogs, but any other unmanageable quadrupeds, why, the thing is as good as done!'

'Tomorrow! tomorrow!' she repeated, impatiently. 'Must I tell you once more that this is no time to delay? Indeed, sir, if I am to be rescued at all, your hand alone can deliver me from this loathly worm!'

I confess I considered she was taking an altogether extravagant view of the relations between solicitor and client.

'If', I said, 'it could be described with any accuracy as a worm, I should not feel the slightest hesitation about attacking it.'

'Then you will?' she said, entirely missing my point, as usual. 'Tell me you will – for *my* sake.'

She looked so engaging whilst making this appeal that I really had not the heart to pain her by a direct refusal.

'There is nothing,' I said, 'that is, nothing in reason, that I would not do cheerfully, for your sake. But if you will only reflect, you will see at once that, in a tall hat and overcoat, and with absolutely no weapon but an umbrella, I should not stand the ghost of a chance against a dragon. I should be too hopelessly overmatched.'

'You say truth,' she replied, much to my satisfaction. 'I could not desire any champion of mine to engage in so unequal a contest. So have no uneasiness on that score.'

On this she clapped her hands as a summons to the seneschal, who appeared so promptly that I fancy he could not have been very far from the keyhole. 'This gallant gentleman', she explained to him, 'has undertaken to go forth and encounter the dragon without our walls, provided that he is fitly furnished for so deadly a fray.'

I tried to protest that she had placed a construction on my remarks which they were not intended to bear – but the old man was so voluble in thanks and blessings that I could not get in a single word.

'You will conduct him to the armoury,' the Princess continued, 'and see him arrayed in harness meet for so knightly an endeavour. Sir,' she added to me, 'words fail me at such an hour as this. I cannot even thank you as I would. But I know you will do your utmost on my behalf. Should you fall—'

She broke off here, being evidently unable to complete her sentence, but that was unnecessary. I knew what would happen if I fell.

'But fall you will not,' she resumed. 'Something tells me that you will return to me victorious; and then – and then – should you demand any guerdon of me – yea' (and here she blushed divinely) 'even to this hand of mine, it shall not be denied you.'

Never in the whole course of my professional career had I been placed in a position of greater difficulty. My common sense told me that it was perfectly preposterous on her part to expect such services as these from one who was merely acting as her legal adviser. Even if I performed them successfully – which was, to say the least of it, doubtful – my practice would probably be injuriously affected should my connection with such an affair become known. As for the special fee she had so generously suggested, that, of course, was out of the question. At my time of life marriage with a flighty young woman of eighteen – and a princess into the bargain – would be rather too hazardous an experiment.

And yet, whether it is that, middle-aged bachelor as I am, I have still a strain of unsuspected romance and chivalry in my nature, or for some other cause that I cannot explain, somehow I found myself kissing the little hand she extended to me, and going forth without another word to make as good a fight of it as I could for her against such an infernal beast as a dragon. I cannot say that I felt cheerful over it, but, anyhow, I went.

I followed the seneschal, who led me down by a different staircase from that I had come up, and through an enormous vaulted kitchen, untenanted by all but black-beetles, which were swarming. Merely for the sake of conversation, I made some remark on their numbers and pertinacity, and enquired why no steps had apparently been taken to abate so obvious a nuisance. 'Alas! noble sir,' he replied, as he sadly shook his old white head, ''twas the scullions' office to clear the place of these pests, and the last minion has long since vanished from our halls!'

I felt inclined to ask him where they had vanished to – but I did not. I thought the answer might prove discouraging. Even as it was, I would have given something for a whisky and soda just then – but he did not offer it, and I did not like to suggest it for fear of being misunderstood. And presently we entered the armoury.

Only a limited number of suits were hanging on the walls, and all of them were in a deplorably rusty and decayed condition, but the seneschal took them down one by one, and made fumbling attempts to buckle and hook me into them. Most unfortunately, not a single suit proved what I should call workmanlike, for I defy any man to fight a dragon in armour which is too tight even to move about in with any approach to comfort.

'I'm afraid it's no use,' I told the seneschal, as I reluctantly resumed my ordinary garments. 'You can see for yourself that there's nothing here that comes near my size!'

'But you cannot engage in combat with the dragon in your present habiliments!' he remonstrated. 'That were stark madness!'

I was glad that the old man had sufficient sense to see *that*. 'I am quite of your opinion,' I replied; 'and believe me, my good old friend, nothing is farther from my thoughts. My idea is that if – I do not ask you to expose yourself to any unnecessary risk – but if you *could* contrive to divert the dragon's attention by a demonstration of some sort on one side of the castle, I might manage to slip quietly out of some door on the other.'

'Are you but a caitiff, then, after all,' he exclaimed, 'that you can abandon so lovely a lady to certain doom?'

'There is no occasion for addressing me in offensive terms,' I replied. 'I have no intention whatever of abandoning your mistress. You will be good enough to inform her that I shall return tomorrow without fail with a weapon that will settle this dragon's business more effectually than any of your obsolete lances and battleaxes!'

For I had already decided on this as the only course that was now open to me. I had a friend who spent most of the year abroad in the pursuit of big game, but who chanced by good luck to be in town just then. He would, I knew, willingly lend me an express rifle and some expansive bullets, and, as an ex-Volunteer and marksman, I felt that the odds would then be slightly in my favour, even if I could not, as I hoped I could, persuade my friend to join me in the expedition.

But the seneschal took a less sanguine view of my prospects.

'You forget, sir,' he remarked, lugubriously, 'that, in order to return hither, you must first quit the shelter of these walls – which, all unarmed as you are, would be but to court instant death!'

'I don't quite see that,' I argued. 'After all, as the dragon made no effort to prevent me from coming in, it is at least possible that it may not object to my going out.'

'For aught I can say,' he replied, 'it may have no orders to hinder any from entrance. As to that I know naught. But of this I am very sure – it suffers no one to depart hence undevoured.'

'But could I not contrive to get out of its reach before it was aware that I had even started?' I suggested.

'I fear me, sir,' he said, despondently, 'that the creature would not fail to follow up your tracks ere the snow could cover them.'

'That had not occurred to me,' I said. 'But now you mention it, it does not seem altogether unlikely. In your opinion, then, I should do better in remaining where I am?'

'Only until the enchanter return,' was his reply, 'as, if I mistake not, he may do at any moment, after which your stay here will assuredly be but brief.'

'You can't mean', I said, 'that he would have the inhumanity to turn me out to be devoured by his beastly dragon? For that is what it would *come* to.'

'Unless, perchance, by dint of strength or cunning you were to overcome the monster,' he said. 'And methought you had come hither with that very intent.'

'My good man,' I replied, 'I've no idea why or how I come here, but it was certainly with no desire or expectation of meeting a dragon. However, I begin to see very clearly that if I can't find some way of putting an end to the brute – and promptly, too – he will make an end of *me*. The question is, how the deuce am I to set about it?'

And then, all at once, I had an inspiration. I recollected the black-beetles, and something the seneschal had said about its being the scullions' duty to keep them down. I asked him what methods they had employed for this purpose, but, such humble details being naturally outside his province, he was unable to inform me. So I returned to the kitchen, where I began a careful search, not without some hope of success.

For a while I searched in vain, but at last, just when I had begun to despair, I found on a dusty shelf in the buttery the identical thing I had been looking for. It was an earthen vessel containing a paste, which, in spite of the fungoid growth that had collected on its surface, I instantly recognised as a composition warranted to prove fatal to every description of vermin.

I called to the seneschal and asked if he could oblige me with a loaf of white bread, which he brought in evident bewilderment. I cut a slice from the middle and was proceeding to spread the paste thickly upon it when he grasped my arm. 'Hold!' he cried. 'Would you rashly seek your death ere it is due?'

'You need not be alarmed,' I told him; 'this is not for myself. And now will you kindly show me a way out to some part of the roof where I can have access to the dragon?'

Trembling from head to foot he indicated a turret-stair, up which, however, he did not offer to accompany me; it brought me out on the leads of what appeared to be a kind of bastion. I crept cautiously to the parapet and peeped over it, and then for the first time I had a full view of the brute, which was crouching immediately below me. I know how prone the most accurate are to exaggeration in matters of this kind, but, after making every allowance for my excited condition at the time, I do not think I am far out in estimating that the dimensions of the beast could not have been much, if at all, less than those of the *Diplodocus carnegii*, a model of which is exhibited at the Natural History Museum, while its appearance was infinitely more terrific.

I do not mind admitting frankly that the sight so unmanned me for the moment that I was seized with an almost irresistible impulse to retire by the way I had come before the creature had observed me. And yet it was not without a certain beauty of its own; I should say, indeed, that it was rather an unusually handsome specimen of its class, and I was especially struck by the magnificent colouring of its scales, which surpassed that of even the largest pythons. Still, to an unaccustomed eye there must always be something about a dragon that inspires more horror than admiration, and I was in no mood just then to enjoy the spectacle. It was hunched up together, with its head laid back, like a fowl's, between its wings, and seemed to be enjoying a short nap. I suppose I must unconsciously have given some sign of my presence, for suddenly I saw the horny films roll back like shutters from its lidless eyes, which it fixed on me with a cold glare of curiosity.

And then it shambled on to its feet, and slowly elongated its neck till it brought its horrible head on a level with the battlements. I need not say that on this I promptly retreated to a spot where I judged I should be out of immediate danger. But I had sufficient presence of mind to remember the purpose for which I was there, and, fixing the prepared slice on the ferrule of my umbrella, I extended it as far as my arm would reach in the creature's direction.

I fancy it had not been fed very lately. The head made a lightning dart across the parapet, and a voracious snap – and the next moment both bread and umbrella had disappeared down its great red gullet.

The head was then withdrawn. I could hear a hideous champing sound, as of the ribs of the umbrella being slowly crunched. After that came silence.

Again I crawled to the parapet and looked down. The huge brute was licking its plated jaws with apparent gusto, as though – which was likely enough – an umbrella came as an unaccustomed snack to its jaded palate. It was peacefully engaged now in digesting this *hors-d'oeuvre.*

But my heart only sank the lower at the sight. For if an alpaca umbrella with an ebony handle could be so easily assimilated, what possible chance was there that beetle-paste would produce any dele- terious effect? I had been a fool to place the faintest hope on so desperate a hazard. Presently he would be coming for more – and I had nothing for him!

But by and by, as I gazed in a sort of fascinated repulsion, I fancied I detected some slight symptoms of uneasiness in the reptile's demeanour.

It was almost nothing at first – a restless twitch at times, and a squint in its stony eyes that I had not previously noticed – but it gave me a gleam of hope. Presently I saw the great crest along its spine slowly begin to erect itself, and the filaments that fringed its jaws bristling, as it proceeded to deal a succession of vicious pecks at its dis- tended olive-green paunch, which it evidently regarded as respons- ible for the disturbance.

Little as I knew about dragons, a child could have seen that this one was feeling somewhat seriously indisposed. Only – was it due to the umbrella or the vermin-killer? As to that I could only attempt to speculate, and my fate – and the Princess's, too – hung upon which was the more correct diagnosis!

However, I was not kept long in suspense. Suddenly the beast uttered a kind of bellowing roar – the most appalling sound I think I ever heard – and after that I scarcely know what happened exactly.

I fancy it had some kind of fit. It writhed and rolled over and over, thrashing the air with its big leathery wings, and tangling itself up to a degree that, unless I had seen it, I should have thought impossible, even for a dragon.

After this had gone on for some time, it untied itself and seemed calmer again, till all at once it curved into an immense arch, and remained perfectly rigid with wings outspread for nearly half a minute. Then it suddenly collapsed on its side, panting, snorting, and quivering like some monstrous automobile, after which it stretched itself out to its full length once or twice, and then lay stiff and still. Its gorgeous hues gradually faded into a dull, leaden-grey tint . . . All was over – the vermin-destroyer had done its work after all.

I cannot say that I was much elated. I am not sure that I did not even feel a pang of self-reproach. I had slain the dragon, it was true, but by a method which I could not think would have commended itself to St George as entirely sportsmanlike, even though the circumstances left me no other alternative.

However, I had saved the Princess, which, after all, was the main point, and there was no actual necessity for her to know more than the bare fact that the dragon was dead.

I was just about to go down and inform her that she was now free to leave the castle, when I heard a whirring noise in the air, and, glancing back, I saw, flying towards me through the still falling snow, an elderly gentleman of forbidding aspect, who was evidently in a highly exasperated state. It was the Princess's uncle.

I don't know how it was, but till that moment I had never realised the extremely unprofessional proceeding into which I had been betrayed by my own impulsiveness. But I saw now, though too late, that, in taking the law into my own hands and administering a poisonous drug to an animal which, however furious it might be, was still the property of another, I had been guilty of conduct unworthy of any respectable solicitor. It was undoubtedly an actionable tort, if not a trespass – while he might even treat it as a criminal offence.

So, as the magician landed on the roof, his face distorted with fury, I felt that nothing would meet the case but the most ample apology. But, feeling that it was better to allow the first remark to come from him, I merely raised my hat and waited to hear what he had to say . . .

'*Are you being attended to, sir?*' was the remark that actually came – and both words and tone were so different from what I had expected that I could not repress a start.

And then, to my utter astonishment, I discovered that battlements and magician had all disappeared. I was back again in the toy-shop, staring into the glass globe, in which the snow was still languidly circling.

'Like to take one of these shilling snowstorms, sir?' continued the assistant, who seemed to be addressing me; 'we're selling a great quantity of them just now. Very suitable and acceptable present for a child, sir, and only a shilling in that size, though we have them larger in stock.'

I bought the globe I had first taken up – but I have not given it to my godchild. I preferred to keep it myself.

Of course, my adventure may have been merely a kind of day-dream; though, if so, it is rather odd that it should have taken that form, when, even at night, my dreams – on the rare occasions when I *do* dream – never turn upon such subjects as castles, princesses, or dragons.

A scientific friend, to whom I related the experience, pronounces it to be an ordinary case of auto-hypnotism, induced by staring into a crystal globe for a prolonged period.

But I don't know. I cannot help thinking that there is something more in it than that.

I still gaze into the globe at times, when I am alone of an evening; but while I have occasionally found myself back in the snowstorm again, I have never, so far, succeeded in getting into the castle.

Perhaps it is as well; for, although I should not at all object to see something more of the Princess, she has most probably, thanks to my instrumentality, long since left the premises – and I have no particular desire to meet the magician.

# CODE NO. 2

## By *Edgar Wallace*

THE SECRET SERVICE never call themselves anything so melo-dramatic. If they speak at all, it is vaguely of 'The Department' – not even 'The Intelligence Department', you will note. It is a remarkable department, however, and not the least of the remarkable men who served – in a minor capacity, it is true – was Schiller.

He was an inventive young Swiss with a passion for foreign languages. He knew all the bad men in London – bad from the violently political standpoint – and was useful to the Chief Secretary (Intelligence), though Bland and the big men – well, they didn't dislike him, but they sort of – I don't know how to put it.

Watch a high-spirited horse pass a scrap of white paper on the road. He doesn't exactly shy, but he looks at the flapping thing very expectantly.

He was never in the Big Game, though he tried his best to get there. But the Big Game was played by men who 'chew ciphers in the cradle', as Bland put it.

In some mysterious way Schiller got to know that Reggie Batten had been shot dead whilst extracting the mobilisation orders of the Fourteenth Bavarian Corps from a safe in Munich – this was in 1911, and the sad occurrence was described as an 'aviation accident'. What Schiller did not know about was the narrow escape which Bland experienced.

The Munich military authorities took Reggie's body up in an aeroplane and dropped it – and the Munich newspapers gave poor Reggie some beautiful notices and said that the funeral would be at two o'clock, and they hoped that all his loving friends would gather round. Such of his unsuspecting acquaintances as did gather were arrested and searched, their lodgings and baggage ransacked, and they were in due course most incontinently sent across the frontier.

Bland, who was in Munich, did not attend the funeral; in fact, he left the beer city without lingering unnecessarily.

He was back in town only a day when Schiller asked for an interview.

Bland, square-chinned, clean-shaven, and wholly impassive, heard particulars of Schiller's application and laughed.

'You are altogether wrong in your view of Mr Batten,' he said. 'He was unconnected with this department and his death was due to a very deplorable accident. Therefore I cannot give you his job.'

Schiller heard and bowed.

'I have been misinformed, sir,' he said, politely.

He went to work in another way and made a carefully-planned attack upon the Chief Secretary, who had reached that delicate stage of a man's career which is represented by the interregnum between the end of a period of usefulness and the consciousness of the fact.

Sir John Grandor had been in his time the greatest intelligence man in Europe, but now – he still talked of wireless telegraphy as 'a wonderful invention'.

Yet Sir John was Chief and a fairly shrewd Chief. His seal of office was Code No. 2, which no mortal eye had seen save his. It lay on the bottom shelf of the safe between steel-bound covers, sheet after sheet of close writing in his own neat hand.

No. 2 Code is a very secret one. It is the code which the big agents employ. It is not printed, nor are written copies circulated, but is learnt under the tuition of the Chief himself. The men who know Code No. 2 do not boast of their knowledge, because their lives hang upon a thread – even in peace time.

Schiller could never be a big agent. For one thing, he was a naturalised foreign subject, and the big men are nationals, trained to the Game from the day they enter The Office. They are educated men, condemned for life to dissociate themselves from the land of their birth, and who they are, or where they live, is known only to three men, two of whom have no official existence.

Sir John liked Schiller and did many things for him. He told him stories of his past adventures, and Schiller listened attentively. In the course of one of these postprandial discussions (he was a most presentable young man, and Sir John frequently took him home to dinner) Schiller casually mentioned Code No. 2. He spoke of it with easy familiarity, and Sir John discussed the code in general terms. He told his guest how it was kept in the special safe, how it was made up on the loose-leaf system, and how it was a nuisance because it was always in disorder, because he had to consult it every day and invariably replaced the sheets he had been using on the top, irrespective of their alphabetical right to that position.

The young man had innocently suggested that he should come to Sir John's office every night and sort them out, but the old man had smiled benevolently and said he thought not.

Bland summoned Grigsby to his office one day, and that florid young man came to the tick of the clock.

'This fellow Schiller is bothering me,' said Bland, in the low tones which are almost second nature in the Service. 'He is a smart fellow and very useful, but I mistrust him.'

'He has a blameless record,' said the other, staring out of the window, 'and he knows little of the bigger things. Sir John is a ditherer, but he's close enough. What is worrying you now?'

Bland strode up and down the room.

'He is inventing a new wireless receiver,' he said, 'and he has got the old man interested. He works all day at it in his room, and at night he carries it down to Sir John's office, where it is most religiously locked in the safe.

'Of course, it is absurd to imagine that the box – it is about the size of a biscuit tin – can contain anything with human intelligence to get out in an airtight safe and walk around, or go squinting at the Code, but somehow I don't like it.'

Grigsby chuckled.

'It's a new one on me,' he confessed. 'I'm not denying that Schiller is clever – he invented a draught-excluder for my room which is a model of ingenuity; but I can hardly imagine a wireless receiver which reads and transmits a code from the interior of a steel safe.'

But Bland was not convinced.

He sent for May Prince. She was holiday-making in Devonshire, but came at once to town, a straight slip of a girl – she looked eighteen, though in truth she was ten years older – with the loveliest smile in the world, a pair of appraising grey eyes, and a mouth which in repose was a little inclined to droop.

'Sorry to disturb you on your holiday,' said Bland, 'but I want Schiller kept under observation. Next week you will be discharged from the Department for neglect of duty. You will retire with a grievance, and you will tell Schiller, whom you will continue to meet, that I am a beast and that I lose a great deal of money backing racehorses. I will have a few bookmakers' accounts prepared for you, which you will show discreetly.'

'Is he to blackmail you?' she asked.

Bland shook his head.

'If he is all I think he is, he will not. No, he might give you confidence for confidence – so long.'

And May with a nod went out.

Schiller's invention took an unconscionable time to develop. Yet he was enthusiastic over its possibilities and inspired the Chief with some of his enthusiasm. He worked in his spare time at the machine, and regularly every evening at five minutes to six he would carry his heavy box to the Chief's office, solemnly deposit his burden on the iron grill which formed the one shelf of the safe, and watch the locking up with a jealous eye.

And May Prince had nothing to report.

Three days before that fatal 1 August which brought so much destruction and misery to Europe, Bland went up to Schiller's room to question him regarding the *bona fides* of a certain Antonio Malatesta suspected of being an agent of the Central Powers. Bland very seldom visited the offices of his subordinates, but on this occasion his 'phone was out of order.

He found the door locked, and knocked impatiently. Presently it was opened by the smiling Schiller. The table was covered with a litter of wire, electric batteries, tools, and screws, but of the great wireless receiver there was no sign.

'You are looking for my wonder-box, sir?' said Schiller. 'She is in my safe – soon I will give you the most remarkable demonstration! Even today I caught a signal from the Admiralty – through a closed window.'

But Bland was not listening. He stood erect, his nose in the air, sniffing.

There was a faint sweetish smell – a scent of camphor and something else. Schiller watched him through narrowed eyes.

'H'm,' said Bland and, turning on his heel, left the room.

A telegram lay on the table. It had been delivered in his brief absence.

SCHILLER IS AGENT IN CENTRAL EUROPEAN PAY. HE IS HEAD OF CRYPTOGRAM DEPARTMENT. HAVE PROOF.— MAY.

Bland pulled open the drawer of his desk, took out an automatic pistol, and raced through the door and took the stairs two at a time.

Schiller's door was open, but he had gone.

He had not passed out through the lobby or the front entrance of the building, but a commissionaire on duty at the side-door had seen him pass and had heard him hail a cab.

Bland went back to his office, and put through a 'phone call to the police.

'Watch all railway stations and docks. Arrest and detain Augustus Schiller.'

He described him briefly, but with a sure touch.

'It is very lamentable,' said Sir John, really troubled, 'but I can't think he has taken away anything of importance. Has he removed his invention?'

'I have that all right, Sir John,' said Bland, grimly, 'and tonight with your permission I am going to see what happens.'

'But surely you don't think—?'

Bland nodded.

'I haven't monkeyed with it at all – but I've listened very carefully through a microphone, and there is no doubt that it contains a clockwork mechanism. It is almost silent, but I have detected the sound. I suggest that we place the box where it is usually put, leave the safe door open, and watch.'

Sir John frowned. All this seemed a reflection on his judgement, and as such was to be resented; but he was too loyal a man in the service, to which he had given forty-five years of his life, to allow his injured vanity to come before his public duty.

At six o'clock the box was placed in the safe.

'Is that where it was always put?' asked Bland.

'I generally – in fact, invariably – put it on the iron grid.'

'Just above Code No. 2. I see, sir.'

The Chief Secretary frowned again, but this time in an effort of thought.

'That is true,' he said, slowly. 'Once, I remember, when the box was placed a little to one side, Schiller pushed it to the centre, which I thought was a little impertinent of him.'

The two men drew up a couple of armchairs and seated themselves before the safe. Their vigil promised to be a long one. Eight, nine, ten o'clock passed, and nothing happened.

'I think it is rather ridiculous, don't you?' asked Sir John, testily, as the quarter to eleven chimed.

'It seems so,' said Bland, doggedly, 'but I want to see— Good heavens – look!'

Sir John gasped.

Immediately beneath the box was Code 2, enclosed in a leather binder, the edges of which were bound, for the sake of durability, with a thin ribbon of steel.

Now, slowly the cover of the book was rising. It jerked up a little, then fell, leapt again, and fell back as though there were something inside which was struggling to get free. Then of a sudden the cover opened and remained stiffly erect, forming, with the contents, the letter L, the upright of which was the cover.

There was a 'click', and the interior of the safe was illuminated with a soft greenish radiance. It threw a glow upon the top page of the code which lasted for nearly a minute. Then it died away, and the cover of the book fell.

'Phew!' whistled Bland.

He lifted the black box carefully from the safe and carried it to Sir John's desk, examined the bottom of the box with a long and patient scrutiny, then set it down.

'Code No. 2 is in the hands of the enemy, sir,' he said.

It was daylight when he finished his investigations. Half the box was taken up by accumulators. They supplied the current which, operating through a powerful magnet, lifted the cover of the code-book. They gave the light to the little mercurial vapour lamps, which afforded the concealed camera just enough light to make an effective exposure.

'The little clockwork arrangement is, of course, simple,' said Bland; 'that sets the time for the machine to work and switches the current on and off. It probably opens and closes the shutters which hide the lens and the lamp and the magnet. I suspected the camera when I smelt the film in his room.'

Sir John, white and haggard, nodded.

'Get me out of this as well as you can, Bland,' he said, gruffly. 'I'll retire at the end of the year – I'm a silly old man.'

He walked to the door and paused with his fingers on the handle.

'There are thirty men's lives in Schiller's keeping,' he said; 'their names and addresses are in that book – I suppose he got through the book. I am so careless, that I changed the order of the pages almost every day, and the devil has been at work for nine months. He ought to have worked through the book by now, for there was a different sheet on top every time.'

'I'll do my best, sir,' said Bland.

Schiller was away, and safely away, before war was declared. He was seen in Holland and was traced to Cologne. There was no possibility of changing the code, and messages were already coming through from agents.

Bland took a bold step. Through a man in Denmark he got into communication with Schiller and offered to make a deal. But Schiller was not selling. In the telegraphed words of the emissary whom Bland had sent:

SCHILLER IS RECEIVING AN ENORMOUS FEE FROM
ENEMY GOVERNMENT FOR DECODING WIRELESS MES-
SAGES THAT YOUR AGENTS ARE SENDING. HE ALONE
KNOWS THE CODE.

Nothing daunted, Bland again got into communication with the traitor, offering him an enormous sum if he would consent to return to a neutral country and retain his secret.

'Meet me in Holland and I will fix everything,' his message ended. It elicited a reply which was characteristic of the ingenious master-spy.

'Come into Belgium and I will arrange.'

A mad suggestion, for Belgium was now enemy ground, but Bland took his life in his hands and a long glass dagger in his handbag and left the same night for the Continent.

Bland went into Belgium by the back door and made a laborious way to Brussels. It would not be in the national interest to explain the means and methods he employed to make his entry into that carefully-guarded land, but it is sufficient to say that he met Schiller, looking very prosperous, in the *estaminet* of the Gold Lion at Hazbruille, a small village on the Ghent–Lille road.

'You are a very brave man, Mr Bland,' complimented Schiller, 'and I wish I could oblige you in what you desire. Unfortunately I cannot.'

'Then why did you bring me here?' asked Bland.

The other looked at him curiously.

'I have a certain code,' he said, quietly. 'I have it complete with certain exceptions: there are three pages missing – what do you want for them?'

Here was a staggerer for a smaller man than Bland.

'That is a fair offer,' he said, calmness itself; 'but what is the particular code you are buying?'

'No. 2,' said the other. 'I thought—'

Bland interrupted him.

'No. 2 Code?' he said, sipping his boch (he was for the time being a Belgian peasant). 'Of course, that's rubbish. Neither you nor I know No. 2 Code; the code you stole was No. 3.'

Schiller smiled superiorly.

'When you get back to London,' he said, 'ask your chief whether "Agate" does not mean, "Transports loading at Borkum".'

'You might have got hold of that particular word by accident,' said Bland, grudgingly.

'Ask him if "Optique" does not mean "Emperor has gone to Dresden",' persisted the calm Schiller.

Bland looked round the room thoughtfully.

'You know a great deal, my friend,' he said.

The woman who managed the *estaminet* came in a little later and found Bland pulling slowly at a rank cigar, his elbows on the table, a half-emptied boch before him.

The woman glanced with a little smile at Schiller.

'He's tired,' said Bland, emptying the boch; 'let him sleep on. And don't let the flies disturb him,' he added, humorously.

Schiller lay sideways on the bench at which Bland was sitting, his face to the wall and over his head was a coarse blue handkerchief.

'He will not be disturbed,' said Madame, and pocketed the five-sous tip that Bland gave her with a grateful smirk.

'When he wakes,' said Bland at the door, 'tell him I have gone on to Ghent.'

Three hours later a German *landsturm* soldier who had come for his evening coffee whisked away the handkerchief which covered the sleeper's face and stammered:

'*Gott!*'

For Schiller was dead and had been dead for three hours. It took even the doctor quite a long time to discover the blade of the glass dagger in his heart.

A week after this Bland was dressing for dinner in his West End flat and had reached the patience stage of bow-tying when his valet informed him that Grigsby had called.

'I told him you were dressing, sir,' said Taylor, 'but he won't take "no" for an answer.'

'Show him up here,' said Bland.

Mr Grigsby came noisily into the dressing-room, though his greeting of Bland was a little cold.

'I've a bone to pick with you,' he said. 'What the devil have you been saying to Lady Greenholm about me? You know my feelings about Alice—'

'Wait a moment, please,' said Bland, sharply, and turned to his servant. 'Taylor, you can go to the General Post Office with the letter you will find on the hall-stand.'

Mr Grigsby waited until he heard the door of the flat close, then walked into the passage and shot the bolt of the front door.

He came back to where Bland was standing with his back to the fire, his hands thrust into his trouser-pockets.

'You're sure he had No. 2?' he asked.

Bland nodded.

Grigsby bit his lip thoughtfully.

'It isn't worth while worrying about how he got it – now,' he said; 'the question is who will get it next?'

Bland opened a cigar-case, bit off the end of a cigar, and lit up before he replied.

'What news have you at this end?' he asked. 'I was across the border before they discovered his death; naturally, I have heard nothing save what our Amsterdam man told me.'

'The Code is in London,' said Grigsby, briefly. 'As soon as he was dead a cablegram was sent to Valparaiso by the authorities in Brussels. It was addressed to a man named Von Hooch – probably a third party. Here it is.'

He took out a pocket-book and laid a slip of paper on the table. The message was short and was in Spanish:

SCHILLER'S LONDON LODGING

'It's rather puzzling,' said Bland. 'Schiller wouldn't have written the Code out – he was too clever for that. And yet he must have given the authorities a guarantee that the secret should not be lost with his death. It has probably been arranged that he should tell some person agreed upon – in this case a man in South America – in what manner the Code was hidden. The exact locale he left until his death, probably sealed up amongst his private papers.'

'That is a sound theory,' said Grigsby. 'He told you nothing more—'

Bland shook his head.

'I had to kill him, of course,' he said, with a note of regret; 'it was pretty beastly, but the lives of thirty good men were in his holding. He probably knew where they were stationed.'

'And the man that comes after will also know,' said the other, grimly. 'We start tonight to make a very scientific search of his lodgings.'

But the flat in Soho Square yielded no profit.

For the greater part of a fortnight three of the smartest Intelligence men (including Lecomte, from the French Department) probed and searched, slitting furniture, pulling up floors, and dismantling cupboards.

And the result was a negative one.

'I'll swear it is there,' said Bland, dejectedly; 'we've overlooked something. Where is May Prince?'

'She's at the Chief Censor's – she has an office there,' explained Grigsby.

'Ask her to come over.'

May came in some triumph.

'I thought you'd send for me,' she said. 'I could have saved you such a lot of trouble!'

Bland was all apologies.

'I've neglected you terribly, May,' he said. 'Do you know, I have never seen you since you sent me the wire about Schiller?'

She nodded.

'I know that. Schiller is dead, isn't he?'

'How did you know?'

She shrugged her shoulders.

'One reads things in the Censor's office – innocent letters from Holland with messages written between the lines in formic acid and milk which become quite visible if you use the correct formulae. Mr Schiller was a remarkable man, and his father was one of the greatest scholars Switzerland has produced, though he was blind. What do you want of me now?'

Bland explained briefly. The girl knew of Code No. 2, and the secrecy which surrounded it, and realised the urgency of the situation.

'By the way, how did you know that he was an enemy agent?' he asked.

'I discovered *his* code,' she replied, cryptically.

Accompanied by the two men she went to the flat in Soho Square. The flooring had been replaced and the rooms were habitable again. She made a tour through the flat, then she returned to the big dining-room.

'This is the room where the Code is,' she said, decisively.

It was a cheerful apartment, papered in a rich brown. A broad dado of a simple design belted the walls and the wainscoting had been painted a chocolate colour to harmonise with the paper. From the ceiling hung an electric fitting, and at this May glanced.

'We've had that down,' said Bland, 'and the wainscot has been taken out – but we've found nothing.'

'Will you leave me alone here for a few minutes?' asked the girl.

The two men withdrew, but they were hardly out of the room before she followed, her eyes blazing with the joy of discovery.

'Got it!' she laughed. 'Oh, I knew! – I knew!'

'Where is it?' demanded the astonished Bland.

'Wait,' she said, eagerly. 'When do you expect your South American visitor?'

'Tomorrow. Of course, the room will be guarded, and he will have no chance of searching.'

Her eyes were still dancing when she nodded.

'We shall see. Tomorrow, I fancy you will have a very frank visitor from Valparaiso, and when he comes I want you to send for me.'

'What on earth—?'

'Wait, wait, please! What will he say?' She closed her eyes and frowned. 'I can tell you his name – it is Raymond Viztelli—'

'You knew this all along?' asked the astonished Grigsby, but she shook her head.

'I knew it when I went into the room,' she said, 'but now I am guessing. I think he will offer to help you discover the Code, and he will tell you there is a secret panel in the wall, and that it will take days and days to make the discovery. And I think he will ask you to be present when he makes his search.'

'He needn't ask that,' said Bland, unpleasantly. 'I think you're very mysterious, May – but I've a kind of feeling that you're right.'

She had a few questions to ask the janitor of the building before she left.

'Mr Schiller did all his own decorations – in the dining-room, didn't he?'

'Yes, miss,' said the man; 'a regular feller he was for potterin' about with a paste-pot or a paint-brush.'

'And he has paid his rent in advance?'

'That's right, miss.'

'And said that nothing was to be done to the flat till he came back?'

'His very words!' said the caretaker.

'I thought so,' said May.

At ten o'clock next morning a card was brought to Bland. It was inscribed:

'Señor X. Bertramo Silva', and written in a corner, 'of Valparaiso'.

Bland pressed a bell, and in a little time Grigsby and the girl came in.

'He's come,' said Bland, shortly, and handed her the card.

The visitor was shown in. He was a dapper little man with a pointed beard and spoke excellent English. Moreover, after the preliminaries, he plunged straight into the heart of his subject.

'I am going to be very frank with you, Mr Bland,' he began, and Bland, shooting a swift glance at the girl, saw the laughter in her eyes.

'I was for some time an agent of the Central Powers – I tell you this because I wish you to clearly understand my position,' he went on. 'Safe in South America I thought no call would be made upon my services. A few weeks ago, however, I received a cablegram which was intercepted by the British authorities.

'I had known, of course, that in certain eventualities, I might be obliged to come to England, to make a search for certain documents, and that I should learn the place where they were hidden by telegram. That telegram came – I am here!'

He flung his arms dramatically.

'I came straight to you on my arrival. I tell you frankly why I came, because I decided, the night before I reached Plymouth, that the game was not worth the candle. I will assist you as far as possible to discover the documents, and then I will, if you will allow me, return to South America.'

It was all very amazing to Bland. The man had said almost all that May had predicted he would say. He looked at the girl again, and she nodded.

'You understand that your search—' began Bland.

'Will be under the eyes of the police?' interrupted the man from Valparaiso. 'I would prefer it!'

'You would like to start your search at once, I suppose?' asked Bland.

'The sooner the better,' said the other, heartily.

'One moment.'

It was the girl who spoke.

'You have a very good memory, *señor?*'

For just a fraction of a second the smile died from the man's eyes.

'I have an excellent memory, madame,' he said, curtly.

They went together in a cab, and were admitted to Schiller's flat by the police officer on guard.

'Have you any theory?' asked Bland, as they stood in the hall.

'Yes,' replied the other, quickly; 'I think the documents are hidden in a recess in the wall behind a secret panel. This is a very old house, and it is possible Mr Schiller chose it for some structural advantage it may have had.'

Again Bland thought rapidly. The frankness of the man – his willingness to help – the talk of secret panels – was all in accordance with the girl's amazing prophecy.

He saw the glee in her eyes – glee at the mystification of her chief.

Then he turned to the little man.

'Go ahead,' he said.

Señor Silva bowed.

'I will take this wall first,' he said, 'and I will search for the evidence of a panel. My fingers are perhaps more sensitive than yours—'

His hand was outstretched towards the dado when—

'Stop!'

At the sound of the girl's sharp warning Señor Silva turned.

'Before you go any farther,' she said, 'let me ask you if you value your life?'

The Chilean shrugged and spread his hands.

'Naturally, madame.'

The girl turned to Bland.

'If this man learns Code 2 – what will happen to him?'

Bland looked from May to the face of the stranger.

'He will certainly die,' he said, simply.

She nodded.

'You may go on if you wish – but you are starting a little too far to the right.'

His face went a ghastly grey.

'To the right!' he stammered.

'The message to you begins at the door, Señor Viztelli,' she said, calmly; 'the Code does not begin until you reach the window. Will you continue?'

He shook his head, having no words.

Bland called in his men, and they hustled the little South American into a cab.

'And now explain,' said Bland.

The girl walked to the wall near the door and touched the dado.

'Feel,' she said.

Bland's fingers touched the wallpaper gingerly. He felt a few pin-point eruptions, passed his hand to the right and felt more. Then the truth dawned on him.

'Braille!' he whispered.

The girl nodded.

'Schiller's father was a blind man,' she said, 'and Schiller evidently took up the study of the alphabet by which blind men read. Silva was informed how the Code had been written, and, by Schiller's instructions, also learnt Braille against the time when it would be necessary to take over Schiller's work.'

She ran her fingers along the dado.

'There are seven lines of writing, and they run round the room,' she said. 'Schiller pasted this dado on himself a bit at a time – as fast as he was able to photograph Code 2. This is how the top line begins.

'To Raymond Viztelli,' she read, 'keep up pretence helping police; be frank as I have told you. Tell them there is a secret panel and you will be able to come often. Code begins, "Abraham" means "new guns have been fitted—"''

Bland caught her hand and gently drew it away.

'If you want to be a nice live girl and dine with me tonight,' he said, half humorously, 'do not pursue your investigations any farther.'

That afternoon Bland did a little amateur paper stripping, and made a good job of it.

# IN MID-AIR

## By F. Britten Austin

ONE BY ONE the machines ran forward from the long line of hangars where the stocking-cap wind-indicators ballooned stiffly horizontal from their staffs. One by one they scudded across the rank turf of the great aerodrome, and one by one, repeating each other's movement like rooks rising from a field, they swung round into the wind, hurled themselves against it, and were borne upward in long, slow spirals until, their height attained, they sped onward, in rapid diminution of size, upon their diverse courses. It was the busy departure hour of the morning at the London terminus used by all the half-dozen competing aerial transportation companies, whether their machines were bound merely for Paris, Brussels, or Amsterdam, or upon the long-distance schedules to Madrid and Barcelona, Marseilles, Milan and Rome, Munich, Vienna, or Berlin.

The somewhat harassed ground-superintendent of the International Airways, Limited, waved a perfunctory farewell to the Madrid-bound machine, which raced, prodigiously roaring, a miniature hurricane in retrograde escape from her, away over the field, and hastened, with quick, self-important little steps, to where the Amsterdam ''bus' lay poised and peaceful in readiness for her flight. The overalled mechanics had ceased their pertinacious irritation of her engines. The last control-wire to aileron and rudder had been tested. Her great wings, fallaciously heavy in the thickness of their appearance, spread themselves wide, contemptuously immobile it seemed, in the gusts of that fresh wind, upon which, in a few minutes, she would soar. The pilot, helmeted and leather-coated, stood at a little distance from her, finishing his last cigarette for several hours, and contemplating, with a mild interest, the passengers who, having been checked off by an official, climbed one by one the ladder into the interior of the aeroplane.

The superintendent bustled up to him, was greeted with a casual nod obviously altogether inadequate to his dignity.

'You've got an important passenger today, Elliott,' he said, with a snappiness of tone that was intended to recall a recognition of his importance, 'so be careful!'

'I've also got a neck,' replied the pilot, unimpressed, 'and I wouldn't hurt it for worlds. It reminds me of carefulness at every minute.'

'Yes, I dare say,' said the superintendent, in a manner sufficiently indicative of his indifference to its continued vertebration, 'but this is serious. I warn you officially, Elliott, that you are to exercise special care on this flight.'

The young man looked at him with innocent eyes.

'What's the excitement?'

'You'll have nearly half a million pounds sterling worth of diamonds on board – that's the excitement,' replied the superintendent, crushingly. 'It's the biggest parcel of precious stones ever carried by air, and its safe arrival will be a stunt advertisement for this company, you understand? You've got to get it there!'

The pilot shrugged his shoulders.

'I'll get it there if I get there myself – and I have no particular desire to remain half-way, I can assure you. They can't be stolen, once we leave the ground – and my responsibility doesn't begin till then.'

The superintendent nodded his head in agreement.

'No, they can't be stolen on the way, Elliott – and that's the reason we are carrying them. These international diamond thieves have been getting so busy of late that the owners are scared of train and steamer transit. Once you're up in the air they're safe till you come down again, that's a sure thing – and we've staked our reputation that you won't come down until you get to Amsterdam. The company is relying on you,' he finished grandiloquently.

'Righto!' said the pilot. 'I'll do my best. Where are the stones? In the luggage-hold?'

'No. The owners are sending a man with them.' He looked around him. 'Ah! there he goes! – I must just speak to him!'

He turned to hurry after a man carrying a small suitcase additionally attached to him by a steel chain that glinted in the sun, who approached the machine. Two other men accompanied him, one on each side, evidently as a protective escort. The superintendent paused for a final warning word back to the pilot ere he caught them up. 'Don't forget, Elliott – we rely on you!'

The pilot smiled in quiet self-confidence, glanced at the weather-sky and then at his wrist-watch, threw away the stub of his cigarette, and walked to where his mechanic stood awaiting him at the foot of the ladder under the open trapdoor forward of the wings.

'All serene, Thompson?' he asked, casually.

'All serene, sir,' replied the mechanic. 'She's tuned up fine this morning. We'll have a good trip.'

'Sure,' said the pilot, as he clambered up the ladder into the cramped cockpit, faced with dials, compasses, and gauges, and slid into his seat. The mechanic followed him, shut down the trapdoor, and slid likewise into the left-side seat. The pilot tested his controls, started first one engine, then the other, kept them running gently, looked over the side of the cockpit in readiness for the signal to start.

The door was closed upon the passengers in the saloon-interior of the aeroplane, and they glanced, curiously or diffidently according to their natures, at each other in the moment of suspense while they were still stationary. There were ten of them, all men, each in his wicker chair at a window of the saloon, five on one side and five on the other, with a narrow gangway between. Their expressions varied considerably. Those who had made air-journeys before leaned back in their chairs and spread their legs with a great assumption of experienced confidence. Those whose first trip it was shifted uneasily and smiled rather sheepishly from faces that were rather white. The man with the suitcase carried it poised upon his knees, his fingers tight upon the handle, and looked stonily in front of him, as though, in the preoccupation of his great responsibility, he was oblivious of his fellow-passengers. The couple of men in front of him, who occupied the forward seat on each side, joked amiably with each other. Some of the other passengers frowned, feeling this levity ill-timed in the solemn silence which filled what was, perhaps, their last minute of safe contact with the earth.

Despite their protracted anticipation, the moment of departure was unexpected when it arrived. A startling blast of violent, all-swallowing noise from engines suddenly accelerated smote the hearts of the nervous passengers with a pang of sharply enhanced apprehension. The roar of the whirring propellers, of the open exhausts from feverishly working cylinders, swelled and broadened as in opening circles of excessive sound, gathering force and volume from instant to instant – maintained itself for a moment or two at a level pitch of intensity that seemed to devastate the senses – leaped yet again to an incredible vehemence. There was a slight bump. They were moving. Ten pairs of eyes looked out of the windows, saw the green field flitting past them, its grass still reassuringly close, its inequalities felt in a series of muffled shocks, but overrun too quickly for vision. Then the trees beyond the aerodrome gyrated swiftly backwards. They were turning. Their speed slackened. One of the engines muted itself suddenly, leaped again with equal suddenness to its full, deep-toned roar. With one last spasm of violently intensified sound, of energy at a maximum of effort, they felt themselves rush over the field at vertiginous speed, bumped twice, thrice – bumped no more. The field at which they stared dropped away from them, the line of hangars sank into safe depression below them as they neared it with apparent recklessness, the trees beyond the aerodrome were suddenly close, small objects foreshortened on a widened landscape – the passengers gripped at their chairs as they nosed down and rose again gently, in a drop and lift upon the slopes of invisible quiet waves, heeled to one side and steadied once more, slowly turning above a diminished world with which they had lost contact.

Cut off from their fellows by the now evenly maintained roar which beat stunningly upon their ears to the obvious exclusion of conversation, the travellers stared out of their windows, lost themselves in the interest of contemplating an unfamiliar world too toylike ever to have been their real habitation. To the patchwork of fields in the vicinity of the aerodrome, absurdly and unworkably small in their cramped quadrilaterals of confining hedges, succeeded suburbs with masses of toy houses neatly blocked-out in squares and crescents and triangles by clearly-defined roads on which diminutive traffic actually moved. Churches, in all the variations of real architecture, lifted midget steeples far below them. Complete railway systems, with a multiplicity of sidings, equipped to the last detail with signals and bridges and railway stations, with moving model trains emitting real steam in exquisite imitation of the real thing, lay flat for their superior vision. They lost the sense of their own speed in the uniform droning roar of the engines which drove them onward. All this silent toy-world seemed to drift slowly beneath them, diminishing imperceptibly as they rose to yet higher levels.

London spread itself beneath them, bisected by the shiningly sinuous snake of the Thames broadening to its head, invisible in the haze far in front, itself veiled by patches of smoke-fog here and there, charted out in a surprising neatness between its main streets, reduced to a scale which permitted recognition only of its most salient features, lost behind them almost as soon as perceived. They left the broad curves of the river to their right, floated, it seemed – so complete was the absence of all shock or friction in this comfortable saloon – over suburbs that thinned into the fields, over fields that succeeded fields in an infinite variation of greens and browns, over small towns clearly islanded in agricultural country, over woods too tiny to seem worth conserving, over long, empty roads thinly ribboned between the patchwork countryside on which occasional motor-cars crawled like insects. Their speed was only vivid to them when they noticed yet again the birdlike shadow flitting far below over plough-land and pasture and realised that it was their own.

The time passed unremarked in the all-drowning roar of the engines, so monotonously maintained that it seemed like an enveloping silence which, here aloft, walled them off from the normal mensuration of terrestrial things, and still the passengers sat absorbed and solitary in their downward contemplation. On a level keel, any variations in height so gently made and corrected that they were imperceptible, the aeroplane roared onwards, profiting by the fresh south-westerly wind. One of the passengers, detaching his gaze from the panorama below, produced a pocket-compass and checked their course. It was east-north-east. The spell of solitary absorption broken by his action, he touched the fellow-passenger seated in front of him and showed him the dial, with a dumb-show gesture of comment. The other man smiled companionably and pointed downwards. They were leaving a thinly foam-fringed coast of pale yellow beaches, drifting over a green-blue ocean where a myriad wave-facets scintillated in the sun. The two men leaned close together and shouted the obvious in a desperate effort at conversation – the North Sea!

The other passengers, vaguely conscious of this breaking of individual isolation, looked round from their windows. One or two of them, ceding to the gregarious instinct hitherto repressed, imitated these pioneers and mouthed ineffectual words supplemented with a smile and nod. It was really very comfortable in this saloon, so comfortable in its solid construction, in its luxurious equipment, that the sense of insecurity thus high in the air was lulled into abeyance. They glanced about them, appraised their environment, their companions, with perceptions no longer blurred by the uneasiness of the moments preceding departure. Electric-lamp brackets provided for the contingency of a flight unduly prolonged into the hours of darkness. A little door in the after-wall led, by its indication, to a lavatory. Another little door, in the forward end, marked 'Private', 'Entrée Interdite', 'Ingang Verboden', aroused a vague curiosity by its suggestion of guarded mystery. As a matter of fact, it opened into a small compartment containing the petrol-tanks, pressure-pumps, etc., and thence communicated with the cockpit where the pilot and mechanic sat, in the open, behind their little glass windscreens. But the passengers in the saloon, their vision bounded by their own immediate comfort, had no more thought of the pilot who conducted them than the traveller in a first-class railway coach has of the engine-driver.

They surveyed each other now with some interest, secretly surprised perhaps to find each other so normal in these unwonted conditions. One or two wrote notes on pieces of paper and passed them to each other, renouncing the excessive effort of verbal conversation. Only the man with the suitcase on his knees remained stonily indifferent to his companions, absorbed in his own thoughts. The two men in the front seats nodded and smiled to each other in the exchange of some idea readily comprehensible to both.

The taller of the pair looked down through his window – they were now over wide sea, dotted with small craft, the coastline far behind – and then rose, with a languid twist of shoulders fatigued by long immobility, to his feet. The other passengers watched him with a mild curiosity. He smiled pleasantly at them – a keen-faced young man with steel-grey eyes under well-marked brows – showing white teeth under his little moustache as his lips parted. So quietly confident, so engaging was his smile that some of the other passengers smiled back, involuntarily, in response. They watched him, with the concentrated, if unillumined, interest of minds undistracted by any other happening in this confined space, as, with a calm deliberation, he extracted a fair-sized card from one of his pockets. His companion had turned in his chair, sat twisted to face the other passengers, a quiet smile on his face also. Eight pairs of eyes turned automatically to the white card in the hand of the man who stood erect at the end of the saloon, his right hand in his jacket pocket. They might have been an audience at a conjuring trick as they sat there motionless in vague half-expectation of his next movement. The man suddenly held up the card with its face towards them. There were words on it in heavy black type – two words – two amazing words – 'HANDS UP!'

Eight pairs of eyes stared uncomprehendingly at this legend, unable for the moment to connect themselves with it. Then, with a variety of sudden facial gesture, eight pairs of eyes found themselves staring as if mesmerised into the muzzles of two automatic pistols, one in the hand of the man who leaned over the back of his chair smiling at them, one in the hand of the man who held the card aloft. The man with the card had ceased to smile; he tapped his announcement significantly with the barrel of his weapon. To those startled passengers it seemed as though the earth had stopped. They forgot the aeroplane in which they were, they forgot everything except the menace of those utterly unexpected pistols. The man with the card smiled grimly and levelled his weapon at the breast of his nearest neighbour. Seven pairs of hands shot up above seven heads. The eighth man sat with his hands stubbornly clasped over the handle of the suitcase on his knees.

The man leaning over the chair-back ran his eyes over the surrendered crowd, marked the recalcitrant, pointed to him with an indicative motion of his pistol, significantly poised, and smiled with meaning. His lips uttered a word inaudible in the roar of the engines, but clearly deducible from their rounded protrusion – '*You!*' The man with the suitcase sat rigid, hands tight over his precious charge, and stared defiantly into the eyes that threatened him.

For a moment or two the group remained posed as for a tableau; the man on his feet still holding up his card; the man leaning over the chair-back still smiling grimly; both with their pistols levelled on their companions; seven pairs of arms held awkwardly aloft; and the eighth man stubborn in a frozen immobility where only his eyes were alive. He had, obviously, no chance. Even protest would have been inaudible. The aeroplane roared onward over the wide expanse of sea far, far below, immensely too high for any jump of escape. They were isolated with their prey, these two well-dressed bandits who smiled with a grim suavity as they dandled their pistols and traversed them over the frightened little crowd. No communication was possible with the pilot even, except through that little door, and they were between it and their victims.

The second man rose lazily to his feet. He nodded to that defiant eighth man with a significant smile which assured him that he would be dealt with in due course, and took a step to the man who sat, hands above his head, in the nearest chair. The victim's eyes bulged with fright as the other man waved his pistol in front of him with a gesture that commanded him to stand up. The confederate ran deft hands through his pockets, produced nothing, shrugged his shoulders, pushed him down into his seat again. He passed to the next man, repeated the procedure, and returned him also to his seat unpillaged. Each of the seven men with their hands above their heads was similarly dealt with, and upon one only was found the article evidently sought – a revolver, which was promptly annexed. Then the pair of confederates, assured against interruption, turned to the man with the suitcase.

He sat absolutely motionless, his hands clenched over the handle in an intensity of grip which whitened the skin between his knuckles. His face was set doggedly in a determination so fixed that he seemed almost unconscious of the man who threatened him. Only his eyes betrayed a silent agony, terrible to look upon, as they stared straight in front of him. The two men stood over him, pistols levelled, and the eyes of all the other passengers turned to watch, fascinated, this drama which played itself soundlessly in the all-drowning roar of the engines which hurried them high above the sea.

One of the confederates tapped him on the shoulder as though recalling him to consciousness. The man's eyes turned from their vacant contemplation to look his adversary straight in the face. They continued to confront him even when the pistol levelled itself at his temple. Deathly pale though he was, not a muscle of his face moved. It was evident that he was exercising all his will-power in a supreme effort, fidelity to his trust a part of himself, hopeless though was his position. The grip upon his suitcase did not relax in the slightest.

The other passengers held their breath as they watched this silent duel. In that suitcase, evidently, was the booty desired by these daring robbers. Nothing else had been taken. They thrilled with a horrible fascination as they saw the pistol come down and press its muzzle tight upon the back of one of the hands that held it.

'*One!*' The word was inaudible in the roar which filled the saloon, its purport only guessed after an instant of deduction from the lip-gesture which produced it.

'*Two!*' The man with the suitcase did not blench. His eyes, fixed terribly upon his tormentor, never wavered.

'*Three!*' The crack of the pistol was a dull detonation in the cease-less roar that swallowed all other sounds, the victim's involuntary yell of pain a cry but faintly heard. The watching passengers, drooping the tired arms still above their heads, saw him sink back in his chair, deathly white. He had fainted.

The two confederates had evidently thought out their plan in every detail. Without a moment's hesitation, one of them produced a file. The chain attaching the suitcase to the messenger's body was cut through in a few minutes of dexterous work.

Then, with a callous indifference to their victim's condition, they left him and went with their plunder to the forward end of the saloon. The man who had exhibited the card turned to the passengers and made a smiling gesture of 'wash-out'. The terrified little crowd dropped their aching arms. What was coming next? How did these two brigands propose to get away with the goods? The question asked itself in seven terrified minds, anguished in a new apprehension of further danger for themselves. The eighth man still lay back in a swoon, blood dropping from his hand to the floor.

The pair of thieves, however, did not seem in the least concerned.

They smiled at each other contentedly, exchanged a word shouted close into each other's ears, and nodded mutual acquiescence. Then one of them placed the suitcase on the floor and sat down in his chair again as though nothing had happened.

The other man opened the little door which led forward and disappeared through it.

Out in the cockpit the pilot sat behind his little windscreen and steered his course through the air that rushed by his head in a roar that mingled with the roar of the engines above and behind him on either hand, a roar that was heard, though muffled, through the close-fitting cap that came down over his ears, all other sounds excluded. Concentrated upon his task, his muscles moved almost automatically in control of the wheel-topped 'joy-stick' that pivoted on its ball-and-socket base as he corrected the deviations, lateral and perpendicular, which registered themselves in a swing of the pointers of the floating compass and the aneroid close under his eyes.

Patches of rain-cloud, torn and heaped by that south-west wind, hung over the sea and he drove into them, moist fogs in which the sense of direction was lost, with faculties quick to perceive any alteration of his level in the changes of atmospheric temperature accompanying them. His arms ached with 'holding up' the heavy machine, which tended to drive forward clumsily in the air-pockets frequent in this stretch of unsettled weather. From time to time the mechanic at his side, posted in vigilant observation of the gauges upon the dashboard, got up silently – conversation quite impossible in this blast of wind – and crept back to the compartment in the rear to attend to the pressure-pumps regulating the flow of petrol and lubrication.

For a longer period than usual the pilot had sat with the seat at his side vacant. He began to speculate uneasily upon possible causes for the mechanic's protracted absence. Had anything gone wrong behind there? He looked at the gauges, saw that they were normal – half-turned his head in a difficult twist from his cramped seat in a questing, but fruitless, glance to the rear. The machine plunged slightly sideways in this relaxation of his control. He pulled her up, renounced the effort to see behind him, concentrated himself for a straight course through the stretch of grey cloud that massed itself upon their track. Fog-wisps flew past him, collected on the windscreen in beads and runlets of moisture that distorted vision.

Ah! at last – Thompson had returned! Without diverting his gaze from his instruments, essential for guidance in this dense fog, he felt the contact of the body that slid into the seat beside him. Confound this clumsy machine! – he cursed to himself as he pulled the wheel close to him in denial of a swing-round of the needle on the aneroid, glanced to the half-gyrating compass-card. A piece of paper was being pushed across it – Good! Thompson's explanation of the irregularity which had detained him. No! What the ——? Utterly bewildered, he read: '*Obey orders or I shoot – fly machine myself.*'

Good Lord! Had Thompson gone mad? He glanced quickly to his left, saw – not Thompson, but a stranger with a young, determined face, the hair of his capless head fluttering in the wind – saw a revolver levelled at his eyes. The machine plunged heavily in his shock of astonishment.

He righted it, glanced again at the stranger. The man nodded emphatically, gesticulated with his mouth, tapped the written message with his left hand, while with the other he held his weapon levelled dangerously. Who in Hades was this? What had happened to Thompson? His brain worked with the quickness of one trained to lightning thought in a school of air-warfare where instantaneous deductions and decisions were vital – those diamonds! But what had happened to Thompson? Thompson was in fact lying stunned in the compartment by the pressure-pumps, but the pilot imagined worse things. He thrilled in a sudden revival of old combative instincts. To blazes with this fellow!

He glanced again at him, saw his mouth frame, emphatically, the words, '*I shoot!*' his eyes flash a stern confirmation of the threat. What was to be done? He could not take his hands from the controls, grapple with this interloper. He thought of the passengers, their lives dependent on him, and was savagely perplexed.

Another scrap of paper was pushed under his eyes. '*Alter course due north – or I shoot.*' Due north! That was out to sea, away from the Dutch coast which they were now nearing! Should he refuse – hold on his course at all costs? He felt the muzzle of that pistol press against the cheek-leather of his helmet.

Lives were more precious than diamonds – he banked her round in a low left-hand turn. They shot out of the fog, roared on between white clouds on a level with them, high above green-blue water mottled with tiny foam-flecks. He glanced over the side to the sea below. It was empty of any shipping except in a far distance. No – what was that long, thin streak of white foam trailed across the waves, a dark spot at its head? From their altitude of three thousand feet it was difficult to distinguish clearly the nature of that tiny craft a long way in front of them to the north. Was it to meet this boat that he had been ordered to change his course?

'*Drop two thousand*' – another message was pushed under his eyes. He hesitated for a moment, then put her head down in a furious suddenness. They plunged headlong with an abruptness that lifted his stomach in the sudden change of equilibrium. In a long, long rushing nose-dive, his weight thrown forward upon the 'joy-stick', they raced down, engines roaring, towards the sea. The pilot smiled grimly. The passengers behind would be sliding out of their chairs, terrified in a prospect of imminent disaster. The man at his side, thrown forward also, tugged frantically at his arm.

The sea was close under them, its waves curiously large. He pulled the wheel of the controlling lever close into him suddenly, threw his weight back, 'held her up' with all his strength. Her nose came up on the bottom curve of an ellipse, and she shot skyward once more like a rocket. The pilot grimly sacrificed the ease of mind of his passengers. His one hope was to shake the nerves of the threatening individual at his side. If only he dared to loop! He speculated for a moment on the strength of the roof above the saloon. Would it bear the weight of nine men suddenly flung upon it? He could not risk it.

The face of the man at his side came suddenly into close contact with his own, its mouth distorted in a full-lunged shout. He just caught the words, '*Quit fooling!*' A left hand clutched at the wheel and the right hand once more brought the pistol into dangerous proximity. He flattened out their soaring, full-engined, skyward rush at a couple of thousand feet.

'*Down!*' shouted the just-heard voice. '*Down!*'

Under the menace of that pistol he dropped her on a steady slant to a thousand, flattened out again at a sign from the man at his side. His one chance, it was obvious to him, was to assume an implicit obedience, ready in the meanwhile to snatch any opportunity of escape that might present itself.

Both men glanced over the side to the sea below. The small craft was close under them, now clearly defined as a swift motor-boat of considerable size. The man in the left-hand seat, still covering the pilot with his weapon, pulled out a Very pistol with his left hand and fired into the air. A star of intense white light shone out suddenly against the blue, sunlit sky, and sank downwards. An answering rocket shot up from the motor-boat that swerved round to follow them.

The pilot obeyed a tug on his arm that commanded him to circle. His captor looked away from him over the side, in an evident computation of distances. The pistol in his right hand, no longer controlled by direct vision of its possible target, waved vaguely at a harmless angle. It was the momentary chance. Abandoning the wheel with his right hand, the pilot reached over in a sudden movement and snatched the weapon, flung it wide overboard.

Then, before his adversary could realise what had happened, he put the machine up on a long, full-powered slant to the south-east, away from the boat below.

A second later a couple of hands were round his throat, choking the life out of him. Suffocating, in an agony of reaction against this throttling-grip, one hand tearing vainly at those which constricted him remorselessly, he fought to keep his consciousness, to keep the machine, with his one free hand, on the upward course whose correctness he, with his head pushed back out of vision of the dashboard, could only determine with the sixth sense of long custom in the air. The machine banked, side-slipped dangerously, and still that grip upon his throat continued unrelaxed. In a flash of intuition at crisis, he understood his adversary's game. He would let her fall into the sea, certain himself of being rescued with his loot – what had happened in the saloon behind? – by the motor-boat evidently at a rendezvous. The pilot, feeling his heart swell to bursting in his suffocated breast, tugged blindly and desperately at the controls with both hands, felt the machine right herself once more.

Then, entirely abandoning the wheel for a moment, his head singing in a whirl of the senses, he made a supreme effort to rid himself of his adversary's grip, half-rising, in blind reaction, from his seat. The machine, uncontrolled, dived suddenly seawards in an awful spin. The pilot, on the verge of fainting, felt her go – felt that the end had come. His hands drooped powerlessly to fumble for the controls.

Suddenly, incredibly, the pressure on his throat ceased. In his first long, full breath of delicious new life, he glanced round with eyes that ached from their sockets, whilst an automatic self seized possession of the controls, struggled desperately to pull the machine out of this fatal, giddy spin. What had happened? Intent, in the urgency of the brief moment or two that separated them from a headlong plunge into the sea, upon a task that demanded all his skill, he only half-glimpsed that it was now his adversary who leaned back, gasping, choking, garrotted from behind.

Thompson? The thought flashed through his mind as, a few feet only above waves that lifted themselves in a run of mobile water where sky had been, the machine suddenly flattened herself into a level course, shot up once more in answer to his tug at the wheel-topped lever. The motor-boat appeared, startlingly close, issuing from under her in a smother of flying foam, oilskin-clad men waving frantically from her hooded deck in expostulation at this threatened crash upon them.

Thompson? He glanced again. No. He saw a horribly mangled hand, black with an explosion and with congealed blood, stretch itself forward from behind, grope over the face of the choking man. He glanced round still farther, saw that a handkerchief was tightly round the throat of his late adversary, saw that its ends were being drawn back with all the strength of a strange man, who thrust his knee into his victim's back and grinned with a horrible exultation of glutted hatred.

The throttled man went over backwards suddenly.

Prior to that first rushing nose-dive, before there was anything to indicate any abnormality in the control of the machine, the passengers in the saloon, left with the man who had taken possession of the suitcase, were too absorbed in the fascination of watching his preparations for disposing of it to notice that its late owner, still apparently in a swoon, was watching also through half-opened eyes. His pistol ostentatiously in readiness on his confederate's chair, the quietly self-possessed brigand occupied himself with attaching two large indiarubber bladders to the suitcase and then inflating them. This done, he produced what was evidently a silken parachute, still closed, and tied it firmly to the handle. Those watching passengers, still too frightened to move, had no difficulty in deducing his intentions. Obviously, he was going to drop the suitcase overboard.

Then came the nose-dive, which sent them all tumbling out of their chairs into a heap upon the floor. The thief, bent over the suitcase, went first, too suddenly surprised to have a chance of retaining his equilibrium. As he sprawled, the man hitherto sunk back in his chair hurled himself upon him, went down with him, his hand groping for the pistol. He seized it by the barrel, struck viciously with the butt upon his enemy's head.

The aeroplane soared up again, righted itself to an even keel. The passengers staggered back to their seats, saw the injured man rising from the prostrate body of his adversary. He retrieved his suitcase, handed it to the guardianship of an emphatically gesticulating passenger, who grinned his courage now that the danger was past, handed him also the pistol for protection in case the stunned man should recover. Then, stumbling and lurching in the now eccentric movements of the machine, he opened the little door in the saloon wall and disappeared into the forward compartment.

A firm of diamond merchants in Amsterdam gave the pilot the dinner of his life that night.

# OUT OF
# THE NIGHT

*By F. Britten Austin*

GEORGE FLEMING was waiting for me on the platform as the train ran into Falmouth station – six feet of honest simplicity attired in a dirty sweater, a pair of disgraceful trousers unevenly turned up, and a battered pair of black shoes irregularly whitened with the incrustations of salt water. His weather-tanned and freckle-yellowed face lit up with a diffident grin as he saw me descend from my carriage.

'Jolly good of you to come, Dickie,' he said, making me wince with his hand-grip. 'I hope you won't be bored to death.'

'Not a bit of it,' I answered, cheerily. I don't pretend to be much of a yachtsman – though I may say I looked the part far more than George – but I had jumped at his invitation to a couple of weeks 'knocking about' in Cornish waters. There is nothing better for city-jaded nerves than a rest-cure on a smart little yacht with a couple of hands or so to do all the rough work. 'I've been looking forward to it.'

Handing over my suitcase to a zealous small boy, my friend and I set out for the waterside. As we walked, I took stock of him. I had not seen him since last winter. My sister had got hold of him then, and, privately announcing her determination to civilise him, had lured him to several dances where he had presented a figure of pitiably uncouth and tongue-tied misery. I remembered that she had startled us to ribald laughter by an alleged discovery that he was 'head over heels' in love with some friend of hers – what was her name? – some Irish girl. It was absurd, of course; George was the sort of fellow that can't look at a woman without getting red in the face. My reading of it was right. There had been nothing in it. The girl had gone back to Ireland, and George – we had rather lost sight of George. He was evasively reticent when I asked him what he had been doing with himself all the year. He had been 'just pottering about' up and down the coast. We arrived at the quay.

'There she is!' he exclaimed, pointing to a small, dingy-sided craft, with what appeared to be a wireless aerial mounted on stick-like

173

extensions of her two masts. She was moored to a buoy out among a flotilla of dainty yachts. 'There's the *Eileen* – the one painted black.' Had she been an America's Cup challenger there could not have been more of affectionate pride in his tone. My heart went down with a bump.

'Why,' I said, with a ghastly attempt at jollity, 'she's a regular liner – wireless and all! That's wireless, isn't it?'

'Yes,' he answered. 'One of my hobbies, you know. I meant to have taken it down, but I had to be ashore pretty sharp this morning to get the stores in. Can't sail with the thing up, you know – gets horribly in the way.'

'Oh,' I remarked (we were now walking along the quay to where a small boy in a dinghy was waving to us), 'you don't use it at sea, then?'

'Good Lord, no! I only rig it up when we're all snugged down.' (George's speech was apt to lapse into horribly clumsy antitheses, typical of him, somehow.) 'I like to listen-in at night, you know, and hear all that's going on – broadcasted concerts and all sorts of things. Makes life heaps more cheery. It gets a bit dull sometimes all by oneself.'

I stopped him on that quayside.

'George,' I said, in alarm, 'you don't mean to say you sail that yacht *alone?*'

He laughed. 'Of course I do,' he replied. 'You didn't expect a skipper and a crew, did you? It's doing things by yourself that makes the fun of it. You'll soon see.'

My conception of fun differed. But there was no help for it now, and I refrained from comment. A few minutes later I had lowered myself gingerly into the dinghy, where a small boy had sat sentry over an immense assortment of parcels, and George was sculling me out into the harbour.

'Here we are! Catch hold!' I grabbed at a rope hanging over the yacht's side. 'Up you go!' By an incredible feat of gymnastics I scrambled on board. 'Stand by for the parcels.' He handed them up to me, followed himself. 'Now, then, we'll just stow all this gear and then' – he burst into cacophonous song – 'A life on the ocean wave – a life on the ocean wave.' His high spirits were a hideous mockery of my own.

'You never could sing, George,' I remarked, by way of giving myself some sort of revenge.

He did not hear me. He had dived down the small companion into the cabin. 'Sling 'em all down to me, my lad,' he shouted out. 'That's the idea.' He encouraged me boisterously as I passed down the stores.

For a minute or two he rummaged about below, and then he called to me, 'Come and have a look round, Dickie.' I squirmed down half-a-dozen steps and hit my head on the hatch. 'Pretty snug, isn't it?'

The man who invented the word 'snug' had a genius for tact. It is a charming way of saying that one is confoundedly cramped. There was a screwed-down table in the centre of the cabin, allowing one just space enough to slither round to an upholstered seat on each side. 'Good head-room, isn't there? when the hatch is up,' he said, cheerily. I thought there might be. 'It's up now, of course,' he explained, and that illusion was dispelled.

'What's that?' I asked, pointing to what looked like a closed desk against the forward bulkhead.

'Oh, that's my wireless set – built it myself,' he said. 'Show it you tonight. Haven't got time now. All hands on deck – and let's get clear of this confounded harbour!'

For the next few minutes I felt horribly in the way as George busied himself with the tangle of ropes on deck. In an amazingly short time the wireless was stowed, the jib and mizzen set, and then, almost before I had realised what was happening, we had cast off our mooring and George shouted to me to go to the tiller while he hauled up the mainsail. We began to move through the water.

'Topping breeze, isn't it?' said George as he came aft and took the tiller from me. 'I hate creeping out in a dead calm. It's a paraffin motor and stinks infernally.'

'You've got an auxiliary engine, then?'

'Yes. Jolly useful, you know, sometimes. It's under there,' he said, indicating with his foot a closed hatch just in front of the tiller. 'Look out for the boom! I'm going to tack.' I dodged to avoid the boom of the mainsail as the *Eileen* came up to the wind and heeled smartly to her new course. She curtsied prettily to the sparkling waves. 'Yes, as I was saying, the auxiliary is jolly useful sometimes. No joke to get becalmed in a fog out in the Channel. Brutes think nothing of running you down.'

He prattled on, thoroughly happy, while I sat on the deck, accommodating myself as best I could to its slope first to one side and then the other, and lit my pipe with more bravado than enjoyment. But enjoyment came to me as we sped over that ruffled sea, just foam-flecked, under the cloudless blue sky, with a kissing splash at our bows and a gurgle under our counter as the yacht lifted and dropped to the swell rolling in from the outer waters. The magnificent Cornish scenery slid away behind us, was soon but a background painted on the lower edge of the blue sky, as beautiful and unreal in the September sunshine as a panorama by an artist with an eye for atmospheric effects.

This is not a panegyric of the delights of yachting but the story of an adventure. George, looking over my shoulder, wants me to put in all sorts of technical details about the course we took, wind and tide and all the rest of it. I should only make a mess of them. Suffice it that to me the day was delightful, and that dusk saw us creeping towards a little cove at the other side of the Lizard where George said we should be snug against anything short of a westerly gale. The wind had gone down with the sun, and we had to use the motor to arrive at our anchorage.

The steak and onions over which, a little later, we sat in the little cabin were the perfect end of a perfect day. When the last morsel had vanished, George pulled out his pipe, filled and lit it.

'Wash up first,' he ordained, 'and then we'll hear what the great world has to say to us.'

The great world seemed immensely remote, unreal, in this secluded cove, where the only sound was the faint *plash-plash* of water against the *Eileen*'s hull as she rocked almost imperceptibly on the incoming tide. Emerging on deck from the lamplight of the cabin, we seemed uncannily suspended in the blue night, far from the familiar earth, the brighter of the myriad stars above reflecting themselves in the glassy calm as though they shone from below us, in an illusion of encompassing cosmic space heightened by the hushed silence. Only at a second glance could the outline of the embracing cliffs be deduced rather than discerned from their dark occultation of blue infinity. As I slung over the washing-up bucket it splashed into ghostly phosphorescent fire.

George's cheery jocularities, making light of the task of washing-up, seemed incongruously out of place in that great silence. The eeriness of it was still upon me as we returned to the cabin.

He went briskly to what had looked like a desk against the forward bulwark of the cabin, lifted off the cover, revealed a complicated array of electrical apparatus, coils and knobs and switches, which utterly transcended my understanding. My ignorance of these matters, familiar enough to nearly every schoolboy nowadays, is singularly complete. The only objects I recognised, or thought I recognised, among those mysterious instruments were three ordinary electric light bulbs fitted upright in a row on a little black board. And when I looked more closely, I saw that even these were different from any I had seen. A little metal cylinder, open at the ends, fitted over the filament of each.

'Pretty good set, that, eh?' remarked George, with a fictitious nonchalance that failed to disguise the pride in his voice. 'Made it myself – every bit of it.'

'Wonderful!' I said, with genuine respect. 'And can you pick up wireless telephony as well as ordinary signals with it?' I expect it was an absurd question – I have a knack of being inane before these technical mysteries – but George only smiled tolerantly.

'Pick up anything that's going,' he said. 'You'll hear presently.' He busied himself with fitting coils of wire into sockets and other little adjustments of the apparatus that were meaningless to me.

'Can you send messages as well as receive them?'

'I *can*,' he answered, frowning abstractedly at some little gadget that was obstinate under his fingers; 'it means starting up the motor and connecting it with the dynamo. Still, there's not much point in it. I don't want to talk to anybody. I only want to hear. But I have found it useful sometimes – got my position more than once when I was in a fog. The shore station will give it to you. Cross-bearings, you know.'

This meant nothing to me, but I refrained from further questioning. George had evidently completed his preparations. He gave me a telephone headpiece, with receivers fitting over both ears, and put on a similar one himself.

'Now listen,' he said. He switched on the three lamps, twisted a knob or two, manipulated a little lever with thumb and forefinger.

I heard a low confused murmuring that rose and fell as he played with that tiny lever, and then suddenly the faint sound of a human voice, out of pitch like a gramophone that is running down. He shifted the lever a fraction farther round the arc it traced, and a man's voice, startlingly loud and distinct, spoke into my ears.

'*Two LO closing down for three minutes!*' it said, with carefully deliberate enunciation. It made me jump, so unexpected was it.

'We've just missed a turn,' said George. 'That's London Broadcasting Station. Concert from eight to nine. Not bad for three hundred miles off, eh?'

'Marvellous!' I exclaimed. To me, that voice coming out of the void was positively uncanny.

'We'll see what else is going on while we're waiting,' he said. 'Would you like to hear the ships talking? They work on a six hundred wavelength. Two LO works on three hundred and sixty.' He shifted the little lever a fraction, and I heard a multiplication of little low-toned raucously metallic buzzings, irregularly and rapidly reiterated. 'That's Morse, of course,' explained George. 'There's half-a-dozen ships talking at once. Can you hear that louder one? That must be quite close – ten miles off. And now the shore station's talking. Do you catch the different note?'

It was weird to sit there in that little cabin of the anchored yacht and listen to those ships conversing with each other, unintelligible to me though were their messages, hundreds of miles away across the ocean some of them. George glanced at his watch and switched the lever back to its former position.

The buzzings of the ships ceased instantly. Instead, came that clearly distinct man's voice, louder than George's close beside me:

'*Two LO speaking. The next item will be a violin solo by Miss Sylvia Smith – Rubinstein's Melody in F. But before she begins I must warn listeners-in that we have again received serious complaints of oscillating valves. Will all listeners-in kindly see that their valves do not oscillate?*' The human touch in that reproof coming out of the night was to me singularly impressive.

A moment later the violin solo began, as full and rich and sweet, the piano accompaniment as ripplingly clear as if the performers were in that cabin with us. And they were three hundred miles away, with no tangible connection to that little yacht hid in a cove of the Cornish coast! And thousands of people in a vast radius from that distant city were listening to that music vibrating noiselessly through the night till it impinged upon a particular juxtaposition of wires connected to a telephone receiver, while all the time, uninterfered with, unperceived, the ships of all nations were talking together. To my mind, naïvely unsophisticated when it comes to the exact sciences, the whole thing was like magic.

I said as much to George when the violin finished and 2LO once more shut down for three minutes.

He smiled. 'You've only heard the fringe of it,' he said. 'We've only been on the low waves. Let's see what's happening on the higher ones.' He took the couple of coils from their sockets, fitted a pair of larger ones, fiddled again with knob and lever.

My ears were filled with a confused mingling of high piping notes, like a lot of distant flutes trying to get themselves in tune. 'D'you hear the difference on the high waves?' he remarked. 'Quite a different note.' He adjusted his lever so that one series came clear, a rapid repetition of one squeaking sound. 'That's one of the transatlantic stations working. You can't pick it up – mechanically transmitted.' He turned the lever again. 'There's the Eiffel Tower – do you catch its call sign – F L – F L?' I took his word for it. 'They work on two thousand six hundred. Now we'll see what Germany's doing. Listen! That's Königswusterhausen, two thousand eight hundred. They telephone only up to five-thirty. They're Morsing now. Nobody but London is telephoning at this hour.'

'Is that the highest wavelength – two thousand eight hundred?' I asked.

'Good Lord, no! Some stations work on a much higher wave than that. Bordeaux works on twenty-three thousand four hundred and fifty. Would you like to hear it?' He fitted a yet larger pair of coils. 'There's no telephony on these high wavelengths. They're mostly used for transatlantic telegraph work.' He manipulated his lever. 'Do you hear it? That's Bordeaux.' I listened to the irregularly-repeated fluting note that had no translatable significance for me.

'And is that the highest your instrument will register?' I queried.

'No. I could catch anything up to thirty-five thousand. But there's no point in listening-in on those high waves. There's no one using them. Bordeaux is about the limit. But still, we'll have a try, if you like. Might hear a message from Mars!' he said, jokingly. 'It was while listening-in on these unused series that Signor Marconi got his mysterious sounds.' He made further adjustments of his apparatus.

There was dead silence. Concert, ships' messages, Königswusterhausen, Bordeaux, all alike were blotted from audition. I wondered whether anything had gone wrong with the instrument, so complete was that cessation of the ether-borne murmurs and pipings to which I had been listening.

'Nothing, you see,' said George. 'That was twenty-five thousand. We'll try a little higher.' Again he altered the adjustment. 'Twenty-eight thousand – nothing.' Dead silence – save for the just-heard *plash-plash* of the waves against our craft. He moved the lever farther. 'Thirty thousand— Hallo! – what's that?' He glanced at me in sharp surprise. 'Listen!'

'*Hallo, hallo, Adler! RHQ speaking. Q Branch wants your report.*' The voice was loud and clear.

'What's RHQ?' I asked.

'Hanged if I know!' replied George. 'Listen!'

Another voice answered in what seemed to be guttural German. We couldn't catch a word of it.

The first voice spoke again.

'*Hallo, Adler! Fetch Mr Maguire,*' it said, on a note of irritation. '*Herr Maguire bringen!*' The amateurish German was peremptory in its utterance.

'*Ja, ja,*' answered the second voice. '*Warten Sie nur.*'

There was a moment or two of silence.

'What have we got on to?' I asked.

'Can't imagine,' said George. 'It's a most unusual wavelength for telephony.' He frowned at the instrument-board while we waited. Suddenly we both jumped at a new voice – a woman's voice on an accent of wild distress.

'*Help! Help!*' it cried. '*Help! – Oh!—*' The voice broke off abruptly, as though the speaker had been snatched away from the instrument. A sharp exclamation from George sent my eyes to him. He was staring in front of him, his broad, honest face twisted in a curiously tense and startled expression. At the same time I thought I heard an indistinct noise of scuffling from the receivers tight against my ears. But it was George's strange look that held my attention for the moment.

'No, it couldn't be!' he muttered, frowning. There was an odd, puzzled alarm in his tone. Before I could ask him what 'couldn't be', a man's voice spoke, a different voice from those we had heard.

'*Hallo – RHQ?*' Then, as though he half-turned his head to someone behind him, '*Take her away! Tie her up somewhere! How did she get loose?*' The voice was again clear and full into the telephone. '*Hallo – RHQ! Maguire speaking. Is that Cassidy?*'

'*Sure!*' came the first voice. '*What's the report?*'

'*All OK. Five thousand rifles, fifty machine-guns, one million SAA, and a hundred cases of grenades landed at rendezvous. Handed over to Captain Flanagan. No interference. We got to sea again at six o'clock.*'

'*Good! Say, Maguire, who was that girl screeching just now?*'

'*She – oh, she's a – a hostage.*' The awkwardness of the reply was plainly evident. '*Some of the boys got loose – burnt a big house nearby. Belonged to a Free Stater. I managed to save the girl.*'

'*She don't seem grateful.*' The voice at the other end was cynical. '*I shall have to report it! What's the name?*'

'*Connolly.*'

'My God!' I glanced round to George. He had sprung to his feet, was trembling violently in every limb. His face was ashen as he stared round at the cabin walls as though expecting to see through them with a vision enhanced to the equivalent of his hearing. 'My God! – did you hear that? Shh!' He stopped my half-uttered exclamation of bewilderment with a gesture of his quivering hand.

That far-off conversation was continuing.

'*What name?*'

'*Connolly – Eileen Connolly. I've got evidence to prove she's an enemy sympathiser.*' The speaker was evidently a little uncertain of the way his action was being received. '*Father was James Connolly.*'

George uttered a wild, inarticulate cry, sank back on to the cabin settee like a man who could no longer stand. His face frightened me.

'*What's happened to him?*'

'*He's dead.*' The voice came with a little ugly laugh. '*The boys burnt him on his own bonfire.*'

'*A Free Stater, you say?*'

'*Sure. It's one less, anyway.*'

'*I'll report the matter. Hold your prisoner for instructions.*' The coldly official voice hinted at disapprobation. '*Your orders stand – you'll proceed to Hamburg and pick up the second consignment. Good-night.*'

'*Good-night.*'

The conversation ceased. There was silence. I turned to George. His face was ghastly, his eyes staring like those of a madman.

'It's her!' he said; 'it's Eileen!'

'But who's Eileen?' I asked, bewildered. 'Not—?' And then it flashed on me – my sister's friend! – Eileen Connolly, of course! – that flirtation of last winter! – the very name of George's yacht! 'Good Lord!' I said, feebly. 'I say, old man, I had no idea there was anything serious between you two.'

'There isn't!' he snapped at me. 'She refused me last winter. My God!' he went on, to himself, 'Eileen! Eileen – in the hands of that murdering scoundrel!' He jumped to his feet, flung the earpieces from his head to the instrument-board, squirmed around the table to the few clear feet at the end of the cabin. I could only watch him helplessly as he paced up and down with his fists pressed hard against his temples. 'Oh, I shall go mad in a minute!'

'But what has really happened?' I said.

'What?' He glared at me impatiently. 'What's happened? You must be an imbecile, man! It's all clear enough. That's a German gunrunner chartered by the Irish Irregulars. Maguire's their agent on board. And the damned scoundrel's been doing a little raiding on his own account.' He griped with both hands in the air. 'If I could only get hold of him!' He took one or two more paces up and down, and then suddenly turned and flared at me. 'My God, Dickie, don't sit there looking like a dummy! Don't you see that something's *got* to be done?' He was like a maniac.

'Yes, but what *can* we do?' I asked.

He stared at me, quietened suddenly.

'God knows!' he ejaculated, and sat down in a sudden lassitude of despair upon the settee. 'God knows!' he repeated, looking around him with hopeless vacuity. 'God knows!' And he buried his face in his hands.

The silence in that little cabin lit by the slightly oscillating oil-lamp continued until I had to break the awful tension.

'George,' I said, as quietly as I could, though I also found myself trembling with the excitement of this crisis that had come to us so suddenly out of the night, 'if we're going to do anything about this, we must have clear brains for the problem. Hysterics won't help us.'

He looked up, sobered. 'You're right, Dickie,' he said. 'We must get our brains to work. I'm all right now.' But he still shook like a man in a palsy, and his face was dreadful in its haggard pallor.

I dug out a bottle of whisky I had brought in my suitcase, poured some into enamel mugs for both of us.

'Now,' I said, 'drink this, and get yourself steady.'

He came to the table, drank it down at a gulp. Then he went again to the wireless set, fitted the receivers again over his ears, listened.

'Nothing,' he said. 'They've shut off. I thought perhaps—' He didn't say what 'perhaps' it was he thought, though I could guess. That girl's terror-stricken voice was still ringing in my ears, too.

He stared at me hopelessly.

'For God's sake, say something, Dickie!' he burst out at last.

'I'm trying to think,' I replied. 'I dare say it's all plain enough to you – but it's anything but clear to me. I'm muddled. There's no doubt, of course, that it was a ship talking?'

'Bound for Hamburg – didn't you hear?' he said, irritably.

'Good. Well – whereabouts is she now?'

He got up, pulled out a chart from the locker. It comprised the southern coast of Ireland. There was a spot on it that had been well thumbed – as George's finger went to it now I had a sudden vision of him brooding alone o' nights in that cabin, bringing himself into a sort of contact with that girl by contemplating on the chart the place where she lived. I said nothing, waited for his words. He glanced up at the cabin clock.

'It's now nine,' he said. 'They put to sea at six. Three hours. She'd be a fast ship to dodge the patrols. Give her twelve knots. On a course for Hamburg, she'd be about here.' He marked a spot on the chart where the fathom-figures were already sparse by comparison with those close to the coast.

'And how far away is that?' I asked.

He got out another chart, placed it upon the table contiguous with the first, measured with a pair of dividers from the indicated point to the Lizard on the second chart.

'About one hundred and sixty miles.'

'She'd pass close here, I suppose?'

'Yes.' He made a mental calculation. 'About ten o'clock tomorrow – if she does twelve knots. About one, if she's only a ten-knotter. But' – he looked up from the chart to me – 'even if she does, how the devil are we going to stop her? We're not a torpedo-boat.'

'No,' I said, filled with a great idea, 'but there are plenty of torpedo-boats at Plymouth. Can't we communicate with the authorities? Surely they would stop the ship?'

His brows puzzled over the suggestion.

'We could talk to the authorities all right,' he argued, 'but I'm sure it would be no good. This is an Irish matter – and who bothers about the Irish these days? I don't think the British Government would interfere. They're only too anxious to let the Irish settle their own affairs. They'd merely suspect us of laying a trap to mix them up in a row – what the Irregulars have been playing for ever since the Free State started.' I wondered at George's knowledge of these matters, and then remembered that he had the best of reasons for close interest. 'Much more likely to send a torpedo-boat round to watch *us*,' he concluded.

It seemed a hopeless problem, and I remarked as much.

'It's maddening!' said George. 'But' – he glared at me as though I were responsible for our impotence – 'somehow or other I'm going to get her off that ship!'

He listened again with the receivers over his head, and I imitated him. There was no sound, except the flapping of ropes overhead thrashing against the mast in a wind that had sprung up without our noticing it.

'It's not commencing to blow, is it?' I queried, uneasily.

George did not answer. All his faculties were absorbed in listening for a sound to come out of the silent night that encompassed our little craft. I imagined that distant ship, one hundred and sixty miles away, throbbing through the dark sea with that girl aboard of her. 'Tie her up!' – that brutal command re-echoed in me. I wondered in what part of the ship she was held prisoner. This thought led me to another. I voiced it.

'I wonder how she – how Miss Connolly got to the wireless?' I said.

George snapped at me.

'Broke loose – didn't you hear that brute say so? I expect she was hiding somewhere round the wireless-house and heard that German fellow telephoning. Directly he went to fetch Maguire she must have dodged in, run to the instrument, and cried for help. Doesn't seem very difficult to me.' He glared at me scornfully. 'I can see her doing it.'

'And why did they telephone in plain speech instead of the usual Morse?' I went on, not rebuffed. I wanted to get a clear picture of the whole thing in my head.

'Oh, don't ask futile, silly-ass questions!' George looked as if he could hit me for this repeated interruption of the silence to which he strained his faculties. 'Why shouldn't they use plain speech? They're on a wavelength that nobody uses – there's no likelihood of anyone listening-in. Can you hear anything now? Of course you can't – and we're on the thirty thousand length. There's nothing doing on it – they've got it all to themselves. They might be talking from one star to another. And unless they use cipher, there's no sense in using Morse. Anyone can pick up Morse. But it's much more convenient to talk straight out – less chance of mistakes. They can talk direct without bothering about operators.' George was irritably voluble once he started to explain, evidently trying to save time by answering in one complete reply any future stupid questions I might be going to put to him. 'You exercise your wits on trying to think of some useful plan, Dickie – and don't worry me with things that don't matter!'

I don't know how long we had sat there in gloomy, baffled silence, when suddenly – I can't recall by what obscure path of thought I had come to it – I found myself contemplating a possibility.

'George,' I said, on an impulse, 'can't you talk to that ship?'

'Talk to the ship?' He puzzled at me.

'Yes.' I was suddenly all excitement. 'Talk to the ship – bluff them – tell them to hand their prisoner over to us. She's passing close by tomorrow morning.'

He jumped up with such impetuosity as to hit his head against the cabin roof.

'By Jove, Dickie,' he cried, 'you've hit it!' He tore off the telephone receivers from his head. 'Keep listening – in case they speak again. I'll start up the motor.'

I stopped him before he had got out of the cabin.

'Wait a minute, George.' I spoke with the confident authority of the accepted strategist. My brain was working rapidly now. 'Don't telephone yet, whatever you do. Those people in Ireland may be listening. We don't want them butting in. Wait till after midnight. They will probably have gone to bed, but there's certain to be someone on duty on the ship.'

'Dickie,' he said, admiringly, 'you're a genius!' He glanced at the clock. 'Two hours.' He looked at me, and the sudden excitement faded out of his face. 'But – man – two hours! How am I going to wait two mortal hours cooped up here? I shall go mad!'

'No, you won't,' I said firmly. I fished a pack of cards out of my suitcase. 'You are going to pour us out a little more whisky – not too much – and play a nice quiet game of piquet with me to pass the time.'

He recovered control over himself.

'All right,' he agreed. 'But keep those earpieces on. We mustn't miss any messages.'

For the next two hours – they seemed an eternity – we sat there, alert for any sound in our ears, playing the most uninteresting game of piquet I have ever sat through in my life. Not a murmur came to us through the instrument. Only the three glowing electric light bulbs reassured us that it was still receptive. Despite the headpieces, we could converse fairly easily, and there were many lapses in our game while we discussed the exact message George was to send to that German gun-runner. In other lapses, too, he told me, shyly and clumsily, something of his feelings for that girl. She was quite evidently the one thing in life that mattered to him. 'It was only natural, of course, that she wouldn't marry a chap like him.' And since he could not have her, he had hidden himself away on his yacht from a world that had become distasteful to him.

'If ever you fall in love, Dickie,' he said, looking at me with honest, simple eyes, 'you'll understand how much a chap wants to be alone. I only invited you because you knew her and could talk about her.'

'Many thanks!' said I, ironically.

Overhead, the cordage drummed against the mast in sharp little puffs of wind.

'I'm afraid you're in for dirty weather tomorrow,' said George, with an anxious glance at the barometer.

We continued our dreary game, forgotten for long intervals in George's halting confidences. 'She'll never have me, of course,' he said, resignedly and miserably.

'Your call,' I reminded him.

We were half through a hand, when suddenly he flung down the cards, sprang from his seat.

'Midnight, thank God! Now we can get busy!'

In a moment he had disappeared up the companion steps. A minute or two later I heard and felt the jerky throbbings of the motor as it whirred and flagged and whirred again in its first uneven revolutions. A nauseating atmosphere of paraffin invaded the little cabin. The motor settled into a steady hum where everything vibrated. George returned, wiping his hands on a bit of cotton-waste.

He went to the wireless, fitted a mouthpiece to a gadget in front of him, manipulated a few more tiny switches. Then, putting on his receivers, he sat down to it again. I drew close, listening also, my heart thumping with excitement.

'Hallo – *Adler!* Hallo – *Adler!*' He leaned forward, spoke into the mouthpiece. I could see perspiration glistening on his forehead. 'Hallo – *Adler!*' He switched to receive the reply.

There was no response. George glanced at me – a quick, scared look. My thought was the same as his. Supposing there was no one listening on board that ship!

'Hallo – *Adler!* – *Adler!* – *Adler!*' He fumbled a little with his tiny levers, altering them a trifle at each utterance of the call. '*Adler!* – *Adler!* – *Adler!*' Again he flicked down the switch which permitted the reply to reach us.

It came – startling us both with its uncanny loudness of direct address.

'*Ja, ja, Adler – ja. Wer ist's?*'

'*Adler* – RHQ speaking. Fetch Mr Maguire. *Herr Maguire bringen!*' He turned to me, whispered: 'What's "at once"?' '*Sofort – augenblicklich,*' I whispered back. '*Sofort – augenblicklich!*' he commanded peremptorily into the telephone.

'*Ja, ja – he sleep – I go wake him,*' came the answer, distinct despite the throbbing of the motor behind us.

George turned to me, the telephone switched off for safety.

'I daren't ask to speak to her, I suppose?'

I shook my head.

'Too risky.'

We waited, through long minutes of silence.

Then again a voice came to us, gruffly, bad-tempered.

'*Hallo – hallo – who's that speaking?*'

George's face went grim and hard as he bent forward to reply. It was as if he felt himself face to face with the owner of that now familiar voice.

'RHQ,' he said, sharply, authoritatively. 'Is that Maguire?'

'*Yes. Is that Cassidy?*'

'No, it isn't.' George, as he explained to me afterwards, tried to speak with the brusque peremptoriness of a wartime 'brass-hat'. 'This is Intelligence speaking. Q Branch reports that you have a prisoner on board – a Miss Connolly. She is urgently required at HQ for examination. A most important prisoner. She is to be handed over without delay. In the meantime, you will be held personally responsible for her safety.'

'*Oh*,' said Maguire – there was a trace of disappointment in his tone – '*shall we put back then?*'

'No.' George made a gesture of 'Heaven forbid!' to me. 'What time do you pass the Lizard tomorrow?'

'*I don't know.*'

'Go and find out from the captain!' George's tone could not have been bettered by the most important of staff officers.

There was a pause in which we listened to nothing but the throb of our own motor working the dynamo.

'*About eleven*,' said the voice suddenly.

'Very well. Tell the captain to go close in to the Lizard. You will be met by a small yawl, flying the signal-flags RHQ. Answer with the same flags, and then send your prisoner aboard of her.'

'*But who am I to hand her over to?*'

'Agents of ours. We've already arranged. All you have to do is to obey your orders.' We were fairly safe in assuming that he would not query what to him would be merely another of the mysterious ramifications of the Irregular organisation. 'Just repeat, please.'

The voice repeated the instructions.

'Very good,' said George. 'Remember – on no account miss that yawl. It might have the gravest consequences – and you will be held responsible. Good-night.'

'*Good-night.*'

There was once more silence.

George turned to me.

'And now to wait till morning!' he said.

We agreed to take alternate watches at the wireless in case any further conversation took place with the *Adler*. George was to have first watch. Utterly wearied by my long day, I rolled myself in a blanket on the settee and was almost instantly asleep.

I woke to find the light of morning pouring through the skylight and George no longer there. The place shook with the throbbing of the motor and the yacht was pitching heavily. I could hear the thud and splash of seas upon the deck. Mystified, I made my way, lurching and scrambling, to the companion stairs, and climbed out. George, still wearing the telephone receivers attached by a long wire which went down into the cabin, was in oilskins, steering the yacht through a smother of spray. No sails were hoisted. She was running on the motor.

'Had to clear out!' he shouted at me. 'Weather's been worsening since dawn. Not a word from the *Adler*. Take the tiller while I get a rag of canvas up. We've got sea-room now and can heave-to for a bit.'

It was a foul morning. A heavy westerly wind drove a grey wrack of mist and rain over a livid green sea that leaped and boiled at us as our motor thudded us through it. The Lizard was a cloudlike mass only faintly to be discerned far astern of us. I kept the *Eileen* bows-on to the sea while George, having put on my head the receivers he had been wearing, struggled with the canvas. At last, close-reefed and helm lashed, the engine stopped, we hove-to for a mouthful of cold breakfast down in the cabin.

He had looked pretty bad the night before. This morning he looked ghastly, dark rings under his eyes, his features pale and drawn. He had not had a wink of sleep. 'No sense in waking you, old chap,' he said. 'I couldn't have slept, anyhow.'

It was an interminable and miserable time waiting for that ship. George lent me a suit of oilskins, and with the receivers on the long wire over my ears I sat on the cabin steps and talked to him while he steered. 'Don't leave them off for a moment,' he had said. 'We mustn't miss a word if they speak. I'll navigate the yacht.'

Directly after breakfast he had set a course for a point just off the Lizard, and then, in heavy blinding squalls of rain, buffeted by a sea that grew worse every minute, we cruised up and down in the vicinity of the spot where we might expect to meet the *Adler*. Our three signal-flags blew stiffly out from the halyards.

'There she is!' cried George, suddenly.

Out of the mist emerged a small and dirty-looking tramp steamer, the black smoke blowing forward over her bows as she wallowed in the following sea. I stood up on the cabin steps to look at her, saw three flags run up to her signal-halyards.

George put the helm over and we came round, beating up towards her, manoeuvring to get under her lee.

'She's stopping,' said George. 'Look! They're getting ready a boat!' I could, in fact, see a little group of figures busy about one of the davits.

George set the motor on at full power, and, pitching and plunging under close-hauled canvas among the waves that crashed over our bows, we came close to her. She had now stopped, was squattering amid creamy-white foam. From her deck men were scrambling into the boat still slung upon the davits.

'There's Eileen!'

George's eyes were quicker than mine, but I also now saw a muffled-up figure hurried by two men along the deck and pushed into the boat. Then they began to lower away. Breathlessly we watched the boat descend on the lengthening ropes, swinging and swaying sickeningly as the steamer lurched and wallowed in the waves. At last it touched the water, was out of sight for a moment, while the davit ropes, released, streamed on the wind.

'Here they come!'

The boat rose on the sea, four oarsmen rowing for all they were worth. Steadily it approached, out of sight one moment, hoisted high the next. In the stern-sheets I could see two figures; one of them, certainly, the girl. George brought the yacht up to the wind, kept her steady with the motor at half-speed.

The boat was a little more than half-way to us when suddenly a voice spoke into my very ear.

'*Hallo, Adler! Hallo, Adler!*'

Intent on watching the approach of the boat from my position on the cabin steps, I had forgotten that the wireless receivers were still over my ears.

'*Hallo, Adler!*'

'They're calling, George,' I cried. 'Calling up the *Adler*.'

He glanced at me, but said nothing. I saw his face set hard as he measured with his eye the distance yet between ourselves and the boat.

'*Ja, ja – Adler! Wer ist's?*' came the reply.

'*RHQ. Where's Mr Maguire?*'

'*Herr Maguire – he vos in boat.*'

'*Boat? What do you mean? I want to talk to him. Fetch him at once. Orders for his prisoner, tell him!*'

The other voice commenced an explanation in broken English.

'Never mind what they're saying,' shouted George. 'Take those things off and stand by to help her out of the boat. I can't leave the helm.'

I did as I was told. The highly interesting conversation between 'RHQ' and the *Adler* ceased for me abruptly. I could only guess at its purport by the figure I saw dart out of the wireless-house and run to the officer on the bridge. A moment later the propeller of the ship began to revolve and I saw a wisp of white steam blow away from half-way up her funnel. The melancholy wail of her siren drifted across to us.

'They've discovered the trick, George,' I shouted, in alarm.

'Never mind,' he said. 'It's too late now. Stand by to pull her on board.'

The boat rose on a wave just in front of us. The men had ceased rowing, were looking back at the ship, puzzled at her signal. The yacht was under way, and the next instant, swung by a deft touch on her tiller, was grinding alongside the ship's boat. A couple of men clutched at the rope we had slung ready alongside. Once more the steamer's siren hooted long and loud. She was moving through the water now, coming straight towards us.

'All right,' I shouted to the man in the stern-sheets. 'There's a destroyer coming up – that's all. She wants you to get back as soon as possible. Pass up the girl.'

There was no time for hesitation with the two boats grinding against one another in that sea. He did the instinctive thing, hoisted the girl upright by main force – she drooped as though she were half fainting – and, seizing the moment, pushed her into my grasp. I dragged her on deck in a tumbled heap.

'All clear!' I shouted, but George had not waited for my word. He set the motor to full speed, put the helm over, loosed the mainsheet ready to his hand. The yacht whipped round like a top. I just heard an angry shout from the boat's crew – and then we were already distant from them.

The steamer was coming for us as though she meant to run us down, sounding her siren in quick and angry blasts.

'Don't matter about them,' cried George, as the yacht flew on before the wind. 'They'll be half an hour picking up their boat's crew – and we're well away. Look after *her*.'

I bent over the girl. She lay huddled upon the deck, staring at me with a face blanched with terror. Then she looked at the man at the helm.

'*George!*' she cried.

Behind us the *Adler* was blotted out in a squall. The *Eileen* changed course slightly, raced, like a living thing, for safety.

# THE KIDNAPPED 'GENERAL'

## By Stacy Aumonier

JIM PARKER and I climbed a stile, walked a hundred yards along a sandy road, and came out on to a glorious common. The common was dotted with clumps of furze, gorse bushes, and beeches. Here and there a sandy pit broke the normal level of the landscape.

The origin of these weekly rambles of ours had been a mutual antipathy to golf. Paying the usual physical penalties of men who lead sedentary lives, we had each been advised by different doctors 'to take up golf'. Now golf may be an excellent game—

I'm not going to argue about it. We did experiment, and lost an enormous number of balls in an incredibly short space of time, but the insistent admonition: 'Ah, old man, what you ought to do is to play golf,' got on our nerves. We met in solemn conclave, and vowed that we would *not* be bullied into playing golf. Eventually we decided to absorb the benefits of golf without undergoing the nervous strain of chasing that absurd little white ball.

We rambled far afield. On this occasion we were just over the border in Buckinghamshire. Jim Parker sighed.

'I wonder they haven't turned this into one of their beastly golf-courses,' he said.

'Touch wood,' I answered. 'We're not across it yet.' But no, there was no golf-course on this nameless common. It was a delightful and deserted spot. We walked across it for half a mile, when we came to a kind of dingle formed by the opening into a long, narrow sand-pit. We were just passing it when Jim remarked:

'There's a queer habitation for you!'

I looked in the direction his stick was pointing, and beheld half-way up the dingle an odd-looking shanty in red and white.

'Um,' I answered. 'Let's go and have a look at it.'

We entered the dingle and approached the rustic dwelling. At first it appeared to be a double-storeyed cabin painted rather gaily, with pots of flowers hanging from a balcony. On closer inspection the truth

193

became apparent. On the lower part of the dwelling, dim but quite perceptible, was the word 'General'. It was an old converted 'General' motorbus! The owner had certainly been rather clever about it. The wheels had either been removed or were buried in the sand. The lower part remained practically intact, except for a surrounding wooden platform. The upper part had been roofed in with timber, and a balcony built out, supported by wooden posts. The woodwork was painted white; there were chintz curtains at the windows, and flowers in profusion in pots and tubs. A gay little dwelling. It was, I suppose, deplorably bad manners for Jim Parker and me to stand there and laugh. But there was something about the association of the 'General' with this obscure and picturesque retreat that was irresistible. We were still laughing when a man came out on to the lower platform and regarded us. He was a tall, strongly-built man, with a neat, pointed brown beard, close-cropped hair turning grey, cold blue eyes, and the skin of a man who lives in the open. He bowed to us gravely, and said:

'Good-morning, gentlemen.'

We pulled ourselves together and responded. Then he added:

'I presume they have sent you from the inn to hear the story of the kidnapped General?'

It was the time of day when it was pleasant to hear that there was an inn in the offing, but we explained that we had come from the opposite direction, and that we were merely explorers, trying to escape from the tyranny of social custom. We had no intention of invading his privacy, but nevertheless the story of the kidnapped General promised an entertaining diversion.

'Come and sit on this bench in the shade,' said the sturdy individual. 'I regret I have no liquid refreshment to offer you, other than water. My medical advisers—' He waved his hand in the direction of the dwelling as though the position explained itself. We all sat down and lighted our pipes.

'My name is McGregor,' he said quite simply – 'William McGregor, but the story of the kidnapped General circles round the character of one Ronny Skinner – Captain Ronald Skinner of the Royal Engineers. Skinner his name was, but the boys called him Grinner. He was that – essentially. He was a man who grinned through life. He grinned through triumph and through disaster. He grinned through battle and when things went wrong. He grinned even when he was bullied or betrayed. He was an irrepressible grinner. A stocky, merry, jolly chunk of a man who never had any luck, except that he always managed to escape with his life. His war record would probably bore you, it was like so many others. He was up to his neck in it the first week, temporarily attached to the RFA as a motor-bike despatch rider. He was a wonderful chauffeur, and could drive any car. You may remember at that time they sent the despatch riders out in couples, one without lights carrying the despatches, the other lighted up as a decoy. Ronny was always the decoy. The war had only been on for five weeks when one night a shell blew his front wheel to pieces. He was captured by the Germans. He spent nine months in a concentration camp at Cassel. I believe he even grinned there. And then one day he and another man escaped, and got across the border into Switzerland. He reported and went back into the line. Does this bore you?'

'Not at all – most interesting,' Jim Parker and I both interjected.

'He was over a year in Belgium, and he grinned when they removed a piece of shrapnel from the fleshy part of his thigh. "Dashed lucky it didn't hit the bone," he said. He grinned when they sent him to Salonika, and kept him hanging about for nine months in a fever-stricken marsh, playing football and cracking lice in his shirt. He even grinned in Gallipoli when the flood came and carried all his kit away, and he was eaten up by savage flying things and poisonous growing things. He didn't grin much when he really got the fever because he was unconscious most of the time. But he grinned when he found himself in a clean bed at Imbros. "Golly! this is fine!" he said, and he hurried up to get well. He wrote to his girl in England. Did I tell you there was a girl? No? Why, yes, there's generally a girl. She was a pretty girl, the daughter of a wealthy provision merchant living quite near here. They were not officially engaged. He had very little money, and he had only just started his career when the war came. The father would not sanction it, and there was no mother. I can't tell you what he wrote to her, or what she wrote to him. But when her letters came he used to grin contentedly, so one assumes the girl was staunch. They sent him off to Egypt after that for another sixteen months and then back to Blighty. Jemini! didn't he grin when he saw the old white cliffs again! But that wasn't for long, mind you. In another month he was in France again.

'The fellow went through everything, right up to the retreat in March 1918, and then the turn of the tide in July. Except for that one wound in his thigh, he was never touched. When the end came he was in the army of occupation on the Rhine, grinning at the Boche housewives, and helping them hang out their clothes to air. And then they demobbed him and sent him back to England. In the meantime his father, who was an architectural sculptor, was ruined by the war. The old man had gone bankrupt, and was living with a married sister, not much better off than himself. There was no one to help the boy.

'When the war started Ronny was nineteen. He was now nearly twenty-five, and he had had no training. He could do nothing except drive a car. London was flooded with unemployed ex-servicemen who could drive cars. He had to get a job anyway, and he went about grinning into all kinds of offices and warehouses. Nobody wanted him. The war was over, and the great need now was economy and retrenchment. The girl was still writing to him, and so he went on grinning and hoping. But the girl's father forbade him to enter the house. He had made a lot of money during the war, and he wasn't going to have his daughter thrown away on a penniless, out-of-work loafer. His God, no, he wasn't.

'I don't know how Skinner eventually managed to get the job he did. Things must have been getting pretty desperate, but one day he blossomed out into a beautiful blue uniform with white piping and large black buttons. He was a driver on a London General motor bus. And there he was sitting up in his box, grinning for all he was worth, responding to the clang of the bell, swerving through the traffic in a most skilful way. The company recognised that he was a good driver, and he was very popular in the yard among the other men. One day he received quite a promotion. There was a special motor bus that used to leave South Hampstead at five minutes to nine in the morning and run express to the City – no stop. They charged a shilling per skull for the trip, and it was very popular amongst stockbrokers and City merchants. The bus was always full, and the men were allowed to smoke inside. There was an express return journey in the evening at five-thirty. To Ronny Skinner fell the great honour of driving this bus. The conductor was a man named Eyles, and they were great pals.'

Mr McGregor paused and looked at us, as though anxious to check the impression of his story on our faces. The impression apparently satisfied him, for he proceeded.

'I am now coming to the amazing crisis of this affair, which, although not kept secret, was never satisfactorily treated, or truthfully chronicled in the Press. It is not altogether surprising. Accounts varied, and when reported they usually appeared so incredible that cautious sub-editors were afraid of their papers being ridiculed. I was one of the few people who knew the truth, and even I never knew the whole truth. I have already told you that there was a woman in the case.

'Ronny Skinner drove that bus every day for just on four months. Every day there was almost identically the same crowd of men. They rushed up a few minutes before it started, with their newspapers and despatch-cases and pipes. They scrambled for the best seats, talked to each other or read their newspapers all the way down. They paid their shillings to the conductor, but no one took the slightest notice of the driver. I don't think any of them would have recognised him. The bus always started to the minute and arrived to the minute. There was never a hitch or an accident of any sort. And yet one day during the first week of July Skinner received a week's notice. No reason was given. The notice merely stated that his services would not be required after the following Friday. The truth was that one of the directors of the company had written to the manager to say that a job had got to be found for a chauffeur who was in his employ, and whom he wanted to get rid of. This story got round. When Ronny heard it, he grinned and said: "Oh, well, I'll have to look out for something else. That's all!" He'd been through the war, you see . . . Now, one thing which affects this story is a letter he received a few days later. It will be better if I don't tell you about this till later on. All that week Ronny grinned, and grinned, and grinned. There never was such a grin. And one night after the last trip, he took Eyles out, and they went down town and did themselves well. The morning of his last day was a glorious summer's day, just like this, gentlemen. The bus was there outside Finchley Road station twenty minutes before its time, with Skinner and Eyles already aboard. The stockbrokers and City merchants began to assemble. It was a very full load, and not only was it full inside and out, but there were five standing up.

'Five minutes to nine – clang went the bell! Grrrh! Grrrh! went the starter. She was off. The stockbrokers started their usual early morning badinage, papers rustled, cigar-smoke curled upwards. Everything was delightfully as usual. The bus went along at its usual pace past Swiss Cottage. A little farther on it took a turning to the right downhill.

'"How provoking!" said the manager of a chain of tea-shops. "I suppose the road is up." Several of the others looked equally provoked, but no one was unduly alarmed. At the end of a few minutes, however, a curious sense of misgiving crept over the company. The bus had taken another turning to the right and *was going back in the direction from which it had come!*

'Exclamations were flying around. "What's the matter?" "Why is he doing this?" "Here, ring the bell." Eyles was appealed to, but he only looked bewildered. He rang the bell. No notice was taken of it. Some of them tapped on the glass, but all they could see was Skinner's face, grinning furiously.

'In five minutes' time they were nearly a mile out of their course, and making for somewhere west of Golders Green. The stockbrokers and City merchants began to get seriously alarmed. It was not only that the bus was out of its course, but it was being driven recklessly. It hardly slackened pace to go round corners. When impeded it dashed along on the wrong side of the road; it lurched through the traffic regardless of consequences. At one corner a policeman held up his hand to stop it, but the bus swerved past him, and at the last second he succumbed to the popular slogan of "Safety First" and leapt out of the way. After that the bus went off the beaten track. It raced along side-streets, and was already getting out into the country. Now, I want you to get firmly fixed in your mind's eye the picture of that company of gentlemen being whirled away from their lawful occasions. I could give you the details of several specific cases. There was, for instance, the chief cashier of a banking establishment in Lombard Street. He had the keys of the strong-room on him. It meant that the bank could do no business until he turned up. There was a barrister who had to defend a fraudulent company promoter at the Old Bailey at eleven o'clock. There was another man with six hundred and fifty pounds in cash in a bag. He had to pay off a ship's company down at Tilbury Docks at ten-thirty. The manager of the chain of tea-shops had to meet his directors at Cannon Street Hotel at ten, and render his annual report. There were innumerable board meeting appointments, business appointments, urgent affairs to be settled that morning, stocks to be disposed of, shares bought, certainties to be acted on, not even bookmakers to be overlooked, and here they all were rushing out into the country captive to the bow and spear (or shall we say wheel and lever?) of a madman!

'Englishmen as a rule have the reputation of taking this kind of adventure philosophically, but there was an element of outrage about this performance which infuriated them. Liberty of the subject indeed! It was the sudden realisation of their utter helplessness which led to a condition of pandemonium. All they could do was to ring the bell furiously all the time, bang on the window, and yell out: "Stop! Stop!" The men on top were no better off. They tried to get at the driver, but he is protected by a solid canopy. They could not even see him. They began to yell out to the passers-by, but the noise was so uproarious and confused, the passers-by merely thought it was some picnic or excursion party cheering, and they cheered back in response and waved their hats. The mad thing got right away into the country. Eyles was being bullied and badgered, but he merely continued to look bewildered and to mutter, "I don't know what's the matter with the chap. *I* can't stop him." Some of the passengers crowded the back-board with the idea of leaping off if the bus slackened its pace at all, but it never went slow enough for that. There was nothing to do but bawl, and yell, and argue. Jagged nerves led to internal dissensions. One man wanted to smash the window and knock the driver over the head, and when it was pointed out to him that such an action would almost inevitably lead to a wreck of the bus, or in any case to a very bad accident, he wanted to fight his opponents, and was only prevented from carrying out his project by being held down on the floor.

'The bus was scheduled to carry twenty-two passengers inside and twenty-four out. In addition to this were the five strap-hangers inside, making a total of fifty-one, of whom only three were women, one being the secretary to the editor of a financial paper, another a clerk in the Admiralty, and the third a lady with a summons to serve on a jury. The three women were neither better nor worse than the forty-eight men. The behaviour of the whole crowd of them can only be described as deplorable.

'I do not propose to weary you gentlemen with a detailed chronicle of the journey. Once well out into the country the grin of Skinner became broader, the venomous expression of the passengers more menacing. All their business and other appointments had gone by the wind. They were collectively buoyed up by the anticipation of some sort of feral vengeance. They gave up hope of any immediate release and simply waited for the mad journey to end, as end it must. They rushed along the country roads, up and down hills, across commons, through little villages, scattering all before them. They ran over three fowls, a cat, and two geese. In one village the left mudguard struck the wheel of a milk-cart and hurled seventeen gallons of good milk into the roadway. These were the only tragedies of note. In other respects it was a perfectly successful and triumphant ride, reflecting the utmost credit on the man at the wheel. Nothing happened, I say, until they reached – this common. Coming round the bend where you gentlemen came, the car began gradually to slow up. When it reached the entrance to this dingle it was travelling at rather less than six miles an hour. Suddenly it turned, swerved to the left, raced up the dingle, and ran nose on into the sand with a pretty considerable bump. And there it stuck, and there it remains to this day.'

Parker and I uttered an exclamation of astonishment, and Mr McGregor paused and critically examined the stem of his pipe.

'And then?' I asked, breathlessly.

'Hats fell off, some of the men were jerked on to the floor, but no one was seriously hurt. When they realised that the tension was over, they scrambled off that bus like madmen. In a body they rushed round and bore down on the chauffeur. Then an unpleasant surprise awaited them. Skinner had already dismounted. He was standing clear of the car, with an insolent grin on his face. In either hand he held a six-chambered revolver. As the crowd approached, he called out: "Stand back!"

'Now, a panic-stricken crowd is liable to do all kinds of unreasonable things, but there is something about the glitter of a shiny little revolver that will steady the most rampageous. The stockbrokers and City merchants, armed with walking-sticks, newspapers, and despatch-cases, drew back and wavered. A white-whiskered City accountant with heavy gold chains hanging over his pendulous stomach bawled out: "What the devil is the meaning of this outrage?" Skinner called out: "Corporal Eyles, get all these men and women into line!" There was then another disconcerting discovery. Eyles appeared from the rear of the bus also carrying a six-chamber. He drew himself up and saluted Skinner. Skinner acknowledged the salute, and then, turning to the crowd, he said: "There are fifty-one of you to two of us. With a little cohesion it would be possible for you to overcome us, but I assure you, before that happened, eighteen of you gentlemen would surely die. My friend, Corporal Eyles, who was with me during the first battle of the Marne, will now get you into line. I will then address you from the top of the bus." A more remarkable sight has surely never been seen on an English common. One of the women became hysterical and ran away, and she was allowed to go. The rest, under cover of Eyles's revolver, were drawn up in two lines of twenty-five. There they all stood, the oddest collection of sizes, and ages, and figures, in top-hats, and bowler hats, and Trilby hats, with newspapers tucked under their arms, holding bags and despatch-cases, and sticks and umbrellas. And the birds were singing overhead, just as they are today, gentlemen, and the bees were humming above the gorse. And there was Skinner, still in his driver's uniform, standing commandingly on the top of that ridiculous red bus. There was a clamour of angry protest from those fifty throats, not unmixed with jeering and even a little laughter. It became necessary for Skinner to flash one of the horrid little revolvers to obtain complete silence. When this desirable condition had been obtained, he spoke in a loud, ringing voice: "Ladies and gentlemen, let me relieve your minds at once of what I know is the dominant fear that possesses you. Eyles and I have not brought you here to rob you. You shall return with all your property intact. Our exploit is rather a spiritual than a material one. We are doing it for your good. If we had not kidnapped you in this way you would now all be grinding and grubbing away in the City, making money, losing it; planning to make it, planning to lose it; contributing nothing of any real importance to the human commonweal. And now here you are on a lovely common with all the day before you, and the sun above your heads. You do not see enough of Nature, you do not learn to live, you do not see facts as they are. You never give yourselves a chance. Your idea of visiting Nature is to motor down to some such place as this, and then create for yourselves a miniature arena of all the petty, fidgeting conditions of your City lives. You stoop over a little white ball. Isn't that the expression you use: 'Keep your eye on the ball'? I ask you, gentlemen, don't keep your eye on the ball, but keep your eye on the stars above you. Soften your hearts, and, when you travel, think of the people who drive you; when you labour and profit and play, think of the people who minister to your necessities. I have mentioned that there are fifty of you to two of us. Well, that represents roughly the percentage of the non-combatant and the combatant element in the Great War. Have you already forgotten that there was a great war, gentlemen? Have you already forgotten Eyles and me? or will you forget us tomorrow? Go, then, all of you, wander the fields and commons, and look into your hearts. Go, and be damned to you!" And without the slightest hesitation, he turned his revolver on to the crowd and fired point-blank into it!

'The panic that ensued is indescribable. The old man with the white whiskers leapt sideways, jumped, and fell into a gorse bush, shot through the heart. No, that is not true, but that was the immediate impression. As a matter of fact he did fall into a gorse bush, but that was only because he caught his foot in a rut. With a wild yell the whole company fled helter-skelter out of the dingle and across the common, followed by shot after shot from three revolvers. None of them was to know that the three revolvers were only loaded with blank cartridges. Was there ever such a sight? Top-hats fell off and were not reclaimed, bags and sticks and newspapers were scattered hither and thither. Someone with experience yelled out: "Scatter! Open out!" They *did* scatter, they *did* open out. Younger men were racing like the wind. Fat old gentlemen were tumbling into sand-pits. The two women were screaming and holding on to the men. The common was dotted with black figures, ducking, doubling, and yelling. No one turned to look back at the assailants. No one saw the broad grin on Skinner's face.'

Mr McGregor again paused, and then he remarked casually:

'We shifted the position of the old bus a little since those days, and removed the wheels.'

'We?' said Parker, faintly.

Mr McGregor seemed hesitating how to shape the crisis of his story.

'I have mentioned the letter,' he continued. 'I cannot tell you the exact contents of the letter. You see, it was one of those sacred missiles – a love-letter, and not written to me. But this I know. It came from the girl – this girl of Skinner's. Her father had died suddenly, and forgotten to make a will. The daughter inherited his fortune. I think there was something in it about a special licence, something about Paris, something about the Italian Lakes. It may seem ironic that a man of Skinner's character should accept money left by a war profiteer. On the other hand, it seemed not altogether unfair that this money should go back to a man who went through it all. I think the girl must have pointed it out to him in the letter. He grinned so happily.'

'But what happened when the stockbrokers scattered?' I asked.

'Everything was so easy after that. A parcel of clothes – two suits – was produced from beneath the front seat of the bus. The two men went behind some bushes in the dingle and changed. You see, the reason why Skinner had come to this particular common was because the girl lived at that little Georgian house just beyond the pine trees over there. You can't see it from here, but it is less than ten minutes' walk away. Thither they both went.'

'But we are still mystified, Mr McGregor,' said Parker, noticing that our informant seemed inclined to leave off. 'How is it that the bus is still here? Why are *you* living here? What action did the passengers take? and the company? Did Skinner get away?'

McGregor sighed pleasantly.

'Ronny Skinner is not the kind of man to go back on a pal. It may simplify things to you, gentlemen, if I tell you that my name is not McGregor – it is Eyles! Skinner did not have the slightest difficulty in getting away. No one recognised in the handsome young man who arrived at Cathay House any resemblance to the driver of the General. They had not even got his photograph, you see, to put in the *Daily Mail*. No one had noticed him very much. That is the advantage of being a nonentity. There was a half-hearted law case between the

passengers and the company, but, as I have said, the majority were
only too anxious to escape the ridicule which the case brought upon
them. As for the bus itself, lawyers argued about it for nearly a year. It
was so damaged that the company was not over-anxious to have it
back. The local Commons Committee tried to make them. In the end
it was found that Cathay House estate – that is to say, the girl – had
certain rights over this particular dingle. The argument went on so
long that the whole thing petered out. About a year later Skinner said
to me: "Eyles, old boy, here is a hundred pounds. You go and make
that bus into a snug little summer retreat, and live there when you
want a change." And Skinner allows me two hundred a year to live
on, for helping him in the exploit. And here I am!'

'You seem a very educated man for a corporal and a bus conductor,' I remarked.

'My experience was almost identical to that of Skinner,' said Eyles.
'When the war broke out I was just leaving Charterhouse. I joined up
as a private. When it was over I was twenty-four, with no training, and
my people had all been ruined. There are lots of others, too, in our
position.'

Parker stood up and shook himself.

'Well, Mr Eyles,' he said, 'I'm sure we are much obliged to you. It's
a most amazing story, and it's delightful to know that it has a happy
ending.'

'Yes,' answered Eyles. 'It has a happy ending. I hope I haven't
bored you. You'll find the inn a quarter of a mile past the crossroads.'

We thanked him profusely and departed. The kidnapped General!
It was a most amazing story. As we tramped along the road we
discussed and dissected the details of it.

'There's one thing that strikes me as queer,' said Parker. 'He said
he was leaving Charterhouse when the war broke out. Say he was
eighteen. When the war was over he would be approximately twenty-
three, so now he should be about twenty-seven. He looks much
older.'

'Yes,' I answered, 'he does, but that may be partly due to the fact of
his hair going grey. A lot of men went prematurely grey during the
war. He looks very wiry and fit.'

'Do you believe it's possible that there wasn't a lot of talk about it in
the newspapers?'

'There may have been some. But you know what it is – one often
reads some fantastic story of that sort, and one simply does not
believe it. It's like freak dinners and explorers' yarns. One thinks
"Yes, yes," and then you turn to see who won the semi-finals at

Wimbledon. It may be true. And then there is a lot in what he says about ridicule. The majority of people would rather be robbed than made to look ridiculous.'

A little farther on we came to the inn. It was a pleasant lime-washed building set back from the road and called 'The Harvester'. A few carters and field labourers were drinking beer in the public bar. We entered and called for bread and cheese and beer. The landlord, a fat, melancholy-looking man in corduroy trousers and a slate-grey flannel shirt, insisted on our having our repast in a little room called a 'coffee-room'. He seemed friendly but not inclined to be very discursive. This may have been due to the fact that his pulmonary organs were obviously in need of repair. He wheezed, and gasped, and panted as he toddled hither and thither in the prosecution of his good offices. It was late and we were hungry, and is there anything in such circumstances so completely satisfying as bread and cheese and good brown ale? We munched in happy silence, both, I believe, still ruminating on the bearded man's strange story.

When we had finished, we called the landlord to settle our reckoning.

Having done so, and come to complete agreement with him that it was a fine day, one of us – I think it was Parker – said:

'That's a queer customer you have out there, living in the motor bus on the common.'

The landlord blinked his eyes, wheezed through the contortions of his breathing apparatus:

'Mr Ormeroyd?'

'No,' one of us answered. 'Mr Eyles, the man in the shanty built on the remains of an old General motor bus.'

The landlord's face twisted into a form that was probably the nearest thing it ever did in the way of a smile. When in control of his voice once more, he said:

'Eyles? Oh, so that's what he calls himself today, is it?'

At this surprising remark we both looked at each other questioningly. Before we had had time to frame any query, however, the landlord added:

'What story did he tell you about the bus today?'

As briefly as possible Parker recounted the story as told to us. When it was finished, we listened patiently to the landlord's lungs. At the end of a few minutes the bellows appeared to give out.

'Oh, so that's the story today, is it? A good one, too. He always tells a different story.'

'What!' I exclaimed. 'You mean to say the whole thing is made up?'

'I wouldn't go so far as that,' said the landlord. 'There is a story right enough, but it has never been told. I've heard tell that if the true story was ever told—'

He stopped and blinked at a small canary in a diminutive cage in front of the window.

We waited for the landlord's version, but it seemed never to be coming.

'Did you say that his real name is Ormeroyd?' I asked at length.

'So I've heard tell,' answered our host. 'They say he is a very clever fellow. He's a very nice fellow, anyway. I've nothing against him. They say he used to be a writer before the war. You know, story-book stuff, tales and so on – made quite a big name, I believe, and lots of money. Now all the stories he invents concern the old bus.'

'But – why? What is the cause?'

'I believe there is a story that, if told, would leave the story you heard today not worth mentioning. D'you remember during the first weeks of the war they sent a whole lot of London motor buses out to help transport the troops? Well, Mr Ormeroyd was a skilful shuvver, and he volunteered, and got the billet to drive one of these buses. I don't rightly know the details. He was only out there six weeks. There was some awful incident – I believe he was the only one of a company saved – he on his old battered bus. There was a score of them buses, men and drivers, and all blown to pieces. It was somewhere in Belgium. He got away back to the lines. But – well, it's a kind of – what do you call it? – you know, got on his nerves, never thinks of anything else. He can still invent his stories, but they always concern the old bus. When they discharged him, I believe he went to one of these here dumps and bought an old battered bus. He says it was his. It may be, for all we know. People up on the common there gave him permission to build his shanty. He lives there, thinkin' and writin'. A clever fellow, they all say.'

'But – hasn't he any friends? Can't they make it better for him?'

'Oh, yes, he's got plenty of friends. The people at the house, for instance – you know Cathay House – they look after him. There's a girl there. They say it is better for him to live as he does – a kind of rest-cure. He's getting better. They say he'll get all right in time. He's got money and his health is otherwise middlin' good. He's a clever fellow. He'll get it all back, they say. His stories get better, you know. I've noticed it. That one about the stockbrokers! Oh, dear! He, he, he!'

Our good landlord was emitting a definite laugh. Moist tears clung to his large, luminous eyes.

'There is a girl, you say?' Parker almost whispered.

'A very nice girl, too, the daughter of Colonel Redding, who owns Cathay House. Why, yes. Oh, I do like that about the stockbrokers!'

The landlord was still chuckling as we took our departure.

When we were once more upon the road, I remarked:

'So this story, also, may have a happy ending, Jim.'

'I hope so,' answered Parker. 'I liked that fellow. I liked the rude things he said about golf.'

And borrowing a match from me, he lighted his pipe; and we continued our pilgrimage.

# AN EVENTFUL DAY
# IN THE LIFE OF
# MISS FAVERSHAM

## By Richmal Crompton

MISS EGERIA FAVERSHAM was the daughter of a dean. He had been rather a thriftless and impecunious dean, and had died without making any provision for his only daughter. He had been fond of a good horse and a good table, and those pleasures are incompatible with large legacies to elderly spinster daughters. The reverend gentleman's own attitude to the question was that the girl should have married. Nor was Egeria herself resentful. She couldn't expect poor Papa to save much money. Poor Papa's income was so small and his needs so many. She had managed to economise greatly for poor Papa in his lifetime by combining in her own person the offices of house-keeper, head-housemaid, and not infrequently cook. Poor Papa, of course, must have his comforts. And as poor Papa said to her on his death-bed, with his wonderful Christian optimism: 'You'll be all right, Geria. There's no money, but you'll be all right. You can teach or marry or something.'

That had been so wonderful of Papa – so cheerful, so thoughtful for others even to the last. Egeria carried that sustaining memory of Papa's last words: 'You'll be all right, Geria,' through life as a kind of amulet against disaster. And she had been very fortunate. She had not married, indeed, but she had taught. A well-to-do couple, Mr and Mrs Smyth-Bruce, who had once been Papa's parishioners, had en-gaged her as governess to their children. It had not been easy work. They were high-spirited children, fond of all sports, and in particular of that sport known as 'baiting Favvy'. And 'Favvy', though eager to impart knowledge, possessed herself only a very small amount of that commodity. Poor Papa had considered education for women a waste of money. It could be spent so much more profitably to all concerned on horses and wines. But Miss Faversham did her best. She loved the children, and she was grateful to her employer, a domineering and rather vulgar woman who treated the cook and housemaids far better than she treated Miss Faversham. That, of course, was natural, because Miss Faversham could be so much more easily replaced. But Miss Faversham was grateful to her employer, as she had been to poor Papa. Like poor Papa, Mrs Smyth-Bruce was 'so kind'.

Miss Faversham, of course, was not attractive. She was one of those women who look fifty before they are thirty – thin, lined, badly-nourished, indescribably prim. She wore spectacles, did her thin grey hair in a tight bun at the back of her head, and wore clothes whose fashions seemed to belong to the last century. Probably they didn't. Any dress Miss Faversham wore would have looked old-fashioned. She was that sort of woman.

When she was fifty-five the youngest Smyth-Bruce had perfected such education as Miss Faversham could impart to her, and Miss Faversham's task in that household was over. She was presented with a large testimonial and a small cheque by Mrs Smyth-Bruce, and went forth gallantly into the world again in search of work. But the world received her coldly. Mrs Smyth-Bruce's testimonial explicitly stated that she was 'hard-working, refined, and conscientious', but it seemed that the world had little need of such qualities. It fought shy of Miss Faversham. It fought shy of her age and her plainness and her old-fashioned appearance. It told her so quite bluntly. And at this stage Miss Faversham more than once quite failed to display that cheerfulness of spirit that Papa had often said was a Christian's first duty (Papa's own Christianity in this respect had reached a high standard), and wept silently and bitterly in the cheap little bed-sitting-room with which Mrs Smyth-Bruce's small cheque provided her. Then (it seemed as if poor Papa must have been controlling her destinies beneficently from above – it made her feel so ashamed of her unchristian despondency) a wonderful thing happened. A brother of Papa's died and left all his money to Miss Faversham – a wonderful amount of money – a thousand pounds. Miss Faversham bought with it an annuity of a hundred pounds. I dare say you say that it isn't possible to live on a hundred pounds a year. But it is. If you know how. Miss Faversham, in her shabby bed-sitting-room in the neighbourhood that Mrs Smyth-Bruce would have called 'slummy', living chiefly on tea and cheap bacon and bread and butter (she always called it 'butter' by courtesy), and still wearing the clothes that she had bought as being 'suitable' to her position as Mrs Smyth-Bruce's governess, was very happy. She was vaguely and expansively grateful to God and poor Papa's brother and Mrs Smyth-Bruce, and for her good fortune. Of course, the other tenants were what Mrs Smyth-Bruce would have called 'not quite—' – except Miss Rossiter. Miss Rossiter was a lady. She was a doctor's daughter. Like Miss Faversham, she had been a governess. She would come into Miss Faversham's room in the evening, where Miss Faversham sat doing crochet work (which she sold to a shop three streets away), take out her knitting (which she sold to a shop in her native town), and would say: 'Well, dear, and how are you getting on?' and Miss Faversham would say in her prim manner: 'Very well, thank you, dear – in my quiet, uneventful way.'

Miss Faversham had just had her lunch. She called it lunch. Lunch sounded so much more refined than dinner, though 'dinner' consisted only of cocoa and bread and butter. She had washed up and put away the things. Her room looked very clean and tidy. Upon the table was the little parcel of crochet work that she had finished the evening before. It was a bright spring day. The sun poured in through the window. It showed up the shabbiness of the little room – the threadbare carpet, the faded table-cloth, the chair whose springs were broken, the discoloured walls.

But Miss Faversham did not notice these things. She was so used to them. She noticed only the transforming brightness of the day, the indescribable sensation of spring in the air, the whiteness of the little clouds in the blue sky, the unusual soaring of her spirits. The first spring day often went to Miss Faversham's head. It made her want to do wild and impossible things, such as dance on the pavement and sing and buy flowers. Quite absurd things, all of them. But she thought she would go out for a little walk, and enjoy the sunshine and fresh air. There'd be no harm in that. She'd take the crochet work to the little shop in the next street but one—

She took her old-fashioned black straw hat from the cupboard and put it on before the little, square, cracked looking-glass that hung on the wall. A very careful observer might have noticed that she took longer than usual to put it on, and that the final result revealed more of her hair than was her custom. Although it was sunny, it was rather cold, so Miss Faversham slipped on her thin black coat, then she took up her little parcel and went down the street.

It was not a 'refined' street. Not even the most highly rose-coloured spectacles would have seen it as a 'refined' street. It consisted chiefly of shops (Miss Faversham's own bed-sitting-room was over a shop) – rather mean little shops, but quite respectable. There was Mr Cripps, the baker, and Mr Frame, the grocer, and Mr

Handley, the draper, and Mr Haslop, who kept the second-hand shop at the corner. Mr Haslop was a little, stooping man with a straggling grey beard and bald head, and dim eyes that peered through large old-fashioned spectacles. Miss Faversham approved of Mr Haslop. She had had certain dealings with him. She had sold him (after great searchings of heart) a silver cigarette case and a gold watch that had been poor Papa's. Mr Haslop had been most respectful in his manner. She felt almost as if she were back again in poor Papa's parish, being looked up to by the less-important inhabitants of Papa's cathedral town.

Miss Faversham walked down the road in the bright sunshine. Had you been there, you would have seen a thin, elderly, dowdy woman, walking very primly with a little mincing step. You wouldn't have known that in spirit she was dancing on the pavement and singing and buying flowers.

Mr Haslop was standing in his doorway.

'Good afternoon, Miss Faversham,' he said. His eyes peered at her through his big round spectacles. Miss Faversham lingered. It was such a beautiful day, and something respectful (was it – was it even admiring?) in his glance joined forces with the beautiful day and made her heart flutter. A faint colour came to her pale cheeks.

'Good afternoon, Mr Haslop,' she said.

He smiled.

'Are you – are you in a hurry, Miss Faversham?' he said. 'I have something in the shop that I think would perhaps interest you.'

She hesitated. She ought, of course, to go straight on. She ought to say she was in a hurry. But – it was such a beautiful day. The flush deepened.

'No,' she said graciously. 'I'm not in any hurry, Mr Haslop. I'd very much like to see it.'

She followed him into the dark shop with a feeling of excitement. It was quite an adventure – quite an adventure to go into this mysterious shop at the invitation of the old man – and such a nice old man. Some faint ghost of sex instinct raised its head in Miss Faversham's dried-up heart – *such* a nice old man – and how nicely he'd spoken to her – almost as if he'd admired her. Again Miss Faversham's heart fluttered.

It was a very dark shop, dark and dusty and cobwebby and piled with what Miss Faversham would have classed as 'rubbish' – great heaps of ornaments and bric-à-brac and small pieces of furniture and boxes, and even a heap of old clothes in one corner – a gloomy refuge of battered and despised household goods, a haunt of mystery. Yet here and there through the gloom came a gleam of something dully rich – the sparkle of jewels from a box on the counter, the sheen of brass and gold from a little table.

Mr Haslop had taken up a piece of carved ivory.

'Now, what do you think of this?' he said. 'Beautiful – eh?'

Miss Faversham looked at it. She was just going to agree when something else caught her eye – an exquisite old vase that stood in the darkest corner of the room.

'That's lovely,' she said, looking at it. She moved nearer.

'It must be very valuable,' she said.

'With its fellow it would be,' said the old man. 'If I get its fellow, they'll be valuable.'

'But how do you get all these beautiful things?' said Miss Faversham, impulsively.

The effect on the old man's face was that of a blind being drawn.

'Oh, they – come sometimes,' he said, evasively, 'sometimes they come.'

Suddenly he moved through the gloom to a door beyond and opened it.

'I was just about to make a cup of tea,' he said. 'I should be honoured if you would join me.'

Miss Faversham's heart more than fluttered. It leapt, it palpitated. The open door revealed a bright little kettle upon a bright little fire. She hesitated – then the spirit of adventure stole down upon her along a ray of spring sunshine through the grimy shop window. She deliberated and was lost; her faded eyes became almost bright. She said, breathlessly: 'Oh, how kind – thank you *so* much!'

As soon as she said the words she regretted them. Have tea alone with a man unchaperoned! She'd never done such a thing in all her life before. But then she'd never been asked to do such a thing in all her life before.

She followed him into the little room and closed the door. Her heart was dancing a war dance in her thin breast. It was terrible. It wasn't respectable. What would Papa have thought? Suppose Papa was watching her now from above. What would he think? Oh, gracious! What *would* he think?

Mr Haslop was pouring the water from the bright little kettle into an aluminium teapot. He had placed a chair for her at the table. She sat down mechanically, adjusting her shabby hat and straying wisps of hair with thin, trembling fingers. The old man went to a cupboard and brought out a tin of biscuits. He opened it, put a few on to a plate, and put the plate on to the table. Then from the same cupboard he brought out two cups.

And as he moved about the room Miss Faversham's agitation vanished. A great wave of pity for his male clumsiness and helplessness came over her. She seemed to lose her identity. She was Woman, mysterious, almost godlike – the genius of the home. He was Man – ineffably forlorn and helpless, a creature of pathos, as strong as a giant, as helpless as a new-born babe. To see him putting out the biscuits and setting the cups on the table sent an almost unbearable pang through her heart. She sipped her tea dreamily. She longed to comfort him in his mysterious male unhappiness, she longed to brush his clothes, to stitch on his buttons, to dust his room. The room was terrible. It couldn't have been touched for weeks. His biscuits were rather musty, but that only increased his mysterious pathos in her eyes.

A glint of sunlight came through the dusty window on to the aluminium teapot. The little room looked cheerful, almost gay. Miss Faversham's shyness and trepidation had vanished. She was actually enjoying it. It was thrillingly mysterious, thrillingly improper. The neglected little room was athrob with romance. Miss Faversham looked across at her host. In her faded eyes was a faint glimpse of sexual provocativeness.

'How do you manage about your housework, Mr Haslop?' she asked.

It was inevitable that she should want to know that. Any woman would have wanted to know that. Nothing appeals to a woman, nothing challenges every spark of sex instinct in her as much as this spectacle of a man living on his own – incredibly, impudently, pathetically independent of her.

'Oh, a woman comes in once or twice a week,' said Mr Haslop. 'For the rest – I manage. Pray let me give you some more tea, Miss Faversham.'

'Your work must be very interesting, Mr Haslop,' she said, almost coyly. Again the veiled look in his eyes behind their great barriers of streaky glass.

'So-so, Miss Faversham. So-so. Only so-so.'

'You seem to get such beautiful things.'

He shot her a quick glance.

'Not often – and they're not easy to dispose of, you know, Miss Faversham, not at all, not at all. People round here can't afford to give their value. It's not an easy life. No, no; not an easy life at all.'

'No life's easy, I suppose,' said Miss Faversham, sententiously, in her best dean's daughter manner.

Somehow that brought back to her the enormity, the terrible impropriety of the whole proceeding. She rose hastily.

'I – I really must go now,' she said in a manner that was half-simpering and half-frightened. 'Thank you so much, Mr Haslop. It was *most* refreshing and *so* kind of you to ask me. No, please don't trouble. I can see myself out – yes, indeed – thank you *so* much.'

She fluttered deprecatingly into the dark little shop and then into the sunny street, murmuring incoherent thanks and farewells. In the street she walked quickly away in sudden panic. Suppose some of the neighbours had seen – what would they think? – what would they say? She'd have no character left. And beneath her panic at the thought was a little thrill of excitement.

At the end of the street she stood still to collect her self-possession. What had she come out for in the first instance? Oh, to take her crochet work to Mrs Blake. She still held the little packet under her arm. She hastened down the street again, passing Mr Haslop's shop with a beating heart and averted head. A gust of wind at the corner nearly knocked her down. As she went she was re-living the moment when she had sat there in that bright, dusty little back-room having tea with Mr Haslop. It had been most improper, but – he'd asked her, he must have noticed her often, he must have liked her, he must have wanted her. Her cheeks flushed, her dim eyes brightened at the thought. No man had ever wanted her – even to share a cup of tea with him – before.

Yes, Mrs Blake was very nice – paid her a shilling each for the doilies as usual. Mrs Blake was respectful in her manner, too, although Miss Faversham was selling crochet work to her. She knew all about Miss Faversham's being a dean's daughter, and she thought a lot of deans. The interview sent Miss Faversham into the street feeling once more calm and respectable.

The only unfortunate thing was that the result was of such short duration. When Miss Faversham reached her bed-sitting-room, she felt as 'unsettled' (that was the word she used to herself) as ever. It was, of course, all the fault of that bright spring sunshine that had first given Miss Faversham the longing to run and dance and sing and buy flowers. It still flooded the little bed-sitting-room. Of course she ought to begin another set of crochet work, but – well, she didn't want to. And that was unusual for Miss Faversham. Usually Miss Faversham did her duty with no regard for her own wishes. But again – it was that mocking spring sunshine that was to blame for it all.

She went to the cracked square of looking-glass and straightened the wisps of grey hair that the wind had blown about her thin, precise little face. She made an effort to obey the call of conscience and sat down with a ball of cotton and her crochet hook. But it was no use. She was back again at once in that little room behind the dark shop. She couldn't do anything but re-live those moments. She couldn't think of anything but that. She fluttered helplessly at the memory. She felt shocked and coy by turns – but always excited. What would he be doing now? She knew quite well. She'd often seen him as she passed the shop in the afternoon. He'd be asleep in the armchair at the back of the shop. He always slept there most of the afternoon. Then the daring idea came to her. She'd do it. She'd slip past him into the back room and dust it for him, and slip out again before he woke. Then – he'd wonder who'd been there – perhaps he'd guess. She put on her coat and hat again and slipped a duster into her pocket. It was quite a new duster that Miss Faversham had not yet marked. As a rule she never used her dusters before she had marked them, but it was rather a dainty little duster; it struck Miss Faversham as looking 'feminine', so she chose it instead of one of the marked ones.

Then, without giving herself time to think over what she was going to do, she went down to the street. The sunshine was brighter than ever. It applauded her idea gaily, it laughed with her in bright friendliness, it filled her with vague longings for adventure and romance.

She went more slowly as she neared the shop. She stood for a moment as though looking in at the window, glancing surreptitiously up and down the street. No one was about. She could see Mr Haslop asleep in the armchair in the darkest part of the shop. The shop door was ajar. The sunshine urged her in, almost pushed her through the door that opened silently and invitingly as soon as she laid her fingers on it. She entered and stood still for a minute, looking around her with beating heart. The shop was very dim and very quiet, but a thousand bright little eyes seemed to watch her enquiringly from the dark shelves and tables. She looked at Mr Haslop. He was sunk in his chair, breathing softly. As she looked at him, the thought of the mysterious helplessness and pathos of his sex surged over her afresh.

She slipped into the back room and began to dust. At once she regretted it. It was full of sunshine, but the sunshine here seemed less sympathetic, less fraught with romance and adventure than it had done in the street. She wanted to run away. But she wouldn't. She'd do it very quickly, now she'd come. She wouldn't be long. She dusted the little sideboard with quick, nervous movements, then stopped, her hand still holding the duster poised in mid-air, her eyes full of horror. There came the sound of movement and talking from the shop. Mr Haslop and another man – they were coming through the shop towards the door. Miss Faversham was for a moment literally paralysed; then she fled, fled without thought or design, in sheer panic terror, through a farther door into – heavens! a man's bedroom. She was in a man's bedroom. It was only by a great effort of will that Miss Faversham prevented herself from fainting then and there. She'd no time to faint. The voices did not stop in the little sitting-room. They advanced towards the bedroom door. Miss Faversham gazed desperately around. She thought of hurling herself dramatically out of the window – anything, anything rather than be discovered in a man's bedroom – she, Miss Egeria Faversham, the dean's daughter. The whole thing was like a horrible nightmare. There was a curtained recess of the little bedroom where hung Mr Haslop's clothes, and into this Miss Faversham darted, just as the door opened. She stood there behind the curtain quivering and moistening her dry lips. Two men entered – Mr Haslop and another younger man, short, thick-set, thick-lipped. Mr Haslop locked the door. 'We'll be safer in here,' he muttered as he did so. They sat down on two chairs at a small table by the door. At first Miss Faversham was too horrified to listen to what they were saying. She was not only in a man's bedroom, but in a man's wardrobe among a man's coats and trousers. The impropriety, the unmaidenliness of it! Never, never, never would she be able to hold up her head again. What would Papa say if he knew? What would the Bishop say, the dear Bishop who sometimes visited Papa and preached such beautiful sermons and was such a good judge of wine? Or – and this was far more to the point – what would Miss Faversham herself say if she were discovered? Waves of successive heat and cold chased each other up and down Miss Faversham's person at the thought. She put her duster to her lips to steady herself, then was terrified at the sound this made.

But the two men were absorbed in their conversation. Gradually Miss Faversham grew calmer in her unmaidenly retreat, and peeped curiously through a little rent in the curtain that was in the neighbourhood of her eye.

Upon the table at which they sat was a vase exactly like the one Miss Faversham had admired in the shop that afternoon.

'Well, it's the one yer wanted, i'n't?' the younger man was saying hoarsely.

'Exactly, exactly,' said Mr Haslop. 'How did you manage it?'

'Just 'appened,' said the other, 'jus' 'appened to see it – the big brown 'ouse beyond the green – I was on a job near there an' I see it through the winder and—'

'What else have you got?' said Mr Haslop.

The other man opened a bag at his feet.

'Valu'bles,' he said; 'antique silver – fetch a lot – an' miniatures – old 'uns – fetch a lot, too; and see here, old cock, you can choke up a bit more'n you did lars' time. It's me runs the risk, not you, mind—'

'No, no,' said the old man, whimpering; 'it's very dangerous trying to sell them – very dangerous indeed. You don't understand how dangerous. And so near where you do your – jobs. I have to let things go for quarter their value—'

'Don't tell *me*,' said the other with a growl. 'I know yer – yer plants 'em off with another fence across London, yer does, an' yer gets yer money's worth an' covers up yer tracks. Wily ole bird. I knows yer. Yer've gotter give me more'n yer gave me lars' time, I tells yer.'

'But I can't, I can't,' quavered the old man. 'You don't understand—'

'I understan' all right. You're a damned miser, that's what you are. Yer *made* of money. Wot's ter stop me bashin' yer over the head an' takin' what I want, eh? Where d'yer keep yer money? That's all I wanter know, yer old miser.'

'Now don't get violent. Please don't get violent,' said the old man. 'I'm a very poor old man. I can only just manage to get along. I pay you more than I can afford for the things you bring me. It's all very dangerous – very dangerous, very dangerous indeed. I take all the risk. I – but bring your bag into the room behind the shop and I'll pay you as much as I can afford to – oh, yes, I'll pay as much as I can afford.'

They went out, the younger man grumbling threateningly. The vase still stood on the little table. Miss Faversham stood behind the curtain, panting. She was horrified. She had entirely forgotten the impropriety of her position. This nice old man wasn't a nice old man. He was a criminal. She'd sat having tea with him, she'd hidden among his coats and trousers, and he was a criminal – a receiver of stolen property. She must get away at once – at once. She was horrified. He was worse than a thief. Miss Faversham felt a wave of righteous indignation surge over her. He'd *stolen* the vase. He mustn't keep it. Just as in the old days she had confiscated the tops with which naughty little boys played in Sunday school, so she instinctively caught up the vase from the table as she passed it on her hurried flight to the door. It wasn't his and he mustn't have it. At the door she paused. The shop was empty. Voices came from the little inner room at the very back of the shop – the young man's voice angry and threatening, the old man's smooth and deprecating. With a shudder, still clasping the vase, Miss Faversham slipped through the dim shop and out into the street. She must get away as quickly as possible. She hastened down the street, and into the street that went off at right angles from it. She must get out of sight of that dreadful place. Then she stood still for a minute to gain breath and consider the situation.

The spring day had been as treacherous as spring days often are. It was now cold, dark, and beginning to rain. The sun which had lured Miss Faversham upon her path of spring madness now deserted her, left her standing at the corner of the street, her hair blown wildly about her, her hat on one side, her prim face full of bewilderment and horror, clasping to her breast the stolen vase. She became suddenly horribly conscious that she was holding the stolen vase. She didn't know what to do with it. She didn't know why she'd taken it. She daren't take it back to the shop. She daren't take it home. She daren't take it to the police station. She felt that any minute a policeman might appear and take her to prison – her, Egeria Faversham, the dean's daughter, the preceptress of the little Smyth-Bruces. Distractedly she looked up and down the dark, empty street. What *should* she do? She swallowed and blinked and clasped the vase still more tightly. It was like a nightmare – only she knew she'd never wake up. She wished she'd died when poor Papa had died and then this terrible thing wouldn't have happened to her. The rain began to fall in no mere tentative sprinkle now, but in a real downpour. That decided Miss Faversham. She couldn't stand there for ever, getting her death. She must get rid of the thing somehow. She must take it back where it belonged. 'The brown house beyond the park.' Of course she knew it – a big, brown-painted house standing in a small garden. Without stopping to think, Miss Faversham set off through the beating rain. It was a long way. She bent down to the wind as she went. Once she passed a policeman and trembled so much that she could hardly walk.

At last she came to the house. She walked up to the front door and rang the bell. And then she realised that she had no idea what she was going to do or say. She turned hot and cold. 'Excuse me, is this the vase that was stolen from your house?' 'Good evening. I've brought back your stolen vase.' No – it sounded dreadful. They'd simply detain her and send for the police. She'd never be able to prove that she hadn't taken it. They'd put her in prison. She'd never live it down. What *would* they think of her – Miss Rossiter, the Smyth-Bruces, the Bishop, dear Papa's spirit? Footsteps were coming towards the door. The perspiration stood out on Miss Faversham's face. With a sudden quick movement she put down the vase on the mat in front of the door and turned and ran – ran with all her might down the darkening drive to the gate. When she was at the gate she heard the front door being opened. She ran down the road, holding up her skirt, her hat flapping over one ear. At the end of the road the silence told her that no one was pursuing her and she slowed down. At the end of the next road the delighted jeering of a street urchin told her that her appearance was such as to attract public attention, and she leant against a wall to gather up her straying wisps of hair, adjust her hat, and take breath.

Ten minutes later she entered her bed-sitting-room.

Twenty minutes later she was sitting by the fire, prim and tidy, just beginning on the next set of crochet work for Mrs Blake.

And just then Miss Rossiter entered, carrying her little bag of knitting.

'May I come in, dear?' she said. 'Have you heard of the terrible tragedy at the little shop at the corner – Mr Haslop's?'

'N – no,' gasped Miss Faversham.

'He's been murdered,' said Miss Rossiter, as she sat down comfortably in the chair by the window. 'They don't know by whom. He was found murdered about half an hour ago. I was passing at the time and stopped. The woman who used to char for him was there. She'd just found a sort of duster in the shop that she said wasn't one of hers' – Miss Faversham gasped – 'but the police didn't seem to attach any importance to it as a clue—' Miss Faversham gulped. Heavens! Suppose she'd taken one of the marked ones! 'The object was robbery. The secret safe that he evidently kept under a board in the floor was broken into and empty—You look a little pale, dear.'

Miss Faversham recovered her self-possession with an effort.

'Only the spring, I think,' she said, faintly. 'These early spring days are rather trying, are they not?'

'And how have *you* been getting on today?' said Miss Rossiter, playfully, taking her knitting out of her little bag.

Miss Faversham looked back over her day. She saw a series of pictures – herself taking tea in Mr Haslop's sitting-room, herself hiding among Mr Haslop's coats and trousers, herself standing in the rain clutching a stolen vase, herself running down an empty street – and she dismissed them as incredible. Things like that simply couldn't have happened to her. She must have dreamed them or read about them. They couldn't really have happened. She took up her crochet work again.

'Oh, very well, dear,' she answered, still rather faintly, 'very well – in my own quiet, uneventful way.'

# MIRAGE

## By W. Somerset Maugham

I HAD BEEN TRAVELLING in Indo-China, and presently made my way to a town in Tonkin called Haiphong, intending from there to take a boat to Hong Kong. It was a dull little place, and I was hard put to it to find anything to do. For the sake of exercise I walked briskly along its straight wide streets. Haiphong is traversed by canals, and sometimes one caught a glimpse of a scene which in its varied life, with all the native craft on the water, was multi-coloured and charming. And there was a canal, with tall Chinese houses on each side of it, that had a curve pleasant to the eye. The houses were whitewashed, but the whitewash was discoloured and stained; with their grey roofs they made an agreeable composition against the pale sky. The picture had the faded elegance of an old water-colour. There was nowhere an emphatic note. But it was none too warm, and I spent most of the day in the café attached to the hotel, reading whatever I could lay my hands on. There was a local paper, a small dingy sheet with stubbly type, the ink of which came off on your fingers; and it gave you a political article, the wireless news, advertisements, and local intelligence. I read it from end to end. But the editor must often have been hard pressed for matter, since he printed daily the name of everyone who had arrived in Haiphong or left it. I suppose he got a list from the *préfecture de police*. Mine looked odd between a Chinaman's and that of a Tonkinese.

On the morning of the day before that on which my boat was to sail for Hong Kong, as I was sitting in the deserted café drinking a Dubonnet before luncheon, the hotel boy came in and said that a gentleman wished to see me. I knew no one in Haiphong and asked who it was. The boy said he was an Englishman and lived there, but he could not tell me his name. The boy spoke very little French, and it was hard for me to understand what he said. I was mystified, but told him to show the visitor in. A moment later he came back, followed by a white man, and pointed me out to him. The man gave me a look and walked towards me. He was a very tall fellow, well over six feet high, rather fat and bloated, with a red, clean-shaven face and extremely pale blue eyes. He wore very shabby khaki shorts, and a stengah-shifter unbuttoned at the neck, and a battered helmet. I concluded at once that he was some stranded beachcomber who was going to touch me for a loan, and wondered how little I could hope to get off for.

He came up to me and held out a large red hand with broken, dirty nails.

'I don't suppose you remember me,' he said. 'My name's Grosely. I was at St Thomas's Hospital with you. I recognised your name as soon as I saw it in the paper, and I thought I'd look you up.'

I had not the smallest recollection of him, but I asked him to sit down and offered him a drink. By his appearance I had first thought he would ask me for ten piastres, and I might have given him five, but now it looked more likely that he would ask for a hundred and I should have to think myself lucky if I could content him with fifty. The habitual borrower always asks twice what he expects to get, and it only dissatisfies him to give him what he has asked, since then he is vexed with himself for not having asked more. He feels you have cheated him.

'Are you a doctor?' I asked.

'No; I was only at the cursed place a year.'

He took off his sun-helmet and showed me a mop of grey hair, which much needed a brush. His face was curiously mottled and he did not look healthy. His teeth were badly decayed, and at the corners of his mouth were empty spaces. When the boy came to take the orders he asked for brandy.

'Bring the bottle,' he said. '*La bouteille.* Savvy?' He turned to me. 'I've been living here for the last five years, but I can't get along with French somehow. I talk Tonkinese.' He leaned his chair back and looked at me. 'I remember you, you know. You used to go about with those twins. What was their name? I expect I've changed more than you have. I've spent the best part of my life in China. Rotten climate, you know. It plays hell with a man.'

I still had not the smallest recollection of him. I thought it best to say so.

'Were you the same year as I was?' I asked.

'Yes. 'Ninety-two.'

'It's a devil of a long time ago.'

About sixty boys and young men entered the hospital every year; they were most of them shy and confused by the new life they were entering upon; many had never been in London before; and to me at least they were shadows that passed without any particular rhyme or reason across a white sheet. During the first year a certain proportion for one reason or another dropped out, and in the second year those that remained gained by degrees the beginnings of a personality. They were not only themselves, but the lectures one had attended together, the scones and coffee one had eaten at the same table for luncheon, the dissection one had done at the same board in the same dissecting room, and *The Belle of New York* one had seen together from the pit of the Shaftesbury Theatre.

The boy brought the bottle of brandy, and Grosely, if that was really his name, pouring himself out a generous helping, drank it down at a gulp without water or soda.

'I couldn't stand doctoring,' he said. 'I chucked it. My people got fed up with me and I went out to China. They gave me a hundred pounds and told me to shift for myself. I was damned glad to get out, I can tell you. I guess I was just about as much fed up with them as they were with me. I haven't troubled them much since.'

Then from somewhere in the depths of my memory a faint hint crept into the rim, as it were, of consciousness as on a rising tide the water slides up the sand and then withdraws, only to advance with the next wave in a fuller volume. I had first an inkling of some shabby little scandal that had got into the papers. Then I saw a boy's face, and so gradually the facts recurred to me; I remembered him now. I didn't believe he was called Grosely then; I think he had a one-syllabled name, but that I was uncertain of. He was a very tall lad (I began to see him quite well), thin, with a slight stoop. He was only eighteen and had grown too fast for his strength; he had curly, shining brown hair, rather large features (they did not look so large now, perhaps because his face was fat and puffy), and a peculiarly fresh complexion, very pink and white, like a girl's. I imagine people, women especially, would have thought him a very handsome boy, but to us he was only a clumsy, shuffling lout.

Then I remembered that he did not often come to lectures. No, it wasn't that I remembered; there were too many students in the theatre to recollect who was there and who wasn't. I remembered the dissecting room. He had a leg at the next table to the one I was working at, and he hardly ever touched it. I forget why the men who had other parts of the body complained of his neglecting the work; I suppose somehow it interfered with them. In those days a good deal of gossip went on over the dissection of a 'part', and out of the

distance of thirty years some of it came back to me. Someone started
the story that Grosely was a very gay dog. He drank like a fish, we
said, and was an awfully gay dog. Most of those boys were very
simple, and they had brought with them the notions they had
acquired at home and at school. Some were very prudish, and they
were shocked; others, those who worked hard, sneered at him and
asked how he could hope to pass his exams; but a good many were
excited and impressed. He was doing what they would have liked to
do if they had had the courage. Grosely had his admirers, and you
could often see him surrounded by a little band, listening open-
mouthed to stories of his adventures. Recollections now were crowding upon me. In a very little while he lost his shyness and assumed the
airs of a man of the world. They must have looked absurd on this
smooth-cheeked boy with his pink-and-white skin. Men (so they
called themselves) used to tell one another of his escapades. He
became quite a hero. He would make caustic remarks as he passed
the museum and saw a pair of earnest students going over their
anatomy together. He was at home in the public houses of the neighbourhood and was on familiar terms with the barmaids. Looking
back, I imagine that, newly arrived from the country and the tutelage
of parents and schoolmasters, he was captivated by his freedom and
the thrill of London. His dissipations were harmless enough. They
were due only to the urge of youth. He lost his head.

But we were all very poor, and we did not know how Grosely
managed to pay for his garish amusements. We knew his father was a
country doctor, and I think we knew exactly how much he gave his
son a month. It was not enough to pay even for the drinks he stood his
friends in the Criterion bar. We told one another in awestruck tones
that he must be getting fearfully into debt. Of course he could pawn
things, but we knew by experience that you could not get more than
three pounds for a microscope and thirty shillings for a skeleton. We
said he must be spending at least ten pounds a week. Our ideas were
not very grand, and this seemed to us the wildest pitch of extravag-
ance. At last one of his friends disclosed the mystery: Grosely had
discovered a wonderful system for making money. It amused and
impressed us. None of us would have thought of anything so ingenious or have had the nerve to attempt it if he had. Grosely went to
auctions – not Christie's, of course, but auctions in the Strand and
Oxford Street and in private houses – and bought anything portable
that was going cheap. Then he took his purchase to a pawnbroker's
and pawned it for ten shillings or a pound more than he had paid. He
was making money, four or five pounds a week, and he said he was

going to give up medicine and make a regular business of it. Not one among those boys had ever made a penny, and they regarded Grosely with admiration.

'By Jove, he's clever!' they said.

'He's just about as sharp as they make them.'

'That's the sort that ends up as a millionaire.'

They were all very worldly-wise, and what they didn't know about life at eighteen they were pretty sure wasn't worth knowing. It was a pity that when an examiner asked them a question they were so nervous that the answer often flew straight out of their heads, and when a nurse asked them to post a letter they blushed scarlet. It became known that the Dean had sent for Grosely and hauled him over the coals. He had threatened him with sundry penalties if he continued systematically to neglect his work. Grosely was indignant. He'd had enough of that sort of thing at school, he said; he wasn't going to let a horse-faced idiot treat him like a boy. Damn it all, he was getting on for nineteen and there wasn't much he didn't know. The Dean had said he heard he was drinking more than was good for him. Cursed cheek. He could carry his liquor as well as any man of his age; he'd been blind last Saturday and he meant to get blind next Saturday, and if anyone didn't like it, he could do the other thing. Grosely's friends quite agreed with him that a man couldn't let himself be insulted like that.

But the blow fell at last, and now I remembered quite well. The shock it gave us all! I suppose we had not seen Grosely for two or three days, but he had been in the habit of coming to the hospital more and more irregularly, so if we thought anything about it I imagine we merely said that he was off on one of his bats. He would turn up again in a day or so, rather pale, but with a wonderful story of some girl he had met and the time he had had. The anatomy lecture was at nine in the morning, and it was a rush to get there in time. On this particular day little attention was paid to the lecturer, who, with a visible pleasure in his limpid English and admirable elocution, was describing I know not what part of the human skeleton, for there was much excited whispering along the benches and a newspaper was surreptitiously passed from hand to hand. Suddenly the lecturer stopped. He had a pedagogic sarcasm. He affected not to know the names of his students.

'I am afraid I am disturbing the gentleman who is reading the paper. Anatomy is a very tedious science, and I regret that the regulations of the Royal College of Surgeons oblige me to ask you to give it enough of your attention to pass an examination in it. Any gentleman, however, who finds this impossible is at liberty to continue his perusal of the paper outside.'

The wretched boy to whom this reproof was addressed reddened to the roots of his hair and in his embarrassment tried to stuff the newspaper in his pocket. The professor of anatomy observed him coldly.

'I am afraid, sir, that the paper is a little too large to go into your pocket,' he remarked. 'Perhaps you would be good enough to hand it down to me.'

The newspaper was passed from row to row to the well of the theatre, and, not content with the confusion to which he had put the poor lad, the eminent surgeon, taking it, asked:

'May I enquire what it is in the paper that the gentleman in question found of such absorbing interest?'

The student, who gave it to him without a word, pointed out the paragraph that we had all been reading. The professor read it, and we watched him in silence. He put the paper down and went on with his lecture. The headline ran: 'Arrest of a Medical Student'. Grosely had been brought before the police-court magistrate for getting goods on credit and pawning them. It appears that this is an indictable offence, and the magistrate had remanded him for a week. Bail was refused. It looked as though his method of making money by buying things at auctions and pawning them had not, in the long run, proved as steady a source of income as he expected, and he found it more profitable to pawn things that he had not been at the expense of paying for. We talked the matter over excitedly as soon as the lecture was over, and I am bound to say that, having no property ourselves, so deficient was our sense of its sanctity, we could none of us look upon his crime as a very serious one; but with the natural love of the young for the terrible there were few who did not think he would get anything from two years' hard labour to seven years' penal servitude.

I do not know why, but I did not seem to have any recollection of what happened to Grosely. I think he may have been arrested towards the end of a session, and his case may have come on again when we had all separated for holidays. I did not know if the case was disposed of by the police-court magistrate or whether it went up for trial. I had a sort of feeling that he was sentenced to a short term of imprisonment, six weeks, perhaps, for his operations had been pretty extensive; but I knew that he had vanished from our midst, and in a little while was thought of no more. It was strange to me that after all these years I should recollect so much of the incident so clearly. It was as though, turning over an album of old snapshots, I saw all at once the photographs of a scene I had quite forgotten.

But, of course, in that gross elderly man with grey hair and mottled red face I should never have recognised the lanky, pink-cheeked boy. He looked sixty, but I knew he must be much less than that. I wondered what he had done with himself in the intervening time. It did not look as though he had excessively prospered.

'What were you doing in China?' I asked him.

'I was a tide-waiter.'

'Oh, were you?'

It is not a position of great importance, and I took care to keep out of my tone any note of surprise. The tide-waiters are *employés* of the Chinese Customs, whose duty it is to board ships and junks at the various treaty ports, and I think their chief business is to prevent opium-smuggling. They are mostly retired ABs from the Royal Navy and non-commissioned officers who have finished their time. I have seen them come on board at various places up the Yangtse. They hobnob with the pilot and the engineer, but the skipper is a trifle curt with them. They learn to speak Chinese more fluently than most Europeans, and often marry Chinese women.

'When I left England I swore I wouldn't go back till I'd made my pile. And I never did. They were glad enough to get anyone to be a tide-waiter in those days, any white man, I mean, and they didn't ask any questions. They didn't care who you were. I was damned glad to get the job, I can tell you. I was about broke to the wide when they took me on. I only took it till I could get something better; but I stayed on, it suited me. I wanted to make money, and I found out that a tide-waiter could make a packet if he knew the right way to go about it. I was with the Chinese Customs for the best part of twenty-five years, and when I came away I wouldn't mind betting that lots of commissioners would have been glad to have the money I had.'

He gave me a sly, mean look. I had an inkling of what he meant. But there was another point on which I was willing to be reassured; if he was going to ask me for a hundred piastres (I was resigned to that sum now), I thought I might just as well take the blow at once.

'I hope you kept it,' I said.

'You bet I did. I invested all my money in Shanghai, and when I left China I put it all in American railway bonds. Safety first is my motto. I know too much about crooks to take any risks myself.'

I liked that remark, so I asked him if he wouldn't stay and have luncheon with me.

'No, I don't think I will. I don't eat much tiffin, and, anyway, my chow's waiting for me at home. I think I'll be getting along.' He got up, and he towered over me. 'But look here, why don't you come along this evening and see my place? I've married a Haiphong girl. Got a baby, too. It's not often I get a chance of talking to anyone about London. You'd better not come to dinner. We only eat native food, and I don't suppose you'd care for that. Come along about nine, will you?'

'All right,' I said.

I had already told him that I was leaving Haiphong next day. He asked the boy to bring him a piece of paper so that he might write down his address. He wrote laboriously in the hand of a schoolboy of fourteen.

'Tell the porter to explain to your rickshaw boy where it is. I'm on the second floor. There's no bell. Just knock. Well, see you later.'

He walked out, and I watched him get into a rickshaw. I went in to luncheon.

After dinner I called a rickshaw and, with the porter's help, made the boy understand where I wanted to go. I found, presently, that he was taking me along the curved canal, the houses of which had looked to me so like a faded Victorian water-colour; he stopped at one of them and pointed to the door. It looked so shabby and the neighbourhood was so squalid that I hesitated, thinking he had made a mistake. It seemed unlikely that Grosely could live so far in the native quarter and in a house so bedraggled. I told the rickshaw boy to wait, and, pushing open the door, saw a dark staircase in front of me. There was no one about, and the street was empty. It might have been the small hours of the morning. I struck a match and fumbled my way upstairs; on the second floor I struck another match and saw a large brown door in front of me. I knocked, and in a moment it was opened by a little Tonkinese woman holding a candle. She was dressed in the earth-brown of the poorer classes, with a tight little black turban on her head; her lips and the skin round them were stained red with betel, and when she opened her mouth to speak I saw that she had the black teeth and black gums that so disfigure these people. She said something in her native language, and then I heard Grosely's voice.

'Come along in. I was beginning to think you weren't going to turn up.'

I passed through a little dark ante-chamber and entered a large room that evidently looked on the canal. Grosely was lying on a long chair, and he raised his length from it as I came in. He was reading the Hong Kong papers by the light of a paraffin lamp that stood on a table by his side.

'Sit down', he said, 'and put your feet up.'

'There's no reason I should take your chair.'

'Go on. I'll sit on this.'

He took a kitchen chair and, sitting down on it, put his feet on the end of mine.

'That's my wife,' he said, pointing with his thumb at the Tonkinese woman who had followed me into the room. 'And over there in the corner's the kid.'

I followed his eyes, and against the wall, lying on bamboo mats and covered with a blanket, I saw a child sleeping.

'Lively little beggar when he's awake. I wish you could have seen him. She's going to have another soon.'

She was very small, with tiny hands and feet, but her face was flat and the skin muddy. She looked sullen, but may only have been shy. She went out of the room and presently came back with a bottle of whisky, two glasses, and a siphon. I looked round. There was a partition at the back of dark unpainted wood, which I suppose shut off another room, and pinned against the middle of this was a portrait, cut out of an illustrated paper, of John Galsworthy. He looked austere, mild and gentlemanly, and I wondered what he did there. The other walls were whitewashed, but the whitewash was dingy and stained. Pinned on to them were pages of pictures from the *Graphic* or the *Illustrated London News*.

'I put them up,' said Grosely; 'I thought they made the place look homelike.'

'What made you put up Galsworthy? Do you read his books?'

'No; I didn't know he wrote books. I liked his face.'

There were one or two torn and shabby rattan mats on the floor, and in a corner a great pile of *The Hong Kong Times*. The only furniture consisted of a wash-hand stand, two or three kitchen chairs, a table or two, and a large teak native bed. It was cheerless and sordid.

'Not a bad little place, is it?' said Grosely. 'Suits me all right. Sometimes I've thought of moving, but I don't suppose I ever shall now.' He gave a little chuckle. 'I came to Haiphong for forty-eight hours and I've been here five years. I was on my way to Shanghai really.'

He was silent. Having nothing to say, I said nothing. Then the little Tonkinese woman made a remark to him, which I could not, of course, understand, and he answered her. He was silent again for a minute or two, but I thought he looked at me as though he wanted to ask me something. I did not know why he hesitated.

'Have you ever tried smoking opium on your travels in the East?' he enquired at last, casually.

'Yes, I did once, at Singapore. I thought I'd like to see what it was like.'

'What happened?'

'Nothing very thrilling, to tell you the truth. I thought I was going to have the most exquisite emotions. I expected visions, like De Quincey's, you know. The only thing I felt was a kind of physical well-being, the same sort of feeling that you get when you've had a Turkish bath and are lying in the cooling room, and then a peculiar activity of mind so that everything I thought of seemed extremely clear.'

'I know.'

'I really felt that two and two are four and there could not be the smallest doubt about it. But next morning – oh, God! My head reeled. I was as sick as a dog, I was sick all day, I vomited my soul out, and as I vomited I said to myself miserably: "And there are people who call this fun."'

Grosely leaned back in his chair and gave a low, mirthless laugh.

'I expect it was bad stuff. Or you went at it too hard. They saw you were a mug and gave you drugs that had been smoked already. They're enough to turn anybody up. Would you like to have another try now? I've got some stuff here that I know's good.'

'No; I think once was enough for me.'

'D'you mind if I have a pipe or two? You want it in a climate like this. It keeps you from getting dysentery. And I generally have a bit of a smoke about this time.'

'Go ahead,' I said.

He spoke again to the woman, and she, raising her voice, called out something in a raucous tone. An answer came from the room behind the wooden partition, and after a minute or two an old woman came out carrying a little round tray. She was shrivelled and old, and when she entered gave me an ingratiating smile of her stained mouth. Grosely got up and crossed over to the bed and lay on it. The old woman set the tray down on the bed; on it was a spirit lamp, a pipe, a long needle, and a little round box of opium. She squatted on the bed, and Grosely's wife got on it too and sat, her feet tucked up under her, with her back against the wall. Grosely watched the old woman while she put a little pellet of the drug on the needle, held it over the flame till it sizzled, and then plugged it into the pipe. She handed it to him, and with a great breath he inhaled it. He held the smoke for a little while and then blew it out in a thick grey cloud. He handed her back the pipe and she started to make another. Nobody spoke. He smoked three pipes in succession and then sank back.

'By George, I feel better now. I was feeling all in. She makes wonderful pipe, this old hag. Are you sure you won't have one?'

'Quite.'

'Please yourself. Have some tea, then.'

He spoke to his wife, who scrambled off the bed and went out of the room. In a little while she came back with a little china pot of tea and a couple of Chinese bowls.

'A lot of people smoke here, you know. It does you no harm if you don't do it to excess. I never smoke more than twenty to twenty-five pipes a day. You can go on for years if you limit yourself to that. Some of the Frenchmen smoke as many as forty or fifty a day. That's too much. I never do that, except now and then when I feel I want a binge. I'm bound to say it's never done me any harm.'

We drank our tea, pale and vaguely scented and clean on the palate. Then the old woman made him another pipe and then another. His wife had got back on to the bed, and presently, curling herself up at his feet, went to sleep. Grosely smoked two or three pipes at a time, and while he was smoking seemed intent upon nothing else, but in the intervals he was loquacious. Two or three times I suggested going, but he would not let me. The hours wore on. Once or twice while he smoked I dozed.

He told me all about himself. He went on and on. I spoke only to give him a cue. I cannot relate what he told me in his own words. He repeated himself. He was very long-winded, and he told me his story confusedly, first a late bit, then an early bit, so that I had to arrange the sequence for myself; sometimes I saw that, afraid he had said too much, he held something back; sometimes he lied and I had to make a guess at the truth from the smile he gave me or the look in his eyes. He had not the words to describe what he had felt, and I had to conjecture his meaning from slangy metaphors and hackneyed, vulgar phrases. I kept on asking myself what his real name was; it was on the tip of my tongue, and it irritated me not to be able to think of it, though why it should in the least matter to me I did not know. He was somewhat suspicious of me at first, and I saw that this escapade of his in London and his imprisonment had been all these years a tormenting secret. He had always been haunted by the fear that sooner or later someone would find out.

'It's funny that even now you shouldn't remember me at the

hospital,' he said, looking at me shrewdly. 'You must have a rotten memory.'

'Hang it all, it's nearly thirty years ago. Think of the thousands of people I've met since then. There's no reason why I should remember you any more than you remember me.'

'That's right. I don't suppose there is.'

It seemed to reassure him. At last he had smoked enough and the old woman made herself a pipe and smoked it. Then she went over to the mat on which the child was lying and huddled down beside it. She lay so still that I supposed she had fallen directly asleep. When at last I went I found my boy curled up on the foot-board of the rickshaw in so deep slumber that I had to shake him. I knew where I was, and I wanted air and exercise, so I gave him a couple of piastres and told him I would walk.

It was a strange story I carried away with me.

It was with a sort of horror that I had listened to Grosely telling me of those twenty years he had spent in China. He had made money, I do not know how much, but from the way he talked I should think something between fifteen and twenty thousand pounds, and for a tide-waiter it was a fortune. He could not have come by it honestly, and little as I knew of the details of his trade, by his sudden reticences, by his leers and hints, I guessed that there was no base transaction that, if it was made worth his while, he jibbed at. I suppose that nothing paid him better than smuggling opium, and his position gave him the opportunity to do this with safety and profit. I understood that his superior officers had often had their suspicions of him, but had never been able to get such proof of his malpractices as to justify them in taking any steps. They contented themselves with moving him from one port to another, but that did not disturb him; they watched him, but he was too clever for them. I saw that he was divided between the fear of telling me too much to his discredit and the desire to boast of his own astuteness. He prided himself on the confidence the Chinese had placed in him.

'They knew they could trust me,' he said, 'and it gave me a pull. I never double-crossed a Chinaman once.'

The thought filled him with the complacency of the honest man. The Chinese discovered that he was keen on curios, and they got in the habit of giving him bits or bringing him things to buy; he never made enquiries how they had come by them, and he bought them cheap. When he had got a good lot he sent them to Peking and sold them at a handsome profit. I remembered how he had started his commercial career by buying things at auctions and pawning them.

For twenty years by shabby shift and petty dishonesty he added pound to pound, and everything he made he invested in Shanghai. He lived penuriously, saving half his pay; he never went on leave because he did not want to waste his money. He would not have anything to do with the Chinese women, he wanted to keep himself free from any entanglement; he did not drink. He was consumed by one ambition, to save enough to be able to go back to England and live the life from which he had been snatched as a boy. That was the only thing he wanted. He lived in China as though in a dream; he paid no attention to the life around him; its colour and strangeness, its possibilities of pleasure, meant nothing to him. There was always before him the mirage of London, the Criterion bar, himself standing with his foot on the rail, the promenade at the Empire and the Pavilion, the picked-up woman, the serio-comic at the music-hall, and the musical comedy at the Gaiety. This was life and love and adventure. This was romance. This was what he yearned for with all his heart. There was surely something impressive in the way in which during all those years he had lived like an anchorite with that one end in view of leading again a life which was so second-rate and vulgar. It showed character.

'You see,' he said to me, 'even if I'd been able to get back to England on leave I wouldn't have gone. I did not want to go till I could go for good. And then I wanted to do the thing in style.'

He saw himself putting on evening clothes every night and going out with a gardenia in his button-hole, and he saw himself going to the Derby in a long coat and a brown hat, and a pair of opera-glasses slung over his shoulder. He saw himself giving the girls a look over and picking out the one he fancied. He made up his mind that on the night he arrived in London he would get blind – he hadn't been drunk for twenty years; he couldn't afford to in his job, you had to keep your wits about you. He'd take care not to get drunk on the ship on the way home. He'd wait till he got to London. What a night he'd have! He thought of it for twenty years.

I do not know why Grosely left the Chinese Customs – whether the place was getting too hot for him, whether he had reached the end of his service, or whether he had amassed the sum he had fixed. But at last he sailed. He went second-class; he did not intend to start spending money till he reached London. He took rooms in Jermyn Street, he had always wanted to live there, and he went straight to a tailor's and ordered himself an outfit. Slap up. Then he had a look round the town. It was different from how he remembered it; there was much more traffic, and he felt confused and a little at sea. He went to the Criterion and found there was no longer a bar where he had been used to lounge and drink. There was a restaurant in Leicester Square where he had been in the habit of dining when he was in funds, but he could not find it; he supposed it had been torn down. He went to the Pavilion, but there were no women there; he was rather disgusted, and went on to the Empire; he found they had done away with the promenade. It was rather a blow. He could not quite make it out. Well, anyhow, he must be prepared for changes in twenty years, and if he couldn't do anything else he could get drunk. He had had fever several times in China and the change of climate had brought it on again; he wasn't feeling any too well, and after four or five drinks he was glad to go to bed.

That first day was only a sample of many that followed it. Everything went wrong. Grosely's voice grew peevish and bitter as he told me how one thing and another had failed him. The old places were gone, the people were different, he found it hard to make friends, he was strangely lonely; he had never expected that in a great city like London. That's what was wrong with it. London had become too big; it wasn't the jolly, intimate place it had been in the early Nineties. It had gone to pieces. He picked up a few girls, but they weren't as nice as the girls he had known before, they weren't the fun they used to be, and he grew dimly conscious that they thought him a rum sort of cove. He was only just over forty, and they looked upon him as an old man. When he tried to cotton on to a lot of young fellows standing round a bar, they gave him the cold shoulder. Anyway, these young fellows didn't know how to drink. He'd show them. He got soused every night; it was the only thing to do in that damned place, but, by Jove, it made him feel rotten next day! He supposed it was the climate of China. When he was a medical student he could drink a bottle of whisky every night and be as fresh as a daisy in the morning. He began to think more about China. All sorts of things that he never knew he had noticed came back to him. It wasn't a bad life he'd led there. Perhaps he'd been a fool to keep away from those Chinese girls; they were pretty little things, some of them, and they didn't put on the airs these English girls did. One could have a good time in China if one had the money he had. One could keep a Chinese girl and get into the club, and there'd be a lot of nice fellows to drink with and play bridge with and billiards. He remembered the Chinese shops, and all the row in the streets, and the coolies carrying loads, and the ports with the junks in them, and the rivers with pagodas on the banks. It was funny; he never thought much of China while he was there, and now – well, he couldn't get it out of his mind. It obsessed him. He began to think that London was no place for a white man. It had just gone to the dogs, that was the long and short of it, and one day the thought came to him that perhaps it would be a good thing if he went back to China. Of course it was silly; he'd worked like a slave for twenty years to be able to have a good time in London, and it was absurd to go and live in China. With his money he ought to be able to have a good time anywhere. But somehow he couldn't think of anything else but China. One day he went to the pictures and saw a scene at Shanghai. That settled it. He was fed up with London. He hated it. He was going to get out, and this time he'd get out for good. He had been home a year and a half, and it seemed longer to him than all his twenty years in the East. He took a passage on a French boat sailing from Marseilles, and when he saw the coast of Europe sink into the sea he heaved a great sigh of relief. When they got to Suez and he felt the first touch of the East, he knew he had done the right thing. Europe was finished. The East was the only place.

He went ashore at Djibouti and again at Colombo and Singapore, but though the ship stopped for two days at Saigon he remained on board there. He'd been drinking a good deal, and he was feeling a bit under the weather. But when they reached Haiphong, where they were staying for another forty-eight hours, he thought he might just as well have a look at it. That was the last stopping-place before they got to China. He was bound for Shanghai. When he got there he meant to go to a hotel and look around a bit and then get hold of a girl and a place of his own. He would buy a pony or two and race. He'd soon make friends. In the East they weren't so stiff and stand-offish as they were in London. Going ashore, he dined at the hotel, and after dinner he got into a rickshaw and told the boy he wanted to find a girl. The boy took him to the shabby tenement in which I had sat for so many hours, and there were the old woman and the girl who was now the mother of his child. After a while the old woman asked him if he wouldn't like to smoke. He had never tried opium, he had always been frightened of it, but now he didn't see why he shouldn't have a go. He was feeling good that night, and the girl was a jolly little thing; she was rather like a Chinese girl, small and pretty, like an idol. Well, he had a pipe or two, and he began to feel very happy and comfortable. He stayed all night. He didn't sleep. He just lay, feeling very restful, and thought about things.

'I stopped there till my ship went on to Hong Kong,' he said. 'And when she left I just stopped on.'

'How about your luggage?' I asked.

For I am perhaps unworthily interested in the manner people combine practical details with the ideal aspects of life. When in a novel penniless lovers drive in a long, swift racing car over the hills and far away, I have always a desire to know how they managed to pay the bill; and I have often asked myself how the characters of Henry James in the intervals of subtly examining their situation coped with the physiological necessities of their bodies.

'I only had a trunkful of clothes. I was never one to want much more than I stood up in, and I went down with the girl in a rickshaw to fetch it. I only meant to stay on till the next boat came through. You see, I was so near China here, I thought I'd wait a bit and get used to things, if you understand what I mean, before I went on.'

I did. Those last words of his revealed him to me. I knew that on the threshold of China his courage had failed him. England had been such a terrible disappointment that now he was afraid to put China to the test too. If that failed him, he had nothing. For years England had been like a mirage in the desert. But when he had yielded to the attraction, those shining pools and the palm trees and the green grass were nothing but the rolling sandy dunes. He had China, and so long as he never saw it again he kept it.

'Somehow I stayed on. You know, you'd be surprised how quickly the days pass. I don't seem to have time to do half the things I want to. After all I'm comfortable here. The old woman makes a good pipe, and she's a jolly little girl, my girl, and then there's the kid. A lively young beggar. If you're happy somewhere, what's the good of going somewhere else?'

'And are you happy here?' I asked him.

I looked round that large, bare, sordid room. There was no comfort in it and not one of the little personal things which one would have thought might have given him the feeling of home. Grosely had just taken on this equivocal little apartment, which served as a house of assignation and as a place for Europeans to smoke opium in, with the old woman who kept it, just as it was, and he camped, rather than lived, there still as though next day he would pack his traps and go. After a little while he answered my question.

'I've never been so happy in my life. I often think I'll go on to Shanghai some day, but I don't suppose I ever shall. And, God knows, I never want to see England again!'

'Aren't you awfully lonely sometimes for people to talk to?'

'No. Sometimes a Chinese tramp comes in with an English skipper or a Scotch engineer, and then I go on board and we have a talk about old times. There's an old fellow here, a Frenchman who was in the Customs, and he speaks English; I go and see him sometimes. But the fact is I don't want anybody very much. I think a lot. It gets on my nerves when people come between me and my thoughts. I'm not a big smoker, you know; I just have a pipe or two in the morning to settle my stomach, but I don't really smoke till night. Then I think.'

'What d'you think about?'

'Oh, all sorts of things. Sometimes about London and what it was like when I was a boy. But mostly about China. I think of the good times I had and the way I made my money, and I remember the fellows I used to know and the Chinese. I had some narrow squeaks now and then, but I always came through all right. And I wonder what the girls would have been like that I might have known. Pretty little things. It's a great country, China. I love those shops, with an old fellow sitting on his heels smoking a water-pipe, and all the shop signs. And the temples. By George, that's the place for a man to live in! There's life.'

The mirage shone before his eyes. The illusion held him. He was happy. I wondered what would be his end. Well, that was not yet. For the first time in his life, perhaps, he held the present in his hand.

# PYJAMAS

## *By Sinclair Lewis*

I HAVE A PREJUDICE against being taken for a ride, with the muzzle of an automatic jabbed into my ribs, so I shall not reveal the name of the city where all this happened. But as I was saying: I was going out to California, last winter, to recover from my operation.

The first two nights out from New York, I slept fairly well; but on the third night, when the train was barging into the farther reaches of the Middle West, I could not drop off for more than an hour at a time.

You know how it is.

Here you have been asleep and happy, dreaming that your Almanacs Inc. stock has again risen to twenty and that the flexible flapper with whom you danced at the Wishepamoggin Country Club, last Tuesday, really liked to dance with you, and did not regard you as the father of a large family.

Just then, the driver decides to have some fun with the passengers.

'Aw, what the deuce!' he thinks. 'Here's all these millionaires, bankers and magazine editors and advertising men and college presidents, all of 'em sleeping in their nice warm beds, while I'm here alone at the wheel of the doggone train, having to change from third to low and jam on the brakes every time a farmer tries to beat the game at the crossing. What an idea! Perfectly ridiculous! *Formez les bataillons!* While they're sunken in their gilded and decadent slumbers, they'll find there's one guy awake on this train!'

So, as the train quivers into the next station, the driver slams on the brakes, the train comes up all standing, and the passengers awake with a low moan.

Anyway I did, that night, and with frequency.

Oh, for the wings of a dove, that I might describe how a Pullman lower berth feels and looks and smells, especially smells, when you can't sleep and you turn on the light! In the polished wooden bottom of the berth above you, you are reflected as a cotton doll. Your face looks long and melancholy, and your pyjamas look – well, they look

241

like wrinkled pyjamas. As the train starts again, sometimes mooing and sometimes yowling and all the time clanking sardonically, 'Awful luck, awful luck, awful luck, awful luck,' it begins to sway, and the coat and vest and trousers which you have carefully draped on the hanger against the green curtain sway with it.

'Oh, ho!' my coat seemed to sneer, as it flipped a horribly empty sleeve at me. 'All these years since you bought me at Moe's Piccadilly Suiterie, Climb One Flight and Save $16.75, I've wiggled and bent at the elbow when *you* wanted me to. Not no more! No sir!' And it frivolously waved its sleeves at me, while the trousers trembled with derision.

I ignored them. Nor was I shaken by realizing from time to time that the train had run off the track, caught fire, hit a motor-car, and just generally taken to playing leap-frog. No! In fact, the only thing that disturbed me was the steady, methodical, earnest snoring of the man across the way. The train clanked and belched and fell upon points with a furious desire to destroy them, but all through this clamour, the subdued and inescapable snoring went on: 'Garrhh – *woof*; garrhh – *woof!*'

But I got so lonely in my cell that I welcomed even this proof that there was still one soul, besides myself, living in the world of roar and chaos.

European observers of America have asserted that the trouble with our sleeping-cars is that the curtains which divide you from the person opposite – who may be a safe-blower, a suicide, a member of the W.C.T.U., or any equally dangerous stranger – do not give you sufficient privacy. The fact is (for, if you take European or British views of America exactly by opposites, you will be reasonably accurate) that the trouble with our sleeping-cars is that they are too confoundedly private.

To lie awake in a Pullman berth is to be stranded on a desert isle without the coconuts. If you are travelling by steamer, you can always go up and be thrown off the bridge by the first officer. In New York there are, day and night, coffee-stall waiters, policemen, evangelists, authors, and bartenders with whom you can talk. In Sauk Center, you can all night long find the bus-driver awake at the Palmer House. But on an all-Pullman train, there is apparently no one awake besides the porters, and the driver, who would almost certainly not welcome you if you climbed over the coal into his cab and demanded: 'Do you think that Humanism will give a more austere purpose to American letters?'

So I reconciled myself to reading a detective story.

It was a nice story.

I reached the page which ran:

'A shot rang out on the mysterious nocturnal stillness of Lime-house, and smote Detective-Inspector Simms full on the forehead. "Oh, I say," grumbled the inspector, quietly brushing the bullet away, "that isn't quite the thing, now, is it?" Then he started. He looked keenly at the Chinaman who had shot him. He said, gently: "Now, Wung Chung Lug, we mustn't have any more of this. Not at all sir. Because I perceive that you are not Wung Chung Lug, nor even Wung Chung Low, but none other (although, sir, in disguise) than Brig.-Gen. Sir Arthur Plupe, DSO, KCMG, RAC." '

Oh, hang it. I'd read this story before!

Of course! I remembered Sir Arthur Plupe, who from time to time appears in the tale disguised as Wung Chung Lug, as Lady Bonaventure, as Michael Arlen, as Hiram P. Scroug of Indianola, Indiana, and even, though less convincingly, as Brig.-Gen. Sir Arthur Plupe. He hasn't done the dirty deed, though good old Inspector Simms (CID), who happens to be on the spot, has seen him rising with a bloody Malayan dagger from beside the corpse of his uncle, Lord Neversly.

And I had nothing else to read. The man across the way was now snoring, 'Urf – *keek*!' and the car-wheel beneath me was not only obviously flat, but likely to fly to pieces, wrecking the train. I tucked on my slippers, pulled my dressing-gown over my pyjamas. And they were lovely pyjamas, given to me by my wife at Christmas, checkered green and yellow, while the dressing-gown, fortunately warm, as it was now February, was a nice domestic thing of pink wool edged with mauve cord.

I swayed, occasionally catching at the curtains for support but not awakening more than two or three apprehensive old maids, along the dim tunnel to the smoking-room. It was occupied by the porter, and a row of shoes, which looked curiously collapsed and dead. I lighted a cigarette and glanced doubtfully at the porter. He had taken one look at me, and his expression suggested that the one look would last him the rest of his life.

'Cold evening,' I said, politely.

'Yes, it's pretty cold if you have to get out at every station and help off passengers!'

The way in which he said 'passengers' made them sound in a class with blow-outs, rent-bills, sticking typewriter keys, and the *Xenopsylla cheopis* Rothsc., or Indian Rat Flea.

I tried again: 'Interesting work you have, isn't it!'

'It isn't.'

'I mean, meeting such types, varieties, and assortments of people.'

'I don't.'

'But going to so many places.'

'Why?'

'Oh, yes – well, I see.'

'And furthermore—' He raised his eyes from a light natty gent's Oxford, looking at me for the last time, and observed: 'And furthermore, my name is not George, the train is not on time, I do not know how late we shall be when we reach Denver, the train for Colorado Springs goes out of the same station, I am not a graduate of Hampton, and the city through whose miserable suburbs we are now staggering is—'

And having named the scene of the strange and romantic adventures that I am going to chronicle, he threw down the natty tan shoe as though he did not care for it, changed into a blue jacket, and left me as one without sorrow.

'I see,' I said.

The train stood in the huge city station. The blinds of the smoking-compartment were up, and uncouth workmen stared in at me, at my dressing-gown and pyjamas, with crude unworthy derision. The little room was filled with the smell of dead cigar-smoke, perished soap, and that curious mouldy smell of sleep. Cold though it was, I ventured out into the vestibule for a slice of fresh air. The snow had sifted under the bellows between vestibules and lay in a pointed streak across the iron-bordered linoleum. I shivered, and was going in, when I saw a restaurant just across the platform.

There was no one in it save one male waiter, who would presumably not be demoralized by my pyjamas, and a cup of coffee would be good. I knew that in the city of Blank the train must stop for at least ten minutes. I might have asked the porter standing down beside the train, but I felt that he and I weren't pals any more.

I flashed across the platform, the wind very playful with my ankles. As I guzzled the coffee I was horrified to see my train pulling out.

'Don't worry. Just shunting. They're taking on the coach from Kansas City,' the waiter comforted me.

'Does it come back on the same platform?'

'Usually. Plenty of time, anyway, brother.'

I almost burst into tears at again being recognized as a human being, and ordered three doughnuts. I even ate part of one of them, and then, feeling like a man of the world, I stepped briskly out on the platform.

And I had forgotten the name and number of my Pullman!

The Pullman now drawn up in front of the restaurant was christened 'Phagocytosis'. I had a notion that my car had been named 'Werewolf', or 'D'Annunzio', or 'Hoboken', or something like that, but this certainly looked like mine, and the porter looked like mine, at least, he was coloured and had a blue coat with silver buttons. He was yelling: 'All aboard!'

I leaped up – I don't know what the thing is that they use for circus bears to sit on and for Pullman passengers to climb on, but that was what I leaped up on to, and, shivering, I pranced into the grateful warmth of the train.

Just inside I met the conductor, growling, 'Tickets!'

'My tickets are in my berth – Lower 4.'

'Say, what's the big idea? There's no one in Lower 4. Hasn't even been made up.'

'I'm probably on the wrong car. Anyway, my berth is Lower—'

The conductor looked at the chart which the Pullman conductor held out to him. 'Then if you're in the only other Lower 4 on this train, your name is "Mrs S. Bezelius and daughter". Maybe you're them. You look like it! Say, what train do you think you're on?'

'The Platinum Plate Limited to 'Frisco, of course.'

'It isn't called " 'Frisco of course." It's called San Francisco. And this is the train for Jefferson City. You'll find your train back on platform seven. Except that it'll be gone when you get back there!'

He pulled the communication cord like an executioner.

'Hey, you can't put me off this train – not out into the night!' I tried to make my voice warm and menacing, but it skidded, just as the train seemed to rear up its whole length from the track and come down with a bang.

The conductor said nothing. The Pullman conductor said nothing. The porter said nothing. The three of them merely propelled me toward the vestibule, in the tomby stillness that had settled down on the train.

But plenty was said by the passengers. Heads popped from between berth curtains, and a bald man informed a lady who had done up her hair in a small fishing net: 'He's a pickpocket; they caught him stealing watches.' With a cold swiftness, like going down a shoot-the-chutes in November, I was galloped through the vestibule, down the steps, into the city of outdoors – and already the train was heaving ahead.

Busy though I was at shivering, I appreciated what a lot of loneliness and cold there was everywhere, and what a distinct lack of warm berths. I was at the end of what seemed to be a million miles of railway yards, all in a modernistic picture – rails that swooped on me like rays of light, red lanterns and green arc-lamps overhead, and the headlights of locomotives that grew in size as though they were exploding, and pointed me out as though they were hunting me down. And all this illumination made the spaces between signal boxes and tool-shacks only the darker and more forlorn.

Impossible to find my train there, even if it had not gone. I must get help somewhere in the city. And I knew no one in the city!

Stumbling across lines, just leaping aside as a vast train burst by me, viciously cold at ankle and wrist and throat, I found a watchman's fire with no one near it just at the moment, and stopped a second to explore my pockets. I possessed, besides the dressing-gown and pyjamas and slippers, a now deflated cigarette package with three wrinkled cigarettes, a quarter-box of matches, three doubtful hand-kerchiefs, ever so many cigarette-crumbs in one pocket, and a piece of paper which, anxiously examined over the fire, was discovered to be a note from our maid: 'Cabbages will be delivered tomorrow.'

It was my sole identification.

And I found five cents – my change after coffee and doughnuts at the restaurant. I looked at it with proud wrath, and hurled it on the ground. Instantly I realized what a huge sum five cents could be. With it I could get a telephone call, a newspaper, or in many Five and Ten Stores, a beautiful tin fire-engine with three red firemen. I scrabbled in the dust and cinders, savagely, ready to kill any interloper; I found the five cents and slipped it into my pocket. And thus I came on something even more important: a particular filthy strip of old Brus-sels carpet. I shamelessly stole it, wrapped it about my bare head and neck, and started for the wilderness beyond the railway yards.

I fell into a few ditches, crawled through a fence, came to a street given over to malt-and-hops emporia, pool-rooms, and lunch-rooms, whose refined neon signs of '*Eats*' mocked my misery. I flickered along it. I had never moved quite so fast. At home, in Pelham, that highly select and indeed I may even call it exclusive suburb of New York, I have been rebuked by my wife, and by Edgar, my eldest son, for my sloth in playing tennis. Sometimes when a ball is returned to me, I miss it entirely, because I am thinking of the relationship of Walter Lippmann to St Polycarp, or the curious use of the squint in the tower of the Cistercian Abbey at Monmonkshire. But this night I could have received and returned a ball six times before my opponent even knew it had been served, so rapid was I.

After perhaps two miles of greyhound coursing, without having time to ask myself just where I was going, I emerged into a district of respectable houses which, because they had two-car garages with cement drives and 'we've subscribed to the Red Cross' placards in the windows, showed that they belonged to the kind of people I knew. I felt safe! Here I would surely find people who would appreciate the fact that I had been graduated from Ohio Wesleyan University, that I had an automatic oil furnace in Pelham, that I had lost money in the panic, like the most aristocratic people, and that my Uncle Herbert was one of the best eye, ear, nose, throat, heart and skin specialists in Trenton, NJ. They would recognize me as one of their own class, and rescue me.

My connexion with the medical profession through Uncle Herbert made me stop hopefully in front of a delightful residence of brown-stained shingles, with a carved greystone porch, on which was a tasteful illuminated glass sign, lettered: 'F. Smilie Lockland, MD, Phys. & Surg.' Though it was now (I guessed) five in the morning, there were lights in the lower storey, indicating that someone was about.

'Good old F. Smilie!' I muttered. 'There he is, succouring the unfortunate! What sort, type, or category of public-spirited citizen soars superior to a phys. and surg.? Perhaps even now he is operating on some poor sufferer, saving his life, being meantime utterly regardless of his own comfort, slumber, and rest. I'll go right in!

'Smilie will know the name of Dr Herbert Smouse. Perhaps he will have read Uncle Herbert's paper on "Comparative Fees in 567 Cases of Tonsillectomy", in the *New Jersey Medical Aegis*. Anyway, his house will be warm. O God, I hope it'll be warm! I must ask him how many square inches of radiation he allows to the cubic foot of room contents. Ought to be more.'

But putting these carping criticisms aside – who was I to criticize a man like Smilie Lockland? – I strode up the sandstone steps, and rang the bell. I threw my vulgar scarf of Brussels carpet into the areaway as the door opened – just three inches.

Of the lady who was peering out at my dressing-gown, I enquired pleasantly: 'Is the doctor at home?'

'He is not!'

'Then I'll just come in—'

'You will not!'

Oh, Smilie, Smilie! F. Smilie Lockland, Phys. and Surg.! Where was your oath of Hippocrates then? What of your little woman who shut out from the temple of healing a man who had lost even his Brussels carpet? For she slammed the door, and I stood alone and frigid; and when I looked I couldn't even find the carpet.

I wavered down the street that a moment ago seemed so friendly and secure. Bah! I knew now what it was that made Bolsheviks! These cursed bourgeois, snug and warm in their beds, with every luxury at hand – sweaters, overcoats, radiators, cans of soup, hot-water bottles, aviators' helmets, wristlets, volumes of Eddie Guest, kerosene stoves, blankets, comforters, gin, woollen socks and fire insurance – while I staggered amid them, cold . . . Cold!

Not till now had I seemed criminal, but as dawn crept grey over the tin roof of the Pentecostal Tabernacle, I was forced into disorderly conduct. I had turned from Maplegrove Street, in which lived that treacherous and abominable F. Smilie Lockland, into the great thoroughfare of Lindbergh Avenue. A young lady alighted from a tramcar. She had a grey suit and amiable ankles. Later reports indicate that she was a telephone supervisor, coming home from a late trick. She said 'Good-night' in ever so jolly a voice to the tram conductor, and frisked up Lindbergh Avenue, till she looked back at me. She gave a slight squeal, and started to run.

I was nettled. Look at it this way! Ask any man in the Men's Club of the Fourth Baptist Church, Pelham, NY. Ask any pastor, grocer or bootlegger who has ever dealt with me. Am I a man to go out deliberately and get into pyjamas and dressing-gown and ruffled hair at five-thirty a.m. and chase down Lindbergh Avenue in the city of Blank, or in any other city, merely to frighten a respectable female telephone supervisor?

I was annoyed. I hastened after her.

Or ask—

I have concealed this from you till now, because I do not like to boast, but the fact is, I am no *Babbitt*. I am a literary man. I do the financial, religious, and baseball notes for the *Employing Steamfitters' Chronicle*. And you may freely ask any man on the staff of the *Chronicle* if I am likely to pursue phone girls down Lindbergh Avenue, or even Maplegrove Street!

Speeding after her merely to explain this, I saw a large policeman emerging from a hallway. He glanced at Miss X (as by now I was romantically calling her); he glowered at me, and unwound his truncheon. I slipped into an alley, into a cross-alley, out into a street, and found myself again in front of the house of Dr F. Smilie Lockland.

The glass sign and the lights on the ground floor still beamed their treacherous greeting. They *had* to save me! Again I burred at the bell; again I faced the small and resolute lady who had previously thrown me out.

'I must see the doctor! I want to pay my bill before I leave town!'

She threw wide the door. 'Oh, do come in!' she crooned, and as I hurled myself into that deliciously warm hall, as I sat shivering on an oak bench, which, though unpadded, was wonderfuly free of conductors, policemen, and telephone girls, she remarked: 'You may pay me, if you wish. The doctor is out. It won't be necessary for you to wait for him.'

'I see. Rather! I take it, as you are waiting up for him so late – and what would we do without our devoted little women? – that he is out on a case of incomparable importance. And when he comes home, you will soothe his jangled nerves, you will heat up a tasty cup of soup with your own fair hands—'

'I will not! I'll tell him what I think of him! With my own fair tongue! The old hellion is out playing poker! And now, about that little bill of yours—'

'Madam, I may as well confess all.'

I did, starting with my boyhood in Oklahoma, briefly describing my bonny little Swiss chalet in Pelham and the better trains to take into New York, making harsh but justified remarks about conductors from Jefferson City, and emphasizing the importance of my Uncle Herbert.

She was a crisp, brainy little woman, Mrs Lockland, though too hard on poker. As I finished, indicating that she could prove the truth of my extraordinary story by looking for the strip of Brussels carpet in her own areaway, she snapped:

'Who – or whom – do you know in this city?'

'No one.'

'Whom could you phone in New York?'

'None of them awake yet.'

'Couldn't you rouse this wife of yours that you talk about, and the three children in Pelham, wherever that is?'

'Alas, they have gone off to my Aunt Ethelberta's, in Maine, and you know how it is with Aunt Ethelberta – she never would have a phone.'

'What if I wired the conductor of your train? He would have your name on his chart.'

'I'm afraid not. I got my ticket at the last moment. I don't think he has my name.'

'I see. Well, I'll think of something. But I mustn't keep you here. You'll be more comfortable in the sitting-room.'

She led me into the cheerful, warm little room at the end of the hall. 'Just sit here while I get you something hot to drink,' she murmured. I sat down gratefully; she rippled out – and I heard her lock the door!

She hadn't trusted me! Still, it was warm there, and I dozed until I heard violent voices in the hallway. It was the doctor's lady, greeting her returning husband.

'So, this is the time of morning you choose for getting home! Of course, it doesn't matter what happens to me! You sit there all night, drinking and smoking and gambling, while I wait up for you and get visited by a lunatic!'

'Well, thass all right with me! Whiss lunatic was it – your father, or your brother Joe?'

'Will you listen to me? Will you kindly try – just *try*; that's all I ask – will you kindly just try to clear your brain from the horrible fumes of smoke and liquor and try, at least *try*, to understand that while you were away, playing your games of chance – and I hope that, for once, you didn't lose, although you will never learn not to try to fill an inside straight, and your weakness for a four-card draw amounts to antinomianism – and me, I wait up for you, and a lunatic breaks in here and I have him locked up in the sitting-room right this minute!'

The doctor's voice sounded as though he were shocked into sobriety.

'I'll go in and treat him right away. Do you know anything about his credit?'

'I do not. First he says he comes from Pelham, Massachusetts, then that he's from New York. He says he's a steam-fitter. He says a conductor bounced him off a train for eating doughnuts. He's wearing frightful pyjamas and bathrobe now, but he says that ordinarily he wears a Brussels-carpet suit.'

'Clear case to me – *dementia praecox*, with an Oedipus complex. Before I see him I'd better get the cop on the beat, in case he turns violent.'

I heard nothing more for ten minutes. In my anguish, I had smoked my last three cigarettes; and in my rage I had torn up and flung upon the floor the note which I had found in my pocket, asserting that the cabbages would be delivered tomorrow. I went berserk. I burst the tame bonds of civilization. I had always been known for politeness and my love of dumb animals, but suddenly I was a ferocious demon. I wanted a smoke, and I was going to get it. All the urbanity of Pelham dropped from me, and I surged through the sitting-room, looking for cigarettes. Ruthlessly I opened the drawer of the centre table, rummaged behind books, and even fearlessly searched the pockets of a medical-looking alpaca jacket hanging on a peg.

And there I found two more cigarettes.

I was sitting with a proud, cold expression on my face, puffing a cigarette and trying to remember that, after all, I came from Pelham and that I needn't stand any rudeness from these hicks in the city of Blank, when the door was unlocked and the doctor edged in, followed by a particularly loutish policeman.

'Good-morning, my boy!' the doctor said airily. He was a small man, with a shredded moustache, and his voice sounded as his moustache looked. 'I'm sorry to have kept you waiting. I've been out on a serious case.'

'Lost much?'

'I don't know what you're talking about!' He turned and winked at the policeman with a wink that said: 'You see? Absolutely batty!'

'Listen!' I raged. 'My uncle is Doctor—'

Oh, I don't know why I got so mixed up. But my night of wretchedness, and the codfish eye of the policeman, confused me, and in horror I heard myself saying: 'My uncle is Doctor Sherbert House – I mean, Doctor Shoubert Hearse – I mean, Doctor Werbert Wows, of Jersey, New Trenton—'

The policeman sat on a small gilt chair, like a bullfrog perched on a goldenrod, and looked as though he was wondering whether to start beating me up now. He stared, and panted fatly. Yet he annoyed me less than the sprightly doctor, who sprang at me and, with those offensively soothing tones we use to children, breathed: 'Just a moment, my dear fellow, just a lit-tle mo-ment!'

Before I could resist, he had got a thermometer into my mouth, had seized my wrist, and was counting my pulse. But I saw that there was something wrong with this picture; and in that muffled voice which comes from talking with a clinical thermometer in your mouth, I gurgled:

'Look here, Doc! You think you're timing my pulse by your wrist-watch. You aren't! You haven't got a wrist-watch on! You lost it playing poker tonight – last night – well, anyway, whatever the darn' night is – and you're still too lit to notice it! And unless you help me out I'll tell your jolly little wren of a wife about the watch!'

He yanked the thermometer from my mouth, looked slyly at the policeman, saw that by now he had gone gently to sleep and whispered: 'I think you're already recovering from your attack. Your case is not *dementia praecox*. You're just a nice old maniac depressive. That will be ten dollars, please.'

'It will not be ten dollars, please! His name is Doctor Herbert Smouse – my uncle, I mean – the well-known stomach, cardiac, boil and diet specialist; and I would have told you before if you hadn't come in scaring me with a cop who would have been in the butcher business if he'd been a little brighter! But I mean: I want you to listen to my story.'

'That's so. I did sell that watch to Ramon Cowley, for nineteen bucks, and bought another stack, and then Doc Murphy had four aces. Go on!'

I told all.

The doctor said pleadingly, 'Don't you think it might be amnesia?'

'Certainy not!'

'Just a little amnesia? Listen, brother, I'd love to have a case of amnesia. *You* know. For the County Medical Society!'

'No. No amnesia.'

'Not the least little bit? But when you pinched the Brussels carpet – there must have been some amnesia then!'

'Not the slightest. The Smouses have been in every war for the Republic, but they have never had amnesia.'

'Oh, all right! You needn't shout at me! After all, this is my house. (It is, isn't it? Of course it is! There's my copy of *Lady Chatterley's Lover*. I *told* Doc Murphy I'd get home safely!) But I mean: Do you often see spots, flecks or dazzling particles before the eyes?'

'Well, flecks, yes. But no spots or particles.'

'I see. Do you hear strange noises? Do you have a feeling that you are being persecuted? Do you feel that a person, or persons, unknown are plotting against you? Do you sometimes fancy yourself as a person of vast power, as Mussolini, Will Hays, or a golf pro?'

'Why—'

'Exactly! Do you fear high places, enclosed places, rapid transit, or eating oysters?'

'Why, sometimes—'

'It's a perfect case! Officer!' He woke the resentful policeman. 'Just keep watch a moment, will you, while I find a timetable.'

The doctor returned, sprightlier and more detestable than ever.

'I find,' he said, 'that your train will reach Omaha in twenty minutes. I always like a sporting chance . . .! And then you to rebuke me about the wrist-watch! Just to show you, I'll phone to Omaha and get the conductor of your train, and see if your pocket-book, tickets, pants, copy of detective story, *et cetera*, are actually in Lower 4 on the car called – what did you say its name was?'

'Oh, heavens, how can I remember—'

'Loss of memory! Do you often find yourself leaving umbrella, packages, wife, *et cetera*, in strange places?'

'I do not! I was saying: That Pullman. Its name was either "Pickerel" or "Marcel Proust", or "Piquenaba" or – *you* know! Have the conductor look in all Lower 4s.'

'Right, my dear fellow! If you'll just wait!'

The policeman spoke the first words of which he had been capable:

'Say, Doc, I gotta ring in at the station.'

'Splendid, Officer, splendid! Come with me!'

The two of them vanished – that is, the lively little physician vanished, though the policeman trundled out more like an ice-wagon. I heard the door locked. I paid no attention. By this time I was hardened to crimes, and sneering quietly I got busy rifling the room.

I found one more cigarette, perhaps a trifle flattened, which had been used as a bookmark in *Minor Diseases of the Duodenum*, and behind Cruden's Concordance I found a flask with three hundred c.c. of gin, which helped greatly. When the door was opened again, I was gravely reading an article on 'Opisthorchis Felineus and Its Relationship to Hepatic Distomiasis', in the *Journal of the American Medical Association*. Perhaps I flatter myself, but it seemed to me that I looked as a man with a Swiss chalet in Pelham should look.

Yet I was disturbed.

For Dr Lockland returned, not with the elephantine cop, but with three other officers, headed by a police lieutenant.

'Ah, there you are my lad! Always reading, ain't you?' said the lieutenant.

I tried to ignore him. I looked at the doctor.

'Did you get the conductor?'

'I did.'

'Did he have my ticket, money, identification papers, *et cetera*, to say nothing of my trousers? God, how I want my trousers.'

'He did not. He looked at all the Lower 4s on the train, and they were either empty or filled with people who were not you.'

'None of them were not me? Not one? I mean—'

The lieutenant and his three hirelings exchanged dirty glances with the doctor, and moved nearer to me, fingering their revolvers in a suggestive way.

Later, checking up, I found that the doctor and the conductor were right. Someone had stolen everything from my berth, though whether it was a passenger or a station loafer is one of the mysteries that will go down unsolved in history, along with the Man in the Iron Mask, the Dauphin, and the reason why many quite respectable persons regard O. Henry as a better writer than P. G. Wodehouse.

'Well, it doesn't matter,' I purred, trying to calm their savage breasts. 'It's about the right hour now, with the difference in time, for someone to be at my office in New York who'll recognize me.'

'Huh? In those pyjamas?' crowed the lieutenant.

'By my voice, idiot!'

'Did you say I was an idiot?'

'I did not!'

'Didn't he say I was an idiot?' the lieutenant demanded of his gallant squad.

'Sure he did, Lieut.! Shall we soak him?'

'Let's get him to the police station first.'

'Besides,' groaned the doctor, 'who would pay for a long-distance call to New York? Speaking of that, brother—I didn't quite catch the name—my call to Omaha will cost you just one dollar and thirty-eight cents. If it wouldn't inconvenience you, my dear fellow?'

From my pockets I brought out the dirty handkerchiefs, a matchbox with seven matches still left in it, and my nickel. 'That's all I've got, though I think the strip of Brussels carpet is still in your areaway.'

The doctor was a good sport. He didn't take the nickel.

The lieutenant did, on the way out.

'Well, we'll just shoot him along to the police station,' said the lieutenant, 'and we'll have him up before the insanity commission today, and tomorrow he'll be in the pecan pen playing mumble-de-peg with Julius Caesar. Come along, laddie, but say, Doc, shall I put the wristlets on him? Is he likely to get dangerous?'

'No,' said the doctor, and it seemed to me that his voice was a little weary, a little sad. 'No, not dangerous. But—my wrist-watch, and now one dollar and thirty-eight cents! Take him along!'

At the telephone in the shiny oak hallway, the lieutenant rang up the station for the police car, and from the station he apparently received exciting information.

He leaped up from the telephone, ordering his battalion: 'Hold him tight!' He bellowed at the doctor: 'You got the wrong idea about this baby! Say, he's one of the most dangerous homicidal maniacs who ever landed in this town! The station has a report about him—yuh, same guy, all right—tall, skinny fellow, washed-out brown hair, dressed in foolish-looking pyjamas and bathrobe, chased Mrs Clairmonteneaux O'Kelly, night telephone supervisor, age thirty-seven, address corner Lovers' Lane and Kloefkorn Street, down Lindbergh Avenue, early this morning, utterin' horrible shrieks, also profanity and blasphemy. Same fellow! Hold him, boys!'

Till then, the officers of the law had regarded me, and my costume, with what might almost be called contempt. Now, as they gripped my arms, as one of them handcuffed me, I felt that they viewed me with the respect of terror.

I saw it all. I had been too meek!

I kicked wildly. I shouted: 'Woe betide begone whurrip!'

And the lieutenant, whose tones had been so cold, said almost caressingly: 'Yes, yes, ole fellow, it's all right. Come ridey-ridey and see nice movies?'

They dragged me out, fondly promising to take me to the zoo, to a speakeasy, to the Museum of Assyriological Antiquities, to the county waterworks, and every other historical sight in Blank, while I kept on kicking as much as an enfeebled constitution and a worn pair of slippers permitted, and shrieking in what I flatter myself must have been an admirable imitation of a maniac: 'Yale beat Harvard! Two-and-six down on the income tax! Let's keep the red flag flying! It's minion, I tell you, minion, not nonpareil! Reach for a sweet! Yes, lettum look for the body under my garage!'

It was curious with what a sweet, quaint, idyllic respect they treated me as they sat about me in the patrol wagon.

'Cigarettes!' I shouted.

'I think he wants a smoke!' sighed one policeman.

'By thunder, Montmorency, I believe you are right! I'll see you get your sergeant's stripes for this!' said the lieutenant nervously. He hastily lighted a cigarette and handed it to me.

Did you ever try smoking a cigarette, at seven of a cold winter morning, in a police car, clad—I mean I was clad, not the car—in dressing-gown and pyjamas, with handcuffs on your wrists? You haven't missed much.

And in the meantime to have to keep up the maniac talk, muttering: 'Twelve cents per kilowatt hour! Snoutrage! And yet—Hey, you demons, listen or I'll treat you the same way! Yurrup! Gloo! Steel handcuffs—non-rustable handcuffs—down on heads of cops and killum. And yet I'm sorry I killed that reater—meter—that teeter-fleeter—I mean that meter reader. Killedum! With can-opener! Blap! Under garage floor! Cement, see?'

At the police station I was escorted in as delicately as if I were Aimee McPherson or King Carol.

'Morning, Lieut.,' murmured the desk sergeant.

The lieutenant panted: 'I've got the Lindbergh Avenue murderer! And I've found that he's committed two as yet, or so, from my knowledge of criminal annals, I should imagine, undiscovered murders. The corpses will be discovered buried in cement under his garage, in Pelham, New Jersey!'

'Is that a fact?'

'Surest thing you know!'

'This means promotion for you, Lieut.!'

'It oughta! I took him single-handed. Where are the reporters? Well, call 'em up, and when they come, tell 'em I have nothing to say, and then see I see 'em. Now where shall we put this poor guy? Nice fellow, but a chronic murderer.'

'Well, we ought to put him in a superior cell, then, don't you think?' said the sergeant. 'You know we've had to haul in Zoppo Innocente, and he's in Cell de Luxe A.'

'You mean—' I have never seen a man more angrily shocked than the lieutenant. 'You mean you've pinched Zoppo? What a swell-elegant bunch you've turned out to be! I suppose you know that Zoppo is merely the most disingenuous gunman west of Chicago? I suppose you know that this will mean the deduction, or shall I say subtraction, from the forces of civic righteousness of you and me, and a lotta guys I won't mention, but God help the mayor and the chief!'

'Sure, Lieut., I know! I know! By the way, if I may be permitted an apparently tangential remark, I should highly appreciate it if you would pay me the twenty-five hundred bucks you owe me. I would like a nice funeral. But here's what happened. The flying squadron caught Zoppo just as he was bumping off Maggiociondolo Grattaculo, though old Zop was as careful as ever. He'd took Maggi for a ride out to Sycamore Plaza. But just as he was shooting, along comes an inspection party of the Anti-Saloon League, with Bishop Skaggs and Ermen Plush in it.'

'Not Plush?'

'The same.'

'Not the guy that devotes all he makes from the sale of cocktail-glasses, shakers, and juniper flavour to the Prohibition cause?'

'Yes. Him. They'd been out on a big crusade. They'd found a coloured gal that was selling beer. She'll get six years. They'd found a GAR veteran with a half-pint of gin. He'll get life! So they was going along, all cosy about five this morning, when they see Zoppo bumping off Maggi. And just then the flying squadron comes along, and the Bish and Plush complains and so Inspector Pjysky had to pinch Zop and bring him in. And believe me, Lieut., Zop is plenty sore. Of course he'll get off in the magistrate's court, this morning, but he says he's lost ten cargoes of beer, and he'll have all our badges. Now listen, Lieut. You say this poor mutt you just brought in is a regular killer?'

'Worst I ever saw! Murdered a train-conductor, a reater-meader – I mean a meter deeder – and six cops and a Pullman porter – oh, yes, and a dealer in Brussels carpets, and has 'em all buried under his garage.'

'Neat place for it, too! Now listen, Lieut.! What about putting him in the same cell with good old Zoppo? Maybe he'll bump him off for us.'

'Serg., you said it!' the lieutenant chanted; and to me: 'Lookit, baby! We're going to put you in with a bad guy. Get me? Baddy, baddy mans! Here's my pocket-knife. If that guy insults you, just 'tend to him, like a good fellow. He hates Brussels carpet, that fellow – get me?'

The handcuffs were snapped off my wrists. I was thrust into a large cell, simply furnished with two beds, a portrait of Hoover, and an expanding bookcase. From his pillow, one of the most extraordinary men imaginable raised his head – a small, square man, very swarthy. Black curly hair almost met his eyebrows, and those eyebrows were a straight menacing line. He glared at me, and slapped his hand against his trousers-pocket, muttering something like: 'Well, baby, Maggi?'

'Certainly not! I am no Maggi!' I sat down aloofly on the other bed.

'Well, hootahell are you?'

'My name is Harry S. Smouse, I am a literary gentleman.'

'Oh! Drunk?'

'Certainly not.'

'Bootlegging?'

'Certainly not. Have you a cigarette?'

'No, dear heart! What do you think of bootleggers?'

'They are, I suppose, a low and perhaps even dastardly race.'

'Did you say dastardly?'

'I did.'

'Oh. My mistake.'

And the extraordinary man flopped over and went to sleep.

I tried to, but so distraught was I that I was still wide awake when a deputation of three gentlemen peered into our cell.

'Good-morning. I am the mayor of the city. Is Mr Zoppo Innocente awake? No, he seems asleep,' said the roundest of the three.

'Are you a friend of his? May I venture to introduce myself? The sheriff,' the second observed to me.

'And I,' said the third with a friendly smile, 'am secretary to the Fly-screen Adjusters and Porch-painters' International Brotherhood, Local seventeen, and I wish to be the first to say that Zoppo has been very much misunderstood indeed. I have ventured to bring him – you both, rather – some cigars, some scarcely worn copies of the *Atlantic Monthly*, and some nice oranges.'

Mr Innocente snorted awake, looked at them sharply, groaned disgustedly, and slammed his pillow over his head.

'Good-morning, Mr Innocente!' they chorused.

'Won't you have an orange?' begged the labour organizer.

Mr Innocente sat up and threw his legs over the side of his bed in one quick, alarming motion. 'Get out of here!'

'A nice orange. Fresh!'

'Beat it!'

'Look here, Zoppo,' begged the mayor. 'You know it was all a mistake. You'll be let out this morning. Honest, old fellow, we had to do something to pacify Ermen Plush.'

'Did you have to run me in like I was some vagrant? Get out!'

Mr Innocente sank his face sobbingly in his pillow. The stately delegation departed, and three young men in sweaters and plus-fours appeared before our bars.

'Zoppo! Hey, kid! Zop!' crooned one of them, in a tender voice.

Mr Innocente looked up. He seemed displeased. 'How you bozos get here?' he sighed.

'Just sweetened the serg., baby,' murmured the centre one. 'Give our regards to Maggiociondolo, will you?' And drawing an automatic revolver from a pocket most ingeniously concealed in the slack of his plus-fours, he shot Mr Innocente three times, and they all went away.

Mr Innocente fell over on the bed. There was a lot of scurrying about of doctors and police officers and reporters for a while.

The doctors said that it would not be safe to move Mr Innocente. And a lieutenant thanked me – I never did quite know why – and gave me a whole new packet of cigarettes.

Mr Innocente and I were alone in the cell, with the door open, when two unpleasant new visitants walked in, also young and sleek and swarthy. Zoppo grinned at them.

'Who done it, boss?' said one of them. 'This guy here?'

I really did feel uncomfortable as the man jerked his thumb in my direction, but Zoppo grinned again. He spoke, with difficulty: 'No. He's me new bodyguard. New leader of the gang – get me? Stick right to him!' A sinister mirth seemed to mingle with his agonized expression.

'Hardest-boiled egg in New York,' he wheezed. 'Talks like a gent, but he's all right. He'll get the Maggi gang. Name Heinie Hipple. Get him out of here, and do what he tells you to.'

And I swear Mr Innocente winked at me.

The other gangster said: 'Look, Heinie, my name is Pete Costola. I'll fix it up to get you out right away. What's the charge?'

'Involuntary *dementia praecox*.'

'Gee, that sounds serious. I'd better see the mouthpiece.'

They went. I slept. I was awakened by Pete Costola, Dr F. Smilie Lockland, the lieutenant of police, the sergeant who had booked me and a new man – a lawyer, it appeared – entering our cell.

The lawyer demanded of Dr Lockland: 'You say this gentleman acted in a mad, irrational, maniacal manner to you? Do you want to go into the witness-box and make a positive statement to this effect?'

'Well, no,' fretted Dr Lockland.

'Do you wish to change the charge, then?'

'Well, I guess I better. I guess I was tired, just a wee bit tired, and misunderstood our friend here. My fault! Glad to withdraw the charge!'

Still in dressing-gown and pyjamas, I was released from the police cell, and at nine in the morning was riding in a taxi-cab with Pete Costola. Pete, who wore an automatic in his coat-sleeve, a pineapple bomb attached to his watch-chain, and carried a sawed-off shotgun in his polished-seal brief-case, looked at me admiringly. Why shouldn't he, I decided – I had been a homicidal maniac. I had worn the Brussels carpet. I was Zop's successor!

'Look, chief,' asked Pete. 'Where did you lose the clothes?'

I put my arms akimbo. I honestly did! I glared at him like Richard Coeur de Lion. 'Any of your business, Pete? Are you *asking* me anything?'

'No! Gee! Excuse me, chief!'

'Then listen! I got me reasons, see?'

'Sure!' he breathed.

'Then listen! Whatsa programme today?'

'Well, I guess first bump off Maggi's successor, Batata Muffioni. We meet the council of the gang at the Hotel Magnifico.'

'Fine, Pete. But first you get me some things to make up for what I lost in the killing last night.'

'Killing? Oh, excuse me, chief!'

'Well, as I was saying, get me a private suite, and bring me some clothes, two hundred and fifty bucks, a toothbrush, and a detective story – a new one, mind you – and don't go bringing me the latest S. S. Van Loon, because I've read it, see!'

For a second I fancied he doubted me as a chief of gangsters. So I rose, dangerously – as much as you can rise in a taxi-cab. The look of doubt vanished.

'Yuh, sure, how about one by Edgar Wallace? Or do you think there is more imagination in the tales of Agatha Christie?' said Pete, hastily and meekly.

'Fine. Now gimme a gun!'

He handed over a large dangerous-looking object. 'Say, chief,' he begged, 'you ain't going to bump off nobody till we meet the council?'

'You keep your mouth shut!'

'Sure, boss! Please to excuse it!'

We rode in silence to the Hotel Magnifico.

Pete got me up tactfully in the freight elevator. We got out on the thirty-seventh floor, and Pete telephoned for the assistant manager – an elegant person in morning clothes, who purred at me: 'Good-morning, Mr Hipple, so sorry to hear of the loss of Mr Innocente. Would you care to try Suite B 7 in which to change your clothes, sir?'

I twisted my jaw round to the right, and hoped I made my 'Awright, shoot!' adequately tough.

It was a nice suite with a serving-hatch, a radio, an electric refrigerator, a bathroom in purple and lemon tiles, an electrical cocktail-shaker, and an electrical orange-squeezer, a hydraulic corkscrew, an original Matisse, a map of Scythia in AD 1267, a quite small and awfully nice private vacuum cleaner for coat-collars, a Gideon Bible bound in crushed morocco, and some beds.

Not more than half an hour later Pete Costola dashed into my suite with the money, a suit that fitted me reasonably well, haberdashery, shoes, a cup of coffee, and a copy of Mrs Belloc Lowndes's *The Lodger*.

'Fine, Pete,' I said, as I hastily drew on the new garments. 'You're a good kid, and I hope to be able to give you a little surprise.'

'Well, say, that's fine of you, boss. Now come meet Pasquale, your new lieutenant.'

Slipping Pete's automatic into my side-pocket, I followed him one flight upstairs. With some notion of escaping down the stairs I stopped at a window and murmured: 'How lovely is the prospect of insurance buildings, chain groceries, and YMCAs, Pete!'

I had thought he would be bored. But in Pete Costola there was something of the poetic soul of his countrymen, Dante and Goethe and Virgil.

'Yeah,' he breathed, ''s a fact. To say nothing of the beautiful marble morgue where Batata will lie in about one hour and a half from now, if to our salt and steel we shall be true! Let's go!'

We entered the suite in which sat the Executive Council of the Zoppo Innocente Literary and Distributing Association, Inc.

Around a large mahogany table sat six young gentlemen with sixty-candle-power eyes. One who looked like Pete Costola, but much more so, arose. 'Hey, whatsa game?' he said to Pete. 'Wherjuh getta idea this guy is Zop's successor? Whoozee?'

I really felt uncomfortable.

Pete faltered: 'He's Heinie Hipple. He's a homicidal maniac – s' what Lieutenant O'Killalay at Station Three said.'

'Hm! We'll see about that!' murmured the unpleasant young man. He telephoned, he got my lieutenant friend and he spoke:

'H'lo. Lieut.! Pasquale Ringabbiare. How's a boy? I hear your eldest son Claude is doing fine on the radio, broadcasting the beef arrivals at the stockyards. I bet he wins the Academy of Arts and Letters medal . . . Huh? No, no, nothing much; they just knocked off two truckloads of beer . . . No, the wife and I have taken up backgammon. Drop around some evening . . . No, the bullet just nipped my ear. Nothing much . . . No, I haven't read much of his stuff. We like Thornton Wilder better . . . Say, listen, Lieut., what dope you got on a guy called Heinie Hipple? . . . He did? Killed a conductor and a doctor's wife and the president of the telephone company? And a man named Russell Scarpet? Thanks, Lieut.!'

Pasquale beamed at me. 'Honestly, I apologize, old fellow! Your demeanour was so gentle that I got you wrong! *Morituri*, in all probability, *te salutamus!* Now what are your orders about bumping off Batata?'

'I'm doing this job alone,' I said.

'But my dear commander, Batata will be surrounded by redoubtable bodyguards!'

'Hear what I said?' I snarled. Pasquale quailed before me. After I enjoyed his quailing, I said, forgivingly: 'It's all right, Pasq, my boy. Now you laddies all wait for me here, understand? Don't stir till I phone.'

'Good luck to you, *mon colonel*!' they chorused, and all shook hands with me as if they didn't expect to see me again.

They didn't.

At eleven that morning I was on the Del Monte Special, bound for San Francisco, sitting in the saloon car chatting to a very pleasant stranger – superintendent of schools in Altheimer, Arkansas, he told me.

'Fine town,' he said. 'Fine educational opportunities.'

'Yes, you certainly get a lot of education in that town,' I said.

'Splendid water-supply system.'

'Is that a fact?' I said, happy having returned to an intellectual milieu.

I gave a glance at the copy of the *Morning Sun* on my lap, noted various headlines, 'Telephone Girl Chased by Maniac', 'Zoppo Innocente Dies of Heart Failure', and went back to watching the peaceful landscape slide by.

I wondered if Pasquale and the boys were still waiting for me.

# MAGIC

## By A. E. W. Mason

I

MR COLIN SAUNDRY, CMG, started out as usual upon his circuit through the Barotse country at the end of the rainy season. He went with his usual pleasure at a few months' freedom from routine. But his pleasure was not shared by everyone in that forest-covered province. There were others besides malefactors who sighed with regret when they saw the first of his caravan and relief when they saw the last of it. Tall, lean, loose-limbed, with an odd, ugly monkey face and a voice which creaked like a rusty machine, he had a way of setting a lonely settlement rocketing with excitement. He was Commemoration Week, Eton and Harrow, Ascot, and a Court Ball all in one. To the wives he was romance and adventure and a whisper from old days. To the men he was an interference and a blatancy. He was too obviously The Great Big Noise, and too arrogantly explicit that nothing but his career must stand in the way of his pleasures.

On this occasion, however, he brought two guests along with him, a Major George Hardacre, and his wife, Carmel. He had found them two days out from his Headquarters sitting disconsolately at a fruit farm which had never begun to be anything but a failure.

'We hadn't enough capital or enough knowledge,' Hardacre had said, pulling moodily at his moustache. He was a retired cavalry officer of thirty-six years, heavy, vacuous, and just as unfitted for the work of a pioneer as a man could well be.

'And we hadn't the resources in ourselves which might perhaps have made up for the want of the other things,' Carmel added, gently enough; but there was a gleam in her eyes which Colin Saundry was quick to notice. Also, she was tall and slim and no more than twenty-eight years old, dark of hair and eyes, full-lipped, and rather beautiful. To Colin Saundry a challenge. So he made his suggestion.

'You both ought to get away from here at once. You can't see things in their proper proportion with the litter of a failure about you. If you come along with me, you'll have the leisure to make your plans, and I shall be very glad of your company.'

They locked their door and came along. Colin Saundry was in no hurry. He was quite content to let the contrast between his easy efficiency and Hardacre's moody helplessness loom up into something very large and important. He went about the work of administering his district, and for a week saw little of his companions until the day was done. In the end a night came when Hardacre maundered with more than his usual monotony.

'I can't really forgive myself, you know. I didn't play fair with Carmel. You can see that for yourself, Saundry. I got her to put her little bit of money into that farm with mine. It seemed the right sort of thing to do after the War. Try the new lands, eh? But I wasn't the man for it.'

And suddenly Carmel rose up with a look of exasperation upon her face.

'Oh, what's the use?' she cried.

They had been sitting in their camp-chairs about a big log fire built in the open. Behind them were their sleeping huts. A little way off, Saundry's police and his servants were chattering about a fire of their own. Carmel took a few steps away from the fire and spoke again with her back towards them.

'Don't let's talk of it! We'll only spoil this lovely night.'

Saundry got up quickly and joined her.

'I'll show you something,' he said; and he led her across the grass and between the bushes to the foot of a little hill. As they climbed it a thunderous muffled noise as of enormous engines revolving beneath the earth reached their ears and grew louder. On the top they halted, and Carmel drew in a deep breath, throwing her head back. Forest and open glade and scattered bush were spread out before them under a silver moon.

'It's magical,' she said. 'Listen!'

Far away in a stretch of forest a baboon mumbled and barked.

'It's the country of magic,' Saundry returned. 'Look!'

Far away to the south-east above a hollow a white mist hung and swirled and changed its shape like a great canopy in a wind; and every now and then some corner of it flashed brightly as though the canopy disclosed an edge of glistening embroidery.

'The spray of the Falls,' he said.

For a little while they watched, held by the enchantment of the scene. Then suddenly Carmel cried:

'If he'd only turn on me just once and tell me I was no more use to him than a wet rag, I'd love it. I don't believe I'd mind if he smacked my face. But he's on his knees – always. Oh!'

And he was on her nerves, Colin Saundry could have added. The devout remorseful lover! Could there be in the world a person more exasperating to a young and beautiful woman in the ruin of her fortunes? What she wanted was courage, resolution, a definite plan to set things right. Instead she got a whine.

'How did it happen?' Colin Saundry asked.

'Our marriage?' said Carmel. She looked at her companion thoughtfully. She had no wish to belittle herself in his eyes by imitating her husband's whine. On the other hand she did not want him to think her an empty-headed fool who had been caught by the old glamour of a uniform. As they turned and walked back towards the camp she replied, choosing her words and watching her companion's face.

'You must go back to the War, no doubt, to understand it,' she said. 'I was eighteen. We were all easily carried away. The same sort of spirit brought us out here to Africa. A new Britain! A new world!'

She laughed half in scorn, half in regret, remembering those vanished enthusiasms, and then suddenly caught Saundry by the arm. They were half-way down the hill.

'Look!'

'I have been looking for some while,' Saundry answered in an odd voice.

'At George there by the fire?'

'At George before he went to the fire.'

Hardacre, his pipe in his mouth, was leaning forward in his camp-chair fiddling with the lighted boughs of the camp-fire, pushing one into the heart of the blaze, shifting another to one side, and all with such method that the little pyramid of flame and smoke might have been to him the most important thing in existence.

'Oh, can't you do something, Colin?' she cried, passionately, and looked at him. Saundry was standing very still at her side with his eyes upon her; and she was suddenly alarmed. She drew back, conscious of a shock. She repeated, rather to break the silence than to compel an answer:

'Can't you do something?' – and this time she omitted the Colin.

'Yes,' he replied. 'I can. This, as I told you, is the country of magic.'

And now she was almost sorry that she had put the question. As they returned to the fire, Hardacre took his pipe from his mouth.

'I say – you two! I've been thinking.'

'You have? Yes?'

There was a lively eagerness in Carmel's voice. After all, then, he had been working out some plan whilst fiddling with the branches of the fire.

'I've been thinkin' that since we've got to get a move on pretty early in the mornin', it's about time we did a little shut-eye, what?'

Carmel turned abruptly away, so that the look upon her face was hidden. Colin Saundry answered:

'There's no hurry. We shan't, after all, be starting until the afternoon. A little thing has happened today. I meant to have told you about it at dinner. But I forgot.'

He went at once across the clearing, and spoke to the head man of his police. It seemed that he, too, had not been warned of this change of plan. Carmel wondered, with a small stab of fear, whether Colin Saundry could have told them at dinner of the little thing which had happened; and whether it hadn't happened within the last hour. She watched Saundry anxiously as he returned to the camp-fire.

'Tomorrow,' he said to her, 'I'll present to you the most remarkable woman, except yourself, north of the Zambesi River.'

II

The three of them rode half a mile the next morning, and dismounted at the gate of a palisade which surrounded a native village of some thirty huts. In front of the most important of these huts, a plump young woman, black and sleek as a new silk hat, sat on a mat in her best beads and awaited her visitors with dignity.

Colin Saundry strode up to her and bowed twice.

'N'Gamba, great chief,' he said in the only sort of English she could understand. 'Dis judge,' and he tapped himself upon the breast, 'he catch complaint.'

Away went N'Gamba's dignity. She clapped her hands delightedly, her round face creasing and crumpling like a baby's. She was N'Gamba, of course. She ruled thirty poverty-stricken Barotse families by the mere lift of her eyebrows. But here was the great magistrate with the voice like a rusty chain, pretending to appeal for her protection. Could anything be more entrancing? She took him up in his own style. She shot one wicked little glance at the tall, slim white woman with the wedding-ring and replied sedately.

'N'Gamba make mammy palaver one time.'

Before she could utter another word, Colin Saundry interrupted sharply.

'Hold your tongue, N'Gamba.'

N'Gamba giggled, whilst Saundry mopped his face with his handkerchief.

'The little devil!' he said. 'She's too quick by a lot.'

Mammy palavers dealt with divorce and compensation, and the questions asked of the parties were as a rule primitive and impolite.

'Mammy palaver finish,' he said, sharply, and now some of the fun died out of her face. 'Money palaver begin,' he continued, slowly, and now all the fun had gone. N'Gamba sat very still, her face wiped clean of expression, her eyes lowered – waiting.

Carmel Hardacre waited, too, oddly disturbed, so swift and complete a change had clouded that interview. There was something serious to be proposed, and perhaps to be refused – something unknown but alarming.

'For three days, N'Gamba, I camp by your village, and go about my business.'

'One, two, t'ree days,' said N'Gamba, with a nod.

'During those days eighty-five pounds of my Government's money are stolen. I want that money back.'

Again N'Gamba did not reply. But she raised her eyes and kept them fixed and unwavering upon Colin Saundry's face. There was neither appeal in them nor fear. She watched him – sounded him, seeking – or was it not rather already knowing – the depths and the shallows of his nature. At the first, Carmel was conscious of a sense of outrage. The little naked black girl, mistress of thirty miserable Barotse families lost in a forest, was actually sitting in judgment over the white magistrate who had the high justice and the low in all these parts! By some strange mutation the proper authority of the one had passed into the possession of the other. Or so it seemed to Carmel – until she looked at Colin Saundry, and was reassured.

He stood at his ease, now slightly contemptuous, his left hand in his riding-breeches pocket, his right hand holding his switch hanging motionless at his side. If those two wills were fighting it was the man's which won. For it was N'Gamba who spoke now, not he.

'My people t'ief half a bit, yes, but big t'ings, no,' and now her face was all appeal that he should be content and let his accusation fall.

But Saundry shook his head.

'It won't do, N'Gamba. I can't lose eighty-five sovereigns of my Government's money. For if I lose, I must pay.'

In the quiet which followed, Carmel suffered a new discomfort. She became aware that though N'Gamba's eyes never wavered from Colin Saundry's, and her face with all its prayer and appeal was turned to him, the prayer and appeal were now being diverted to her and with an overmastering force. It was no affair of hers, she tried to argue, but with a sting of indignation she felt that she was being drawn into it – enlisted to plead by the side of N'Gamba that the enquiry should cease here and now. Against her will, indeed, she took a little step towards Colin, but before she could speak he turned to her, and the mere arrogant look of him broke the spell which had been laid upon her. He turned back to N'Gamba.

'Listen to me! I go from here tomorrow upon my work. In seven days I return. When I return you find for me the money and the thief. It is an order.'

It seemed that as he had released Carmel Hardacre from the compulsion put upon her, so he had broken down N'Gamba's opposition. As the fun had once died out of her face, so now did the appeal and the prayer. But it was not submission which took their place. On the contrary, Carmel had the illusion, that though no physical change took place, the little black plump girl grew into a creature formidable, potent. Carmel said to herself, wonderingly: 'I thought her a little figure of fun.' She saw her now as the immemorial wise woman of all the ages and all the races – the woman with all the secrets of the future locked away behind her eyes. It was no longer the theft of eighty-five sovereigns which was in question – but something of vast moment at which she could not guess.

N'Gamba stretched out her hand, and said in a curiously toneless and gentle voice:

'Baas, I do what you say. But I catch some prayer.'

'That I leave it all alone?' Saundry asked.

N'Gamba nodded her head.

'Baas – some t'ings – you meet 'um so. I t'ink Goddy go do 'um.'

Colin Saundry received the message with a harsh burst of laughter.

'Isn't that just what a child cries,' he exclaimed, 'who's asked to explain how the apples have vanished?'

'But it wasn't a child who cried it,' Carmel objected.

'It's a child, at any rate, now,' George Hardacre added, with a grin. It was his only contribution to the dispute, and certainly he seemed to be right. For as they turned away to the gate in the palisade, scream upon scream followed them; and there was N'Gamba rocking her body from side to side upon her mat, beating the ground with the palms of her hands and sobbing like an infant in a paroxysm of passion. Colin Saundry smiled as he looked back.

'But she'll find the thief and the money,' he said, with the completest confidence; 'they're all frightened to death of her.'

'Why?' Carmel asked.

'She's the greatest rainmaker in these parts, and for people who live on mealies, rain at the right time in the proper moderation is a very important thing. The natives travel miles to give her presents and ensure her goodwill. As you saw, she's getting a little too fat and prosperous.'

'How in the world can she make rain?' said Carmel, and Colin Saundry shrugged his shoulders.

'That's her secret and her father's before her. I can't tell you how it's done or whether it's done. All I know is that she flew into a rage once and told her Barotses that they shouldn't have any rain. And they didn't. Then when they argued with her that they were starving, she flew into a greater rage still and told them she'd bring down so much rain upon them that she'd wash their mealies out of the ground for them. And she did.'

Hardacre laughed loudly.

'Oh I say, I say, old fellow. A bit of a fairy-story, what?'

'South Kensington would call it a fairy-story, no doubt,' Saundry replied, dryly. 'But these things happened here in Africa.'

Carmel felt again the little stab of fear. She, at all events, had not lived north of the Zambesi without knowing of mysteries not to be solved by the rules of logic.

'This is the country of magic,' he had said, and she looked at him, the magistrate, and wondered whether it had not taken him to itself and taught him some of its dark secrets.

They were to break camp after an early luncheon. Carmel finished her packing quickly and crossed to the hut which they used as a mess-room. There she found Saundry alone, and put a question to him at once.

'What did that girl mean when she spoke of a mammy palaver?'

Colin Saundry chuckled.

'She was a bit too quick, wasn't she?'

'Why? What did she mean?'

'She meant – how many oxen I ought to pay your husband.'

'I see.' She lowered her eyes from Saundry's face, and added, 'None, of course.'

Colin nodded his head ruefully.

'No, none.'

It seemed that he had upon the tip of his tongue the word 'yet' to add to his 'none'; and Carmel drew back a step as though he had uttered it. She had not yielded to him – yet, but she was not sure that she wasn't going to. The vividness of the man almost swept her off her feet, lifted her on to her toes, at all events. There were comparisons forced upon her each hour of each day. Even now she must glance back through the doorway to the hut in which her husband was packing. It wanted just some small extra thing to push her one way or the other. But she was conscious of a queer enmity towards Colin Saundry. She disliked where she almost loved.

It was her enmity which spoke now.

'That money? You are quite sure you've been robbed of it.'

Colin Saundry's face flamed.

'Of course,' he said, and there was certainly nothing but indignation in his voice. 'I'm not likely to make a mistake in a matter like that. There were hundreds of opportunities. You and Hardacre were out shooting. I was on my circuit with my police. The camp has been practically deserted all day whilst we've been here.'

Carmel agreed.

'That's true,' she said. 'Here's George.'

'And here's luncheon,' added Colin Saundry.


### III


On the evening of the seventh day the party returned to the same camp. The theft had been avoided as a topic during the week by some sort of tacit agreement between Carmel and Colin Saundry, whilst Hardacre had become more and more silent and morose. But Carmel had not forgotten it, and now that they were back in the camp again the odd conviction seized upon her that they were all concerned in some alarming way with a matter of much deeper importance than the recovery of the money. An uneasy excitement made her restless, and touched Colin Saundry too. He sent a messenger into the village to announce his arrival to N'Gamba, and a little time afterwards lifted his head for silence.

'Listen!'

From a distance came the tapping of a solitary drum.

'Well, we've heard that a good many times and in a good many places during the last weeks,' said Hardacre, with a shrug of the shoulders.

'I know,' answered Colin Saundry.

But he still listened anxiously. They went out into the open after dinner. Above the trees half a mile away the loom of the village fires reddened the sky. From that quarter came the beating of the drum. It was louder now and they could all distinguish changes in its rhythm as though it sent a message in a code. For now it was spaced and monotonous, now it hurried, the taps following upon one another like sparks from an anvil; now the tap merged in one prolonged roll like a summons or an alarm. Colin Saundry listened with his head on one side and a frown upon his face.

'How far would the sound reach?' Carmel asked in a low voice.

'For miles. It fills the night.' Then he tried to laugh. 'I was wondering for a moment whether N'Gamba had taken it into her head to make some trouble for me tomorrow. But she wouldn't dare. No, I am sure. She wouldn't dare.'

Trouble of the kind which Colin Saundry feared, N'Gamba certainly did not make. For no more quiet and orderly assemblage could be imagined than that which the village presented to the magistrate and his friends the next morning. It was, in fact, too quiet and orderly. For it was panic-stricken.

Carmel could not make head or tail of the spectacle. It seemed to her that a sort of performance was being given which held the tribe spellbound, and she was sure that it was entirely displeasing to Colin Saundry. For she heard him curse N'Gamba under his breath, and add: 'Well, it's got to go on now.'

The tribe was seated on the ground in a semi-circle, with N'Gamba at the central point of the arc; and it watched a hideous old man who was mumming in the open space – watched him as though death waited at every turn of his feet. He was clothed in a leopard skin; dirty rags decorated his arms and ankles, and a string of shark's teeth hung about his neck. His hair was twisted up on the top of his head and bunched there with ivory skewers, and he held a calabash in his hands half-filled with old screws and bits of broken iron, and rattled it as he slowly twisted and stamped.

'Who's that comedian?' Hardacre asked, and suddenly Carmel knew. The three of them were standing at one end of the semi-circle and she had a clear view. The terror stamped upon the faces of all those savages squatting upon the ground told her, and explained, too, the anger of the official at her side. N'Gamba had called in a witch-doctor to find his money for him.

The old man, bent and decrepit and thin as a baboon, ceased his dance and sat cross-legged on the ground. From his calabash he fetched out four bones, tossed them in the air, caught them like a juggler, and then set them in the shape of a diamond in front of him, altering them from time to time so that now the point of the diamond was directed to one man, now to another. And whilst he juggled with his bones, he whined rather than crooned some monotonous old chant which held in it the melancholy and the despair of all the ages.

'Curiouser and curiouser,' Hardacre quoted.

From Colin Saundry there came a sharp hiss.

'Keep still!'

He knew his people and Hardacre did not. These Barotses, to a man, were bound in a spell by stark fright. What if the spell broke? And a little thing might break it. What if frenzy followed upon fright? A massacre might come of it. Even now a man half rose to his feet with a whimpering cry and squatted down again, as though he dared neither flee nor stay.

The witch-doctor unslung from his shoulders a buffalo horn. He took from his basket a rusty spoon, and, of all incongruous paraphernalia for a magician – a dirty old jar which had once held Keiller's marmalade. Comic enough, no doubt, elsewhere than in a forest of Africa amongst a tribe of panic-tortured savages. Here every commonplace, familiar little implement gave an added touch of the macabre to the whole ghoulish exhibition. Carmel knew from a sharp movement at her side that the climax of the grotesque rite was at hand. As terror chained that black sweeping curve of men, so suspense held her – or all of her but her throbbing heart.

The old pantaloon scooped from the jar a pitch-like grease, so rank that the evil smell of it tainted the air even where Carmel stood. He filled each end of the buffalo horn with it.

'That's his magic,' said Saundry in a low voice, and the witch-doctor rose to his feet. Balancing the horn in his hands, he scuttled suddenly with a quite horrible quick run to the point of the semicircle opposite to Carmel. Before the first man he halted, and she witnessed a ritual which shocked her as an unexpected blow might do and drained her cheeks of all their colour. The old man extended the horn, and the other, his teeth chattering, his body trembling, took it with a humble reverence like one upon his knees. For a little while he held it upon the palms of his upturned hands, whilst standing over him the wizard muttered and whined. Carmel had, for a moment or two, a horrible illusion that she was present at and condoning by her presence a filthy parody of the sublime mystery of her faith. But the ceremony was too real to all these participants for such an error to persist. Because it was terrifying and real to them, it became real to her, real and compelling. The centuries fell away behind her. She was assisting at some ordeal which had been repeated and repeated in this still, sunlit glade in the forest, long before even the men from Babylon passed southwards to quarry their diamonds and their gold. And it could not fail! She was sure of it. She watched the old and hideous magician pass his buffalo horn from man to man, stooping, muttering. At some moment a man would rise, unable to endure his torment for one more second, and, flinging up his arms, avow his guilt. She was sure of it. She waited for it with clenched hands and parted lips.

If only that had happened!

Right round the semi-circle the witch-doctor practised his sorcery in vain. He came to the last of the tribe and failed with him. He stood, a noisome creature to be imagined in a nightmare, his small eyes glinting, his wizened body an offence.

'Let me look at that horn,' cried a voice by Carmel's side – and a strange voice it seemed – a voice which spoke under compulsion. Carmel turned towards her husband. It was he who had spoken, and he had the appearance of a man in a trance. Carmel looked suddenly at N'Gamba. N'Gamba was squatting on the ground, her head lowered upon her bosom, her eyes veiled. She was motionless as a statue. The recollection of the power which that little black girl had exercised over Carmel on this very spot flashed back into Carmel's mind. She would have yielded to it but for Saundry's interruption. He would interrupt again – yes – yes! Carmel looked at Saundry hopefully, but the man was rattled; he was angry; he was alarmed. For one fatal hour his easy assurance failed him. In the contest between these two, the wise woman with the lore of Africa and the white man from the West, the white man lost. Carmel saw her husband reach out his hands. She tried to cry out; her dry throat refused a sound. And the odious, horrible catastrophe happened in a second. As Hardacre grasped the horn, it leapt and twisted in his hands. Before even Colin Saundry could have seized and held him, he was out there in the open space, wrestling like a madman with a buffalo horn which no one held. There could never have been such ignominy. He was dragged about like a doll. Carmel was hardly aware that all the black men were on their feet leaping, screaming, laughing in their reprieve from fear, or that N'Gamba sat like an idol of stone, her head lowered, her arms crossed upon her breast. But she heard Colin Saundry's voice raised in a loud anger, she saw him cross to N'Gamba and fling at her some passionate words; and when she came to herself she was outside the palisade and one of Saundry's police was holding the stirrup of her horse.

\*

They rode back to the camp without a word. But when they reached it, Hardacre said:

'My hut must be searched.'

Colin Saundry waived the suggestion aside.

'It was a trick . . . No doubt they have some queer powers, these witch-men. Powers we don't understand. N'Gamba set him to it. By God she shall pay.' He slipped his arm through Hardacre's. 'You mustn't mind, Hardacre. We shall be away from here tomorrow.'

Hardacre drew his arm away.

'I insist.'

His pallor under the sunburn gave him the look of a man sick to death. Colin Saundry dropped his arms to his side.

'I wouldn't have had a ridiculous thing like this happen for ten times eighty-five pounds. You shall have your way, of course.'

And that night as they sat silently smoking about the camp-fire, Saundry's head man came forward to them carrying a bag of sovereigns which he had just dug out of Hardacre's hut.

For a while no one uttered a word. A silence weighed about that fire such as might follow a dread verdict in a court of justice. A turtle dove, startlingly near, called suddenly from a bough of a tree and far away a baboon mumbled, and then by the fire Saundry shook the bag so that the sovereigns in it rattled. If he had been seeking for the one extra jolt which should thrust Carmel into a more definite position between the two men, he could have found nothing more decisive. He had got his money back, yes, but Carmel hated him.

'Of course it was a plant,' he said. 'N'Gamba must have found the thief, and then buried the money, knowing that we should return. I'll get it cleared up on my next circuit. Meanwhile here's the money and no harm done. There's absolutely no motive, of course . . .'

He spoke with generosity, knowing – it must have been so – that there was all the motive in the world. But he was not allowed to expand his argument. Hardacre stood up and pulled at his moustache. Even at that moment he could not be impressive. He alarmed neither of his companions. He did not even look at them. He just said in a dull voice:

'I've had about enough of this.'

Then he pulled a pistol out of his pocket, blew out his brains and pitched forward into the fire. Fortunately Carmel Hardacre fainted.

The affair, of course, could not end there. Slowly the facts were put together. Finally N'Gamba spoke. Saundry had sent her a message summoning her to meet him in the forest two days before he returned to his camp by her village. He came to the appointed place riding in great haste and alone. He bade her accuse Hardacre of the theft. No blame should fall on her, for the money would certainly be found in Hardacre's hut. N'Gamba wept, pleaded, yielded. But she chose her own way. She called in her witch-doctor. She used her own dark gifts. You may give them what name you will, magic, witchcraft, mass hypnotism. It is wiser perhaps to accept the experience of Colin Saundry and say that the fairy-story in Kensington happens in Africa. But from first to last N'Gamba never wavered from this assertion. She could have done nothing whatever had Hardacre been innocent.

Colin Saundry, however, got no profit from his scheme. He lost Carmel at the moment when he chinked the bag. He lost his position when N'Gamba told of their meeting in the forest, and thereafter he fell upon difficult days.

Some years afterwards, when rather drunk at a shabby party in his lodgings behind the Bayswater Road, he was asked for his explanation of the story. He said, 'Hardacre, of course, stole the money all right. I saw him going from my hut to his when I came down a hill towards the camp-fire one night. The next morning I missed the money. Oh, yes. Hardacre stole the money all right.' Then he laughed foolishly and bibulously, and added:

'Some t'ings – you meet 'um so. I t'ink Goddy go do 'um.'

# THE MYSTERY TOUR

## By 'Sapper'

THE LANDLORD of the Angler's Rest contemplated his preparations with pride. Underneath a huge tree was set a long table, groaning with good fare. Cold salmon and cucumber, meat pies and salad, with a Stilton cheese as the central *pièce de résistance*, went to make up a meal of much merit – a meal which he felt did credit to the famous hostelry he owned.

The order had been somewhat of a surprise. Well-known though he was for the excellence of his food, his principal customers were fishermen. Through his land there flowed the Weldron, which, as all the fishing world knows, is one of the best trout streams in the south of England. And since the cost of a rod is considerable, it followed that most of his guests were men of means and leisure, who like peace and quiet in which to tell their lies. So that he wondered how this sudden influx would be viewed by the three who were staying with him at the moment.

And it had indeed been sudden – so sudden that he contemplated with justifiable pride his response to such an unexpected commission. Only four hours in which to prepare a genuine old English spread for thirty people was asking a good deal. And that was all the time he had been given. At four o'clock that afternoon a car had drawn up outside his hotel, and from it had descended a well-dressed and pleasant individual who had ordered dinner for thirty at eight o'clock. And it was to be no ordinary dinner, since it was no ordinary party. Simple and plain the food might be, but it must be of the very best. For, as the gentleman had pointed out, the atmosphere of a hundred years ago could be obtained with the genuine article just as well as with tinned salmon and tough beef,

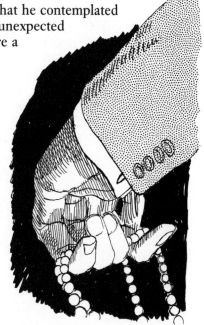

279

and with far more beneficial results to the digestion. And when he had proceeded to pass over a tenner as advance payment before getting back into his car, mine host had wasted no time.

'Great heavens, Jackson! What is this ghastly thing I see before my eyes? Have you got a charabanc party coming?'

He swung round: three men, their footsteps noiseless on the grass, were standing behind him contemplating the long table with horror.

'Not a charabanc, Captain Drummond,' he said. 'Money no object, sir. Old English fare, and of the very best. They're coming at eight.'

'You'd better give 'em that trout you stunned, Hugh,' said one of the three. 'Have you ever seen Captain Drummond fish, Jackson? Or I should say, "Have you ever heard him?"'

'Can't say as I have, Mr Darrell.'

'It sounds like a gramophone record – the departure of a troopship. First there is a loud crack and a branch behind him is torn off. That is followed by a medley of oaths, and the noise of a large cable hitting the water. Then the waves begin to break all round you.'

'My dear Peter,' said Drummond, languidly, 'your insults leave me cold. I caught a fish – true, not a large one. But alone I did it.'

'I should damn well think you were alone,' remarked Darrell. 'I was a mile from you, and only great agility saved me from drowning in the bore you started.'

Drummond waved a vast hand.

'Beer, Jackson, beer. Lots of beer. And then tell us about your party. Algy, don't finger the food, you filthy beast.'

Algy Longworth returned from the table, his mouth full of meat pie.

'Definitely good, old jolly-belly,' he assured the landlord. 'Tell the varlet to feed those to me at dinner.'

'But joking apart,' said Darrell as the landlord went inside, 'what has the silly ass let us in for? It's sacrilege on an evening like this.'

'It is life,' answered Drummond, taking a pie himself. 'Life in this land of ours today. Here we sit, 'neath the old oak tree, surrounded by our trophies of the chase. The sun is sinking in the west; the shadows lengthen, throwing into gentle relief the rugged beauty of our features. All is peace; nought is heard save the gentle babble of the brook . . .'

'Sit on his head,' said Algy. 'That's Eliza having a bath.'

'Where did I get to? Brook . . . The babbling brook. And what does the future hold for us? Is it pleasing converse with fair ladies and brave men clad in knightly armour telling of glorious deeds in derring-do? Is it Dick Turpin bidding us ride the road with him as darkness falls? No, sir, it is not. It is the descent upon us of hordes of women, clasping grubby-nosed and puling brats to their bosoms, whilst from their foul conveyance a portable abomination will give us the fat stock prices. England, my England.'

'Beer, sir?' said the landlord at his elbow.

'Tell me, old friend of my youth,' continued Drummond, as he took a tankard, 'where is the spirit of adventure today? Rich and riotous adventure . . . Does no red blood still flow in our veins? Passing over my battle today with that monster of the deep . . .' He peered into his creel. 'By the way, where the hell is my fish?'

'Hidden under the third blade of grass,' said Darrell. 'Look here, Jackson, what on earth induced you to wish a beanfeast on us?'

'It's a funny sort of beanfeast, gentlemen, that stumps up a tenner in advance.'

'Worse and worse,' cried Algy. 'It's a gathering of absconding goose-club treasurers.'

'Hardly that,' came a suave voice. 'I can assure you, gentlemen, that our guests will not trouble you in the slightest.'

With a smile and a little bow the speaker crossed to the table and inspected the contents.

'He's the gentleman who gave the order, sir,' said the landlord in a hoarse aside to Drummond before joining the newcomer at the food. 'The best I could do, sir,' he remarked, 'at such short notice.'

'And a very good best too,' said the other approvingly. 'Let us have plenty of ale and cider. And whisky for those who prefer it.'

He lit a cigarette and sauntered back to Drummond's bench.

'What a charming spot!' he remarked.

'Very,' agreed Drummond shortly. 'So quiet as a rule.'

Once again the man smiled.

'I see that you fear the worst,' he said. 'And I admit, gentlemen, that you will have to put up with a party of thirty for an hour or so. But I can promise you that there will be no banana skins or orange peel thrown about, and that everybody will be strictly sober. You will excuse me?'

With another bow he turned and went indoors, leaving the three men to their beer.

'That man', said Drummond apropos of nothing, 'is not English. Algy, you hound of hell, go in and get these refilled. The whole staff is running round in circles over this damned party.'

'What about feeding somewhere else, Hugh?' said Darrell as Algy went obediently. 'The prospect is not inviting.'

'Not a bad notion, Peter. Let's lower another can and think about it. Though I admit I'm curious to see who the preparations are for.'

'We'll give 'em the once over and then push off,' suggested Darrell. 'Don't slop the beer, Algy.'

'Slop be blowed,' said Algy, putting down his tankard. 'Look here, you boys, our foreign friend seems a bit curious about us.'

'What's that?' cried Drummond.

'I was getting the drink through the hatch place, and he was round the corner in the bar having a quick one with Jackson.

'"You know them, Mr Jackson?" I heard him say.

'"Very well, sir," answered the old boy. "Mr Darrell often comes here to fish, and the other two gentlemen are friends of his."

'And then Eliza gave me the tankards and they saw me, and shut up. But why should the organiser of this bun-worry be interested in us?'

'Why indeed?' agreed Drummond thoughtfully.

He relapsed into silence as Darrell gave him a warning kick under the table: the gentleman in question was approaching.

'I have just heard from the landlord', he said, 'that you are frequent visitors here. And so I felt I must really come and express my regrets at this invasion of your privacy.'

'Don't mention it,' said Drummond. 'We are full of curiosity . . . Now was that genuine?' he continued as the man moved away. 'Or was it an endeavour to explain his curiosity, knowing he'd been overheard in the bar by Algy?'

'We ought to know soon,' said Darrell. 'Here are the competitors arriving.' And then he gave a grunt of disgust. 'Good Lord!' he cried. 'It's one of those confounded Mystery Tours.'

'What are they?' asked Algy vaguely.

'My dear man, they've been going for years. You buy a ticket and get into a bus, which then starts off for some unknown destination . . . You finally arrive at Stonehenge at dawn, where you are bitten all over by mosquitoes and the other passengers.'

The luxurious motor-coach drew up opposite the door. In front was a notice – MYSTERY TOUR: behind, standing by the open door, was the organiser of the party. And with languid interest they watched the guests descend – an interest which became slightly more animated during the process. For by no stretch of imagination could they visualise the occupants of the coach biting one another at Stonehenge. Or throwing banana skins about. For almost before a babel of voices broke out to proclaim their nationality it was obvious that the party consisted of well-to-do Americans.

The majority consisted of young people, but there was a leaven of older ones who were evidently parents. And from the fragments of conversation that came drifting to the ears of the three spectators it was clear that one and all of them were tickled to death with the whole performance. In fact, when the oldest inhabitant of the village, clad in a smock, appeared at the door of the inn, smoking a long clay pipe, a positive cheer went up from the younger members of the party.

'Ladies and gentlemen, will you please be seated.'

The voice of the organiser rose above the general hum of conversation.

'Sit where you like,' he continued. 'I am sure you can all sort yourselves out better than I can. And now,' he went on when all the chairs were occupied, 'I am just going to say a few words before our worthy host begins to serve the dinner. On our trip over in the *Begonia*, you were good enough, sir,' – he turned to a grey-haired man on his right – 'to bet me that I would not stage for you something out of which you would get a kick. That I think was your exact phrase.'

'Sure,' agreed the American.

'You were good enough to say that you would put yourselves unreservedly in my hands. And I asked you to assemble at Hyde Park Corner this afternoon, and get into the motor-coach which would be awaiting you there, so that you could embark on a mystery tour. I gave strict injunctions to the driver and his mate that they were not to tell you where you were going – not even this half-way mark. Because I can assure you, ladies and gentlemen, that I should not consider I had seriously tried to win my bet if this was the finish of my entertainment. That comes later.

'But since we poor mortals must feed, I decided to try and introduce – even to such a prosaic thing as dinner – a certain novelty: to give you something as far removed from the Ritz and Claridge's as I could. And mercifully our fickle climate has been kind.

'Ladies and gentlemen, I want you to throw your minds back into the past. Seated where you are under that same tree were the men who watched the beacons light on the hills yonder, as the Spanish Armada approached our shores over three hundred years ago. Seated where you are under that same tree were the men who awaited the latest news of Buonaparte. And they were eating the same fare as you will be eating tonight; and drinking the same. No cocktails, ladies and gentlemen: I forbid it. There is English ale, English cider, and I have stretched a point over Scotch whisky.

'There stands the inn as it stood then; there flows the stream as it flowed then. Nothing has changed save that you came in a motor-coach and not on horseback. You are dining in a little piece of untouched England.'

'If he says "God save the King",' whispered Drummond, 'I shall burst into tears.'

He was saved that, however: a burst of applause signified that the oration was over.

'What's stung you, Peter?' Drummond asked. For Darrell was staring thoughtfully at the table, his forehead wrinkling in a frown.

'You see that elderly grey-haired woman sitting two from the end,' he said, and Drummond nodded. 'I'm trying to think where the devil I've met her . . . Somehow or other she's connected in my mind with cricket . . . Wait: it's coming . . . That team I went out with to America two years ago . . . It was then I saw her . . . In Philadelphia . . . Mrs . . . Mrs . . . I've got it: Mrs Walmeyer.'

'Who is Mrs Walmeyer?' asked Algy.

'Wife of Mr Walmeyer, the grey-haired bird who made the bet, and who is one of the ten richest men in the States. Her pearls, which she's got on now – incidentally she is reputed even to have her bath in 'em – are insured for five hundred thousand dollars. And the rest of her stuff is in keeping.'

'None of 'em look as if they were qualified for the dole,' said Drummond as he rose and stretched himself. 'But they seem harmless enough, so let's feed here if there's anything left to eat. I'm going to wash.'

He lounged indoors, leaving the other two over their beer.

'Going to introduce yourself to the girlfriend?' asked Algy.

Darrell shook his head.

'Not I,' he said. 'I don't suppose for a second that she'd remember me, and I'd hate to butt into the party. You know, I rather take off my hat to that fellow, whoever he is. I'll bet it's a novelty to this crowd.'

'Depends on the second part of the programme,' said Algy. 'What's stung Hugh? I want my dinner.'

And at that moment they saw Drummond beckoning from the door.

'Boys,' he said happily as they joined him, 'I have impinged on a fairy. Going up to my room I became aware of a faint but delightful scent. And as I stood sniffing the ozone, a door suddenly opened and I perceived a positive peach framed in the light. "Is that you, Paul?" she said.

'I assured her that to my undying regret it was not, but I naturally placed what poor services I could render at her disposal. She thanked me adorably, and I asked her if she would like me to teach her fishing tomorrow. She seemed to think it was a capital idea, and on that high note of optimism we parted.'

'Was she a member of the party?' asked Algy.

'No, dear boy, she was not. I at once looked out of my window, and found that the mystery tour was all present and correct.'

'When did she arrive?' demanded Darrell.

'That is not the point. When will she leave?'

'On the spot, when she sees you by daylight,' said Algy. 'What have we got to eat? Your trout?'

'And you have the frightful gall to tell the poor child you'll teach her to fish?' Darrell gave a hollow laugh. 'If I did my duty, I'd summon the police.'

'Jealousy, jealousy,' said Drummond sadly. 'Jackson, old host, bring some of the fish Mr Darrell bought in the village this afternoon.'

They sat down by an open window, from which they could see the table outside. Dinner, there, was nearly over, and the younger and more impatient members of the party were beginning to agitate for the next item on the programme. They were clamouring for a hint as to what it was going to be. But the organiser was adamant. Smilingly he shook his head; everything would be discovered in due course. The whole show would be ruined if it was given away beforehand.

'But I can promise you all', he said, 'that it will come up to your expectations. If it doesn't,' he added with a shrug of his shoulders, 'I lose my bet. Now – are we all ready?'

There came a pushing back of chairs, followed by a general exodus towards the motor-coach.

'And we shall never know', said Drummond, 'whether he wins his bet or not. But the ghastly thought that assails me is that he is Paul. That laden tomorrow with American dollars he will insist on attending my fishing lesson . . . My God!'

The other two stared at him in amazement, for he had jumped to his feet and was staring out of the window like a man possessed. And the next moment he had left the room.

'What's the matter with him?' said Algy, bewildered, and Darrell shook his head.

'No good asking me,' he answered. 'Here he comes again.'

Gone was the Drummond of a few moments before, and they looked at him even more bewildered.

'Listen to me,' he said curtly. 'The two drivers on that coach have been changed. They're not the same men that brought it down from London.'

'What of it?' cried Algy feebly.

'They never send four men on a coach, you fool: only two. Why have they been changed? And who has taken the original men's places?'

He swung round as the landlord came in.

'Jackson – where are the two men who brought down that coach? I saw them having their dinner a quarter of an hour ago.'

'A dreadful thing, sir, has happened.' The worthy man was wringing his hands. 'They've both of them drunk too much. Luckily there were two others here who were qualified to take their places.'

'Very lucky,' snapped Drummond. 'Let me see the two originals.'

And most assuredly they had drunk too much if appearances were to be believed. Snoring stertorously, they were sprawling over a bench, and Drummond took one look at them.

'Drugged, or I'm a Dutchman,' he cried to Darrell. 'And you don't drug men for fun. Get the car, Algy, and jump to it!'

He let out a bellow of laughter.

'Adventure, boys: rich, riotous adventure after all.'

'But what's the game, Hugh?'

'That, old lad, remains to be seen. All that matters at the moment is that Paul – if it is Paul – has abducted a perfectly good party of American millionaires. Look here, Jackson,' he continued as Algy sprinted out of the room, 'what did these two sportsmen have to drink?'

'A pint of beer each, sir.'

'Was it laced with anything?'

'Not that I know of, sir.'

'Even if it were doped with gin, Hugh,' said Darrell, 'one pint wouldn't produce *that* effect.'

'I agree. And where did the two substitutes spring from?'

'They'd been here some time, sir. And when Mr Verrinder saw what had happened they volunteered to drive instead.'

'Is Verrinder the name of the man who organised the show?'

'That's right, sir. Mr Paul Verrinder.'

Drummond smiled.

'And the lady upstairs?'

'A friend of his, sir. She went off in a car with another gentleman about ten minutes ago. Is anything wrong, sir?' he added anxiously as Algy appeared in the doorway to say the car was ready.

'That's what we're going to find out, Jackson. Did anybody drop a hint as to where they were going?'

'I heard the lady say something about it being five miles beyond Romsey, sir.'

'Good. We should overtake 'em by then. Come on, boys.'

They tumbled into the car, and set off in pursuit. It was a quarter of an hour before they saw the lights of the coach in front of them. Drummond at once slowed down. To overtake the party would be fatal; to sit close on their tail might arouse the driver's suspicions. And so with dimmed lights he kept two or three hundred yards behind, only drawing nearer when they came to Romsey itself.

The coach took the Winchester direction, and Drummond fell back again. From now on more care was necessary, since the actual destination was unknown. And so when the coach suddenly swung right handed along a narrow road, he was only about a hundred yards behind.

For two miles they continued, then once again the coach swung right – this time through lodge gates into a drive flanked on each side by an avenue of trees. And very cautiously, with lights extinguished, Drummond swung in after them.

In the distance they could see the dim outline of a big house against the sky. It was in darkness, as was the lodge; evidently the place was empty. And as Drummond turned the car on to the grass verge and ran her in between two trees he chuckled joyfully.

'What the devil is the game, chaps? Or can it be that the show is genuine?'

The party had dismounted by the time they reached the house: the motor-coach, lights switched off, was standing by the front door. And keeping in the shadow of the trees, the three of them skirted round the edge of the drive.

Suddenly Drummond paused, his hand raised warningly. From close by had come the sound of voices and a short laugh; then two figures loomed up and disappeared in the direction of the house.

A moment or two later Drummond came upon a fast sports car carefully hidden behind some shrubbery.

'Can it be that it just grew there?' he continued. 'Or is it for a rapid getaway? In either event, I think we will tune it up.'

He opened the bonnet, and under the ministrations of three experts the car gave up any claims to fastness. In fact, its maximum speed would now be that of a cart-horse towing it. Then conscious of work well done they continued their progress towards the front door.

It was open, and they cautiously entered the hall. Practically empty of furniture, the house smelled of disuse. In front of them they could dimly see the stairs, with a stained-glass window at the top: on each side doors opened into lofty rooms empty as the hall. And then from the back of the house they heard Paul Verrinder's voice.

'Ladies and gentlemen.'

'Come on,' whispered Drummond. 'The curtain is going up.'

'Ladies and gentlemen,' continued the voice, 'you are now in the banqueting hall of Strathray Place – one of the seats until quite recently of the Earls of Strathray. Above us, at the far end of the room, is the musician's gallery, untouched since the terrible tragedy that took place over a century ago.'

Without a sound Drummond and his friends crept towards the door and stood outside. A faint light filtering in through the mullioned windows on to the floor only seemed to throw into greater darkness the rest of the room. And when for a moment the voice ceased, a sudden nervous giggle from some girl came almost as a relief.

'Silence, please!' Verrinder was speaking again. 'It is essential that you should try to attune yourselves to the atmosphere of the place. And to help you I will tell you the story of that night. For in the room where we now stand a very strange drama was being enacted.

'Picture to yourselves a long table, on which burned countless candles. It was laid for a party of thirty. The historic Strathray plate was adorning it in all its magnificence. The major-domo and the footmen stood motionless in their places, though had one looked at them closely, one would have noticed that here and there a finger twitched, a jaw clenched unnaturally. For grim things were in the air that night, and the men sensed it.

'Seated at one end of the table was their master – the eighth earl. Dressed in the height of fashion, with the candle-light glinting on his aquiline features, he seemed to be enjoying some secret joke as his eyes wandered from one to the other of his two companions, who sat on each side of him. The remaining chairs were empty.

'On his right was a beautiful girl; on his left a young man, whose plainer clothes betokened a less exalted rank than that of his host. A handsome youth with sensitive hands and face, he kept shooting little glances first at his host and then at the girl opposite, who kept her eyes fixed steadily on her plate.

'Slowly the meal dragged on, each course ushered in with the pomp and ceremony habitual to the household, but it was noticeable that the only one of the three who spoke was the earl. And after a while he frowned.

'"You are silent, my love," he said suavely to the girl. "I trust nothing ails you."

'"I thank you, no, my lord," she answered. "But I am wondering what can have happened to your lordship's other guests."

' "Surely, my dear, the company of your husband and Mr Ludlow is ample compensation for the absence of others. What say you, Mr Ludlow?"

' "That I greatly appreciate your lordship's hospitality," said the young man.

' "Long may your appreciation continue," remarked the earl. "Put the wine upon the table." He signed to the major-domo. "And then begone. And now we can talk undisturbed," he continued as the servants left the room. "I understand that you are a musician, Mr Ludlow."

' "In my poor way," said the other with a bow.

' "Excellent. I did well to countermand the players. And since you too, my love, perform so charmingly upon the harp I shall be privileged to listen to a duet later."

'The eyes of the two young people met, held for an instant and then fell apart. But in that instant the message had flashed between them. The earl knew. How he had found out that they loved one another did not matter; he knew.

' "A duet played in the musicians' gallery, with an audience small but most appreciative. Incidentally, my dear wife, small though the audience may be, it will be larger than many you have both played to."

' "I don't understand you, my lord," she whispered through dry lips.

' "Don't you?" he sneered. "Then your brains are hardly in keeping with your beauty."

'He clapped his hands.

' "Bring Mr Ludlow's violin," he ordered the servant who had appeared. "And her ladyship's harp."

' "My Lord," stammered the youth. "I am not in the mood . . . I . . ."

' "To play with a lady! Zounds, Mr Ludlow, what an ungallant remark! But I fear I must insist." ' '

Paul Verrinder's voice ceased, and even as it did so a faint light began to illuminate the musicians' gallery and a little sigh of expectation whispered through the party. For there, seated by the rail, clad in the costumes of a bygone day, were a girl and a man.

' "Play!" the harsh voice rang out again. "Play – damn you – your last duet!" ' '

But no music followed. Instead there came a splintering crash, and the two figures seemed to fall through the floor of the gallery into the darkness below. Two dreadful thuds: the dying twang of a violin string: then silence – save for a sardonic laugh.

'The last duet! Admirably played.'

For a moment there was a stupefied silence, then pandemonium broke loose. Women screamed, men shouted for lights. So that it was not surprising that in the general uproar the noise of a short sharp struggle near the door passed unnoticed. And when Paul Verrinder's voice rose above the tumult calling for silence, the struggle was over.

'Ladies and gentlemen, be silent, I beg of you. Everything is quite all right. Neither of them is hurt. Look!'

He switched on a torch, and there, carefully placed under the floor of the gallery in such a position that it had been invisible, was a net. On the floor lay two dummies, a harp and a violin: the two performers had disappeared. And as the full realisation of how they had been spoofed dawned on the party, a burst of applause broke out.

'Gee! Mr Verrinder,' cried Walmeyer, 'that gave me one of the nastiest turns I've had for some time. I sure thought there had been an accident.'

'And do I win my bet, Mr Walmeyer?'

'You certainly do. It was worth all of five thousand dollars. And if you call round to the Porchester tomorrow I'll have the greatest pleasure in handing 'em over.'

'But surely', came a cheerful voice, 'the entertainment is not yet over, Mr Verrinder?'

And at that moment the headlights of a car shining through the windows lit up the room clearly. The whole party swung round. Standing at the top of the three steps leading down into the banqueting hall was Hugh Drummond. In his hand he held a small bag, the sight of which caused Paul Verrinder's face to turn a delicate shade of green.

'Who the blazes are you?' said Mr Walmeyer.

'Just a helper in the party,' answered Drummond affably.

'I've seen him before,' cried one of the men. 'He was having dinner at the Angler's Rest.'

'Quite right,' said Drummond. 'And now, Mr Walmeyer, I gather from what you said a few moments ago that the entertainment up to date has been worth five thousand dollars.'

'That is so.'

'Well, if we can give you a further entertainment, where the thrill will, I think, be as great – even if not from the same cause – as the one you have already had, would you be prepared to make that five thousand ten?'

'Yes. I would,' answered the American after a pause.

'You see, Mr Verrinder thinks of everything. And supposing something had gone wrong with the admirable little play he staged for you tonight, he had another card up his sleeve. Shall I begin – er – Paul?'

'Of course,' said Verrinder, contorting his face into a smile.

'Now, your pearls, Mrs Walmeyer,' continued Drummond. 'You know – I don't see them round your neck.'

Her hands flew to her throat.

'John!' she screamed. 'They've gone.'

Drummond held up his hand.

'Please, don't be alarmed! Peter! Mrs Walmeyer's pearls, please. Will you hand them to the lady . . . Thank you. And now exhibit B.'

He groped in the bag and extracted a bulky pocket book.

'Someone seems to have lost this. Marked J. B. W. Any claims?'

'My wallet,' howled John B. Walmeyer.

'And mine's gone . . . Mine too . . .' came in an excited babble from the other men.

'Sort them out, gentlemen . . . Peter, put the collection on the floor. Now, Mr Walmeyer,' he continued as the others crowded round the bag, 'I leave it to you to decide whether we deserve that extra five thousand dollars or not. My friend here, Mr Algernon Poltwhistle, the most famous pickpocket entertainer in the world, was specially hired by Mr Verrinder tonight, to put the finishing touch to the evening's performance . . . Algernon Poltwhistle . . .'

He pushed Algy forward, who bowed deeply.

'His other well-known trick is a lifelike imitation of bath water running away, but as the hour is late, and he wishes to get back to his wife and eight children, we will not call on him for that. However, Mr Walmeyer, as I see that you have considerably more than the sum at stake in your pocket book – may I be permitted to extract ten thousand-dollar notes?'

John B. Walmeyer looked at him with shrewd blue eyes: then he looked at Verrinder. And then, like little Audrey, he laughed and he laughed and he laughed.

'What are you going to do with the ten thousand?' he asked, when he had recovered.

'It will come in most handy for Mr Poltwhistle's ninth child,' answered Drummond blandly.

'Help yourself,' said John B. Walmeyer resignedly. 'And may Heaven preserve me from being anywhere in the neighbourhood when he has his tenth.'

'A most satisfactory ending, Paul, to a charming evening,' remarked Drummond a few minutes later.

The mystery tour had departed on its way back to London, amidst general hilarity, after voting the performance a howling success.

'There is one thing, however, that I would like to know,' he continued. 'How did you propose to do your own getaway? It wouldn't have been long before someone spotted that he'd been robbed.'

'By car, confound you,' said Verrinder with a grin. 'Along with the two drivers of the coach. I was going to leave the whole outfit here.'

'A little difficult,' remarked Drummond. 'We have already attended to it.'

'The devil you have. Incidentally, what have you done with Joe Parkins?'

'Is he the engaging gentleman who pinched the stuff?'

Verrinder nodded.

'I dotted him one, Paul. My fist crashed against his jaw. He's in a flower bed outside. But a little arnica, or one of those excellent advertised preparations, should soon put him right. Ah! And here is the fair accomplice. My congratulations, angel face. Is the fishing still on?'

The girl lit a cigarette.

'What put you wise, big boy?' she asked.

'Drugging the drivers, darling.'

'It was a risk, I know,' she said. 'But if we were going to leave the crowd here, it had to be done.'

And then she looked at him curiously.

'Why didn't you give us away?'

'Because I haven't enjoyed myself so much for a long while,' said Drummond with a grin. 'Most reprehensible, I know – but there you are.'

'What about the ten thousand bucks?' cried Verrinder.

'What, indeed?' said Drummond grinning still more.

'Damn it – you might go fifty-fifty. I've paid for the dinner, and the coach, to say nothing of mugging up English history till I was faint from brain fag.'

Drummond roared with laughter.

'Nothing doing, old boy, absolutely nothing. Your sole reward must be the consciousness of tomorrow's good deed.'

'What do you mean?' cried Verrinder, looking puzzled.

'Acting on your instructions, Paul, I shall tomorrow send ten thousand dollars to one of the Village Centres for Disabled Soldiers and Sailors. Unless, of course, you have another charity you fancy. Well? . . .'

'I leave it to you,' said Verrinder resignedly. 'I suppose my overdraft in Paris is not on the approved list.'

# LAST JOURNEY

## By *William C. White*

T H E Y  S A Y  A T  T H E Deuxième Bureau, which is the French Intelligence Office, that Captain Dufresne, who heads the Western European division, is a very wise man. But Jeanne Rohan doubted his wisdom one afternoon as they sat on a bench in a secluded corner of the Luxemburg gardens.

'You never hesitated before at any assignment,' the captain said, surprised at Jeanne's reaction.

'This is different.' She hoped he would not ask an explanation.

'Indeed!'

'It isn't that I'm afraid to go to Berlin.'

'Fear? My dear!' Dufresne, remembering assignments in Vienna, Oslo, Tunis, and Rome, brushed that aside.

'The point is', Jeanne said bluntly, 'that having to see Paul Perel in Berlin will be embarrassing. He and I – that is – well, four years ago in Normandy – I was on holiday. At any rate, it was all over after a month. I have not heard from him since.'

Dufresne looked so sorry. '*Mais oui*, my dear, I had forgotten.' He smiled apology and understanding. 'Of course, I do not insist that you go, but there is no one else I can send . . .'

After registering at a small hotel off Potsdamer Platz, Jeanne spent the first two days going about the city. If anyone were assigned to follow her, and it was important to determine that, he had for his pains a fairly comprehensive tour of museums, art galleries, and historical buildings. No one followed, so far as she knew. Half a dozen times each night she left the hotel to walk along deserted streets and, from time to time, to look behind. No one followed.

On the third day she telephoned a few publishing houses to say that she represented a French publisher who wanted to translate and publish children's books. Several firms sent representatives to her hotel, and she talked with them until mid-afternoon. That established a legitimate reason for being in Berlin. That night she went out alone and no one followed her.

She came back to her room, content. No German agent in Paris, so far as she could judge, had wired Berlin to watch a woman named Jeanne Rohan. That was a good sign; one could never be certain. Never! From each of the journeys in the past there had been a return, but one day one of these journeys might be a farewell to Paris for ever. Telling herself that she would never know that it was a last journey until the knowledge was too belated to matter, she turned on the desk lamp and switched off the overhead light. Now she could begin work. The softer glow in the room added something to her face; it smoothed the straight stern line of the mouth, it set a spectrum of tints in her black hair, it touched away a few years from the late twenties.

She took a piece of writing paper, but she stared at it for some time before writing. Then, as if it were something that could not be postponed any longer, she wrote hurriedly, 'Dear Paul, Surely you remember Jeanne Rohan? I am in Berlin combining a vacation with business and I should greatly enjoy seeing you.'

Sealing the note so lightly that a messenger could easily open it and reseal it, she addressed it to Paul Perel, Assistant Military Attaché of the French Embassy. A messenger would deliver it in the morning. The sternness and the cold certainty left her face as she looked at the note. Paul had certainly changed; he would find that she had changed, and in that change the remnants of memory of a summer four years before would not be dangerously stirred. Yet it was unpleasant to think of Paul other than as he had been that summer. They had separated after a quarrel, and that was that, and he had not written. For him, at least, there had been summers and springs and autumns since then.

An invitation to call at his flat in a side street off Kurfurstendamm reached her by return messenger. In the late afternoon Jeanne rode towards the west of the city. The pavements were crowded now, the cafés filling rapidly. In Berlin, as in Paris, people at this hour were leaving business to get home, far from any concern with international problems, people who lived all their days without ever knowing a moment when life might hang waveringly on one wrong word, one artificial gesture, one thoughtless turn into a wrong street. Jeanne watched them hurry by, and as always she realised how lonely her own work was, how lonely it had to be, how far it put her from these untroubled crowds.

Jeanne paused at the entrance to the flat. Paul might resent her coming, he might misunderstand, he might even think that she had accepted the assignment on the chance of seeing him again. She would let him know at once that she came on business. Then she rang the bell and a servant opened the door for her and led her into a little living-room.

A moment later Paul appeared, still slender, still seeming young for thirty, with that same broad smile that was half a question, half a defence.

'Jeanne!' He came forward so quickly and took her hand. 'Let me look at you – I am so glad to see you!'

He was free of any strain or embarrassment, and Jeanne was annoyed at the fact that she noticed that he had changed.

'What are you doing here?' he asked.

'Business and pleasure.' Then, almost inaudibly, 'Is it safe to talk?'

'Well!' He shrugged his shoulders. 'As safe as anyone can tell in this country. Perhaps you would like to go driving?'

She agreed, and they got into his car and turned west. At once he asked, 'You haven't tired of working for Captain Dufresne yet?'

'No,' she smiled. This so easily led to conversation of four years ago. 'Not yet.'

'Why do you stay in it, Jeanne?'

She had no ready answer. 'It gives me some sort of deep emotional satisfaction, I suppose.'

'Yes,' he agreed without comment. 'Aren't you afraid to come here so openly? The Germans would count you a very valuable catch.'

'I am interested in children's books, so the Gestapo can find out, should they bother to investigate me. *Bien!* And what am I doing now except to talk to one of my fellow-countrymen?'

He smiled. 'Sometime you may decide to tell me what you are really doing here. Is there any help I can give you?'

'Probably,' Jeanne said drily. 'Captain Dufresne spoke about the amount of information you have sent him in the last nine months.'

'Particularly those last reports?' he asked eagerly. 'I hoped they would please him.'

Jeanne nodded. Without having to ask any questions that might have aroused his suspicions, those reports had come into the conversation.

'I was very fortunate to get them,' Paul added modestly. 'They are valuable, *n'est-ce pas?*'

'Most valuable,' Jeanne agreed. 'They', as Dufresne had carefully explained to her, were two reports showing the location of hidden fortifications, pillboxes and cement cellars fit for artillery mountings, behind the Rhine. Then she asked carelessly, 'You are certain they are authentic?'

Paul gripped tightly at the wheel in surprise and the car wavered. 'Authentic?' The question had a shade of defiance, as if he felt that in some way his own reputation had been attacked. 'I got them from the same source that furnished me a year ago with the story of the row between General von Kruft and General von Helgman. And the same source gave me the report on the amphibian tank last spring. Weren't they authentic?'

'Yes, but fairly unimportant. These latest reports will force our General Staff to make changes in our own military plans at once.'

'Naturally,' Paul said. Then he repeated, 'Of course they are genuine.'

Jeanne had nothing more to say, and they drove on in silence. It was vital, and Dufresne had emphasised it, to go carefully and not to arouse Paul's suspicions. Here was a lovely afternoon and a clear road ahead. Four years ago they had driven together like this, but with bubbling conversation rather than question and answer, and in place of grimness, laughter.

'Do you mind if we turn back now?' Paul asked suddenly, slowing the car. 'A friend of mine is coming to my flat.'

'Certainly.' Then, trying not to be too personal, 'I'm sorry my question hurt you.'

'It did not hurt,' he said shortly. 'My friend is a Fraulein Tiedner. I'd like you to meet her.'

'I should like to.' Jeanne tried to put aside any personal curiosity or feeling at the thought of meeting his Berlin friends. She only remembered what Dufresne had said: 'The girl who is always with him is said to be so lovely. *C'est triste*, but beauty and brains do not always guarantee honesty!'

The girl waiting in the living-room was a blonde, attractive at first glance, with a round face and light blue eyes. Hers was almost a peasant face, but something in it denied peasant simplicity.

She seemed surprised to see Paul enter with a woman, but her face could change expression with sudden speed; at the introduction she became instantly gracious. 'I'm so glad to know any of Paul's old Paris friends,' she smiled, but the air of possession with which she took his arm was a little too obvious. 'You're in Berlin for the first time?'

Jeanne was ill at ease. It was not the certainty that this girl had heard the same things that Paul had said during that Normandy summer; it was the certainty that the girl sensed instantly that Jeanne was in Berlin for a purpose.

While coffee was served conversation flitted from one full stop to another. Whenever Madga had a chance she questioned Jeanne. 'You live in Paris? Where are you staying here? Will you be here long?' Of course, it might be the narrow interest of a woman who sees her man's old friend turn up. It might be the interest of someone who wanted to be hospitable and helpful. Every question was asked with a pleasant smile, but the smile had only the appearance of warmth in it, the warmth of vapour that comes from ice.

As Jeanne went back to the hotel alone, she wanted to wire Dufresne that she was returning to Paris at once. It had been much harder to meet Paul than she had foreseen; he had changed, but the things she liked in him had not changed. Everything only reminded her that, but for a silly quarrel four years ago, they would have been married. Now she had to face this girl and a situation not of her own making or wish.

Dufresne suspected that Paul had been careless in his work, and it was up to Jeanne to prove it. Madga was obviously suspicious; and why should any German girl run the dreadful risk of intimacy with a foreign military attaché? One answer was obvious, but it had to be proved: because the police encouraged the friendship and paid the girl to cultivate it. It was hard to believe that Paul was so stupid as to fail to recognise that. But to prove it meant delving into his own personal affairs and perhaps being told brutally, 'None of your business!'

A telephone call late that evening surprised her. She heard Paul ask, 'How would you like to see something of Berlin by night?'

For just a second she felt that it would be better to have no contact with Paul except the most formal sort. Yet this night might give her a chance to get a speedy answer for Dufresne, who was waiting. She agreed.

Paul came quickly. 'We'll go for a drive, if you don't mind.'

That certainly meant more than just a pleasant evening together. It meant nothing that soft lights and dance music could assist, but something that had to be said far from any ears that might overhear.

'I called you because I had to talk to you,' he began awkwardly. Then, breaking clumsily through restraint, 'What did you think of Madga?'

'She is very nice and attractive.'

'She's different.' He was approaching laboriously whatever it was that he wanted to say. 'She asked me about you – I didn't realise that she was jealous. She asked me why I had never mentioned you to her before.'

'Why should she be interested in me?' Jeanne's mouth tightened at the thought of the girl asking questions. She *was* suspicious.

'I told her about that month in Normandy.'

At least he had not forgotten that there had been such a month.

Then, awkwardly, nervously he asked, 'Will you be here long?'

'Meaning that the longer I stay the more I am liable to complicate you and Madga?'

'I did not know she was so jealous,' Paul said lamely.

Jeanne held back her own feelings. The girl might be jealous; on the other hand, she might use jealousy as a means to get information. No matter how distasteful the situation was, it had to be faced. Determinedly Jeanne asked, 'Have you known her for a long time?'

'More than a year.'

'I should suppose that it would be dangerous for any German girl to be seen too much with a foreign military attaché.'

'They probably assume that she's harmless,' Paul said non-committally. 'Neither the Gestapo nor anyone else has bothered her.'

It was unbelievable that he, a French army officer, would be serious about her. And it was unbelievable that the Gestapo would not keep a close watch over every one of his friends. Jeanne had to ask questions and hope that he would not resent them. 'What does Madga do?'

He did not seem to be annoyed. 'She works in the accountants' office of one of the big department stores.'

'She lives alone?'

'Yes.'

He had turned the car into the suburbs. The only noise now was that of the motor and the hum of tyres on concrete, the only lights, the little self-sufficient lights on the dashboard.

The next question might cause a quarrel, but Jeanne had to take that chance. 'Are you sure that she is trustworthy?'

He did not resent that, but he sounded hurt. 'I understand. I know that it isn't the best thing for an attaché to have a close friendship with a German girl. Some of the Embassy staff have spoken to me about it.' He continued, 'But several of her relatives have been jailed early in the Hitler regime.'

'And she is anti-Nazi?'

'Naturally. Like so many people here, she says nothing about her feelings, but she is bitter.' He lowered his voice. 'I can prove that she's trustworthy. She has been my most valuable assistant. It is she who was able to get the reports I sent Dufresne!'

That was what Dufresne had suspected! From habit, Jeanne turned round quickly to make sure that even here in the car no third party was listening. 'Where did she get them?'

'From army officers whom I could not have met myself.' Everything he said sounded honest, without the careful phrasing, the unconscious halting of an impromptu story. 'But for her I should never have had those reports. Thanks to her, our General Staff will have to change at once our own military plans.'

'*Would* have to change,' Jeanne said quietly.

Paul jerked forward, as if he saw imminent collision ahead. 'Would have?'

'They would have to be changed,' Jeanne emphasised each word, 'if we were certain that the reports are genuine. Dufresne is sure that they are false, that they were given us purposely to fool us.' Then, bluntly, 'I was sent here to determine that.'

He jammed on the brakes and the car stopped beside the dark road. 'Why should the Germans furnish us with false reports?'

'To have us believe them genuine and to make corresponding changes in our own plans,' Jeanne explained. 'The Germans would then know the changes and could be prepared accordingly. That is nothing new in espionage.'

'I don't believe it,' Paul said huskily. 'The reports last year were genuine, weren't they? Madga got those for me.'

'They were unimportant,' Jeanne said quietly. 'She may have given you those to make you believe in her honesty, and all the while the Gestapo supplied her with the information.'

'Do you take me for a fool?' Paul exploded. 'Do you think I can't judge another human being? It is outrageous for you to come and make such a suggestion.'

'It is not I,' she said, sure that he misinterpreted her interest. 'Captain Dufresne suggested it.'

'And you've come here to check up on me?' Paul asked sharply.

Jeanne spoke softly, hoping that he would understand. 'I was sent here against my wish to determine the accuracy of the reports – that is all that matters.'

'You put your profession before your feelings once again,' Paul said slowly. 'Remember?'

'I remember.' Over that they had quarrelled four years before. She would not promise to quit her profession after marriage. 'My feelings have nothing to do with this now – all that matters is the authenticity of those reports.'

He drove on in silence. Then he said, 'I have known Madga for a year, and I have had a chance to judge her. I believe her honest, and I shall ask her to give you proof that the reports are genuine.'

That was so childish. 'What proof can she give you?' Then, suddenly concerned, 'If she does work for the Gestapo, what is to prevent her from reporting me to them as soon as she finds out I work for Dufresne?'

Paul did not answer but drove on, his hands tight on the wheel. 'I shall find some way to show you that Madga is honest.'

Jeanne could hope so. If not, then in Madga's hands might be the power to make this a last journey from Paris.

Jeanne left the hotel the next morning to walk about the streets aimlessly, too intent on her problems to notice either passers-by or shop windows. It was hard to follow one pattern in her thoughts; too many things had become so quickly interwoven. Foremost were the reports, but they were connected with the honesty or the dishonesty of Madga, with Paul's interest in the girl, with her own safe return to Paris.

Thinking of Paul, Jeanne realised why she had dreaded the trip to Berlin: to see him meant to realise a little more clearly the loneliness of her profession. As she turned down the Linden, her whole world in her mind, she knew very well how she felt about him. It had been so ridiculous to quarrel; nothing, not even her work, really mattered compared with him, but she had found that out too late. The quicker she settled the authenticity of those reports and left Berlin, the less unhappy she would be. Away in Paris, she might be able to go on again quietly and unemotionally.

She came back to the hotel about noon, tired and glad to be tired, with no definite plan of procedure, with no way to get at the girl. There was a message for her, asking her to telephone Paul. Over the 'phone she heard him say one sentence. With a gasp she answered, 'Let me come and talk to you first!'

She was at his flat as quickly as a taxi could take her.

'You asked for proof of Madga's honesty,' he said. 'Well, I've considered marrying her for some time, but I hesitated. You know – career, and marriage to a German girl, and all that!'

Jeanne nodded dumbly and said, 'Of course.'

'This morning I decided that marriage to her would be all the proof that you and Captain Dufresne would need.'

'Proof?'

'Of her honesty,' Paul said seriously. 'If she works for the Gestapo, they will never let her marry a foreign attaché. They would arrest her first. They would be sure she had sold them out.' His logic seemed to please him. 'If we are able to marry, then you will know that she has no Gestapo connections and that those documents are authentic.'

'She will marry you?' Jeanne asked, trying hard to hold back any trace of her own feelings.

'I rang her up this morning and she agreed.'

She knew she had to choose the most impersonal arguments. 'It won't necessarily be proof. The Gestapo might be very pleased to have one of their employees married to a French attaché.' Then, as if grasping at something, 'I doubt if you can remain attaché if you marry her – your career will end.'

'If Captain Dufresne insists that I resign, I shall do so.'

'And give up your career?' She spoke eagerly. This argument might yet persuade him. 'Very few marriages are recompense for a discarded career.'

'So you once told me, *ma chérie*,' he said bitterly.

Jeanne winced. That hurt.

'There is something more important than my career. What can I believe in if Madga is dishonest?' He was scornful. 'Why aren't you pleased? What better proof of her honesty can you ask?'

'I can only tell you', Jeanne said firmly, 'that it is not proof. The Gestapo may not know of her marriage until it is finished. But you can't throw away your career!' Repetition only made her realise how hopeless it was. 'I doubt if Captain Dufresne will accept it as proof of the authenticity of the reports. And if you marry her, we shall have no further chance to check up on her work.' She could only hope that Paul would not guess why she seemed so frantic about the marriage. 'Before you marry her, let me talk with her, please. Won't you tell me where she lives?'

As she went to a flat apartment near Nollendorfplatz, she realised that this would be a duel in which she would need new weapons. This was the first time she had had to face another woman; the tricks she had used on men, the flattery, the appeals to a man's vanity, were valueless. Madga would know all those and, if she were really suspicious, she too would be trying to get a meaning from every gesture, every inflection, every flutter of the eyes.

It began like the most unpleasant of interviews. 'I want to talk about Paul's marriage,' Jeanne said bluntly.

'If he wishes to marry me,' Madga answered coldly, 'I do not see that it concerns you.'

'I am interested in his career. He will have to resign his position.'

'He can find something else,' Madga said. 'We have talked about marriage for almost a year.' Then, almost savagely, 'Just why are you interested, Mademoiselle Rohan?'

The direct question was unexpected and Jeanne knew that she showed her embarrassment and that the girl understood it; her smile showed that. Then, in her confusion, Jeanne saw a way out, a seemingly direct answer that would save her pride, and that seemed important now. And that answer might offer a way to trap the girl, but to make it Jeanne knew that she would have to forget herself, any fear for herself, any certainty of return to Paris. For a moment she hesitated, then she said, 'I am interested in Paul for professional reasons. We are proud of the work he has done and we do not want to see him end his career so suddenly.'

Magda snapped at it. 'You are in the Deuxième Bureau?'

Jeanne nodded. Let the girl have that to take to the Gestapo! If she did, then it would be clear who her employers were.

'It must be difficult work,' Madga said as if that settled it. 'I have helped Paul before. I could make him a valuable wife. I am ready to do whatever will make him happy, and if he marries me' – she said it definitely – 'he will be happy!'

It was best to leave it at that. The next twenty-four hours would show the girl's honesty.

As Jeanne drove off she felt chilled. She had given Madga a piece of knowledge she could use, and if she used it, then this was a last journey from Paris. But, more important, it would reveal the truth about the reports, it would stop the marriage and save Paul's career, and some day he might realise that and be thankful.

Then Jeanne let herself think what she had done; she had forgotten herself completely and her own safety. She was suddenly aware of the sun, of the people on the streets, of the traffic swirling by, and she felt as if she had shut herself away from this open world. The German prisons along the Baltic are grey and damp.

Then she stopped herself – she had never sentimentalised over any risk before and she would not begin now. There was an excellent chance that Madga might see the trap and avoid it, but Jeanne was too exhausted to think about that. It was enough to know that she had baited a trap and that she had used herself for bait.

She went at once to Paul. It was important for him to know what she had done so that if she were arrested secretly and taken off, he would know what it meant. The thought that he might warn the girl to avoid the trap occurred to her, but she felt that she could believe in his honesty if not in his judgement. It hurt, though, to think of seeing him, and possibly for the last time.

She asked him bluntly, 'Do you agree that it makes a good test for her?'

'I tell you, no test is necessary,' he said firmly. 'You will find her honest. Nothing will happen to you.' Yet he was nervous. 'You should not have put yourself in that position; if they should arrest you now by chance, on someone else's report—!'

Jeanne returned to the hotel, uncertain how to spend the next hours. If Madga were to report her, she would probably do it at once. It would be better to wait where the police might most easily find her. Facing arrest now was not as she had once imagined it would be. In such a desperate moment, she had always believed, she would be doing her utmost to avoid it, her brain more alive than ever before, trying one chance then another, turning this way and that. Now, in fact, she had to sit quietly, studying the wallpaper, almost wishing that the police would come quickly if they were coming. Then again – and this only intensified the suspense – they might not come. Knowing that Jeanne's arrest would jeopardise her marriage, Madga might not report her. Through the long afternoon, the longer evening, no one knocked at the door. No one telephoned except Paul. He called several times and he seemed nervous. 'I just wanted to ask if you were all right,' he said, or 'I only wondered if you had gone out.'

'I think I shall go out for a walk,' she said. If someone followed her, she would know that a watch was being kept on her.

She went out but no one followed.

It was the longest of nights. The footsteps of a passer-by sounded like the tramp of police, and she waited in cold perspiration until they passed her door. The noise of a car stopping in the street made her run to the window to see if it was a police wagon. This was the end; never again would she face arrest. If the morning came and she was able to return to Paris, she would tell Dufresne that she was finished. She thought of Paul, and she remembered how they had quarrelled. She had chosen her profession, which led to this night of fear, which would lead to Heaven knew how many more nights like it, in other cities, in other circumstances.

She woke in the morning, not quite convinced that she was still in the same room, that no one had disturbed her during the night. After the surprise passed, she had to face the obvious: the police had not come, the trap had not worked. Either she was wrong about the girl or the girl was too clever. Paul telephoned early and when he said, 'It's a pleasant morning,' he sounded relieved. He obviously did not want to say anything definite over the telephone.

It was paradoxical to feel depressed and defeated now because the threat of arrest seemed imaginary. Nothing was really settled, not the authenticity of the reports, nor Madga, nor the wedding. Possibly a telegram to Dufresne asking advice might help, but no advice could stop the marriage. Then, at the thought of a telegram to Dufresne she smiled. She considered it further and she laughed and went to the telephone.

'I shall return to Paris today,' she said to Paul. 'I should like to entertain the prospective bride and groom at lunch before I go.'

'We'd be delighted.'

'It would be wise to choose a place where we should not be overheard. Shall we drive to some place on the outskirts of the city?'

Then she rang for a page and asked for a telegraph form.

During the drive to the suburban inn only Madga seemed free from tension. She was lively and gay, but most of her remarks were to Paul. Not until lunch was nearly over did Jeanne feel that she could take over the conversation. She began, 'I owe you an apology, Madga. I have misjudged you.'

Paul interrupted, 'She felt you must be employed by the Gestapo.'

'That was ridiculous,' Madga said.

Jeanne agreed and took a folded telegraph form from her pocket. 'I want to give both of you a little wedding present. I am sending this this afternoon to Captain Dufresne.' She offered Paul the opened telegram.

It read: 'Have just met Paul's fiancée. Will make him charming and especially valuable wife. Wire him permission to marry and to remain in service.'

Paul reacted first, simply and naturally. 'That's awfully nice, Jeanne. Isn't that nice, Madga?'

The girl did not answer at once, and Jeanne felt her pulse beat faster. This hesitation might mean that Madga saw the implications in that telegram. Then Madga said, hurriedly, 'You must not send that openly. Do you want the telegram censor here to know that you are in contact with an officer in the Deuxième Bureau?'

'Madga's right,' Paul insisted. 'You can send the telegram in Embassy code.'

'I prefer to send it openly,' Jeanne said coolly. 'I will face any risk.' She was almost sure that she had Madga caught. She explained, 'The censors will read this telegram, of course. You see, Paul, if by chance

Madga does have Gestapo connections they will wonder what bargain—'

'You have no right to say such a thing,' Madga exploded.

'—she has made in order to secure official permission for your marriage. If she has no connections, naturally, they will ignore the message, so far as it concerns her.'

'That's nonsense,' Madga snapped. 'Please don't listen to her.'

'You will listen!' She had the girl now. 'If you have no Gestapo connections, you need not fear this telegram. If you have, then you will be accused of having dealt with us in exchange for official approval of your marriage, and you may expect the police to arrest you at once to prevent the marriage.' She faced Madga. 'Now, shall I send it?'

'Of course you will send it,' Paul said, as if understanding for the first time. 'Madga has nothing to fear.'

For a moment the three sat silent. Jeanne fumbled with the telegram.

'No!' Madga was on her feet. 'She shall not send it. I admit, Paul, I deceived you.' Then, even more bitterly, 'She has done this for one reason, so that she could marry you herself. I saw it in her face when I first met her.'

Jeanne looked at the girl, then at Paul. His face was white and his forehead throbbed.

'She's clever,' Madga continued, 'but not clever enough. I saw your trap yesterday. But', she began to laugh, 'I shall see that you do not leave Germany. And I shall probably be rewarded for catching such an important French agent as you.'

Before Jeanne could say anything, she saw Paul's face tighten and a new strength was set in it. 'I think that Jeanne will arrive back in Paris safely, Madga. Unless she does, I shall see that the Gestapo learns that it was you who admitted that those reports were false. For that betrayal, the charge would be treason, *n'est-ce pas?*'

Madga's face turned pale. Then, unsteadily, she reached for her handbag and walked slowly away.

For a long time Paul said nothing. Then, 'I shall go with you to Paris tonight.' He reached for the telegram. 'Tell me, were you really going to send this?'

'What does it matter?' Jeanne smiled. 'She thought so!'

They faced Captain Dufresne hand in hand. 'I want to tell you that I have made my last journey,' Jeanne told him. 'Paul and I are going to marry at once.'

'*Tiens!* I am very glad,' Dufresne smiled. Then, as if to show the wisdom for which he is famed, he added, 'I might say, I sent you to Berlin hoping that that would happen.'

# THE NEWS
# IN ENGLISH

## By Graham Greene

LORD HAW-HAW OF ZEESEN was off the air.

All over England the new voice was noticed: precise and rather lifeless, it was the voice of a typical English don.

In his first broadcast he referred to himself as a man young enough to sympathise with what he called 'the resurgence of youth all over the new Germany', and that was the reason – combined with the pedantic tone – he was at once nicknamed Dr Funkhole.

It is the tragedy of such men that they are never alone in the world.

Old Mrs Bishop was knitting by the fire at her house in Crowborough when young Mrs Bishop tuned in to Zeesen. The sock was khaki: it was as if she had picked up at the point where she had dropped a stitch in 1918. The grim comfortable house stood in one of the long avenues, all spruce and laurel and a coating of snow, which are used to nothing but the footsteps of old retired people. Young Mrs Bishop never forgot that moment: the wind beating up across Ashdown Forest against the blacked-out window, and her mother-in-law happily knitting, and the sense of everything waiting for this moment. Then the voice came into the room from Zeesen in the middle of a sentence, and old Mrs Bishop said firmly, 'That's David.'

Young Mary Bishop made a hopeless protest – 'It can't be,' but she knew.

'I know my son if you don't know your husband.'

It seemed incredible that the man speaking couldn't hear them, that he should just go on, reiterating for the hundredth time the old lies, as if there were nobody anywhere in the world who knew him – a wife or a mother.

Old Mrs Bishop had stopped knitting. She said, 'Is that the man they've been writing about – Doctor Funkhole?'

'It must be.'

'It's David.'

The voice was extraordinarily convincing: he was going into exact

311

engineering details – David Bishop had been a mathematics don at Oxford. Mary Bishop twisted the wireless off and sat down beside her mother-in-law. 'They'll want to know who it is,' Mrs Bishop said.

'We mustn't tell them,' said Mary.

The old fingers had begun again on the khaki sock. She said, 'It's our duty.' Duty, it seemed to Mary Bishop, was a disease you caught with age: you ceased to feel the tug tug of personal ties; you gave yourself up to the great tides of patriotism and hate. She said, 'They must have made him do it. We don't know what threats . . .'

'That's neither here nor there.'

She gave weakly in to hopeless wishes. 'If only he'd got away in time. I never wanted him to give that lecture course.'

'He always was stubborn,' said old Mrs Bishop.

'He said there wouldn't be a war.'

'Give me the telephone.'

'But you see what it means,' said Mary Bishop. 'He may be tried for treason if we win.'

'*When* we win,' old Mrs Bishop said.

The nickname was not altered, even after the interviews with the two Mrs Bishops, even after the sub-acid derogatory little article about David Bishop's previous career. It was suggested now that he had known all along that war was coming, that he had gone to Germany to evade military service, leaving his wife and his mother to be bombed. Mary Bishop fought, almost in vain, with the reporters for some recognition that he might have been forced . . . by threats or even physical violence. The most one paper would admit was that if threats had been used, David Bishop had taken a very unheroic way out. We praise heroes as though they are rare, and yet we are always ready to blame another man for lack of heroism. The name Dr Funkhole stuck.

But the worst of it to Mary Bishop was old Mrs Bishop's attitude. She turned a knife in the wound every evening at 9.15. The radio set must be tuned in to Zeesen, and there she sat listening to her son's voice and knitting socks for some unknown soldier on the Maginot Line. To young Mrs Bishop none of it made sense – least of all that flat, pedantic voice with its smooth, well-thought-out elaborate lies. She was afraid to go out now into Crowborough: the whispers in the post office, the old faces watching her covertly in the library. Sometimes she thought almost with hatred, why has David done this to me? Why?

Then suddenly she got her answer.

The voice for once broke new ground. It said, 'Somewhere back in England my wife may be listening to me. I am a stranger to the rest of you, but she knows that I am not in the habit of lying.'

A personal appeal was too much. Mary Bishop had faced her mother-in-law and the reporters: she couldn't face her husband. She began to cry, sitting close beside the radio set like a child beside its doll's house when something has been broken in it which nobody can repair. She heard the voice of her husband speaking as if he were at her elbow from a country which was now as distant and as inaccessible as another planet.

'The fact of the matter is . . .'

The words came slowly out as if he were emphasising a point in a lecture, and then he went on – to what would concern a wife. The low price of food, the quantity of meat in the shops: he went into great detail, giving figures, picking out odd, irrelevant things – like Mandarin oranges and toy zebras – perhaps to give an effect of richness and variety.

Suddenly Mary Bishop sat up with a jerk as if she had been asleep. She said 'Oh, God, where's that pencil?' and upset one of the too many ornaments looking for one. Then she began to write, but in no time at all the voice was saying, 'Thank you for having listened to me so attentively,' and Zeesen had died out on the air. She said, 'Too late.'

'What's too late?' said old Mrs Bishop sharply. 'Why did you want a pencil?'

'Just an idea,' Mary Bishop said.

She was led next day up and down the cold, unheated corridors of a war office in which half the rooms were empty, evacuated. Oddly enough, her relationship to David Bishop was of use to her now, if only because it evoked some curiosity and a little pity. But she no longer wanted the pity, and at last she reached the right man.

He listened to her with great politeness. He was not in uniform: his rather good tweeds made him look as if he had just come up from the country for a day or two, to attend to the war. When she had finished he said, 'It's rather a tall story, you know, Mrs Bishop. Of course it's been a great shock to you – this – well – action of your husband's.'

'I'm proud of it.'

'Just because in the old days you had this – scheme, you really believe . . . ?'

'If he was away from me and he telephoned "The fact of the matter is", it always meant, "This is all lies, but take the initial letters which follow . . ." Oh, Colonel, if you only knew the number of unhappy weekends I've saved him from – because, you see, he could always telephone to me, even in front of his host.' She said with tears in her voice, 'Then I'd send him a telegram . . .'

'Yes. But still . . . you didn't get anything this time, did you?'

'I was too late. I hadn't a pencil. I only got this – I know it doesn't seem to make sense.' She pushed the paper across. SOSPIC. 'I know it might easily be coincidence – that it does seem to make a kind of word.'

'An odd word.'

'Mightn't it be a man's name?'

The officer in tweeds was looking at it, she suddenly realised, with real interest – as if it was a rare kind of pheasant. He said, 'Excuse me a moment,' and left her. She could hear him telephoning to somebody from another room: the little ting of the bell, silence, and then a low voice she couldn't overhear. Then he returned, and she could tell at once from his face that all was well.

He sat down and fiddled with a fountain-pen: he was obviously embarrassed. He started a sentence and stopped it. Then he brought out in an embarrassed gulp, 'We'll all have to apologise to your husband.'

'It meant something?'

He was obviously making his mind up about something difficult and out of the way: he was not in the habit of confiding in members of the public. But she had ceased to be a member of the public.

'My dear Mrs Bishop,' he said, 'I've got to ask a great deal from you.'

'Of course. Anything.'

He seemed to reach a decision and stopped fiddling. 'A neutral ship called the *Pic* was sunk this morning at 4 a.m., with a loss of two hundred lives. S.O.S. *Pic*. If we'd had your husband's warning, we could have got destroyers to her in time. I've been speaking to the Admiralty.'

Mary Bishop said in a tone of fury, 'The things they are writing about David. Is there one of them who'd have the courage . . . ?'

'That's the worst part of it, Mrs Bishop. They must go on writing. Nobody must know, except my department and yourself.'

'His mother?'

'You mustn't even tell her.'

'But can't you make them just leave him alone?'

'This afternoon I shall ask them to intensify their campaign – in order to discourage others. An article on the legal aspect of treason.'

'And if I refuse to keep quiet?'

'Your husband's life won't be worth much, will it?'

'So he's just got to go on?'

'Yes. Just go on.'

He went on for four weeks. Every night now she tuned in to Zeesen with a new horror – that he would be off the air. The code was a child's code. How could they fail to detect it? But they did fail. Men with complicated minds can be deceived by simplicity. And every night, too, she had to listen to her mother-in-law's indictment; every episode which she thought discreditable out of a child's past was brought out – the tiniest incident. Women in the last war had found a kind of pride in 'giving' their sons: this, too, was a gift on the altar of a warped patriotism. But now young Mrs Bishop didn't cry: she just held on – it was relief enough to hear his voice.

It wasn't often that he had information to give – the phrase 'the fact of the matter is' was a rare one in his talks: sometimes there were the numbers of regiments passing through Berlin, or of men on leave: very small details, which might be of value to military intelligence, but to her seemed hardly worth the risk of a life. If this was all he could do, why, why hadn't he allowed them simply to intern him?

At last she could bear it no longer. She visited the War Office again. The man in tweeds was still there, but this time for some reason he was wearing a black tailcoat and a black stock as if he had been to a funeral: he must have been to a funeral, and she thought with more fear than ever of her husband.

'He's a brave man, Mrs Bishop,' he said.

'You needn't tell me that,' she cried bitterly.

'We shall see that he gets the highest possible decorations . . .'

'Decorations!'

'What do you want, Mrs Bishop? He's doing his duty.'

'So are other men. But they come home on leave. Sometime. He can't go on for ever. Soon they are bound to find out.'

'What can we do?'

'You can get him out of there. Hasn't he done enough for you?'

He said gently: 'It's beyond our power. How can we communicate with him?'

'Surely you have agents.'

'Two lives would be lost. Can't you imagine how they watch him?'

Yes. She could imagine all that clearly. She had spent too many holidays in Germany – as the Press had not failed to discover – not to know how men were watched, telephone lines tapped, table companions scrutinised.

He said, 'If there was some way we could get a message to him, it *might* be managed. We do owe him that.'

Young Mrs Bishop said quickly before he could change his mind: 'Well, the code works both ways. The fact of the matter is . . . We have news broadcast in German. He might one day listen in.'

'Yes. There's a chance.'

She became privy to the plan because again they needed her help. They wanted to attract his notice first by some phrase peculiar to her. For years they had spoken German together on their annual holiday. That phrase was to be varied in every broadcast, and elaborately they worked out a series of messages which would convey to him the same instructions – to go to a certain station on the Cologne–Wesel line and contact there a railway worker who had already helped five men and two women to escape from Germany.

Mary Bishop felt she knew the place well – the small country station which probably served only a few dozen houses and a big hotel where people went in the old days for cures. The opportunity was offered him, if he could only take it, by an elaborate account of a railway accident at that point – so many people killed – sabotage – arrests. It was plugged in the news as relentlessly as the Germans repeated the news of false sinkings, and they answered indignantly back that there had been no accident.

It seemed more horrible than ever to Mary Bishop – those nightly broadcasts from Zeesen. The voice was in the room with her, and yet he couldn't know whether any message for which he risked his life reached home, and she couldn't know whether their messages to him just petered out unheard or unrecognised.

Old Mrs Bishop said, 'Well, we can do without David tonight, I should hope.' It was a new turn in her bitterness: now she would simply wipe him off the air. Mary Bishop protested. She said she must hear – then at least she would know that he was well.

'It serves him right if he's not well.'

'I'm going to listen,' Mary Bishop persisted.

'Then I'll go out of the room. I'm tired of his lies.'

'You're his mother, aren't you?'

'That's not my fault. I didn't choose – like you did. I tell you I won't listen to it.'

Mary Bishop turned the knob. 'Then stop your ears,' she cried in a sudden fury, and heard David's voice coming over.

'The lies', he was saying, 'put over by the British capitalist Press. A country governed by Jews cannot believe in national unity. There has not even been a railway accident – leave alone any sabotage – at the place so persistently mentioned in the broadcasts from England. Tomorrow I am leaving myself for the so-called scene of the accident, and I propose in my broadcast the day after tomorrow to give you an impartial observer's report, with records of the very railwaymen who are said to have been shot for sabotage. Tomorrow, therefore, I shall not be on the air . . .'

'Oh, thank God, thank God,' Mary Bishop said.

The old woman grumbled by the fire. 'You haven't much to thank Him for.'

'You don't know how much.'

All next day she found herself praying, although she didn't much believe in prayer. She visualised that station 'on the Rhine not far from Wesel': and not far either from the Dutch frontier. There must be some method of getting across – with the help of that unknown worker – possibly in a refrigerating van – no idea was too fantastic to be true: others had succeeded before him.

All through the day she tried to keep pace with him – he would have to leave early, and she imagined his cup of *ersatz* coffee and the slow war-time train taking him south and west: she thought of his fear and of his excitement – he was coming home to her. Ah, when he landed safely, what a day that would be! The papers then would have to eat their words: no more Dr Funkhole and no more of this place, side by side with his unloving mother.

At midday, she thought, he has arrived: he has his black discs with him to record the men's voices, he is probably watched, but he will find his chance – and now he is not alone. He has someone with him helping him. In one way or another he will miss his train home. The freight train will draw in – perhaps a signal will stop it outside the station. She saw it all so vividly, as the early winter dark came down and she blacked the windows out, that she found herself thankful he possessed, as she knew, a white mackintosh. He would be less visible waiting there in the snow.

Her imagination took wings, and by dinner-time she felt sure that he was already on the way to the frontier. That night there was no broadcast from Dr Funkhole, and she sang as she bathed and old Mrs Bishop beat furiously on her bedroom floor above.

In bed she could almost feel herself vibrating with the heavy movement of *his* train. She saw the landscape going by outside – there must be a crack in any van in which he lay hid, so that he could mark the distances. It was very much the landscape of Crowborough – spruces powdered with snow, the wide dreary waste they called a forest, dark avenues – she fell asleep.

When she woke she was still happy. Perhaps before night she would receive a cable from Holland, but if it didn't come she would not be anxious because so many things in war-time might delay it. It didn't come.

That night she made no attempt to turn on the radio, so old Mrs Bishop changed her tactics again. 'Well,' she said, 'aren't you going to listen to your husband?'

'He won't be broadcasting.' Very soon now she could turn on his mother in triumph and say – there, I knew it all the time, my husband's a hero.

'That was last night.'

'He won't be broadcasting again.'

'What do you mean? Turn it on and let me hear.'

There was no harm in proving that she knew – she turned it on.

A voice was talking in German – something about an accident and English lies, she didn't bother to listen. She felt too happy. 'There,' she said, 'I told you. It's not David.'

And then David spoke.

He said, 'You have been listening to the actual voices of the men your English broadcasters have told you were shot by the German police. Perhaps now you will be less inclined to believe the exaggerated stories you hear of life inside Germany today.'

'There,' old Mrs Bishop said, 'I told you.'

And all the world, she thought, will go on telling me now, for ever . . . Dr Funkhole. He never got those messages. He's there for keeps. David's voice said with curious haste and harshness: 'The fact of the matter is—'

He spoke rapidly for about two minutes as if he were afraid they would fade him at any moment, and yet it sounded harmless enough – the old stories about plentiful food and how much you could buy for an English pound – figures. But some of the examples this time, she thought with dread, are surely so fantastic that even the German brain will realise something is wrong. How had he ever dared to show up *this* copy to his chiefs?

She could hardly keep pace with her pencil, so rapidly did he speak. The words grouped themselves on her pad: 'Five Us refuelling hodie noon 53.23 by 10.5. News reliable source Wesel so returned. Talk unauthorised. The end.'

'This order. Many young wives I feel enjoy giving one' – he hesitated – 'one day's butter in every dozen . . .' the voice faded, gave out altogether. She saw on her pad: 'To my wife, goodbie d . . .'

The end, goodbye, the end . . . the words rang on like funeral bells. She began to cry, sitting as she had done before, close up against the radio set. Old Mrs Bishop said with a kind of delight: 'He ought never to have been born. I never wanted him. The coward,' and now Mary Bishop could stand no more of it.

'Oh,' she cried to her mother-in-law across the little over-heated, over-furnished Crowborough room, 'if only he were a coward, if only he were. But he's a hero, a damned hero, a hero, a hero . . .' she cried hopelessly on, feeling the room reel round her, and dimly supposing behind all the pain and horror that one day she would have to feel, like other women, pride.

# DRIVER!

## By Hilton Brown

*Rowley was as tough a desperado as Rhodesia had ever known. Yet he rode in to the police one morning and gave himself up. This story tells why.*

AT MWONUKO, that Sunday morning of late February, the Rhodesian police were having an easy. The neat little mud-and-whitewash buildings basked in a sunshine as peaceful as Buckinghamshire. Cotter, who was in charge, was lying in a deck-chair outside the office, enjoying it; the sunshine had followed heavy thunder rain and he was wondering if the Sebute river would have gone down enough to let him ride over to check the next station before evening. He was just deciding – regretfully – that it would, when he saw the solitary horseman approaching him – a lean, dark man on a lean, dark horse. They both looked dead weary.

At first he thought nothing of it; weary horsemen were a not uncommon sight in Rhodesia in those days. Then suddenly he stiffened; his hand went to the empty holster on his belt; he scrambled out of his chair and went forward.

The horseman rode straight at him almost as if Cotter were invisible. He stopped and slid from his saddle in a single movement. Cotter, his hand still feeling for that absent revolver, said, challenging:

'You're Rowley!'

The dismounted horseman stood in front of him, staring like an idiot. He looked like a man in the throes of malaria; he was shaking all over. He said:

'Sure. I'm Rowley . . . Y' don't need no gun . . . Y' can take me in.'

Cotter grinned – as he well might.

'I'll take you in all right, my boy.' He paused and looked at his captive. 'Where's Reits?'

A sort of spasm shook the man in front of him; his eyes rolled upwards in their sockets, almost out of sight; his face went the colour of old ash.

'Reits!' he said. 'That's why I'm here . . . I'll – I'll tell y' about Reits.'

If you travelled today from Abercorn to Shabani and said at intervals 'Rowley and Reits', the probability is that not one soul would know what you meant. Yet at the time when all this happened these two names were terror. To the managers of outlying mines, to the proprietors of lone up-country stores, to the wayside station-master, they meant a clatter of horses' hoofs in the dark – or even in broad day – a crash on the door, the entry of a tall, dark man and a short, stocky one, a blow or a shot, and the disappearance within five minutes of all the money in the till or the safe or the wallet.

You never knew when, you never knew where. To the half-distracted police, Rowley and Reits meant a legend that everyone knew, a couple of figures as easily identifiable as Pork Pie Mountain and as elusive as ghosts. You never knew when, you never knew where, you never knew *how*. If they dropped, on their lean horses, out of the sky; if they melted, with all their accoutrements, into the soft Rhodesian air, they could not be more intangible. They struck somewhere; they vanished. You thought they were gone; you prayed they were gone. They came back – somewhere else. Robbery with violence here, robbery with murder there; and the police chiefs at Salisbury and Livingstone cursing and raging, and the police subordinates riding and riding and riding – and all for nothing.

It was easier, of course, in those days. Railways were new, roads negligible, telegraph offices few and far between. But even allowing for all that, Rowley and Reits must have had genius. How did they link up in that queer partnership that sounded like a music-hall turn? Nobody knew. Rowley was an Australian; he was said to have tried unsuccessfully to revive bushranging in the old Ned Kelly country; like Ned Kelly, he was said to wear steel plate under his clothes. Reits was Afrikaner – from Hoopstad and the Vet river. But you never thought of 'Rowley', you never thought of 'Reits'; it was 'Rowley and Reits', the perfect partnership, the invincibles.

Rowley and Reits; they were the devil and all his angels. Or two of them, anyway.

'Slick's the word'; that was the Rowley-and-Reits motto. You came in, you did it, you went. Five minutes, ten perhaps if you had to search round, never more than twenty. They were like a bolt of light-ning – as quick, as lethal, as blinding. They prided themselves on a technique that worked to split seconds . . . It was so, that February Friday, at Gout's Store at Nsangi, three miles south of the Sebute river drift.

Gout's Store was easy – or should have been. It was a solitary tin-roofed tumbledown shack with nothing near it but some native kraals. Gout, a half-caste, was old and fat and sleepy and sozzled. There was not a great deal to be got – fifty pounds at the most. But that was part of the Rowley-and-Reits technique: little and often was how they liked them . . .

They came down on Gout's Store about half-past nine at night in pitch darkness and pouring, drenching rain. Gout had nothing but an oil-lamp, but it was enough to show where the safe was – if you could call it a safe.

But there was something that Gout's lamp didn't show. Early that morning, one Flitch, a miner on tramp, had appeared at the Store on his weary way to Mwonuko. He had proceeded to drink a bottle of Gout's Cape brandy; he was now sleeping this off in a stable at the back. He must in fact have nearly slept it off, for Gout's shrill lamentations – the partners themselves never made a sound – woke him up. Completely befuddled, he stumbled out into the pouring rain; he heard horses moving off in the dark; he loosed off a couple of wild shots. Then he staggered into the Store and surveyed Gout's dirty old figure, raging with terror and grief. Flitch said:

'Reckon I hit something.'

Gout paused for a moment in his stream of blasphemies.

'How could you hit? In this dark.'

'Reckon I did, though. Some feller yiked anyway.' He perceived, on the table, an open bottle of brandy, and promptly forgot all else.

Darkness was one of the many things that made no odds to Rowley and Reits; in the thundering rain, which grew always heavier, they rode north as straight for the Sebute rift as if it had been shining sunlight. Far away down river there were flickers of lightning, blue undulations along the horizon; Rowley and Reits neither needed nor heeded them. They rode unhurriedly at any easy trot for perhaps a mile; then Reits said, in a queer flat voice,

'Slim! I been hit.'

Rowley reined back a little. 'Bad?'

'Don't know. Think so. Me legs is goin' dead.'

Rowley swore. It was hard luck. A chance shot in the dark – cruel bad luck on a pair who had more than once run untouched from police rifles in broad daylight. But then that was the way Fate got you. He said:

'Does it hurt?'

'Not what y'd call hurt. I don' *feel*. It's in me back somewhere.'

'Can y' go on?'

'Got to, ain't it? How far's the drift?'

'Two miles. Bit less.'

'I'll go on. But if we get through, I'll have t' lie up a bit somewhere.'

Rowley said, 'Right. There's plenty places.' *If* we get through! he thought; that's not like Gus. Of course we'll get through. No sane or sober man would have faced the Sebute drift that night; but again, that was part of the Rowley-and-Reits technique; they did what no sane or sober man – what no human man *would* do. We've done it before, thought Rowley, we'll do it again. He said kindly, for he was fond of Reits:

'Walk the horses a bit, Gus. There ain't no hurry.'

Reits said, his teeth grinding a little, 'That —— with the gun.'

'Blast his gun! He won't worry us. Come on, pard, we'll do it.'

They rode on again in silence. The rain roared. Rowley thought – that river's going to be big.

It *was* big. In the dark you could see nothing, of course; but you could hear. You had the sense that in front of you land finished and there was a vast area – moving. And you could tell the first eager lap and swirl of it as it met you on the down slope to the drift. Much sooner than it should have done.

Reits said – and his voice was weaker:

'Gimme y'r belt or something, Slim. He might fall with me and – I can't hold the saddle.'

Rowley uncoiled a short length of rope from under his right leg and passed it over.

'Take an end o' that. Put it round y'. I'll lead . . . All right?'

'All right. So far.'

Rowley set his horse at the water – a deeper blackness in the mirk ahead of them. The beast slipped and scrabbled. Rowley said, 'We'll have t' swim this bit. Come on.'

There was nothing new in that; they had done as bad – or nearly as bad – before. But Reits wailed suddenly that he was frightened, and that *was* new. Rowley said, 'What y' frightened for? Crocs?' and led forward. The water lapped and splattered and gurgled. Above the noise of the river, Reits said, 'I'm done, Slim. I can' grip. I can' feel a thing. Don' leave me, Slim.'

Rowley said nothing, leaning forward on his horse's neck, peering into the gloom. A bank of ground rose suddenly in front of him; low bush at whose branches the river was tearing, the tops of reed-beds. He forced his horse on to it, dragging the other after him. With a splash and a splatter both animals reached dry ground.

Reits said, with sudden strength, 'God! We done it.' But Rowley shook his head.

'We ain't. This ain't the bank. It's Kobse's island. We're off the drift. We gone downstream. I c'n see that old shack o' Kobse's agin the sky.'

Reits said with a groan, 'Island or no island, here I gotta stop.' There was a crash and a splash as he fell sideways from his horse. Rowley heard his voice screaming out in sudden panic.

'Slim! Slim! I can' get up. I can' get up. Don' leave me, Slim.'

Rowley dismounted and went to him; he seemed to be wriggling the top of his body but his legs were immovable struts spread V-shape in front of him. Rowley said:

'I won't leave y', pard. Let y'self go slack an' I'll heave y' up again.'

He tried, tried again; but it was useless. Nothing would get Reits into the saddle; having once lost his balance there, it seemed he could not regain it. He fell once, twice, crying out each time in agony as he hit the ground. What next, then? He could be slung across his saddle face downwards like a sack; but the rope wasn't long enough to tie him on, and with the other arm of the river to cross and the current running fast and the horse slipping and plunging, how long would he stay there? Thirty seconds, with luck. I could take him up somehow behind me, thought Rowley; but – no horse is going to get through this with two men on his back. We'd founder half-way . . .

A new squall of rain, the fiercest yet, like a bucket thrown in one's face, came roaring down river like a train. Kobse's island shook with it.

Rowley let his partner gently to the ground, withdrew his arms from under his shoulders. 'It's no go,' he said, 'I'll have t' get a cart . . . Look! Let's get y' into that old shack o' Kobse's. Y'll be all right there till mornin'. I'll swim over both the horses.'

'*Both* horses?' said Reits sleepily.

'Sure! 'Case someone's lookin' for us, see? Great brute of a horse wanderin' about Kobse's island – give y' away. I'll swim both the horses on; I'll get a cart down t' the far bank.'

'Where'll y' get a cart?'

'You leave that t' me. I'll be back soon after daylight. This water'll be down by then. We'll do it. It's pie. Come on, chum, I'll give y' a heave.'

Reits cried out in pain as he was lifted to his useless feet; cried out again twice on the short journey to the deserted shed. 'It's me back!' he said, gasping. Inside the shed, Rowley struck a match. The place was bare and empty but relatively dry – more so than one would have expected. In one corner stood the remains of a native bed. Rowley, by main strength, heaved Reits on to it; it sagged but stood. Rowley stepped back, grinning.

'Bloomin' hotel, this is. *You'll* be all right. Take a shot o' brandy and go bye-byes. I'll be back 'fore y' know. Come on, pard; it's pie.'

As he moved again to the river, riding one horse and leading the other on the rope, he heard Reits, lying helpless on his back on the bed, cry out again that he was frightened. He stopped with his horse fetlock-deep in the first swirl of water.

'Wot y' frightened for? Crocodiles? There's no croc 'd eat *you*, y' ugly old ——!'

He went boldly forward.

No man who desired to go on living refused anything to Rowley in a certain mood. Certainly at Kobse's kraal on the north bank of the Sebute they did not refuse him a country cart and a couple of bullocks and a cartman. But inasmuch as they were Africans, not even Rowley, black and terrible as the night itself, could make them hurry.

It was past three in the morning when they came back to the river, the cart creaking and bumping in front, Rowley behind with the horses. In the meantime the night had cleared as if by magic; a skyful of stars showed Rowley the flood water rippling past. The river had obviously and markedly fallen, but now that you could more or less see it, it was even more frightening than before. Rowley, however, was not easily frightened, and it was the narrower arm of the river. They had got over the wider and worse half of it. In the starlight he could make out dimly the dark bulk of Kobse's island; he even thought he could see the roof of the shed. He stood on the bank considering.

The immediate future was clear enough. I'll leave the horses here, Rowley thought, and swim it myself; I'll get Gus over easier that way. I can tow him along on my back like the old life-savers on Manly. Pie! . . . Yes, but then what? How bad was Reits? The bullet must have got him in the spine somewhere; might be still in it, might have just glanced off. That could be dealt with; Rowley and Reits had their lying-up places and their medical service. Still, the remoter future wasn't going to be easy. Well, one thing at a time.

With the first glimmer of dawn – having taken the precaution of tying the cartman securely to a tree – Rowley slipped into the Sebute waters. He had no fear of crocodiles, or at all events he did not allow himself to think of them. The river was falling fast; it was easier even than he had expected. He reached the island almost, it seemed, at once. His teeth chattering a little with the cold, he coo-eed loudly. There was no reply, but that was not surprising; probably Reits, inside the hut, couldn't hear him. Quite confidently Rowley stepped ashore; then he stepped back again – hastily.

Right in front of him, between him and the hut, there was an enormous snake; a black snake as thick as his arm. But the terrible thing about this snake was that he could see twenty yards of it; it stretched, writhing, through the bush grass as far as he could see on either hand. It seemed to have a million scales, each scale in tiny fluttering movement. Black as ink among the bush grass, the great rope of a thing, hideously alive, rippled and flowed like running water.

'My God!' said Rowley. 'Driver!'

For the black living rope in front of Rowley was no snake; it was ants – the black pincered flesh-eating 'driver' ants that are one of the horrors of Africa. Everything in the African bush gives way to driver: lion, buffalo, rhino – when that thick purposeful million-headed column comes thrusting along, they give it the road. Driver will go through a bungalow in a matter of hours and leave it stripped of anything edible, swept clean of insect life, rats, mice – and even bigger things than these. When you see driver coming, you quit.

Rowley stood a moment, gaping at the procession. Where was it coming from, where was it going? You couldn't say. It just drove forward in that endless purposeful rush; it wanted meat, it would get it. It seemed to be coming from the centre of the island and heading downstream towards its eastern end; but it might be circling round the other side. Could it get off the island? Perhaps. They said driver could make a rope bridge of themselves and cross the Zambezi. As he stood there irresolute, nauseated, as everyone is by that seething fester of life, it seemed that the column halted, tested the air, swerved a little. Suddenly he felt himself bitten, bitten again.

Without a second thought, he jumped straight back into the river. There *were* crocodiles in the Sebute, but crocodiles are better than driver; at least they come singly and at least you can see them. He went in up to his neck, holding himself braced against the current by the branch of a small tree. Lead-grey in the early light, the Sebute swirled and nestled against him like – like a column of driver.

'Reits!' he shouted. 'Reits! Are y' there?'
There was no answer.

The day grew – as is the fashion of tropical days – by fits and starts, as if someone went round a room lighting a succession of candles. Now one sprang up, now another. Brightness came in a series of waves – and with each wave time, precious time, went by.

Twice Rowley pulled himself on shore and went forward; but the driver were still there streaming endlessly on; millions upon millions of them. Kobse's hut was on the far side, the south side, of the island. It was only a matter of fifty yards or so; but ten thousand ants could get on to you in less than fifty seconds . . . Look at it how you liked, there was no getting Reits out of it till those driver went by; and if Gout had called out the police or the troopers by now – well, there it was.

At his second landing Rowley was desperate enough to go forward and chance it, but almost instantly he felt himself bitten on the legs and fled back into the water, panicking. At his farthest point, perhaps ten yards from the bank, he called Reits by name repeatedly; but again there was no reply. Still, the river was making a good deal of noise; Reits might not hear; in any case, at the best he must be feeling too bad to make himself heard in reply. He could be unconscious. He could be asleep. Meanwhile the police . . .

Just on the back of seven o'clock Rowley made his third landing, and this time the driver were – gone. Where to? God only knew. They might have made one of their rope bridges and crossed the river; they might have gone into the ground. At all events, that seething black rope no longer lay between Rowley and Kobse's hut. Now for it.

In the bush grass the ants had left a trail clear and hard-beaten as a road; Rowley followed it. As he went, he shouted aloud, as much to hearten himself as to cheer his partner. 'Stick it, pard!' he yelled, 'Slim's comin'.' Or, 'Here we are, Gus; here we are!' But presently the horrible quiet of the island daunted and silenced him.

For a score of yards the ant-trail led him along the bank of the river; then it swerved sharply to the left, straight inland. He followed it; it was the way he wanted to go. Suddenly in front of him he saw the white-washed walls of the shed shining through the bush. Tough as he was, Rowley would have given five years of his life to turn tail on that insignificant building and re-swim the river and leap into his saddle and ride – away and away. But, chattering now with something more than the cold, he forced himself forward; he flung back the rickety door of the shed.

For a moment, after the daylight, there was semi-darkness; then – all too well – he saw. No one now lay on the bed where Reits had been left. But in the corner behind it there crouched a Thing that was almost a skeleton; that would have been better if it had been a skeleton altogether. Much better. It crouched doubled-up in the angle of the wall into which it had, by some superhuman effort, jammed itself. Its arms, Rowley saw, were crossed over what had been its face.

'My God!' he said again. 'Driver!'

'That's why I've come,' said the lean, dark man to Cotter, sitting in the pleasant sunshine outside the Mwonuko police station. 'That's why I've come. A chap don' go on after a thing like that. No.'

'I can see that,' said Cotter. He was white in the face himself. 'Yes, I can see that . . . Well . . .'

He thought for a minute. A score – a hundred – decent harmless people robbed, battered, beaten up, maimed, murdered, terrorised over a term of months. You couldn't be sorry for Reits. But . . . willy-nilly, his mind carried him into that hut on Kobse's island. In the dark. In the flood. Helpless. *No!* . . .

He shook himself together. Up, Cotter! Action. Good healthy rewarding action. Get on with it. Thank God for a villain – two villains – fewer in the world; and no more thinking about – *that.*